BRENT LIBRARIES

Please return/renew this item
by the last date shown.
Books may also be renewed by
phone or online.
Tel: 0333 370 4700

AN UNEXPECTED SCANDAL

JULES BENNETT

ONE WILD KISS

JESSICA LEMMON

MILLS & BOON

First Published in Great Britain 2020
by Mills & Boon, an imprint of HarperCollinsPublishers,
1 London Bridge Street, London, SE1 9GF

An Unexpected Scandal © 2020 Jules Bennett
One Wild Kiss © 2020 Jessica Lemmon

ISBN: 978-0-263-27920-7

0420

MIX
Paper from
responsible sources
FSC® C007454

This book is produced from independently certified FSC™ paper to ensure responsible forest management.

For more information visit: www.harpercollins.co.uk/green

Printed and bound in Spain
by CPI, Barcelona

AN UNEXPECTED SCANDAL

JULES BENNETT

This book, and this entire series, is dedicated to the other half of my brain, Jessica Lemmon.

I'm thankful for boat-ride plotting, FaceTime chats when we look our absolute worst and a special friendship that goes well beyond books.

One

The cool spring rain pelted Nick Campbell's back. The unopened envelope in his hand held a secret he'd yet to discover...and part of him wanted to shred it and let the secret die with his mother.

Nick stood over Lori Campbell's pearl-white casket and stared down at the spray of pink roses cascading in every direction. She had left him this letter and told him there were two more to be delivered to the others.

So many secrets, so many cryptic deathbed messages.

Honestly, he didn't care about any of that right now. The yawning ache in his heart over losing his mother trumped all other emotions.

But he'd vowed he would read the letter once she was gone. She had passed five days ago, and he still hadn't opened it. For days he'd carried the envelope around in his pocket, thinking he'd look at it, but one thing led to another. Arrangements were made, insurance dealt with, so many details for a funeral. Nick just hadn't had the time or the energy.

Anticipation and worry gnawed at him, and he knew the moment had come. He had nothing else waiting on him, nothing pressing right this second...and he'd promised his mother.

Nick tore his eyes from the casket and gazed down at the wrinkled envelope in his hand. He tore the seal open and pulled out the letter. With a deep breath, he started to read.

Shock, anger, confusion...so many emotions rolled through him that he had nowhere to channel everything. Nick read through the letter once again, slower this time, hoping he'd read it wrong.

What the hell? How could he process her death and this, too? It was all too much to take in—and he didn't want to accept any of it.

When he'd realized his mother was indeed going to pass only a few short weeks ago, he'd closed in on himself, not wanting to even think of a future without her...let alone finishing the resort she'd started renovating with his help.

The resort that had led him to Silvia.

For one night, Silvia Lane, lead architect on the resort project, had been more than an associate, more than an acquaintance.

She'd been passionate, giving, so damn sexy that he couldn't stop thinking about every single detail. Her hair sliding over his body, that naughty grin she'd tossed him just before she'd let her pencil dress slide down her body. And he'd never forget the way she'd cried out his name as her pleasure took over.

That heated encounter had played over and over in his mind the last four weeks. The morning after, she'd slipped back into her dress, and they'd both agreed there would be nothing beyond that night. She was new in town and building her career. She couldn't afford for anyone to know she'd slept with a client. And he sure as hell was in no position to add another complication to his life.

But she'd comforted him when grief had overtaken him. And part of him wished for more comfort from her now.

Nick's eyes scanned back over the page until the handwritten words blurred together. He wanted to shred the letter, as if that would make this entire nightmare go away. If only things could be so easy…

Unfortunately, Nick knew his mother wouldn't lie. The woman didn't have a deceitful bone in her body, and she would never purposely hurt him, not even with the bombshell she'd left him with.

That didn't mean he understood why she'd kept the truth from him for so long. Or why she'd chosen to share it with him only after she was gone and he could no longer get answers. And what had she meant about two other letters?

Nick pulled in a shaky breath and shivered against the cold rain. He'd said his private goodbyes and it was time to go. He had to move on, to continue to honor his mother's wishes, and carry out her plans.

The crunch of leaves had him jerking around, coming face-to-face with Silvia…the woman he hadn't seen since their one-night stand.

* * *

Silvia had stood back beneath the covering of a lush tree and watched as Nick clearly had a private moment over his mother's grave. He'd pulled an envelope from his pocket and studied it for some time.

Gripping her umbrella, Silvia decided she couldn't stand here forever like some stalker. She had to approach him now before she lost her nerve.

For the past five days she had tried to contact him, but then she'd learned about the death of his mother, and she knew the timing of her news couldn't be worse. She understood why he was not responding to her texts or calls.

It hadn't been because she'd broken their promise to keep it to just one night.

He was grieving, just as he'd been that night everything had changed.

She wanted to go to him, to place a hand on his shoulder to comfort and console, but everything was different now.

They'd had a strong working relationship for the past few months, and then one night in his office, he'd broken down about his mother, and one thing led to another.

There had been attraction building since day one, when he'd hired her as the lead architect for the renovation of his mother's resort.

Being the professional she was, she had kept her erotic fantasies to herself...until that night when she hadn't.

Now look where that had landed her.

How had she fallen for his charms? It wasn't as if she hadn't been charmed by men before. Maybe it was

Nick's vulnerability that night. Perhaps coupled with the impossible-to-ignore sex appeal, she'd really been fighting a losing battle.

Silvia gripped the handle of her umbrella now and shoved her other hand into her jacket pocket. The spring rain and gray skies matched her mood as she took one courageous step and then another.

Nick jerked around, his bright eyes met hers and her mind instantly flashed back to that night they'd taken their business meeting from his leather office chairs to his oversize desk...

She hadn't seen him since, but he'd always been in the forefront of her mind.

"What are you doing here?" he asked, his voice thick with emotion.

Silvia had never seen him so dressed up. He typically wore jeans and a button-down dress shirt, but now he wore a charcoal suit with matching shirt and tie. His dark blond hair perfectly styled, even in the rain, his usually scruffy jaw clean shaven.

And those glasses.

No matter the anguish he was going through, those glasses stopped her cold. She'd knocked those dark frames off his face when she'd jerked his shirt over his head that night.

Focus, Silvia. You're not here for a reunion, and he's hurting.

Neither of them could afford to get more involved than they'd been for those few hours.

He'd disappeared after, and Silvia's heart ached for him during this loss. The timing of this little secret could not be worse. She'd never lied in her life and she certainly wasn't about to start now, not even to save him from more shocking news.

"I'm checking on you," she told him honestly. "I didn't want to smother you during the service. I saw so many people, and I just… I don't really belong here, but I had to come."

Understatement.

"I called and texted," she went on as the rain continued to pelt her umbrella. "I figured this was the only place we could talk."

Droplets clung to his darkened hair, normally a dirty blond when dry. He seemed oblivious to the fact that he stood before her absolutely soaked, with raindrops dotting his lenses.

He still looked too damn good.

"Talk?" Nick shook his head and removed his glasses. He wiped a hand down his face, flinging the moisture aside. "Work is going to have to wait. I know I was pushing for this project to be done, but—"

"I'm not here about work."

His eyes widened for a split second before his lips thinned. "We can talk in the car."

Guilt tugged at her. He stood at his mother's casket, saying his final goodbyes, and here she was, demanding they talk.

If her news weren't so life changing, she wouldn't be here.

"I can go wait in my car," she told him, then nodded toward the casket. "You take your time."

She turned and walked away, not giving him a chance to argue or ask questions. She'd told him they had to talk, and he'd agreed—now she and her bundle of nerves just had to go and keep each other company until he joined them.

The moment she slid behind the wheel, Silvia closed her eyes and willed herself to remain calm. Getting worked up would not change the circumstances, and she had to maintain control. Getting emotional or hysterical wouldn't help and she prided herself on being professional. Now that her professional life had rolled into her personal life, she still had to maintain her composure.

Silvia had only been in her car a couple minutes when the passenger door opened and Nick leaned in.

"I'm soaking wet. Just follow me back to my place. I'll change and we can talk."

He slammed the door before she could say a word, and Silvia dropped her head back against the headrest. She'd followed him here in the rain for a number of reasons. She didn't want to go to his house, didn't want to be on his turf when she broke the news, and she didn't want to wait.

So she didn't.

Silvia opened her car door and stepped out, sans umbrella. She jerked the knot on her trench coat and marched toward Nick's menacing black SUV. Nerves and fear swirled together, but she swallowed back the emotions to focus on the task.

"I need to talk now," she demanded to his back.

He turned, clearly stunned that she had not obeyed his command to just follow him home. But she was done waiting and keeping this secret to herself. She always tackled issues head on, and she was ready to start planning the inevitable changes that were to come.

There was no right time to say it, so she just said it. "I'm pregnant."

Nick slowly turned all the way around to face her, his eyes never wavering. Silvia practically held her breath, waiting on him to say something or have some reaction other than a blank stare.

"Nick?" she finally said.

"Meet me at my house."

And with that he turned, got into his truck and drove off. Looked like she would be following him to his house after all, but the first order of business would be teaching Nick Campbell that she didn't take commands from anyone.

Two

If this day could get any worse, Nick sure as hell didn't want to know how.

First, he laid his mother to rest.

Second, he'd read the final words of his mother in the form of a letter that had left him reeling and shaken.

And finally…this was the real kick in the gut. The lead architect on his mother's multi-million-dollar resort and the only woman he'd ever had a one-night stand with informed him she was pregnant.

He pulled up the long, curvy drive leading to his private mountain home overlooking the Great Smoky Mountains National Park. The tall red spruce and Fraser firs flanked each side of the drive and he'd been sure to leave as many untouched as possible when he'd cleared his lot for his three-story cabin.

This place had always been a tranquil escape from

his hectic life and travel as a business mogul and investor. But now, even the sight of the cozy stone home that he'd had built only a few years ago didn't calm him. His nerves were all over the place, coupled with guilt and pain.

A child.

He was going to be a father? Supposedly, anyway. He knew nothing about parenting. He'd never even wanted a family.

For nearly forty years, he'd wondered who his own father was, but his mother had always said he was better off not knowing. How ironic that now he was sliding into a role he knew absolutely nothing about.

And to become a parent with a woman he had only been intimate with once?

Oh, he'd fantasized about her plenty before that night. Her quick wit and smart business sense had been total turn-ons, not to mention they meshed perfectly together while working on the designs for the mountain resort he would be opening in the fall.

Even his mother had adored Silvia.

Those two had laughed and really seemed to be on the same page when it came to the minute details of the elite, yet cozy mountain getaway. Nick had loved seeing his mother so happy in her final days, but from his vantage point, having Silvia penetrate another layer of his life wasn't smart. A quick fling was one thing, but getting too personal, too permanent, could be a disaster.

Clearly they were entering dangerous territory if he was indeed the father of her child. And, honestly, he didn't believe she would lie about this. He trusted Silvia or she wouldn't be on this project…and he wouldn't have slept with her.

Nick pulled into his garage and left the door open for Silvia to follow. He had no clue what to say. Hell, on a good day he wouldn't know how to react to the news that he was going to be a daddy, but today he was emotionally drained and had nothing left to give.

He stepped from his SUV and removed his suit jacket, then unbuttoned the top two buttons of his dress shirt before rolling up the sleeves. Damn thing was too confining. He certainly wasn't a suit type of guy on a normal day.

His cell vibrated in his pocket, and he pulled the phone out, only to ignore the caller. Rusty Lockwood's office. Of course they'd call *now*, when Nick's world seemed to be falling apart.

He had been demanding a meeting for weeks.

Rusty had been the proverbial thorn in Nick's side for far too long, and today was not the day to deal with that mess. The moonshine mogul and CEO of Lockwood Lightning ruled the resorts and bars of this upscale area with an iron fist. You served Lockwood moonshine or you served nothing at all. Anyone who refused to bow down to Rusty didn't receive a liquor license. And since the grade-A bastard had refused the liquor license for Nick's mom's resort, Rusty was also Nick's main nemesis.

One crisis at a time.

He turned back to Silvia to take care of the current, more pressing crisis.

"I tell you I am pregnant and you just drive off?" Silvia stated as she stepped into the garage and smoothed her wet hair from her face.

"Did you want to get into this at the cemetery?" he countered, the fear and uncertainty raging inside of him.

When she only stared, Nick turned and headed inside—again, he left the door open for her to follow. He heard the most unladylike growl behind him and cursed beneath his breath. He was being an ass, and she didn't deserve it. His emotions were all over the place and he had to take a deep breath and get himself under control.

It wasn't until she'd stepped into the kitchen that Nick realized she'd gotten completely soaked from the downpour. He was soaked, too, but he'd been numb most of the day anyway. She shouldn't have to be miserable.

"I'll grab us some towels," he muttered as he headed down the short hallway toward one of the guest baths.

Nick also grabbed the thick white robe off the back of the door and turned to find Silvia standing in the doorway.

"Are you running from me?" she asked, blocking his exit and holding his gaze.

He handed over the towel and the robe. "I'm not running," he corrected. "I'm trying to get us dry."

And maybe he needed to stay busy to ignore all the emotions he wasn't ready to face.

Silvia clutched the items in her hands and continued to stare at him. Even with her hair hanging in ropelike dark crimson strands, her wet clothes plastered to her shapely form and her face void of most makeup, she was still a damn knockout.

He'd often wondered how he would feel when he saw her again after that night. Now he knew. Even with everything going on, he wanted her. Apparently, nothing could diminish the pull between them.

"I'm not purposely being a jerk," he started as he

raked the towel over his head. "I'm just… Hell, I don't even know what to say."

"I'm not sure what can be said at this point." Silvia patted her face and squeezed her hair with the towel. "I tried getting in touch with you, but you were busy with your mother. I hated showing up at the cemetery, but I knew I would find you there. I purposely waited until everyone else was gone."

In the pouring rain, she'd waited. He'd never met anyone as determined as she was.

"I just want you to know that I don't expect anything of you," she went on. "I mean, if you want to be part of our lives, that's up to you, but I'm not trapping you and I'm not—"

"Stop."

Nick dropped his towel to the floor and reached for hers. She had draped the robe over her arm, but water still dripped from her hair, droplets clinging to her light lashes. Those bright blue eyes remained locked on him as he took her towel and dried her hair. His body reacted, as it always did when she was around, but somehow, knowing she was carrying his child only made him crave her more.

He stepped back because his emotions were too raw, too intense.

"My mother raised me by herself." Nick handed her the towel and watched her slide it down the darkened red strands. "She struggled, sometimes working two jobs, but she never missed my ball games and was always my biggest cheerleader. I never felt like I lacked a father. She was an amazing woman."

Speaking of her in the past tense seemed so strange, so painful…so foreign. She should still be here, alive and vibrant, and finalizing plans on the Smoky Mountains resort she'd always dreamed of opening. And how would she have reacted to the possibility of being a grandmother?

Nick swallowed and went on. "As I got older, I appreciated her drive and determination. That's why I'm so successful today."

"Are you bragging?" Silvia asked, her mouth kicking up in a slight grin.

"Stating facts," he corrected. "What I'm saying is that my mother was a kick-ass woman, and I believe you're just as stubborn and driven."

Silvia blinked. "Um…thanks?"

"Listen, you won't be doing this alone." Nick stepped closer again and gripped her shoulders. "I know what it's like to grow up without a father, but this child will not."

He waited for her to say something, to argue or thank him…hell, he didn't know what to expect. None of this was familiar territory, but he never backed down from a responsibility, and he sure as hell wasn't going to start now with the most important role of his life.

He might not know what it was to have a good father, but he'd try his damnedest to be one.

After that night, when they'd both claimed it was a mistake, neither of them had wanted anyone to know what had taken place in private. Now, though, keeping that secret would be impossible. He couldn't stand by her side without people noticing.

"I want you to have as much of a role as you want," she told him. "But I have to put the needs and the security of the baby first. So if you're going to be around for a little bit and then shirk your daddy duties, I'd rather you not be around at all."

Shirk his duties? Not likely. Clearly she didn't know him very well.

"I'm not going anywhere," he assured her.

She might not believe him, she might have her doubts, but he'd show her with his actions. This child would never question where his or her father was. Nick would always be present and available. Never before had he even thought to put something or someone ahead of his work, but from this moment on, his baby would come first.

Even though his world had seemed to come to a halt with losing his mother, the fact was, Silvia's had kept going and she'd been holding this in until they could speak.

"How are you feeling?" he asked, truly wanting to know how she felt.

Silvia jerked as if the question stunned her. "Oh, well, fine, I guess. I mean, I'm tired, but that's normal, from what I've read. I don't have morning sickness, so I hope that doesn't happen."

She looked amazing. Not a dark circle, not a pale complexion…nothing. Silvia Lane epitomized class and beauty, even when soaking wet and dealing with an unexpected pregnancy.

And if not for a moment of weakness and a few gin and tonics with extra lime, this sexy architect might not have given a rough country boy like him the time of day. Oh, he had money—more than he would ever know what to do with—but that didn't change his roots, a mountain childhood with a struggling single mom.

Silvia was the total opposite with her polished look

and her Ivy League degrees. Her background was likely full of cotillions and dinner parties while his had been frozen dinners in front of the television.

"What was that letter I saw you with earlier?"

Her question pulled him back. "What?"

"At the cemetery," she added. "You were reading a letter, and you seemed, I don't know, angry or hurt. Both."

Hurt? Yeah, that he hadn't been told the truth before his mother passed away.

He'd read the letter twice and already had the damn thing memorized. There was no way he could ever forget his mother's final words, her final confession. The one that would forever alter his life from this moment forward.

Nick,

I'm sorry I couldn't tell you this while I was alive. Maybe I'm a coward, but I just wanted to spare you the pain of the truth for as long as possible. Now, though, I want you to have all of the information available to move forward. You're the smartest, bravest person I know, and I trust you will continue to do the right thing.

For years you asked about your father, and I never wanted you to know the truth. With me gone, you deserve to know everything, even if it's not what you expected or what you want to hear. I hope you don't hate me, and I hope you don't think badly of me.

Rusty Lockwood is your biological father.

Nick despised the man. He had been butting heads with the arrogant prick for the past year. Everyone in

Tennessee knew who Rusty Lockwood was and how conniving he was in business. His moonshine distillery drew in thousands of tourists a year, but Rusty was always under the microscope and dodging rumors of illegal actions.

Nick would bet his private jet that the man didn't have one truly loyal friend. Rusty was as crooked and as underhanded as they came. His millions stemmed from distributing backwoods moonshine long before the white lightning was legal. He'd only kept his head above water because he had certain politicians and the city council in his back pocket.

And now he was the power behind this place. Nick refused to let this go on any longer than necessary. Rusty had to be stopped.

How the hell had Nick's mother gotten mixed up with Rusty Lockwood to begin with? Had he used her and discarded her? Had they actually had a relationship?

Nick recalled the final portion of the letter.

I know this is a shock to you, but I'm telling you the truth. I wish I could tell you your father was anyone else, but I can't. I just want you to be careful. He's vicious, but I can't say I regret my past because it gave me you.

He paid me fifty thousand dollars when I told him about you. He gave me money to leave him alone and keep his name off the birth certificate. I'm not ashamed I took the money—that's how I was able to buy us that small home.

I found out over the years that he fathered two other sons. I'm pretty sure he knows nothing about them, and I hope you all find your way to each other. I've sent them letters as well, and what they decide to do will ultimately be up to them. Continue making me proud. Get my resort up and running. I wouldn't trust anyone else to that task.

I'll love you even in death, Nick. Stay safe.

Nick pulled himself back to the moment. Silvia stared at him, still waiting on an answer.

"It was nothing," he lied.

Because the life Nick had known before this day was gone. Now he had choices to make as his past and his future collided.

Three

"And don't forget to have that to me by the end of the day," Clark said with a wink. "You don't want to mess up your six-month probationary period when you're so close to the end."

Silvia stared at the doorway long after her boss slunk away. Every time he winked that damn wink, she expected an air gun with his hand. And that snarky laugh grated on her every nerve. But she was still fairly new to Green Valley, Tennessee, and she needed this job. She'd moved here from Charlotte, wanting to be closer to the mountains she'd always visited as a child. Why not live in the most peaceful place she could think of?

Granted she wasn't feeling much peace right now.

Clark wasn't her favorite person, not by any means, but this firm was the best in all of Tennessee, so she was thankful for the position. Not to mention she was the only woman in the entire office; even the assistants and the interns were male. She liked to think that said something about her work ethic and her killer skills, but who knew. They likely were worried about a lawsuit, so they needed a woman to prove they were inclusive.

Silvia hadn't yet told her boss that she was expecting. Since the pregnancy was still early, and she hadn't finished the probationary period he'd tried to joke about, she didn't see the need—plus, she didn't think her personal life was any of his business...yet.

She hadn't seen Nick since she'd spoken to him yesterday after his mother's funeral. He'd looked so lost, so stricken with grief, but she couldn't keep the baby a secret from him.

She wouldn't.

She also couldn't turn off her damn hormones where he was concerned. The way he'd gently dried her hair really shouldn't have turned her on, but her body had responded just the same as when he'd taken her on his desk in his office a month ago.

As if she needed another reason to feel a pull toward the man who'd given her the best sexual experience of her life.

That whole rugged, I-don't-give-a-damn attitude really turned her on in ways she couldn't explain. And the glasses, she couldn't forget those. He didn't wear them all the time, but when he did...

Maybe she was tired of proving herself to men like her boss. Maybe the way Nick actually valued her opinion was refreshing. He listened to her, he'd sought her out for this particular project and she could tell that he hadn't been wanting to get in her pants from the get-go. He'd always treated her with respect.

Or maybe she'd just had enough of controlling her emotions, and when he had let that twinge of vulnerability show in his office that night, she'd taken advantage. She'd taken what she wanted.

Now she was pregnant.

Her one and only one-night stand, the one time she'd let herself bend the rules just a bit, and her life was altered forever.

But she didn't have regrets. Regretting any situation wouldn't change the outcome, and regrets always meant looking in the past. She didn't have time for that.

Silvia came to her feet and circled her desk in her tiny office with no window. That was definitely one of her next goals in this building was to secure a window view. It seemed such a shame to work in such a picturesque place and have no view of the mountains.

After flicking the lock into place—because she didn't want anyone barging in while she was making an appointment with an obstetrician—Silvia pulled out her cell.

Her hands shook. While she frequently made regular doctor's appointments, she'd never made a call like this.

Sleeping with a client was a serious no-no, especially for a newbie to the firm like her. But getting pregnant? Silvia had yet to find that chapter in the company handbook.

But she would remain professional about all of this—she had to. Having been raised in foster care, Silvia had always felt like she had to work harder to measure up, to prove herself. Maybe that was all in her own mind, but the self-imposed pressure to do her best at all times was all she'd ever known.

Moments later, Silvia's appointment was made, and

she felt a little more in control of this situation. As much as she would love the fun of going online and making a Pinterest board or searching for the perfect maternity clothes and best baby must-haves, she still had a demanding job to do.

Graduating at the top of her class from Cornell University meant she could manipulate design plans in her sleep and construct a draft like a champ. But for this situation, she just didn't know what steps to take next. Given her upbringing, or lack thereof, she had to be cautious and ensure each decision worked for the good of her child. Bouncing around from foster home to foster home had taught her so much—life's lessons learned the hard way.

She wanted an easier life for her child. She wanted the stability that she'd never had. She wanted her baby to enjoy being a kid and not worry about where he or she would lay their head at night or if mommy and daddy loved them.

Shaking away some not-so-pleasant memories, Silvia glanced to her computer and stared at Nick's name highlighted in yellow for their on-site meeting this afternoon. She hadn't forgotten about it, but they hadn't discussed getting together when she'd seen him yesterday. Would he want to reschedule? He'd just laid his mother to rest and found out he was going to be a father. Jumping back into work seemed a bit soon, didn't it?

No, someone like Nick would want to push forward. He had started this particular project in honor of his mother. Her dream had always been to own a posh mountain resort, and Nick was making every bit of that dream happen—with Silvia's help.

Silvia had absolutely loved Lori Campbell. The

woman had been in poor health by the time Silvia entered the picture, but Lori had still insisted on coming to as many design meetings as possible. A few were even done via video conference so she could attend and continue to give her input. Lori had been a determined woman, and Silvia could appreciate that. She respected Lori so much for going after what she wanted, even as a single mother who had clearly worked hard to give her only son a successful life. She had always been serious a go-getter, or Nick would not have turned out so headstrong and driven.

After their one-night stand, Silvia had worried about how she and Nick would continue their working relationship. She'd never slept with a colleague or a client, and this job was her step up. She'd worked hard to become an architect and had taken a risk moving to a place where she knew nobody.

And now there was so much more to consider.

Like the fact that seeing him again had only reminded her that their one passionate night had definitely not been enough.

Nick pulled his work truck into the site and killed the engine. It had taken all of his willpower not to cancel his meeting with Silvia so he could confront Rusty Lockwood.

But this bit of shocking news would take some time to process. He needed to formulate a flawless, effective plan. With this news, Nick suddenly had an edge up on Russ, which was exactly the way he wanted, no needed, to keep things.

Before this, they'd been butting heads over a liquor license issue, but not even Russ's dirty hands in the pockets of the city council would stop Nick from pursuing what he needed for his resort. He owed his mother.

Besides, he loathed people like Rusty, who bullied simply because they had the power and the money. Someone needed to take Rusty down, and Nick did not mind being the one to step up to the plate.

Even so, barging into Rusty's office with his life-altering news now would only be a mistake.

He could put this information to better use.

And he'd be talking to Rusty soon enough. Through some scouring, Nick had discovered there was a poker game between local bigwigs that took place in the back room at the Rogue Wingman bar every Friday night. Nick had instantly taken an interest in the game. Rusty would be there, and so would Nick.

A flash of red hair caught his eye, and Nick watched through the windshield as Silvia walked out of the front door of the old, historic building. She had on a black jumpsuit that she probably deemed professional, but it just looked sexy as hell to him. With all of that red hair hanging down her back in a mass of waves…

Yeah, one night definitely hadn't been enough if he was still fantasizing about how those silky strands felt across his skin.

She stared up at the building and shielded the late-spring sun from her eyes with her hand. The wind tossed around her curls as she continued to study the area.

Nick had no clue how to shift from lover to co-worker—to father—but he better get used to all of that, because now he owned all the hats.

Instead of sitting there like a creeper, Nick exited the truck and pocketed his phone. Despite the turmoil that his life had become—the discovery of a supposed father, possibly some half brothers, his own impending parenthood and a woman he couldn't seem to forget—Nick would see this project through. At least this resort was one damn thing he could control.

His mother had worked at some of the finest establishments across the nation, but she'd landed in Tennessee as a maid at a local hotel. No matter how poor they were or how they struggled to make ends meet, his mother always valued her job and worked her ass off. She used to tell him about her dream of being able to afford to stay in an elegant place where she could order room service and watch the sun rise over the mountains.

She had the simplest of goals, and Nick had wanted her to live long enough to see this historic building transformed into her dream.

She'd never see it, but he'd build it for her anyway.

Before Nick reached Silvia, she'd disappeared back inside. He hadn't been to the site in a few weeks, what with his mom's declining health and then the funeral arrangements. He was anxious to see the progress and get back to some semblance of normal...or at least figure out his new normal.

The moment he stepped through the old double wooden doors, his breath caught in his throat. Maybe there wasn't so much progress as there was destruction. The place had been stripped down, and piles of rubble lay here and there. The wide, curved staircase proudly stood directly ahead—that was one of the main things Lori hadn't wanted touched other than to refinish it to its original state. Between the location of the building, which was perched on top of one of the Great Smoky Mountains, and the grand staircase, Lori had fallen in love with the place the first time Nick brought her here. He had to admit, he had fallen in love himself. This was the perfect location for an upscale getaway with a million-dollar view.

A muttered curse from behind the stairs had Nick watching his step as he made his way over the roughened wood floors.

"Silvia?"

"Back here," she called.

Nick followed the string of curses until he found her, and he quickly realized her problem. That sexy jumpsuit had just gotten even sexier with a rip down the side, exposing a red strap that no doubt belonged to a thong…if his memory served him correctly, that was her favorite style of underwear. He could fully admit he was a fan himself.

But then he noticed a nasty scratch on her hip. Nick stepped over the pile of rough boards to close the distance between them.

"I just took the tag off this outfit," she grumbled, attempting to hold the two pieces together like that would solve her problems.

"Let me see." He swatted her hands away until the fabric hung around the wound. "How did you do this?"

Nick bent down to examine how deep the cut was.

"The edge of that pile over there. I looked right at it and still managed to snag a corner."

Nick straightened and met her bright eyes. "And you're not wearing your hard hat."

She laughed, crossing her arms over her chest. "Yours is a pretty shade of…oh, wait. You're not wearing one, either."

Nick didn't want to get into an argument—he seriously didn't have the energy today. How could he keep her safe when she volleyed comebacks that were so on point?

And it was that damn strong-will that had first attracted him. Now he didn't find it so sexy when he was the target of her stubbornness.

"I haven't been here in weeks, so I didn't know there was such destruction," he defended. "You knew better."

Silvia shook her head. "Relax. My hard hat is over there with my stuff, and the crew isn't coming in until later. I do know how to do my job."

"Then put on the hat."

"Because that would have saved my leg from being scratched?" she threw back. "Listen, maybe we should reschedule this meeting. You've got so much going on—"

"No."

He wasn't rescheduling, and he was not going to let her tell him what he needed. He needed to work, damn it. He needed to get some regularity back in his life, and this was the only area he currently had control over.

After so many years living in poverty with his mother, he'd finally made it. With his career as an investor and renovator, he had made a name for himself, and he was damn good at what he did. He worked at something he could be proud of.

His personal life? That was something he was going to have to work on...starting with the woman carrying his child.

"Nobody would think anything if you took time off," she added, her voice softening.

He hated pity. He'd had that soul-sucking emotion thrown out at him as a child, and he'd come too far to revert back to it now. Pity for being the poor, hillbilly kid with clothes that had seen better days. Pity for not having a dad. He'd pushed through that web of pity. It had held him down for years. Until he'd gone to college on a baseball scholarship, earned a degree in half the time, and made wise investments before turning all that money around to help others. Determination and drive made all the difference.

It would make the difference now, too.

"I had time off," he reminded her. "My mother would want me to move on and see this through."

When Silvia opened her mouth, he went on. "Get the hard hat on. Better yet, we shouldn't be meeting here, not in your condition. I can wait on the foreman to arrive if you'd like to get back to the office."

Something Nick didn't recognize swept over her features as she squared her shoulders and tipped up her chin.

Well, hell. He didn't know what he'd said that had pissed her off, but he had a feeling he was about to find out.

Four

If Nick Campbell thought for one second that she would be a pushover or let him rule her every move simply because she was pregnant with his child, he was a damn idiot. But, because she was feeling generous and knew he was going through a difficult time, she opted not to throat punch him.

"My office is where I do creative work," she started. "My office is also where I sometimes meet clients for the first time or answer emails. But when I schedule an on-site meeting, I tend to need to go to the actual site. You never had an issue working with me on this project before."

"You weren't carrying my baby before."

Silvia ignored her instinct to think his statement was sweet in some new-dad-worry kind of way and tried to figure out how to shut down this conversation. She didn't want them talking so openly about this. Anyone could walk in and hear, and she needed to keep her pregnancy—and her intimacy with Nick—a secret for now.

She'd worked too hard for her current position to be unprofessional now. And sleeping with a client was the furthest thing from professional she could think of.

Still, that had honestly been the most passionate, hottest night of her life. She'd let her guard down one time, allowed herself to enjoy the hell out him, and now her whole life had shifted. Not only did she have to find a way to prove she was the best at her job, she also had to figure out how to make it all work with being a mother.

"I am still more than capable of working," she countered. "If you're worried about my health, maybe you shouldn't purposely be trying to piss me off. You're raising my blood pressure."

Nick's lips twitched, but he said nothing as he turned on his heel and crossed over to her things, which she'd set on a pile of boards. He grabbed the hard hat, came back, and plopped it down on her head.

"Now, tell me what's been going on the past few weeks."

Damn it. She wanted to be irritated at him for attempting to tell her what to do, but he didn't continue arguing to get his point across. Nick was definitely more a man of action than words.

It was those actions that she kept replaying over and over in her mind.

He'd been fair to his workers, and went out of his way to be kind. That was the sign of a true leader.

But the way he'd looked at her with desire during the beginning stages of this project, yet still managed to be professional had completely turned her on in ways she still couldn't explain. She still couldn't quite get her footing where her need for Nick was concerned.

How could one night of passion have such an impact? How could she still want him despite everything? They'd both agreed it wouldn't go further than one night, but now she had a child to consider. There wouldn't be any grand gestures of romance from either of them. They both had very lucrative careers they were married to and past baggage. Didn't everyone have a load of baggage? Well, she wasn't in the mindset to take on anyone else's...no matter how much she wanted him.

"As you can see, the entire lobby area has been gutted, but we are resurfacing the old hardwoods and keeping the copper ceiling." She gripped the gaping material at her thigh. "You requested we keep as much as possible and restore it, so all of the old trim is being housed in the basement for now and will be cleaned up and put back in place."

Silvia continued to go over what had been done in the past couple of weeks, plus the next steps. All the while, Nick kept those striking dark blue eyes on her.

If she thought he'd been potent before they'd slept together, that was nothing compared to now. She knew the intensity of those eyes during moments of pleasure— she vividly recalled how her body shivered as he raked that hungry gaze over her. She was shivering a little even now remembering how that same gaze traveled over her bare skin.

"Silvia?"

His low voice jerked her back, and she realized she had stopped talking and she'd been staring...remembering.

Great. Just what she didn't need—to lose touch with

what was important here, and it wasn't her desires. Nick trusted her with this project. He'd chosen her because he trusted her work, and because she was a woman and he wanted someone who could relate to his mother's vision. There was pressure to get this right. Added to that, several coworkers at her firm were just waiting on her to fail so they could swoop in and save the day...and gain the healthy paycheck that came from working with world-renowned mogul Nick Campbell.

Silvia had to honor the vow she'd made to herself way back in foster care—she would always rely only on herself and rise above any obstacle. She wouldn't depend on anyone to hold her up or escort her through life. And she wasn't going to start now. She refused to rely on Nick, not financially and not emotionally.

Just because she kept thinking back to their night together and fantasizing didn't mean it could happen again.

"As I was saying," she went on, clearing her throat. "I remember, too."

Silvia stilled. Her heart thumped heavily; her hand gripped the torn material even tighter. His low tone washed over her, thrusting her back to that night when he'd whispered sultry words in the dark.

"I recognize fantasizing," he added, taking a step forward, his eyes never wavering from hers.

Silvia didn't back up—she refused to seem weak or intimidated, because she already looked absurd standing here in a hard hat and a torn jumpsuit.

"Who says I was daydreaming?" she asked, cursing herself when her voice cracked.

Nick settled his hand on her hip and stared down into her eyes. He made her feel almost...well, protected.

She'd never felt completely protected in her life, and she was not going to let herself get comfortable with the feeling now. All the years of taking care of herself had hopefully prepared her for the next role she would take on as mother and provider.

She couldn't add lover or girlfriend or anything else to the mix. Getting swept up in hormones would not benefit anyone long-term.

"You don't have to say a word," he murmured as he leaned in closer. "Your face is full of expressions…and I recall each and every one from our night together."

Silvia's body heated with his words, his delicate touch, his nearness. She placed a hand on his chest and stared into those mesmerizing eyes.

"We're having a baby," she reminded him. "Everything has changed. But still, we can't do this again."

"Why not?" he countered. "The desire hasn't gone away."

He inched forward, his lips merely a breath away. Her body ached for him to touch her, to prove to her that everything she recalled was real and perfect.

Why couldn't they do this again? She was having a difficult time remembering with him standing so close.

The slam of a truck door pulled Silvia back. She jerked away as reality smacked her in the face.

"Because we're working together," she stated, reminding herself. "This is my first project with a new firm. I can't afford to get tangled with a client."

Something harsh washed over his face. "Too late."

He barely got the words out before the foreman for the project came strolling in wearing his hard hat, work boots, and denim overalls. Silvia gripped the material together at her thigh and skirted around Nick. She had to remain in control of this situation, of her emotions, or she'd find herself right back where she'd been a month ago.

Naked and in his arms begging for more.

Nick stared at the jewelry on the desk in his home office. He'd requested that his mother's jewelry be returned after the funeral, and his assistant had just dropped the pieces off earlier.

Propping his hands on his hips, he contemplated what to do with them. His mother had always worn the plain diamond necklace. It was the smallest stone in the simplest of settings, but that's what Nick had purchased for her with his first check. He had wanted her to have something nice after all the years of working so hard to take care of him.

As he'd become more successful, he'd tried to get her to choose a new necklace or at least take this one off. She deserved better, bigger, but she'd said over and over that this necklace meant more to her than any other ever would and she didn't want to replace it.

He didn't think the simple gold hoops were worth anything, but she'd always worn them, too.

So now Nick stood in his home office and stared at the last few items of his mother's. Well, and the letter that he had locked away in his safe.

After leaving Silvia at the site earlier, he had driven around, trying to put his thoughts into some nice, neat order, but considering his entire life was in chaos, there was no way to organize his thoughts.

Ultimately, he'd ended up at home. He probably should go in to the office, but there wasn't a thing he couldn't do from home, and he wasn't quite ready to hear the condolences or be on the receiving end of countless hugs. He knew his employees meant well—they had showered him with food, flowers, cards—but he just couldn't see them face-to-face right now.

When his assistant had brought the jewelry, he'd also informed Nick that they had been denied once again for the hard liquor license for the new resort. Not that Nick had believed it would pass for him when it hadn't for others in the area, but he wished he had at least one break right now.

Regardless of all the changes in his life, he wouldn't back down. Rusty Lockwood might think he ran the town and had all the power, but Nick had his own leverage right now. Rusty had no idea about the damning letter left behind revealing the truth.

Would Rusty even care that he had a son? Would he be interested in knowing that there might be others who would come forward?

Nick planned to keep the information guarded until it was time to strike. He wanted to cause the worst possible blow to Rusty Lockwood. That man needed to be knocked down several proverbial pegs. The fact that he continued to monopolize the local liquor world was beyond absurd.

Green Valley and the surrounding areas were rich with moonshine history. The stories of how "white lightning" was once sold illegally until the state realized what an investment it would be to legalize the drink. Tourists traveled from all over the globe for tastings and to experience the atmosphere and beauty of the Great Smoky Mountains.

Nick understood wanting to capitalize on the market, but Rusty couldn't just keep his iron fist clutched around the entire industry.

There was no way Nick would open a resort and not serve hard liquor. A glass of bourbon or even a shot of moonshine was perfectly acceptable, and most definitely expected, in this area. Nick had every intention of making this upscale getaway top notch, high class and every single thing his mother envisioned. He wouldn't let one man with too much power rule over him. There was too much at stake and he'd made his mother a promise he fully intended to keep.

Nick took the small velvet pouch and slid the jewelry back inside then took everything over to his safe, which was behind a section of books in a built-in bookcase. As he opened the safe, his eyes landed on the letter, the envelope crumpled around the edges.

The initial anger and confusion had lessened, replaced by curiosity and worry. His mother had kept such a life-altering secret for decades. Not only regarding the identity of Nick's biological father, but also the fact there were two half brothers out there somewhere.

Were they also guys he knew? Were they in Green Valley, Tennessee? Nick had so many questions, but he would have to have patience. Time would reveal all the answers.

To know that his mother had carried this secret around for so long, plus that she'd gone above and beyond to make sure she provided his every need, humbled Nick. The love that she'd expressed without words, just to try to keep him safe and protected because she truly believed Rusty to be a monster. Likely Rusty would've tried to use his paternity as some type of blackmail if he could have figured out a way to gain anything further for himself.

Nick's mother had been strong—stronger than he'd realized until now.

Which reminded him of another strong woman.

Silvia would do anything for her child, of that he was certain. She'd told him the truth, but she'd also been pushing him away. She would insist on doing everything on her own, simply to prove she could, but he didn't want her to ever for a second feel like she was in this alone. Everyone needed a shoulder to lean on at some point.

Nick knew without a doubt that Silvia would never ask for help or admit that she needed him. That was fine. Her pride and her independence were just two of the qualities he had originally found so damn attractive. Her sexy little suits didn't hurt, either.

Pushing aside his past and focusing on the present, Nick shut the safe and arranged the books back in place. He could mourn and focus on everything that had happened with his mother's death, with the secrets she'd kept, or he could take hold of this information and honor his mother's reasons for protecting him. She'd done what she'd thought was right under the circumstances, and now she'd given him the truth as her final gift.

Nick's cell vibrated on his desk, and he glanced over his shoulder to see Silvia's name.

In two quick steps, he crossed and answered.

"Silvia."

"I'm at your gate," she stated. "Let me in."

Demanding women had never appealed to him before, but damn, this one did. He'd have to tell her about the bell to ring on the keypad that would alert him she was here.

Nick disconnected the call and made a quick tap on his app that unlocked the wrought iron gate at the bottom of the mountain. Nick didn't know what warranted her coming back to his house, but he was certainly not going to complain.

Nick went to the front of the house and waited on the covered porch. He hadn't realized it had started raining while he'd been home, but the darkened skies made it look as if they were in for one hell of a spring storm.

The weather seemed to be a metaphor for his life as of late.

Silvia brought her car to a stop in the curve of the drive closest to the porch steps. The rain pelted the vehicle, and she reached toward the passenger floorboard to see where her umbrella had gone. Those things were never close when she needed them, and lately she had needed them more than usual. Crazy spring weather.

Cursing, she realized she'd just have to run to the porch and become a haggard, wet mess…pretty much just like the last time she was here.

Silvia turned to reach for her handle and screamed.

One second ago Nick had been on his porch, but now he stood at her door with an umbrella, being all southern gentleman and making that speech she rehearsed vanish.

Damn him for being so considerate. Those kind little gestures were definitely not helping her self-control. At least he wasn't wearing his glasses right now. The look of him in those things was pretty much a panty dropper, and she seriously needed to keep those in place.

Nick reached for the handle and opened the door, making sure to hold the umbrella over the opening as she got out.

"Seems to be a theme lately," he told her with a sexy, cockeyed grin.

"I'm not staying long."

She made the statement more for herself than for him, but he merely widened his smile and hooked an arm around her waist. As he led her to the porch, she huddled against his side away from the pelting rain... and instantly knew coming here was a mistake.

She'd wanted to talk face-to-face, to lay down some boundaries about workplace etiquette and how they needed to keep their personal relationship separate from their business one. And by personal, she meant the baby...not the attraction that she needed to ignore and put in the past.

Once on the porch, Nick shook out the umbrella and propped it next to a stone column. Nick's house was exactly like him: bold, masculine and magnificent. Situated up on the mountainside, the place offered spectacular views, even better than her own mountain home only ten minutes away. But he didn't know where she lived, and for now she wanted to keep it that way.

There had to be some division between personal and professional until they had a good foundation for moving forward with this baby bond they'd share forever. She had to curb the attraction until she was positive the future of her child was secure.

"Have you had dinner?" he asked.

Silvia shook her head. "No, but I'm not here for that. I won't be long."

"Well, I'm hungry." He turned and opened the massive wooden door. "You can talk while I cook. If you're still talking when it's done, you might as well stay."

She stared at him, but he extended his arm in a silent gesture for her to come in. Silvia let out a sigh and marched past him. She wasn't staying for dinner...she *wasn't*. Was he purposely trying to seduce her?

Yet again, a man of action.

Without a word, Nick started toward the back of the house and into the kitchen. Silvia set her purse on the table inside the door and followed. There. Her keys and her phone were close to the door through which she would be exiting very, very soon.

Silvia stepped into the kitchen and barely contained a gasp. The entire back wall was one breathtaking view, with sliding glass doors that opened to the most magnificent patio. Even in the rain and under the darkening skies, she could make out a tiered eating area and pool.

This design was most definitely an architect's dream. She wanted to explore further.

"Go ahead and open it up," he told her as he pulled out a round baking stone and set it on the concrete center island. "I love listening to the rain. Thunder and lightning have always fascinated me."

Silvia made her way across the spacious room and slid open first one door and then the other. The refreshing aroma of the rain hit her, and she pulled in a deep breath. There was something so calming about the crisp mountain air. It was nearly impossible to be in a bad mood or let worries consume her.

She'd come to Green Valley for the serenity that only the Smoky Mountains could offer. Visiting a handful of times a year simply hadn't been enough. She wanted to settle here and now that she was expecting, she couldn't think of a better place to raise her child.

"I'm making my famous barbecue chicken pizza," he told her. "The dough has been rising since this morning."

Silvia jerked her head around, fully expecting him to be smirking at her or laughing at the joke, but no. Nick wasn't even looking her way as he worked the dough with his hands, and within moments, he was tossing it up in the air and catching it like a pro. The dough naturally stretched with each fling.

"You make your own pizza dough?" she asked, still stunned. What world had she just stepped into where Nick was this domestic?

"Not only is it healthier than store bought, but it tastes so much better," he informed her. "No processed chemicals here."

O-kay.

"And do you make other homemade things?" she asked. "Soaps, wreaths or perhaps your suits?"

Now he did laugh as he placed the dough onto the stone and started arranging it into place. "You're mocking me," he said. "That's fine. I get it. Not many people know that I am actually a great cook."

"So you flip businesses brilliantly, develop high-class resorts and make self-proclaimed famous pizzas." Silvia crossed to the opposite side of the island and settled on a leather stool. "What other secrets are you hiding?"

His eyes darted to hers. A darkness she'd never seen stared back at her, then he glanced back down to his task.

"I'd say that's for another time over something more than pizza."

Silvia watched those strong hands work and couldn't help but recall exactly how talented he had been with her body. As if she needed the reminder. There wasn't a day or night that went by that she didn't remember in vivid detail how perfect they had been together.

And, yes, there had been alcohol involved, but she'd known exactly what she'd been doing and who she'd been saying yes to. Maybe she'd crossed the line because he'd been at a vulnerable time, but he was a big boy. He had definitely been on board with every single passion-filled touch and everything that followed.

Besides, since day one, when he and Lori had come into Silvia's office, there had been sparks. Lingering glances, extra meetings that could probably have been a simple email or text. She'd thought she could work with him and ignore that spark. She'd been wrong.

But she couldn't afford to be wrong again.

"There goes that memory of yours again," he murmured.

Silvia wasn't going to bother denying it this time. Why should she? They both knew this attraction was still strong, and maybe only getting stronger.

"So what if I remember?" she tossed back. "We both had a good time, but that's actually what I'm here to discuss."

With a quirk of a brow, he stilled his hands and stared at her. "Discuss? I prefer no talking, but I'm game to try something new."

Silvia didn't even try to suppress her eye roll. "We have a working relationship, Nick. That's where we need to focus, and that is where this relationship needs to stay."

Nick flattened his hands on the counter and leaned forward. "How long did you rehearse that?"

"Pretty much the entire way over here," she admitted with a smile. "But I'm serious. I have too much at stake to get personally involved with a client."

"Yet you're having my baby, and you still want me."

"Nobody needs to know this is your baby until the project is complete. Actually, I would prefer it that way."

She wasn't going to acknowledge that last part.

If she thought his stare was dark a moment ago, that was nothing compared to what flashed over his face now. Her words had hurt him, angered him. But she had to be honest. It wasn't her way to play games here.

"I will not lie about being the father, and I sure as hell won't stay back and have you go through this process alone."

Silvia completely understood why he was so quick to irritation. He deserved to be part of the baby's life, too.

"That came out wrong," she amended, folding her arms on the concrete countertop. "I'm not pushing you away from our child, but I can't let my firm know that I'm pregnant just yet, and certainly not that I'm pregnant by a client."

Nick stared another minute, his shoulders finally relaxed as he went back to smoothing out the sauce and adding toppings.

"Women don't have babies in your workplace?"

"There are no other women in my workplace."

His eyes darted up to hers. "Seriously? None?"

Silvia shook her head. "There have been in the past, but they've never stayed long. I've just refused to let them drive me out. I'm damn good at my job, I love Green Valley and I need the prestige behind the Baxter firm's name to launch my career."

"You don't need anyone," he replied. "Your prior projects speak volumes about your ability."

While she wished she could bask in the warm fuzzies of his praise, she still had to stay in touch with reality. And the reality was, she worked in a male-dominated field, and more often than not, as a woman, she had to work twice as hard to get half the recognition.

"I'm new to Baxter, remember?" she asked. "I've only been here six months, and I'm still in the probationary period. Besides, I'm sure they wouldn't like to learn that I slept with my very first client. It's important that I be seen as professional."

Nick said nothing as he took the stone and placed it in the brick pizza oven. Now that she glanced around beyond the view, she realized this was a serious chef's kitchen. He had spared no expense with the eight-burner gas stove, two refrigerators and an impressive wine fridge.

Nick circled the island and came to stand next to her, resting his elbow on the counter. His eyes held hers, and she concentrated on keeping his gaze, not letting her focus drop to his lips.

"You are worried about what they'll think, yet that night, you made the first move."

Silvia shrugged. "Sometimes when I see something I want, I go after it. I'm human, and I couldn't stop myself."

He'd had on those glasses with stubble all across his jawline. The combination of rough and studious had been tempting her since they met. But it had been his sense of vulnerability that night that had pushed her over the edge.

Nick inched closer, his hand settling on her thigh. "Something else we have in common. I go after what I want, too."

And then his mouth covered hers.

Five

He was a damn fool for torturing himself.

Nick knew full well that Silvia had every intention of drawing a proverbial line between them of dos and don'ts, but right now all he cared about was feeling her again.

There was no one to stop them, no crew member who could walk in and interrupt. With the pelting rain outside and the aromas wafting around the kitchen, Nick was as relaxed as he had been in weeks. Something about Silvia calmed him…something he couldn't afford to explore further.

His hand slid up her thigh and over her hip to settle at her waist. Silvia shifted in her seat, turning to get a better angle, and her knees widened, so Nick took the opening and settled in deeper.

The softest moan escaped her, and Nick thrust his

hand into her hair, tipping her head back just enough to have better access. It still wasn't enough. He wanted to consume her, to strip her of everything and lay her out on the counter. He wanted to carry her out into the rain and take her on the chaise. Anywhere he could have her, he wanted her.

Nick hadn't touched her like this in a month, and no matter what she wanted to claim, their chemistry wasn't just contained to one night. And it wasn't the product of a few too many gin and tonics or the desperation of grief.

There was a passion in Silvia he'd never experienced before, and he wasn't done.

Her hands flattened against his chest, and she pushed him slightly. "No. We can't do this."

Actually, they could, because they were, but he respected her enough to stop. She was obviously torn, and he didn't want to make her life more difficult.

"Why would you deny yourself?" he asked.

"Because I have a job to do, and now I have a child to consider," she stated. "Right now, my needs are irrelevant."

At least she admitted she had needs. That was a step in the right direction. He was just going to help her take another step. She felt this heat between them just as he did, and she could only deny herself for so long...

"Obligations are something I understand," he stated. "I wouldn't be where I am today if I hadn't always held firm to my responsibilities. But it's okay to be selfish sometimes."

Her eyes darted away. "I have been selfish my entire life," she murmured.

"I find that difficult to believe."

Nick doubted there was a selfish bone in her body. When someone worked as hard as she did, was as determined as she was, that meant often putting other people's needs first.

"You don't know me, Nick." Her eyes flashed back to his, pain and sorrow settling deep in them. "My childhood wasn't quite as sweet as yours."

Nick eased back from between her legs and settled on a bar stool. He reached across the island and slid his hand over hers. Those words weren't what he was expecting, and he realized he didn't know enough about her. He actually wanted to know more.

More than what it felt like to be with her for one night, more than how much ass she could kick as an architect. Nick wasn't sure what that meant—that he wanted to know everything about her—but he wasn't going to try to label his emotions, not when they were all so raw.

"I grew up pretty damn poor," he told her when she remained silent. "I didn't know just how poor at the time. My mother never let me feel like I was unloved or that we weren't safe."

"Well, I never knew my parents."

A sad smile crept over her face, and it took every ounce of willpower not to haul her into his lap. Nick waited for her to continue, but the pit in his stomach told him he wasn't going to like what she had to say. This shocking revelation was a far cry from the lifestyle he'd assumed she'd had while growing up. Maybe they were more alike than he thought, both having difficult pasts to overcome before finding success.

"I was sent to my first foster home two days after I was born."

Her voice remained strong, as if she'd become numb to the past, or as if she'd given this rundown too many times to be affected and now they were just words. But Nick knew better. Silvia felt deeply; she was invested in this story about how she'd been raised. She'd put up a defensive wall against her past, and that was how she was able to talk about it now. As if he needed another reason to admire her. The more he discovered about her, the more he was piecing together how she'd become so strong and resilient.

"By the time I started school, I had been in three foster homes. From then on, I continued to bounce around. There were times I caused trouble, and I remember a counselor telling the couple I was living with that I just needed more attention."

Silvia's humorless laugh pierced his heart. There was so much pain in the sound, he wondered if she even realized how much.

"Attention was the last thing I wanted," she went on. "I wanted to be left alone. I excelled at school because that's what I threw myself into. The only thing I connected with was reading, so I read everything I got my hands on."

"My mother used to read to me every night," he chimed in, unusually comfortable with talking about his own past. "Even when I was a teenager, that was something I never got tired of. I knew it was something not everyone did, so I never told a soul, but it was our thing."

Silvia offered him a sweet smile. "A little library for the baby is a good idea. I don't think it's ever too early to start showing them how much you care."

From a woman who clearly wanted someone to care.

Maybe that's exactly what she'd always needed. She might put up that steely exterior, but hurt recognized hurt. No matter how much she kept to herself, Silvia deserved someone in her life she could count on...someone she could turn to.

That certainly wasn't him. He wasn't the type of man who had ever longed for family life. He'd watched his mother work hard to save every penny, and she'd taught him how to have a strong work ethic so he could have a better life than anything she could've provided in his early years. She'd instilled in him that his career had to come first because he couldn't always count on a relationship to put food on the table, or for happiness.

Growing up without a father had been a void he never could shake, and now that he knew the truth, that void seemed to be even larger because of who his father really was. There was so much ugliness surrounding Rusty Lockwood, and that bloodline lived in Nick. Maybe that bloodline was more a part of him than he could have imagined. Was Rusty's legacy why he'd failed at his first marriage? Was it why he couldn't see himself as father material? Maybe it confirmed that he wasn't a man worthy to be with Silvia.

Even so, he would provide for her and their child.

Nick didn't like the poignant stirrings swirling like a vortex inside his heart. He couldn't let his emotions get wrapped up in her right now, especially with the state he was in. Now was certainly not the time to make any major life decisions or read too much into what was happening between them. All he could offer her was a physical connection and financial support—he had plenty of both to give.

The timer went off before he could say anything else. Nick stood, and Silvia came to her feet as well.

"I should go."

Nick settled his hands on her shoulders and looked her in the eyes. "Dinner is ready, and it's getting nasty out. Stay."

Her eyes held his, and he waited for her to argue or decline, but she simply nodded.

"I'd like that."

"We're still within budget and on track to open by summer's end," Silvia stated as she leaned back in the Adirondack chair on the covered patio.

Dinner had been amazing, and Nick deserved those bragging rights he'd talked about earlier. Somehow, he'd convinced her to come outside to watch the storm, and she found the longer she sat here, the more relaxed and comfortable she became. So she opted to discuss work and try to keep her mind centered right where it should be.

"That's good news," Nick told her. "I'm sure something will come up with the budget—that's inevitable with older buildings—but I want this done right and exactly how my mom would've envisioned it. I'm not worried about the cost."

No, he wouldn't be. Not only did he have the financial means to do anything he wanted, he would spare no expense in honoring the woman he'd loved more than anyone.

That kind of bond was a true testament to the type of man Nick was. She believed he would be loyal to a fault, but Silvia also didn't know how all of this would work between them and with the baby.

Regardless, she had several months to get a sense of his true feelings about being a father. No matter what, she would provide for their child, whether Nick decided to be in the picture or not.

"Have you been able to lock in that licensing you wanted for the bar?" she asked, keeping the conversation on business...a safer common ground.

Nick let out a snort. "Not yet. Rusty Lockwood is a bastard on his best day, but I'm not done with him. The fight won't end until I've won."

"I haven't met him, but I've been in town long enough to know he has more enemies than friends. The tourists don't seem to mind, though. His establishment is always busy."

"Tourists are there for the tasting experience and the liquor to take home," Nick stated. "They don't care about the type of man Rusty is. And his so-called friends are paid to remain loyal, so I'm not sure how legit those relationships are."

Yeah, she'd heard all about how much of a shark Rusty was. His moonshine distillery brought in thousands of thirsty tourists per month and was good for the local economy, but the man only cared about the bottom line. He'd been under a lot of scrutiny recently, from what Silvia had heard. Only last year he had been fined by the IRS for tax evasion.

Maybe he'd made some enemies way back when he'd first started and moonshine was illegal. Rusty couldn't pay off everybody who passed through that he needed on his side. Silvia was just glad she didn't have to deal with the infamous mogul.

"I'm sure you'll win the fight," she told Nick. "You have more motivation to win than he does."

"I've never lost a fight yet," he informed her. "I sure as hell don't intend to lose this time, not to such an arrogant prick."

Silvia extended her legs out in front of her and crossed her ankles. Lacing her hands over her abdomen, she closed her eyes as she listened to the rain and the roll of thunder. She wondered about the little life growing inside her and could admit she was equal parts terrified and excited.

Even though she'd never really had a solid mother figure, Silvia vowed to do her absolute best where this baby was concerned. Love and stability would go a long way.

Nick's arm brushed hers, and she wished when they'd come out that he'd chosen another seat—he had enough choices, between the benches, loungers, and tables and chairs, but he'd taken up in the Adirondack next to hers.

The nearness did nothing to tamp down her desires. Having him cook dinner for her hadn't helped, either. Getting even more involved with him would not look good to her firm—it was the reason she'd never intended to be intimate with him again—and part of her wondered if they were waiting on her to mess up just like this. Not that they'd ever admit it, because they thrived on having a solid reputation, but she figured Clark was ready to swoop in and take over the project at her first slip.

Fingertips brushed over her arm, then feathered across her cheek.

"Silvia."

Her name sounded so distant, yet so intimate.

"Sil."

Nobody ever called her that. Having her one-time

lover use a special name should have made her want to run away for fear of getting entangled in something she wasn't ready for. But she couldn't run from Nick, not anymore…and she didn't want to.

His fingertips slid over her jawline, and a moment later she was being lifted, cradled.

Her eyes flew open as she realized Nick had swept her up into his arms. "What are you doing?"

"You fell asleep."

With a strength she found ridiculously sexy, he carried her through the house. She slid her arms around his neck for a more secure hold. Maybe just for a minute she'd allow herself to take comfort in his warmth and strength.

"I can walk, you know."

"I'm aware. You actually have quite a sexy strut."

Silvia narrowed her eyes. "I don't strut."

"Oh, you do."

He turned toward the grand staircase and started up.

"What are you doing?"

The stubborn man wasn't even out of breath as he hit the first landing and kept going on up to the second floor.

"Putting you to bed."

"Oh, hell no."

Nick's deep chuckle vibrated against her. "Relax. I have plenty of spare bedrooms. You can even choose which one you want. They all have their own baths and their own views of the mountains."

"I'm not worried about the amenities," she countered. "I can't spend the night."

When he reached the top, he stopped and glanced

down at her. "You said the same about dinner, but you enjoyed it. Two of everything, if I recall."

"I do everything in twos," she muttered, hating that he had noticed that little quirk.

Silvia growled when he remained still and staring. "Put me down."

The arm beneath her knees gave way, and she gripped his neck to keep from stumbling as she found her footing.

"I'm not staying," she repeated.

Nick settled his hands on the curve of her hips and leveled a stare. "I don't recall you being so difficult when we first started working together. In fact, we got along so well."

Yeah, hence the pregnancy. They'd had that whole flirtatious-banter thing going on for months before she decided to make a move.

After all the pep talks she'd given herself on why she couldn't get involved with a client, she'd had a moment of weakness and given in to her desires. Denying Nick wasn't something she could do, and she'd honestly thought one night would simply be just that…one night only. They'd agreed not to discuss it again.

And they hadn't. Until she'd found out she was pregnant. Keeping a personal distance at that point had become utterly impossible.

"Everything has changed," she reminded him. "I work for you. I can't play roommates or have a slumber party with you, too."

His mouth twitched, and she wanted to smack him. "I'm serious," she added.

"Nobody has to know you're here," he told her. "Nobody has to know you're pregnant or that I'm the father until you're ready. I respect the position you're in, and I'm sure we're both going to learn along the way. Don't push me away just because you're scared."

Scared? She had well surpassed scared. There was no plan B if she lost her job. She'd had to depend on herself nearly her entire life, and now was no different. Wait, it was totally different, because now she would have a little human who depended on her for financial stability and loving support.

And Nick wanted her to stay, agreeing to carry over the terms from their one-night stand, not letting anyone in on their secrets.

A good portion of her was tempted to take him up on his offer. They'd been so compatible in bed, and she never ignored warning flags and did something for herself.

But, as tempted as she was, she also had to keep her control in place. One little slip and she'd find herself in Nick's bed before she could even see that red flag waving.

Silvia stared back at him and then shook her head. "I can't figure you out. You say the right things, you do the right things, you're…"

Apparently her exhaustion and attraction had removed the filter from her mouth.

"Don't stop now," Nick said with a sexy grin. "I'm interested in knowing what you think about me."

"Your ego is big enough," she chided. "I'm not feeding it any more than necessary."

Nick smoothed her hair away from her face, and Silvia pulled up all of her control to ignore the urge to turn her face into his touch.

"It's not my ego that needs feeding." His eyes held

hers for a second before he shifted that hungry focus to her lips. "I have other urges." He nipped at her lips. "Other desires."

The dim lights lining the hall set an intimate mood she couldn't afford. The late hour, the storm surging outside, the way he looked at her like he was ready to fulfill her every need, the way she wanted him in spite of her best intentions, all collided into a dangerous situation.

"This is a terrible idea," she whispered, but she found herself reaching up to touch his crisp stubble that would no doubt turn back into the beard he typically sported. "I came here to tell you we couldn't be more than professional colleagues for now and we would work on the whole parenting thing later."

Nick gripped her hips and pulled her closer. "You did tell me, several times, in fact."

"I'm not taking my own advice."

Nick eased closer until his lips were a breath away. "Nobody knows you're here, Silvia. Nobody has to know what we do behind closed doors. And this attraction has nothing to do with business."

Why did his every word resonate with her? Why did she want to ignore everything outside this house and just take what he offered?

Because she was human and she wanted him and resisting Nick had proven to be impossible...not that she tried too hard, but still.

Before common sense could prevail, Silvia framed his face with her hands and covered her mouth with his. Once again, he swept her up into his arms, and this time, she didn't object.

Six

Nick fully expected Silvia to argue or insist on leaving. He'd been ready to accept he might have to let her go, even though taking her into his suite was exactly where he'd wanted her since day one.

Now she was here, and she looked even more perfect than he'd imagined.

Lightning flashed through the wall of windows and doors in his bedroom. He wanted to see her in this light. In the frantic, raging storm. The fury seemed fitting, considering they both were going into this knowing they might be making a mistake, arguing about the reasons they should be more careful, but ultimately agreeing they deserved to take what they wanted.

For two people who had been in the deepest valleys of life as children, they knew that when happiness entered the realm, they had to take hold.

"Tell me now if you don't want this."

Her eyes held his as she reached down and pulled her silky top over her head and tossed it to the floor.

"Just one more night," she told him. "Tomorrow we go back to being architect and client."

Sure, if she wanted to tell herself that, he could play the game. And maybe she even believed the lies she told herself, but there was still too much heat between them. Ultimately there was no way they could keep up the professional charade she was hoping for.

"You're feeling all right?" he asked. "I mean, with the baby?"

"The baby and I are both fine," she assured him. "I wouldn't keep anything like that from you."

Her affirmation of loyalty shouldn't tug at his…

No. His heart wasn't involved.

That was absurd. This was lust and sex. They had limits on their crazy attraction. Neither of them wanted more, and he should be ecstatic she felt the same.

Nick was done talking, because talking only revealed more and more ways they were alike and compatible. He quickly rid himself of his clothes, but when Silvia started to reach for her pants, he swiped her hands away.

"I'll do this."

With expert work on the button and zipper, he had her jeans sliding down shapely thighs, leaving her standing in her satin panties and matching bra.

Nick slid his hands over her curves, grazing his thumbs over her abdomen. He dropped to his knees and kissed the smooth skin just below her belly button.

Silvia's fingers threaded through his hair, and instead of getting wrapped up in the turmoil of his life lately, Nick dipped his head to the curve of her inner thigh and trailed kisses along the delicate elastic seam where her panties met skin. He gripped her hips and inhaled her arousal, his body throbbing with a need he only found with her.

And this time they were both completely sober.

He curled his fingers around the material and pulled her panties down until she lifted one foot then the other to kick them aside.

Nick gripped the back of one leg and lifted it over his shoulder as he buried his face at her core. Silvia's cry and the tug on his hair had Nick grabbing hold of her backside to secure her exactly where they both wanted. He'd had every intention of going slow and properly laying her on his bed like a gentleman.

But when it came to his desires, there wasn't a gentlemanly thought on his mind. Something inside him snapped whenever she moaned or sighed or gave any inclination that every move he was making was the right one. He got so much intense pleasure from *her* pleasure that Nick could continue for hours.

Silvia's hips jerked, and she cried out his name as her orgasm tore through her. Nick consumed her release, making sure she had the best experience, because this was just the beginning of the night. He wanted so much more from this passionate woman.

When her trembling ceased, Nick held on to her as he came to his feet. She swayed a little against him, and he swept her back up into his arms.

Before tonight, he hadn't realized how much he loved doing this, but holding Silvia in such a protective pose made him feel like he could shield her from anything life threw her way. She deserved that, even though she'd argue she didn't need anybody.

"You're determined to carry me everywhere," she murmured, laying her head against his shoulder.

"Oh, I'm determined," he agreed, but his motivation was a little more primal.

Now he did lay her out on the bed, selfishly standing over her to take in that flushed body. With the exterior lights and the random flashes of lightning, he could see her perfectly.

Silvia came up onto her elbows and smiled. "Are you joining me, or do you think I'm going to beg?"

Nick laughed as he climbed up on the bed to settle over her. She fell back and wrapped her arms and legs around him.

"Protection?" he asked, realizing that might be silly at this point, but there were other issues besides an unplanned pregnancy.

"I'm clean," she told him. "You?"

He nodded. "Is this what you want?"

Because going without would put them at an entirely different level of intimacy—one he wasn't sure either of them was ready for.

Yet he couldn't deny his wants or her obvious desire.

Nick joined their bodies and earned a gasp from Silvia as she arched against him. He gritted his teeth as he began to move, confirming that the one night he'd had with her *had* been different…euphoric.

With one hand on the back of her thigh and the other holding his body above hers, Nick shifted against her as she met his thrusts with her own. Her passion matched his, and Nick still couldn't get enough.

Watching Silvia with her head tossed back, biting on her bottom lip, with a sheen of perspiration dotting her chest and neck, was just about the sexiest thing he'd ever seen.

Her hands came up to grip his shoulders, her short nails bit into his skin. She panted his name as her expressive eyes focused onto his, and then she utterly came apart once again. Nick could only appreciate the erotic sight for a moment before his own climax slammed into him.

Nick closed his eyes, afraid of looking at her for fear of what she'd see. He was too raw, too vulnerable right now, but he'd never admit such things. They'd agreed this was just sex, and that's all he was taking from her... all he was willing to give.

"That's two," he murmured against her ear when their bodies calmed and he settled in beside her.

With a soft chuckle, Silvia nestled against him, and it was no time before her breathing slowed. He was left awake, alone with his thoughts about how to tackle his past and not ruin his future.

Nick pulled into Hawkins Bourbon Distillery to meet up with owner Sam Hawkins. This newer distillery had been around for a decade, but that was young in the industry, especially considering how long bourbon needed to age. But Sam's gin, rye and vodka had exploded onto the scene.

Since he couldn't sell in Green Valley, Hawkins was huge in larger cities across the country and trickling into the overseas market.

Now Hawkins was gearing up to launch their first ten-year bourbon while thousands of others continued to age in the barrels.

Sam had made quite a name for himself in Green

Valley, and nationally, for the spirits he pushed out. Nick knew it was true because tours of this place sold out months in advance. This little gold mine produced some of the best gin that Nick had ever tasted, and he wanted it for his resort. He'd had a few samplings that first night with Silvia, but that wasn't something he could dwell on now. Today was all about seeing how he and Sam could make this partnership happen when Rusty was determined to stand in their way.

So Nick was going straight to the top to see if he and Sam could work together in teaming up against Rusty and his band of crooked city cronies. Nick didn't know Sam on a personal level, but Nick had toured the distillery before and was more than impressed with the company.

Nick made his way up the stony path that led to the main building. Sam had made sure to keep the old charm of the brick and stone buildings while adding an updated feel with the thick, square columns leading up to the second-story tasting deck, and he'd added a glassed-in area overlooking the lake in the back. Nick recalled from the tour he had taken before that the offset room was for special parties or elite groups.

The gas lamps on each of the posts and on either side of the fifteen-foot double doors were a perfect nod to the history of the place. Nick appreciated all of the details and wouldn't mind taking some of these ideas back to his own resort.

Sam was expecting him, so Nick bypassed the lines of people waiting to check in for various tours and headed down a long hallway that ultimately ended at the base of a winding staircase. Nick climbed the steps, and at the top was a young man at a desk, who greeted him with a smile.

"You must be Nick Campbell. Sam is expecting you."

The guy gestured to another hallway, and Nick nodded his thanks and headed down. The old wood floors and iron sconces on the gray walls kept that same masculine vibe and old-world theme as the rest of the place. The Hawkins emblem had been embedded into the wood floors.

Nick reached the door and tapped his knuckles on the frame.

"Come in," a voice stated from the other side.

Nick eased open the door and was surprised at the vast office with an entire wall of glass overlooking the creek running behind the distillery. All distilleries had to be near fresh water, rich with limestone. That was just another thing that made Green Valley so perfect for these types of businesses—plenty of fresh water sources.

"Nick Campbell."

Sam Hawkins rose from his desk and came around with his arm extended. Nick crossed to shake his hand and was shocked by the sheer size of the guy. He'd seen pictures, but nothing prepared him for the Jason Momoa look-alike.

"Thanks for seeing me," Nick said as he released the strong grip and adjusted the frames of his glasses. "I won't take up too much of your time."

Sam crossed his arms over his chest and leaned back onto his desk. "Take all the time you need. I'm always eager to discuss bourbon."

The CEO might look large and menacing, but he seemed genuine and certainly didn't have the stuffy appearance and attitude of a stereotypical chief executive. He wore a Hawkins Bourbon tee and jeans, a very non-CEO wardrobe that Nick could easily relate to. Gone were the days of business owners always wearing suits and ties.

"I'll get to the point," Nick stated. "I'm opening a new mountain resort in late August. I want Hawkins to be the exclusive gin and bourbon."

Sam stared for a minute before he laughed. "I'd love to, but you know that's not going to happen with Rusty Lockwood controlling the damn licenses. He'll only approve it if you exclusively use his hard liquor."

"That's why I'm here in person," Nick went on, knowing anything worth having was worth working for. "I think with two powerhouses teaming up, he won't want to take on both of us. Especially if we can show numbers to the city council and provide statistics on how much growth our businesses can and will bring to Green Valley. Money speaks louder than Rusty Lockwood."

Sam seemed to mull over that nugget of information. Nick wasn't about to mention that Rusty was his biological father. That loaded fact would be the perfect blackmail for Rusty should he choose to fight back.

Nick didn't want to lay that card out just yet with anyone...including Rusty.

"That bastard has been a pain in my ass for years," Sam finally said. "He's offered to buy me out countless times, but I'll die first before I let him get his hands on my company."

Nick knew from that statement alone that Sam would be all for this partnership. Just another step forward in gaining everything Nick needed to fulfill his mother's dream.

"He sees me as a threat," Sam went on. "If he could

push his ego aside and understand moonshine and bourbon draw totally different crowds, maybe he'd think differently. Some people like both, but most people prefer one or the other. But he's stubborn, and he's mean. Any business dealings with him are off the table for me. No merging, no partnering, no selling."

Sounded like they were both on the same page in their hatred for the moonshine mogul. Rusty was seriously only hurting himself by trying to monopolize this region.

If Rusty continued to commit career suicide, it was only a matter of time before Nick could come in and take over. Who knows, maybe he'd buy out Lockwood Lightning one day down the road. Wouldn't that be poetic justice?

"I'm popping into a poker game tomorrow night," Nick told Sam. "Rusty plays every weekend with some city council members, and I found out where their boys' club location is. The Rogue Wingman's back room."

Sam nodded and raised his brows. "I'm impressed. You really want this."

A flash of his mother's elegant handwriting on the letter whipped through his mind. "More than anything."

Sam pushed away from the desk and gestured toward the door. "Let's go have a drink and discuss the details. If you're ready to take on Lockwood, I sure as hell am not going to miss that chance. And I agree. With both of us coming at him, he might change his tune."

Nick wasn't going to turn down the drink or the discussion about how they could work together. Maybe this alliance would turn into something even more powerful than either of them expected.

Seven

"Delivery for you."

Silvia glanced up from the design she had been perfecting for the main check-in desk at Nick's resort. She couldn't quite get the layout to present the way she wanted it. Something was off, and she had been staring and staring but still couldn't put her finger on it.

When she spotted the office receptionist, she did a double take at the desk chair with a giant red bow wrapped around it in her doorway.

"Delivery?" she asked, coming to her feet. "A chair?"

"That's what I was told by the guy who dropped it off."

Silvia rounded her desk and glanced at the oversize leather piece. There was an envelope with her name on it dangling from the bow.

She glanced to the receptionist. "Thanks, Kevin. I'll take it from here."

Once he was gone, Silvia wheeled the chair in and closed her door. Most people received flowers or chocolate or a tacky dancing bear or something. But...furniture?

She tore open the envelope and read the card.

"I researched and these were the best chairs for expecting moms."

No signature, but she knew who this was from, and her moment of surprise quickly turned into anger. He couldn't just have a chair delivered here. She was perfectly fine in her old chair. And what if Kevin had gotten nosy and opened the envelope? Considering it was still sealed when she got to it, she knew he hadn't, but he *could have*.

Silvia pushed the chair into the corner and went back to her perfectly fine seat. She tucked the note into her purse to make sure no other eyes saw the message before she pulled out her phone and completely bypassed a text message. This situation warranted a phone call.

"Silvia. I was just thinking about you."

Nick's answer had her gripping her cell and turning to look out the window. "I bet, considering you just had one of your minions make a delivery to my office and then slink out before I caught him."

His low laughter sent a shiver through her. She didn't want those shivers—she wanted to be angry.

"Minion?" Nick asked still laughing. "I'll be sure to let Garret know his new title."

"Listen," she said in a lower tone. "You can't have things delivered here...or anywhere else, for that matter. And you most definitely need to watch what you write and what you say."

The laughter on the other end died, and Nick cleared

his throat. "I didn't even think about that," he stated. "I was up doing some research last night and I wanted you to have the best, because I know how important your work is to you."

Well, damn it. Not only did he recognize her career and its value to her, but he also took the time to see what would be best for her and the baby. Her anger vanished, quickly replaced by a warmth she didn't have room for in her life. She *wanted* to be angry. It was easier. She wanted that sliver of negativity so she could justify pushing Nick away...but he continued to turn everything to the good.

"I can take it back if you don't want it," he added.

Silvia stared at the leather chair with padded arms and a curved back and shook her head. "No. I'm being a jerk when I should have just called to say thank you instead of berating you."

"You're welcome. I'll be more careful, but I won't stop taking care of what's mine."

Silvia opened her mouth, but before she could say a word, Nick went on.

"I'm well aware that you can take care of yourself, but you're carrying my child."

With a whirl of emotions spiraling through her, Silvia crossed her office and sank into the new chair. The leather seemed to hug her body, and she couldn't deny that she was already in love with this darn thing...and she hadn't even hit any buttons to take advantage of all the features.

"I need to go," he told her. "And don't be angry about the next shipment."

The next...

What?

Silvia glanced to the phone and saw he'd disconnected the call. What the hell did he mean by *the next shipment*? She had specifically told him not to do anything else...which clearly meant he had another plan already in play.

Great, now she would be on edge all day waiting for who knew what to show up at her office door. Maybe it would be something as simple as flowers. He couldn't keep sending furniture...could he?

But flowers seemed normal and romantic and not quite right for them. They weren't actually dating or trying to forge a normal relationship. Nothing about this arrangement was normal—but she wouldn't turn down some fresh blooms.

Pushing aside the silly daydream, Silvia wheeled away her old chair and put her new one in place. She'd have to have someone come get this old one, but she wasn't quite ready to answer questions, so she tucked it into the corner for now.

As she stared down at the design she'd been working on moments ago, she couldn't help but wonder what else Nick had up his sleeve...and why she found his tendency to surprise her so damn attractive.

Silvia pulled into her drive and stared at the boxes on her front porch. She hadn't ordered anything, so she had to assume this was Nick's second installment for the day. What on earth had he done now?

At least this present had come to her home and not her office. She'd had to dodge some questioning gazes earlier when she'd had her old desk chair removed. She'd played it off that she just wanted something cozier and she'd had it delivered to herself...bow and all.

Lame, but she couldn't think of anything else.

She pulled her car into the garage and grabbed her purse before heading out and around to the stone sidewalk. She followed the curved path to her porch and recognized the label on the boxes as that from her favorite local restaurant, Mama Jane's.

He'd had food delivered? She certainly wasn't turning that down, and if any of these three boxes had her favorite banana cream pie, she might just propose to Nick Campbell.

Silvia laughed at herself as she unlocked the front door and took her boxes inside, one at a time. Marriage was ridiculous. They'd had amazing sex, they were having a baby, but the food delivery was what drove her to think marriage? Clearly, she had problems.

There was no note with the boxes, but Silvia knew. Other than her coworkers, she really hadn't had time to make friends or go out and socialize since coming to town. Nick was the one constant in her life, both professional and personal.

Silvia took each box into her kitchen and opened them to see what Nick had sent.

As she pulled out the packing that had kept the food cold and fresh so she could cook it when she wanted, she realized there was two of everything…including the banana cream pie. He'd remembered.

The familiar burn hit her throat a moment before her eyes filled. Crazy pregnancy hormones. Who knew cartons of pot pies, biscuits and desserts would set her off?

She put each package into her refrigerator and set the larger packing boxes out of the way. She'd never had anyone go to the trouble of taking care of her before. Part of her balked at the idea of not being solely independent—she'd been on her own for so long—but the other part of her realized Nick wasn't trying to steal her identity. He was trying to help her and feel like he was needed.

There would be some push/pull as they figured out all of this, but Silvia had to remain true to herself and do what was best for the baby. Contemplating a relationship just because she had warm and fuzzy feelings was a complete mistake.

Silvia had once mistaken lust for something more. After coming out of a multitude of foster homes, she'd turned eighteen and set off on her own with her boyfriend of two months. After a quick courthouse wedding and a month of not-so-wedded bliss, she'd realized her mistake.

Since then, Silvia had shied away from anything akin to a relationship. How would she know what was right? She couldn't trust her own judgment, her own emotions, because she had never been shown the right way.

Despite her upbringing, Silvia knew one thing for certain. She would love this baby and always provide a shelter and a safe haven, because no child should ever have to wonder if they were loved or secure.

Just as she reached for her purse to grab her cell, the phone rang. Smiling, she glanced to the screen, fully expecting to see Nick's name. That wasn't the case.

"John, what's up?"

"We have a problem," the foreman from Nick's resort responded. "I tried calling Mr. Campbell, but he didn't answer. There was an accident, and we have an injured worker. The ambulance is here now."

Silvia immediately grabbed her purse and headed

out the back door toward her garage. "I'm on my way. I'll try getting in touch with Nick."

She disconnected the call and prayed the entire way to the site that the worker would be okay and there would be no backlash on her or the firm or Nick.

On-site accidents weren't uncommon, but there were too many variables, and Silvia sure as hell hoped none of this was due to negligence on her end. She could not afford to screw up on her first project, especially not one of this magnitude.

She had so many questions that wouldn't and couldn't be answered until she got to the site. She wondered why they were there so late on a Friday. It was well after six o'clock, and they typically were done by five.

As Silvia made her way to the resort, she tried calling Nick but only got his voice mail. Where was he? The man always had his phone. She'd never had an issue with getting in touch with him about the project before.

Silvia could handle this, but Nick needed to be there—he needed to know what was going on. After two voice mails and an SOS text, she pulled into the site and rushed to the scene to see exactly what she was dealing with.

Rusty Lockwood's tired, deep-set eyes widened as Nick stepped into the closed poker room. That shocked gaze shifted over Nick's shoulder to Sam, and the old bastard nearly dropped his cards.

Oh, the element of surprise was already working in their favor.

"Got room for two more?" Nick asked, not waiting for an answer as he settled in at the round felt table.

The room reeked of cigar smoke and moonshine.

The suits of the town had shed their jackets and ties, and their sleeves were all rolled up. Nick recognized several men—some he had already butted heads with over the liquor license.

Sam took a seat next to him, and they both pulled out their wallets, flashing their Benjamins. Rusty's stare volleyed between Nick and Sam, and it took everything in Nick not to stare in return, looking to find any physical similarities. He'd wondered his entire life about his father, and now he sat in the same room with him but couldn't say a word.

Not that he wanted to. Nick wasn't happy about the paternity facts, and he sure as hell wasn't looking for some loving reunion. Just because Rusty was Nick's father didn't mean Nick needed that bond. That was something in his life he'd never have, but he would be damn sure his child never knew this kind of void.

Nick's sole purpose tonight was to make sure Rusty knew who he was up against and to face the very real reality that Nick wasn't backing down. Ever. Not only was he not backing down, he was building an army to rise up against Rusty. The days of Rusty Lockwood running Green Valley and the surrounding counties were coming to an end.

Nick didn't want to take his business—that had never been the issue. Nick just wanted the old mogul to do the right thing—to open up Green Valley to new blood and to stop being such a dick. Apparently all of that was too much to ask.

Whatever. Nick wasn't intimidated in the slightest and Sam was just another ace in the hole. Nick and Sam had a mutual hatred for the moonshine kingpin.

"Get you fellas a drink?" an older man asked as he

came to his feet and headed to the bar in the corner. He held up a familiar tall, rectangular bottle with a dome-shaped lid. A lightning bolt down the front was a sign everyone easily recognized.

Sam shook his head as he fanned out his cards. "Not much of a moonshine fan."

Nick bit the inside of his cheek to keep from laughing. "I'll take a bourbon."

"Just the white lightning served here," the old guy stated, putting the bottle back on the counter. "Never seen anyone turn down perfectly good moonshine."

"Show me good moonshine and I won't turn it down," Nick joked, which earned a few chuckles, but not from Russ. "Five-card stud? My favorite. Deal us in."

Nick's cell vibrated in his pocket, but he ignored it. On a Friday night, he had nothing else he needed to be doing other than this right here. Besides his unborn child, all that mattered was pushing through to fulfill his mother's wishes and their ultimate goal. Nick planned on fighting this battle not just for his business, but for Sam and for other establishments like theirs.

Over the next half hour, he won a couple hands, Sam won a hand and Rusty grew angrier by the minute. Even his tumbler of moonshine had gone untouched, and his cigar had sat in the tray completely ignored. He must be really pissed…which only pleased Nick further. Good. The man needed to learn that not everything would go his way in life.

The cell in his pocket had vibrated off and on for the past hour, but Nick played on. He'd catch up when he left. He'd waited too long to make his next move and he couldn't let anything interrupt.

"You're the one working on that resort over on Silversmith Mountain, right?"

Nick glanced to the older gentleman who'd initially offered him a drink. "That's me. Should be open at the end of summer."

"This town can always use more places like that, at the rate people flock here."

Nick fully agreed as he motioned for another card. "I'm banking on just that. But my mother had a bigger vision, so we're doing a few extras that other getaways don't have."

"He's about to open a gold mine," Sam stated as he folded and eased back in his seat. "The economy is great around here. More resorts and places to stay means more people coming to the distillery."

Rusty grunted as he folded his hand. He reached for his glass and swirled it around. It was moonshine, not an aged bourbon or an expensive wine. The man seriously needed a lesson in fine alcohol.

Nick rested his hand on the green felt and waited for the other players to reveal their cards. Nick kept his poker face in place as he laid down aces over jacks and raked in the winnings.

"You play often?" another man asked.

"Not as often as I'd like," Nick replied with a grin.

"I doubt I can afford to play with you every week," Sam joked. "But I'll let you take my money tonight."

Nick stacked his chips and weighed his next words carefully as he glanced to Sam.

"Oh, you'll get plenty of my money once we're in business together."

Sam simply nodded without glancing up as he reached for the new cards he'd been dealt. Nick left the veiled statement hanging and didn't even glance up to Rusty. He didn't need to see the old man's reaction to know he'd hit home, and looking across the table would only be seen as a direct threat. Nick figured he and Sam showing up together and that carefully laid-out business venture was warning enough for one night.

After about an hour, and multiple wins, Nick came to his feet. "Well, guys, I'll head on out, but I'll be back next week, if you're taking new members."

Every man in the room, save for Nick and Sam, glanced to Rusty, who looked like he was about to explode—if the red face and flared nostrils were any indicators. He better get used to being pissed off because Nick was going to really upset his perfect little world.

"We're not taking new members," Rusty finally answered, glaring at Nick from across the table. "I don't know how you managed to get in here tonight, but it was a onetime thing."

And he wouldn't find out how Nick and Sam managed to get in. Rusty wasn't the only one with power in this town.

Nick started to ease forward, but Sam put a hand on his shoulder.

"We'll see," Sam stated. "Seems your friends didn't mind the extras."

After a good ten-second stare, Nick pulled back from the table and gave a nod to the other men. Then he followed Sam out of the smoke-filled room and pulled in fresh air once they were out of the back of the restaurant.

"Well, that went well." Sam laughed. "It was tempting to see what you were going to do, but I wanted to get us both out of there in good standing—and I don't have time for jail."

Nick shook his head and flexed his hands at his sides. "I wouldn't have hit him. I've been tempted for years, but I won't let him get the best of me or give him the satisfaction."

They headed down the narrow brick street toward the parking lot.

"So I'll meet you here next week? Same time?" Sam asked.

Nick nodded. "Counting on it."

Sam turned toward where he'd parked, jumped in his car and headed out. Nick turned the opposite way to head to his truck as he pulled his cell from his pocket and saw all the missed calls and texts.

It didn't take long for him to realize he'd missed a hell of a problem while trying to deal with another.

Nick made record time getting to the site and only hoped Silvia was okay and the injured worker wouldn't sue.

Of all the times for him to have gone silent, this was quite possibly the worst. He cursed himself the entire way to Silversmith Mountain. His first thought when he'd seen her name so many times on his screen was that something had happened to her or the baby.

He didn't want to acknowledge what that sickening pit in his stomach told him. He cared about Silvia so much more than he should've ever allowed.

Now what the hell was he going to do about that complication?

Eight

"Well, I'm glad you could make it."

Silvia stood over the broken, splintered floor where the worker had fallen and thankfully only suffered a twisted ankle and some scratches to his arms.

For the past hour and a half, she'd been trying to get in touch with Nick, but he'd obviously been too busy to answer his phone or worry about his business. The longer she surveyed the area and the more she talked to the foreman, the angrier she became. The accident stemmed from a worker who had stayed late on his own to finish some work. Supposedly when he was sanding the flooring, he had mishandled the equipment, resulting in the brittle planks giving way.

Silvia wasn't so sure she knew what to believe, because the inspector had been out multiple times and found the floors were solid.

Since everyone had left, she'd tried to wrap her mind

around the events of the evening, but she was tired and wanted to just go home. This was certainly one drawback of the job she so loved.

She wished Nick had arrived more quickly, wished he would take more care in his responsibilities to this resort, because they had to work as a team…especially now.

Maybe he'd been on a date. The thought slammed into her and caused her pause. They hadn't discussed whether or not they'd see other people and it's not like they were in a committed relationship with each other… right?

She didn't like the weight of jealousy that settled deep within her.

"I came as soon as I could," he told her, carefully stepping over the construction zone. "Fill me in."

Silvia glanced over her shoulder, surprised he already had on his hard hat. "One of the workers was negligent, and he now has a twisted ankle. That's the gist. The long story is that you weren't available when the foreman called or when I called and texted. I'm not sure who she was, but if you could tell your dates that you have other obligations—"

Nick took hold of her shoulders. "Dates? You think I was on a date? If I wasn't pissed at the accusation, I'd think you were jealous."

Jealous? Please. She wasn't jealous.

She *wasn't*. Being jealous would imply that they had a committed relationship to each other—which they didn't.

"From a professional angle, I deserve to have my calls answered," she retorted. "This is your property, and you should have been here."

Nick released her. "I'm here now. I had other resort business I was working on."

For the first time since he arrived, she noted a sadness in his eyes. But more than that, there was a determination layered with the pain. Wherever he'd been, it hadn't been with a date.

And maybe she had let her imagination run rampant with thoughts of him being with another woman while she cleaned up this mess. She was irritable and stressed, but that was no excuse.

"I'm sorry," she told him. "I don't like accidents and I don't like injured employees, especially because this one seems shady. The firm won't like any of this at all, but the incident was out of my control, and the crew member was here alone when he shouldn't have been here to begin with."

"Don't apologize to me," Nick commanded. "And your firm won't blame you. It's not your fault the guy couldn't do his job properly. He's fired as far as I'm concerned."

Silvia nodded, turning her attention back to the hole that opened up to the basement. "The foreman already suspended him without pay until we could further assess the situation."

As she walked Nick through the events, he listened without chiming in, and she noted that he looked at her when she spoke. His eyes held on to hers like every word that came out of her mouth mattered. He wasn't trying to figure things out or looking around to get his own read on things. He was taking her opinion seriously, listening to her story and respecting her as the architect on the project.

The air seemed thick, almost sticky as she kept

talking. Silvia found herself dabbing the sweat off her cheeks. The hard hat certainly didn't help. When black spots danced in front of her face, Silvia closed her eyes a moment and pulled in a deep breath. None of that helped, either. The heat or the altitude must really be getting to her.

The next thing she knew, her world tipped, and strong arms banded around her a second before she was hauled against a broad, firm chest.

"Silvia?"

Nick's worried tone had her wanting to reply, but she couldn't find the energy. What was wrong with her? She felt…she couldn't find the word, but she was hot and sweaty and her body just seemed to lose energy all of a sudden.

As Nick carried her over to the windowsill and sat her down, her hard hat fell to the floor with a thunk. Silvia started to open her eyes, but a wave of nausea swept over her once again.

"Just…give me a minute," she murmured, gripping his shoulders.

His hands roamed over her, then framed her face. "You're clammy and pale. I'm taking you to the emergency room."

"No." She opened her eyes slowly to focus on his worried gaze. "They're only going to tell you I'm pregnant."

"What if something else is wrong?" he asked, his eyes searching hers. "I don't know anything about this, but I don't want to take chances, because I'm out of my element here."

Even though the room wasn't spinning, Silvia still felt more sluggish than she ever had before. She pulled in a deep breath and pressed her hands to Nick's chest.

"Give me some space," she told him. "I'm fine. I just need air."

Nick came to his feet and continued to stare down at her. Those bright blues roamed all over her face.

"What all have you done today?" he asked, clearly trying to figure out what had happened. "Maybe you overdid it."

"I had a 9:00 a.m. meeting, then I worked on restructuring the lobby here. I know you said it was fine, but I still feel like something is off. Maybe it's the archway, maybe that's too feminine? I don't know. I've drawn so many different—"

"Focus," he ordered, smoothing her hair away from her face. "What happened after you were working on the design—which is fine, by the way."

"In the middle of my work at the office, your chair came," she went on. "After all of that, I had another meeting, because my six-month review with the board was this afternoon."

She replayed the review in her mind, the fact that she'd been told she was doing well enough with the Campbell project, but they'd like her to take on more projects and really push harder.

She was already doing more than several of the male associates at her level. Just wait until she informed them she would be taking maternity leave. She really had no clue what to expect at the end of that conversation.

"Oh, when I came home I found your other surprise," she told him. "That was certainly not necessary, but thanks."

"Did you eat?" he asked.

Silvia shook her head. "I had just put it all away when I got the call about the injury here."

"So you haven't had dinner. What time did you have lunch?"

She shrugged. "I didn't get out for lunch, but I had an apple and a granola bar at my desk around eleven."

Nick cursed under his breath. "You can't do that. Skipping meals or half-assing them may have worked in the past, but our baby needs more than a few hundred calories."

Silvia squared her shoulders and came to her feet, proud of herself for only swaying slightly. "I am well aware of how to care for myself and the baby. I got busy. I would've had a normal meal, but I got called here… when they couldn't get in touch with you, by the way."

"I was busy."

His lips thinned, and his eyes narrowed. Silvia propped her hands on her hips and snorted.

"Too busy to check your phone? I know you had it with you."

"My private life is none of your concern," he tossed back.

The jab shouldn't sting—after all, they didn't have a commitment to each other—but that didn't stop the piercing pain. The implication that she wasn't important enough for him to share that aspect of his life hit her hard, even though they had agreed to secrecy…to being physical only. Even though those limits had been her own idea.

"That goes both ways," she replied. "I can take care of myself, so the gifts need to stop, and I can get myself home and make my own dinner. I don't need a keeper. Now, if we're done here, I've had a long day."

Silvia turned and scooped up her hard hat and gathered her purse and phone. Nick's heavy stare remained on her, but she ignored him. Any other man would argue with her or apologize or stop her or *something*. But no. He just stood there staring in that infuriating way, and she used all her willpower not to throw her hard hat at him.

"Are you okay to drive?" he finally asked, his tone low and uneasy.

Silvia glanced over her shoulder and nodded. "Don't worry about me. You might want to check on your injured worker, though, and get to the bottom of what really happened."

She didn't wait for him to reply before she turned and left him standing in the mess. Besides the report she'd have to write and turn in concerning the injury, she'd also have to work on the new floor. She was only thankful this had happened now and not when they were further along.

Not that she wanted anyone to get hurt, but things could've been so, so much worse. No matter whose fault the accident was, nobody wanted this black mark on their name.

She drove home and cursed herself for being a fool where her feelings and Nick were concerned. The sweet gestures, the way he cared for her—could something deeper be developing here? Hadn't she learned her lesson about letting people in? Being tossed around her entire childhood had proven to her that she could only depend on herself.

And there was still that gaping hole that she'd carried with her for thirty-two years. A hole that only love and stability could fill. She had doubts she'd ever be able to fully seal that void…even if part of her couldn't help but hope she would some day.

Silvia might be angry and hurt by Nick's words, but that wouldn't stop her from devouring the food he'd had delivered. Now, if she could figure out what to do with her attraction to him. Because no matter how upset she was, she still felt a pull toward him that had nothing to do with the baby and everything to do with the fact that her body could still feel his touch. Being near him every day only put her even more on edge.

And she could barely admit this to even herself, but when he was near, that gaping hollowness in her life seemed to lessen.

So what would happen if she let him fill that void? Would the day come when Nick would ultimately crush her heart?

Nick shot off the text to the mayor, inviting him to a special meeting at Hawkins Distillery. Nick and Sam were working from all angles, and getting the mayor alone, away from Rusty or any other influencers, would be key in making this alliance work.

He gripped his cell and stared out the windshield at Silvia's mountainside home. He'd finally gotten her address, a necessary move since they had leapt from coworkers to one-night-stand to parenthood. They couldn't keep hiding their personal lives forever.

The beautiful stone-and-log house seemed to be lit up all over. Windows encompassed the entire side addition, and the second-story peak had a glow beaming from the accent window as well. The old-fashioned lanterns flanking the front door seemed inviting, but he wasn't so sure she'd welcome him in.

He deserved to have the door slammed in his face. He deserved her anger. He was here to take all of that.

Whatever she needed to do so they could move on, he would accept.

Nick stepped from his truck. He'd hurt her earlier. It wasn't her fault his entire world was turned in all directions, but he'd lashed out at her like she was the problem.

How was he honoring his mother's memory if he treated Silvia like she didn't matter? One thing he'd loved most about his mother was her ability to make everyone happy, to make everyone feel special.

And Silvia did matter. Damn it, he just wished she didn't matter so much.

Nick wasn't surprised when the front door opened as he stepped onto the stone porch. Silvia had changed into a pair of leggings and an off-the-shoulder tee that was probably meant for comfort, but she looked sexy as hell. In the few months he'd known her, Nick had never been turned off. Everything about this woman kicked him in the hormones, making him feel things he didn't even know existed. She could rock a suit like the badass businesswoman she was and then transform into the girl next door with those bright blue eyes and wild red hair.

Ignoring all the ways she tugged at his heart was becoming more and more difficult.

Nick kept telling himself he was just too vulnerable right now, with his mother being sick and then her passing. Combine that with the news about the pregnancy, and that's the only reasoning that could explain the constant, invisible tug he felt toward Silvia.

"Come to apologize?" she asked, blocking the door.

Nick nodded. "I did."

"Then you can come in."

He had to hide his smile at her bold, matter-of-fact

greeting. This firecracker was surely going to be the one who pushed him over the edge…and he couldn't quite decide if that was a good thing or not.

Silvia turned back into the house, leaving the door open. He wasn't going to ignore that invitation…or those swaying hips. Nick prided himself on his self-control, but when it came to Silvia, he wondered exactly who held the strings.

As he stepped into the open living area, he closed the door behind him. Everything in this space gave him little glimpses into Silvia's personality and lifestyle. The L-shaped stone island had four leather stools tucked beneath it. A bowl of limes sat on the concrete top…no doubt an even number of produce. Straight ahead were floor-to-ceiling windows that stretched up two stories to allow a magnificent view of the mountainside and valley below. But before that view was a spectacular firepit area and pool.

Her living room had more stone surrounding the statement fireplace. A shaggy white rug covered a good bit of the dark wood floors, and her cozy gray furniture held colorful throw pillows in a variety of patterns. She had a little bit of a playful side thrown in with all of the strong elements.

Silvia bustled around in the kitchen, putting things back into the fridge and wiping off her counter. Nick took a seat at one of the stools and rested his arms on the island.

"I was a jerk earlier," he started.

"Yes."

He bit the inside of his cheek to keep from grinning. She wouldn't make this easy, and perhaps that was part of her appeal. She didn't shrink away from challenges or just accept all that happened around her. She took charge while maintaining her dignity. He was positive she'd wanted to throat punch him earlier.

"I don't know how to treat this...whatever is going on between us," he admitted. "You want things kept quiet about the baby, about us. Part of that irks me, but I get it. I do. But I also have some personal issues that I can't talk about yet."

Or ever. Coming to grips with the fact that Rusty was most likely his father was one thing, but sharing that news with the world was a completely different matter entirely. Nick waited each day for a phone call or for someone to show up at his office or home saying they'd received a letter, too, that they might be his half brother. Or should he seek them out? Did he really want to overturn their lives as well?

Did Rusty know any of this even existed?

According to the letter, he knew he was going to be a father, but Nick highly doubted Rusty knew who his son was...or if he did, then he simply didn't care. Nick wasn't going to discount any possibility. At this point, nothing would surprise him.

To say he was on edge was a vast understatement.

"We're both in unfamiliar territory and trying to push through," she told him as she folded her dishrag in a neat rectangle and draped it over her sink. "But you can just say you can't talk about what's bothering you without being a jerk, and I would understand. I'm not asking for a commitment from you or even exclusivity. I mean, I realize you probably want to date and see other women. You shouldn't be tied to me just because—"

Nick was up and around the island before he even

realized he'd moved. Her words died as he caged her in and hovered his mouth near hers.

"Exclusivity?" he growled. "Maybe that's exactly what I want. Maybe I hate sneaking around when I actually want to see you outside of work and behind closed doors."

Which he hadn't even realized he wanted until now. What the hell was happening to him?

"What?" she gasped. "No. That would be a *relationship*. We aren't doing that. Just because I'm pregnant doesn't make *us* a good idea. Neither of us is cut out for long-term, and we hardly know each other on a personal level."

Damn her for being logical when he wanted more. More what, though, he wasn't sure.

"I'm not saying that because you're pregnant," he retorted. "I'm saying it because I want to see more of you, not work related, and not always in the bedroom."

Her eyes widened, then her brows drew in. "But we're not those people. We don't do relationships. I... I can't."

Something in her tone sounded downright terrified, and every part of Nick wanted to push her to tell him why. He wanted to know those nuggets of information that all came together to make up who she was today.

"I was married once," he blurted out. Maybe if he opened up a little, she would feel more at ease to do the same. "It didn't last long."

Realizing he was still hovering over her, Nick took a step back and shoved his hands in his pockets. Maybe that failed marriage was just another example of why he shouldn't mess with Silvia's feelings. Who was he to ask for more? Just look at who his biological father was. Nick had Russ's blood in his veins. Could he ever really be what she wanted, what she deserved?

Even so, he continued.

"We married right out of high school," he stated. Silvia's eyes remained locked on his, so he kept going, hoping she would see just how serious he was about wanting to share with her. "We were in serious lust, but neither of us knew what love meant. I'm not sure I do now, either, but that's beside the point. Her father was livid about us, which only made me want her more."

Silvia smiled. "I could see that. What was her name?"

"Molly. We realized our mistake about two months in. We ignored it, though, because we were both so headstrong and wanted to prove her parents wrong."

"What did your mother think?"

Nick laughed. "She told me I was too young to marry, but she would support any decision I made. She always had my back."

And with that support system gone, now that he needed her more than ever, he was fumbling through his days, his life, trying to find the proper balance.

"So when did you divorce?" Silvia asked.

"We were married six months. We parted on good terms, and she's actually remarried now with four kids."

"Four?" Silvia laughed. "Sounds like maybe you two weren't compatible. I can't imagine you coaching a ball team or schmoozing with parents in the school pickup line."

Nick hadn't even thought of that. Maybe he wouldn't be that kind of parent. He had no clue, but he did know he wanted this child…and for the time being, he wanted Silvia. Who knew what the future held? Life was fleeting, and if he wanted something, he had to take action and not wait.

"I wasn't ready for marriage or a child when we were married."

"And now?"

"Are you proposing?" he asked, smiling.

Silvia jerked, her face scrunched. "Not at all. I'm not marrying now, if ever."

"You have something against marriage?"

She sighed. "I did it once. It lasted about as long as yours, so I'm definitely not looking for a repeat. I learn from my mistakes."

Interesting. The more they chatted, the more he discovered about her, the more he realized they were similar. Every layer he peeled back revealed something else remarkable that showcased her strength and perseverance.

How many more similarities would he uncover before the lines of their lives ultimately intertwined?

Nine

Silvia didn't know how they'd ended up out back with a crackling fire, cozied up with a blanket, sitting in the same oversize lounger. One minute they were sharing pieces of their past, and the next, she was giving him a tour and he'd fallen in love with the outdoor living area…so here they were.

"I'd never leave this spot if I lived here," he told her.

"You have a pretty awesome place yourself," she retorted.

Silvia stretched out her legs and crossed her ankles, trying desperately not to brush against him any more than necessary. Then again, she didn't need to touch him to be utterly turned on and ready to rip his clothes off.

But she tried to stay in control of the situation and not act like a teenager with a crush.

"This view is what sold me on the place," she admitted. "All of the windows on the back of the house and this firepit area, the pool, didn't hurt, either. I've only been here six months, so I missed the autumn leaves. I can't wait to see all the colors this fall. This is the perfect place to grab a sweatshirt and cuddle next to a fire with s'mores. Oh, maybe I need an outdoor rocker— you know, for the baby?"

"This is a great home for raising a child," he told her.

Silvia smiled. "It is. I've already decorated the spare room a hundred times in my head."

Nick shifted, turning toward her. "You're feeling okay now?"

She glanced his way, then back to the flames licking the darkness. "I'm fine. I just needed to eat. The day got away from me, but I promise to be more aware. I'm still getting in the mind-set that I'm not the only one I need to look out for anymore."

Nick slid his hand beneath the thick blanket and covered her flat belly. Silvia tensed, her eyes darting to his, and she found him solely focused on her.

"I respect your independence, but you have to know that I'm going to worry and I'm going to be pushy and I will likely piss you off. It has nothing to do with not thinking you can't do this alone and everything to do with the fact that you don't have to."

Silvia swallowed, unable to form words. Between his comforting touch and intense stare and gravelly voice, Silvia couldn't concentrate. Nick possessed every single quality she didn't want to want. He said and did all the right things...but opening herself to the possibility of hurt was not something she could ever do again.

Neither of them was in a position to make life-altering decisions right now, either. They had a baby to think about, and she had to keep that in the forefront of her mind. She would never allow a child in her care, especially her own, to ever feel unwanted or second best. This baby had to be the top priority, above her wants and dreams and desires, above her fears.

"What are we doing here?" she finally asked, holding his gaze.

"Enjoying the nice evening."

She slid her hand over his and removed it from her stomach. "You know what I mean. I don't want a relationship. And you...well, you're not ready, either."

"Maybe not," he agreed. "Does that mean we can't just go out and enjoy our time together? We get along, Silvia. That's rare these days. I would think that's something you understand more than anybody."

Silvia settled onto her back and stared up at the starry sky. She wished she had all the answers; she wished she had someone she trusted enough to tell all her problems to and seek advice. But she'd been a loner her entire life. She really was used to this empty feeling... she just didn't like it.

"I can't let you in," she finally said. "I have nothing to offer, and anything I do have will go to the baby."

Nick sat up and turned, hovering over her so she was forced to look directly into his eyes. "I have never asked for anything. And I won't."

"You can't promise that."

His silence said more than any words could.

"I get the attraction," she added. "That's difficult to ignore. But we have to accept that it's just temporary."

"Temporary," he repeated, like she'd just offended him. "Because you want to keep me your dirty little secret so your coworkers don't know you slept with me? Fine. Keep me your secret, but for now…keep me."

His lips touched hers almost before she realized he was leaning in. Instant arousal assaulted her, and Silvia arched into that strong, firm body. Everything about Nick pulled her in. No amount of self-talk and mental prepping could hold against such a potent man.

One hand gripped her thigh and the other flattened against the lounger beside her head as he held himself above her.

Nick's lips traveled from her mouth, across her jawline and over her exposed shoulder. Anticipation pumped through her, but she'd known where this would lead. Sex was what they knew, a language they both understood in a time when they were both so confused and emotionally torn.

"However long this lasts," he murmured against her skin, "just let it."

How could she argue with his logic? They both wanted this physical connection; they craved it. Maybe they were using each other to combat all the hurt that had built up in their lives. Whatever the reason, there was no way she could deny either of them this moment…and likely the next one, too.

Nick eased back and stared down at her. With her sole focus on him, Silvia reached for the hem of her tee and pulled it up over her head, tossing it aside without a care. His eyes raked over her, and that heavy-lidded stare was just as potent as his touch.

If he weren't a client, she might be brave enough to put aside her fears and dive headfirst into this unknown territory. But he was, and that was all the reason she needed to keep him at arm's length. She'd worked too hard to get to where she was. Sex she could handle. Sharing custody she could handle. Letting her heart get involved would certainly push her over the edge.

"I don't want to pressure you," he added.

Silvia reached for his shirt, keeping her eyes locked on his. "Do I look like I'm being pressured?"

With a sly grin, he helped her pull off his shirt. In a flurry of hands and laughter, they removed the rest of their clothes, leaving everything in piles dotting the patio.

"I guess this is just a perk of living on a secluded mountainside," she told him as he settled between her legs.

"One of many."

Nick's strong hands held on to the back of her thighs as he barely touched their bodies together. Silvia tensed, waiting for that connection, aching enough that a moan of desire escaped her.

But he didn't merge their bodies; he simply stared at her with one brow quirked.

Silvia nodded. "Do it."

Nick eased into her, and Silvia gasped as her body bowed. He didn't take his time; he didn't slow this down. No, Nick jerked his body against hers as he braced his hands on either side of her. Silvia reached for him, but in the next move he had shifted both of them to his side of the lounger, and she straddled his lap. He moved quickly, but clearly he knew what he wanted.

Silvia curled her fingers around his shoulders as she continued the frantic pace. Every nerve ending in her sizzled with an ache that only Nick could satisfy. His hands cupped her breasts as he tipped his head to capture her mouth once again.

The man kissed with such passion, making her feel every bit of his need. Silvia rose up just a tad, then eased back down, pulling out a long, low groan from Nick. She wanted to make him lose his mind here. She wanted to be the one he fantasized about, the one he couldn't get enough of. For reasons she was too frightened to explain, she wanted to be his everything.

But, since that was an unobtainable dream, she was going to take what he offered temporarily. She deserved every bit of happiness she could hold on to.

The battle she kept waging with herself over Nick and how far she wanted to let this go would have to wait. She just needed to be in this moment, absorbing all the pleasure he was willing to give.

When Nick released her lips and covered one breast with his mouth, Silvia threaded her fingers through his hair and allowed herself to be utterly consumed by Nick's touch, his passion.

The crisp night air washed over her bare body, only adding to the overwhelming sensations. There was something so free, so delicious about being out in the open and completely exposed. She didn't want this to end, but her body climbed to the peak and there was no holding back the euphoric burst.

Silvia cried out just as Nick slid one hand between them to touch her where they were joined. His hips bucked beneath hers as his entire body tensed. Silvia dropped her head back, taking in every bit of their climax.

Nick's lips slid up the valley between her breasts, and Silvia focused her attention back to the top of his head. He mumbled something against her heated skin, but she couldn't enjoy the afterglow *and* decipher words right now.

She finally stopped trembling, and Nick wrapped his arms around her and gathered her against him. Silvia rested her head in the crook of his neck, inhaling his musk and woodsy cologne.

"Let me stay," he murmured. "We have nowhere to be tomorrow."

She should make him leave. She should try to keep some kind of line drawn in this confusing relationship, but she couldn't ignore one very important fact.

Her heart was becoming involved in this entanglement—and she worried she wouldn't be able to prevent another heartache.

Silvia woke to the robust aroma of dark roast. She blinked against the sunlight streaming in through her windows. She'd never slept long enough to be awakened with the bright natural light, so she tapped her phone to see the time.

The sudden movement and the combined scent of coffee and something cooking in the kitchen had her stomach instantly revolting.

She tore off the covers and dashed to her en suite bathroom just in time. Sweat dampened her forehead, and a wave of heat overcame her. Stripping off Nick's T-shirt, which she'd slept in, Silvia welcomed the coolness of the bathroom floor tile.

When she felt confident enough that she wasn't going to be sick again, she sank back on her heels and closed her eyes. Silvia pulled in a deep breath and concentrated on her breathing and waited for the rest of the queasiness to pass. Something would have to be done about those smells.

With a groan, Silvia started to get up, but her legs were weak and she was pretty sure the room was spinning again. She closed her eyes just as heavy footsteps sounded down the hall and entered the bedroom.

Not the morning-after look she'd been going for, but there wasn't much she could do about that now. Apparently, morning sickness was ready to make an appearance at this stage of her pregnancy.

"Silvia." Nick rounded the door frame and stilled. "What can I do?"

She held on to the edge of the sink and shook her head. "Nothing. It will pass, but whatever you're making has to go. I'm sorry."

"Consider it done."

He disappeared, and she was thankful he didn't hang around and insist on helping her. She really wanted to wash her face and brush her teeth alone, and if she was going to get sick again, she truly didn't want an audience.

Thankfully, he left her alone, and Silvia managed to grab a quick shower.

Once she was feeling somewhat human again, Silvia tugged his T-shirt back on and pulled her hair up on top of her head. Silvia padded out into the living area and found her doors and windows open and no sign of the food.

Nick rested a hip against the island and held a cup of coffee. "Water or juice?"

"I can get it," she told him as she moved into the kitchen. "What had you made?"

"French toast. It's in the trash, and I took it outside."

Her stomach grumbled, but there was no way she could put anything heavy in there right now. She reached for the bread and popped a slice in the toaster. Bland and blah would likely become her new diet for the foreseeable future.

"I appreciate you making me breakfast," she told him as she turned to face him. "But listen—"

"Regrets already?" he asked, taking a sip of his coffee like he hadn't a care in the world. "I really thought we were past that."

Silvia gritted her teeth. "No, not regrets. I just think we need to not kid ourselves and think that we can play house."

"I'm not playing at anything." Nick set his cup on the island and started moving toward her. "If you're afraid of these emotions, that's understandable, but don't tell me what we're doing is wrong."

"But it is," she countered. "I'm confused because I want you, but I don't *want* to want you…if that makes sense."

"You're not going to get hurt," he assured her.

Silvia placed a hand on his chest to stop him from coming any closer as she met his gaze. "But what if I hurt you?"

"I've been hurt before." He curled his fingers around her wrist and removed her hand, then laced their fingers together. "We both have experienced divorce and loss, and look at us. We're pushing through. Nothing can keep us down. Are you really afraid to give this a try with me?"

She studied his eyes as his words settled in. "Why do you want this so much?"

Nick's lips thinned, and his jaw clenched before he

spoke. "Because I saw my mother struggle. I saw her try to be two parents at one time. I don't want that for you, and if the two of us can see how we are together, if we could make something work, that will only help the baby."

The baby.

Nothing to do with how he felt about *her*.

Oh, he enjoyed the sex, obviously, but was there anything beyond the physical? Surely he had some inkling of emotion for her or he wouldn't keep going to all of this trouble to be with her, to please her.

But…everything he'd done circled back to what was best for Silvia as a pregnant woman, not Silvia as a woman who was growing much too attached to Nick.

"I'm on board with keeping this just between us," he went on. "But don't push me aside before we have a chance to see if this is the right move."

For the baby.

The words hovered between them just the same as if he'd said them.

But hadn't she wanted them to have emotional distance? Hadn't she thought that would feel safer?

And didn't she want him, temporarily?

Maybe, if it was all about the baby, they *could* try this out, without any heartbreak. She just had to keep her heart protected at all costs.

There had to be some ground rules, though. If he was going to continue to be sweet and open and sexy, then she'd have to have some boundaries—that was the only way to ensure she wouldn't get hurt.

"No more gifts."

Nick nodded.

"No more meals."

He quirked a brow. "I have to eat, too."

She didn't hide her smile. "Then no more meals delivered to my house."

He nodded his agreement. "Anything else?"

"Yeah. If you want to end this, tell me. But until then, this is just physical and completely behind closed doors."

Nick pulled in a deep breath and held up a hand, but she put a finger over his lips.

"That's the deal."

His eyes held hers a moment before he ultimately nodded.

There. At least she would retain some control, and hopefully, if fate was on her side, she wouldn't endure any more heartache.

Ten

Nick pulled into the parking space marked "VIP" and chuckled. Like hell would he be a VIP member of Lockwood Lightning. But he wanted to be petty, and he wasn't apologizing. After all, wasn't he technically heir to this hillbilly dynasty?

Did he have a meeting scheduled with Rusty? No. Did he want to be here? Also no. Did he want to see the man squirm? Oh, hell yeah.

Catching the enemy with the element of surprise was just one of the tools in Nick's arsenal. After the card game the other night, Nick figured stopping in to headquarters was the perfect opportunity to talk to Rusty and keep the old man on his toes. Nick wanted Rusty to be wondering what would happen next. Nothing like an impromptu Monday morning meeting to really catch your nemesis off guard.

Nick slid his hands into his pockets and whistled as he crossed the lot to the back offices. He wasn't completely sure of what he'd say once he got in there, but he wasn't concerned. Nick had come to accept that he'd have to take each day, each moment, one at a time and decide his direction once he was in the moment.

The old two-story brick building sat next to the creek that ran through the back of the property, just like Hawkins. Nick stepped into the main entrance and walked right up to the receptionist. He was hoping for a young lady, but there was a middle-aged man. Okay, fine. He could work with that.

As Nick crossed the open lobby, and the guy glanced up from his computer. "Can I help you?"

"I'm here to see Rusty."

The man glanced back to the computer, clicked a few keys, and looked back to Nick. "What was your name?"

"Nick Campbell."

He had to give the man credit. He only slightly cringed at Nick's introduction. His reputation must have preceded him. Now what had dear old dad been saying about him?

"I don't have you down for an appointment this morning."

"This is a pressing family matter," Nick replied with a smile. "I'm sure Rusty would much rather meet me in private than for me to discuss it here with you or take it to social media."

Okay, so the "family matter" description was a slip, but whatever. Nick could gloss that over later.

"Is that a threat?" the man asked.

The door behind Nick opened, but he paid no attention to whoever came in. He merely tucked his thumbs in his belt loops and shrugged.

"More of a promise," he stated with a wide grin. "Trust me. Rusty would rather we talk in private, and I'm not leaving until we do."

Nick felt someone standing behind him, so he glanced over his shoulder and was greeted with a nervous smile from a twenty-something blonde.

He shifted his focus back to the receptionist. "As I was saying, I can be out of your way in seconds. Just point me toward Rusty's office."

"Security is one call away."

Nick nodded. "They are, but I don't think Rusty would appreciate that. Things will be much better for him if I speak to him. Now."

The guy wanted to argue, Nick could see it plain as day. So Nick didn't move, didn't even blink. He stared back and dared the man to pick up that phone.

Ultimately, the man nodded. "Up the stairs and to your left. The door at the end of the hall."

Nick smiled. "Have a good day."

Mounting the stairs, Nick ignored the nerves curling through him and focused on the sole reason for this visit—his mother. She would want him to see this through. She would want him to fight for what was right. And, really, this push against Rusty went well beyond just trying to serve hard liquor in Nick's new resort. He was doing all of this because Rusty kept his dirty hands in the pockets of the city council and any powerhouse who could benefit him, and Nick was tired of Rusty being a damn bully.

There were plenty of high-class restaurants in Green Valley, but unless Rusty owned them, the establishments didn't have the authority to sell liquor. Rusty wanted to monopolize the multimillion-dollar industry, and Nick wasn't going to just sit back like others had done. He would fight Rusty until the old man either gave in or gave up. Nick had motivation, youth and more money than that old bastard. And money did talk, quite loudly.

Nick reached the wide double doors at one end of the long hall. There were a few offices at the other end, but other than that, this second floor was rather quiet. Nick couldn't imagine working for Rusty—just the thought was a nightmare.

Being the man's son was worse, but only if Rusty found out the truth. Nick had to assume the old man would try to use it against Nick.

Nick didn't bother knocking—no doubt the minion downstairs had already called up to give a report.

He eased the door open. Rusty stood facing the windows overlooking the back of the property.

"You must really want to see me, to bust into my card game and bully your way into my office."

Nick took that as his invitation to come in. He closed the door at his back and crossed the spacious office. Rusty glanced over his shoulder as Nick came to stand on the other side of the wide desk.

"What's it going to take to get you to release your hold on the council members so they will allow a liquor permit for my resort?"

With a gruff laugh, Rusty turned to face him. "I don't have a hold on anybody. They just know a smart business move when they see one, and I happen to have tapped in to the licensing first. Maturity and experience speaks volumes."

So did money and power...both of which Nick had a vast amount over Rusty.

Nick crossed his arms over his chest and adjusted his stance. "Fine, but that their business decisions were made decades ago, and you're no longer the sole distiller in the area. Moonshine is a far cry from bourbon. There's plenty of business to go around."

Rusty stared back, his bushy brows drawn, the buttons straining against the material over his protruding gut. Just when Nick began to wonder if he'd have to repeat himself, Rusty let out a snort.

"You came all the way here to have this same conversation?" Rusty asked, curling his old, chubby fingers around the back of his desk chair. "You wasted your time and mine."

"You won't win this fight," Nick retorted. "You *can't* win it. You might as well make things easier on yourself and just cooperate. Do the right thing for once, or you could regret it."

Rusty raised his busy brows. "Is that a threat?"

Nick dropped his hands and shrugged. "Take it how you want, but you're smart enough to know a formidable opponent when you see one."

"You are nothing to me," Rusty said. "You can't touch me, but watching you try is rather entertaining."

Nothing to him?

If he only knew.

Would the truth even make a difference to him? Would Rusty thaw his cold heart if he knew he had a son? Three sons, if his mother was correct?

Nick stared at the evil man and didn't see one shred of resemblance between them, but he had no doubt his mother had told the truth. She had nothing to gain by revealing the secret after her death. And while Nick wanted to know who his half brothers were, he didn't want to disrupt their lives, and he sure as hell didn't want to take time away from bringing Rusty down and getting that license.

"Entertaining," Nick murmured. "Do you know what will be entertaining? When I reveal the dirt I have on you to your cronies. When I clue them in on what a worthless, selfish bastard you really are."

"What dirt? You know nothing about me."

Nick laughed. "The *facts* and evidence I have on you are something you don't want spread publicly, trust me. Everyone has skeletons, Lockwood. You just have to decide who gets to see yours."

Rusty's eyes narrowed as he stepped around his desk. Nick held his ground. Nothing about this man intimidated him. If he hadn't sold moonshine on the black market before it was legalized, he wouldn't have become a millionaire and he wouldn't have opened this distillery. There was nothing glamorous about the history of white lightning and nothing classy about Rusty Lockwood.

"If you have something on me, let's hear it." Rusty came toward him. They stood toe-to-toe, but Nick towered above the man.

"And let you in on my secrets?" Nick shook his head and laughed. "I don't think so. I'd rather you think about what I could possibly have. What would have the potential to bring you down and destroy all you've made for yourself? I'll even be so generous as to give you two weeks to think it over."

Rusty's jaw clenched as his nostrils flared. "You don't come into my business, my office, and threaten me."

Nick smiled and took a step back. "And yet, I just did."

He turned and headed back to the door but stopped and glanced back over his shoulder. "Two weeks, Rusty. Then your dirty secrets come out for all to enjoy." Nick smiled. "Now that's entertainment."

"The heartbeat is strong, and the baby looks great."

Silvia breathed a sigh of relief. Seeing the image of the baby on the screen made everything seem so real. Hearing the heartbeat had brought a tear to her eye, but she blinked it away.

"How soon until we know the gender?" Nick asked as he stood at her side.

Silvia glanced up at him. "Do you want to find out?"

"If that's okay with you," he replied.

"I actually wanted to wait."

Nick nodded. "Then we'll wait."

He'd insisted on driving her to the ultrasound appointment today. She'd purposely chosen an office thirty minutes outside Green Valley for secrecy's sake.

While she was glad Nick wanted to be involved, there had been something completely off about him since he'd picked her up. He hadn't spoken much, hadn't taken her hand or acted like he was *here*, present in the moment. She didn't know what to expect—they'd agreed they weren't a couple or really in a relationship...mostly because *she* had decided not to go there. Even though they'd discussed rules, there was still no label she was comfortable with putting on whatever was going on here.

But something about him was off.

Once her appointment was finished and she had her

photos in hand, she and Nick stepped into the hallway of the medical complex.

"You want to grab some lunch or something?"

Nick glanced around, then back to her. "I actually need to get to my office. Do you want me to drop you off at your place or the site?"

Disappointment niggled at her. But seriously, this wasn't a date. They weren't going to go grab a nice lunch and discuss baby names and then go back to his house and settle in for a movie and dinner.

"Just take me back to my house," she told him. "I'll get my car."

She didn't know why he'd insisted on driving if he was just going to take her home. Maybe he'd wanted to talk to her about something but didn't know how to bring it up. Maybe he just didn't want to be alone. Or maybe he thought *she* didn't want to be alone. He'd mentioned before that he would be extra protective of her since he'd watched his single mother work so hard. But she didn't want him to just tag along out of obligation. She wanted him to *want* to be here.

Silvia reached out and put a hand on his arm. "You don't have to come to every appointment," she told him. "I know you're busy. That doesn't mean you don't care."

"I am busy, but I'll never be too busy for my child." Those expressive eyes held hers. "And I'm a parent, too. If you're here, so am I."

Okay, well, he left no room for argument. At least he didn't appear to be one of those fathers who acted like the child was the mother's responsibility.

"Is something going on?" she asked. "You seem... off."

He pulled his key from his pocket and started down

the hall toward the parking garage. "I'm fine. Nothing I can't handle."

But he shouldn't have to handle it alone. Wasn't that what he'd been stressing to her? Did he honestly think taking his own advice was a one-way street?

"Maybe if you stopped being so stubborn and actually talked to someone, you would feel better."

He came to such an abrupt halt and she ran into his back.

Nick turned and grabbed her shoulders to steady her.

"Can you take the day off?" he asked.

Silvia blinked and stared, wondering if he was joking. Take the day off? She didn't think a man like Nick even knew what that term meant.

"Um… I probably shouldn't. I already took half a day for this appointment."

Nick nodded, but she saw his excitement vanish.

What had he had in mind? Whatever it was, it had sparked something in him she hadn't seen before.

"I can meet you after work," she suggested, hoping he'd take the olive branch.

"Sure. Yeah. That's fine."

From his tone, she could tell it was anything but fine, and she vowed to find out exactly what was going on with him.

Eleven

Nick stared at his mother's handwriting once again. He had no clue how many times he'd pulled out her letter and read each word. And he didn't really know what he expected to see that he hadn't seen before. Maybe he just wanted to feel that connection with her since this was her final correspondence with him or maybe he just needed to see her handwriting.

Or maybe if he continued to dissect each and every word, he'd figure out her motivation for dropping all of this after keeping the secret for so long.

Nick's cell buzzed with the tone from the front gate. He put the letter back into the safe and pulled his phone from his pocket.

The image of Silvia's SUV filled the screen. He was surprised she was here, but he typed in the code to open the gate. They'd mentioned meeting up, but that had been the beginning and end of that conversation. He'd dropped her off at her car this morning, and she'd headed off to work. He hadn't spoken to her since.

Nick had been feeling irritated for the past two days, ever since leaving Rusty's office on Monday morning. Every moment that passed without a call from Rusty had Nick twitchy. The last thing he wanted to do was drag the old man through the wringer, because Nick's mother would be in that wringer as well. He had to hope Rusty would cave. There was still time, but with each passing day, Nick became more certain that Rusty was calling him on his bluff.

Nick stepped from his office and headed downstairs to greet Silvia at the door. He owed her an apology yet again. He seemed to be doing that quite a bit lately, but he also hadn't been himself since the funeral. The Nick she'd met months ago wasn't the same man he was today.

He hadn't meant to be cranky with her earlier. It wasn't her fault his father was a bastard, or the bane of his existence, or a maniac who had to be stopped. Nick didn't mind taking on Rusty—Nick just wished he could compartmentalize his emotions. He was having a difficult time concentrating on his responsibility to Silvia and their baby because Rusty was consuming his thoughts.

Nick opened the front door just as Silvia's SUV pulled into the circular drive. He stood at the edge of the porch and waited.

As soon as she exited and rounded her vehicle, Nick took in her change of clothes. Earlier she'd had on a sexy pantsuit, but now she had on a simple sundress with a denim jacket and little boots.

"You're turning all Tennessee on me," he joked.

She glanced down and laughed. "I kind of like this vibe. It's comfortable and trendy."

He didn't know much about trendy, but he did know that Silvia knocked the breath out of him and she looked ridiculously sexy.

"I'm sorry that I couldn't take off work earlier," she told him. "I just… I haven't told anyone about the baby yet, and I really had no excuse I could give. This job is important to me and—"

Nick held up his hand. "I get it. I just had a last minute thought. No big deal."

She tipped her head to the side, sending her hair falling over her shoulder. "What was your idea?"

His sour mood instantly switched. There was no reason they couldn't do his plan now. In fact, they both needed the escape and the distraction.

Nick offered her a smile and reached for her hand. "Trust me?"

With a tip of her head, she narrowed her eyes. "Does this involve me losing my clothes?"

"That's not what I had in mind, but I can adjust to your plans."

Silvia took his hand and laughed. "Let's go with your plan first and see how the evening progresses."

He helped her up onto the porch and into the house. Keeping her hand in his, he led her through the entry and toward the garage.

"Where are we going?" she asked, glancing around the house. "Your house is ridiculous, by the way."

He glanced over his shoulder and lifted a brow.

She grinned. "In the best way. It's stunning. I haven't gotten a good look at it like I really want to."

"You'll get the grand tour when we come back," he promised. "I've already pictured you naked on that leather couch in front of the fireplace."

She snorted. "Your seduction technique needs a little work."

He pulled her close, close enough to see those navy flecks in her blue eyes. "I'd say my technique is just fine. You're in my arms right now."

"Touché."

Nick escorted her to the garage and assisted her into his SUV. Once they were on their way, she shifted toward him.

"But really, where are we going?"

He gripped the wheel and rounded the sharp curve heading down the mountain. "You don't do well with surprises, do you?"

"I do...when I know what they are."

Nick laughed and reached for her hand.

"That's not a surprise," he countered. "Just enjoy the ride. We'll be there soon."

"The airport?" Silvia asked. "Nick, I can't leave town. I have a job. One that I have to be at tomorrow morning."

Nick laughed as he pulled up and parked in front of a private plane. "I promise you'll be back before you know it."

Silvia stared at the plane, then looked back to Nick. "I thought you were taking me to show me something or to grab a hamburger or... I don't know. I didn't think I was coming to the airport."

Who did that? Who just picked up on a whim and decided to fly out? This was a lifestyle she wasn't used to living. Her wild nights consisted of making sure all her laundry was done.

Nick got out of the vehicle and came around to get her door. "You're not afraid of flying, are you?"

She stepped out and shrugged. "Not sure. I've never done it."

Nick's mouth dropped. "Never?"

Silvia shook her head. "I guess we're about to find out if I love it or hate it."

She looped her arm through his and started toward the plane. "It will all depend on how good our pilot is."

"You're looking at him."

Silvia jerked to a stop and stared back at Nick. "You fly planes, too? Is there anything you're not good at?"

His mouth quirked into a toe-curling grin. "Well, I've never been a parent, so I'm not sure how I'll be there."

Something tugged at her heart. The more they discussed parenting this baby, the more she wondered just how they could keep going with a physical-only relationship. Because each day that passed, each moment she spent with him, pulled her deeper and deeper into his world. She worried she might never want to leave.

Wasn't that how she'd grown up? Trying to fit into other people's worlds? She'd wanted just one area to call her own. One home, one family. Now with Nick, she was seeing the entire package dangling in front of her. The sexy man who fulfilled her every desire, who made her smile, who would be the father of her unborn child. A family of her own was within her grasp... But what if, just like always, she wouldn't be able to capture it?

"Hey. You okay?"

Nick's question pulled her back to the moment. "Fine. Now, let's see if I like this whole flying thing."

He looked like he wanted to question her further, but he slid his hand over the small of her back and escorted her onto the plane. Silvia opted to sit in the cockpit with him as opposed to in the cabin...which was quite posh and impressive. Rich brown leather sofas, a minibar, even a bedroom in the back.

She didn't want to know how many other women he had taken for impromptu airplane rides just to show off his piloting skills. She wanted to think she was special, that there was something happening here beyond a child and beyond just sex.

Foolish, yes, but she couldn't help her feelings.

Nick explained everything he was doing as he started the plane. Several moments later, he was heading toward the runway, flanked by lights. Silvia couldn't help but stare at him. He seemed so at home here. She'd never known this about him. Clearly he had a passion for flying, or he wouldn't own his own plane and know how to pilot it. He muttered to himself about a preflight check and tapped on various controls and gadgets. Who knew how sexy this would be? She already loved flying.

The moment the plane lifted, Silvia's attention turned to the side window. In an instant, the airport got smaller, the roads were just mere lines and there were lights everywhere. The orange glow from the sunset seemed to light up the world.

"This is gorgeous," she exclaimed, her eyes darting around to try to take in all of the breathtaking views at once. "Is this what you wanted to show me?"

"No. I had no clue you'd never flown or I would've taken you before now."

"So where are we going?"

He glanced her way and offered her a grin. "Just enjoy the mountain views from above."

As he glanced back to the controls, Silvia took his advice. But she couldn't take her eyes off him. The strong jaw, the glasses and the stubble, the intensity and passion rolling off him. This was a man who knew what he wanted, what he craved. Somehow, she'd slid into that role in his life, and she wondered if she could stay there. Was she so foolish as to hope something long-term could come from this?

Before she knew it, they were landing at another airstrip. Silvia had no clue where they were. She figured they'd been flying for about thirty minutes.

"Can you tell me now?" she asked, once he brought the plane to a stop and shut it down.

Nick reached over and squeezed her hand. "I thought you trusted me."

"With this? Sure."

It was everything else she worried about.

"Silvia—"

She smiled and put her finger over his lips. "Let's not say anything else. Just take me to my surprise."

Worry flashed through his eyes a moment before he took her hand from his mouth and kissed her fingertips. Part of her wished she would've let him talk, but the other part—the damaged part—worried about what he would've said.

Twelve

Nick stared across the tiny booth at Double Down Donuts and watched as Silvia thoroughly enjoyed a honey cruller. When she let out a moan and licked her fingertips, Nick readjusted in his seat to alleviate the uncomfortable war between his anatomy and his zipper.

"Does this surprise meet your approval?" he asked.

Her eyes darted to his as she grabbed her napkin and swiped the glaze off her lips. Shame. He'd been looking forward to removing that himself with his own lips.

"Feel free to surprise me anytime with double donuts."

Nick laughed and reached for his iced coffee. "I figured you'd appreciate the whole even number factor, especially with donuts."

"You already know me so well."

He was learning each day, and not only about Silvia, but about himself as well. He wanted more, but more of what he didn't know. He did know that he was still in a vortex of confusion. He was wading through a chapter in his life that felt as if someone else was writing it.

"This was my mother's favorite donut shop," he told her, trying to get out of his own head. "I'd bring her here once a week until she got too sick to travel. She loved sweets and she loved to fly, so it was a perfect day for her when we came."

Silvia reached across the table for his free hand. "I'm sorry. Does being here bring up bad memories?"

Lacing his fingers with hers, he leaned down and took a drink, then shook his head. "Not at all. I haven't been here in a few months. It's nice to be back."

"I take it this is the booth you always sat in?" she asked.

"Actually, she would usually want to sit at the bar so she could watch them bake in the back. The owner, Stan, he got to the point he would just invite her into the kitchen. He actually closed the café the day of her funeral, and the entire staff attended her service."

Silvia's eyes welled with tears, and her chin quivered as she bit her lip.

"I didn't tell you that so you'd cry," he said with a laugh, not at her, but because tears made him nervous. "I'm just saying that it's nice to be back here and I'm glad I could share this with you."

And he hadn't been quite sure how he'd feel coming back until he'd walked in the door, but having Silvia at his side was a balm he hadn't realized he needed. She settled something in him, filled a void he hadn't known existed. Not the void from losing his mother. No, Silvia had entered the picture before that.

There was something sexy about her intelligence

and business sense. It pulled him deeper. He loved that she was making a name for herself in a mostly male-dominated world. That's exactly the type of mother he wanted for his child...a fearless leader and an independent woman.

"Why are you looking at me like that?" she asked, her brows drawn in.

He pulled her hand to his mouth and kissed her knuckles. "Just wondering how soon we can get back to my place."

Awareness and desire flashed through her eyes. "If I recall, there's a bedroom on that plane."

Could there be a more perfect woman? Their parallel thoughts were just another significant turn on.

"I love how that smart mind of yours works."

Nick couldn't get out of the donut shop fast enough. He grabbed their boxes and tugged at her hand, leading her out to the car he'd driven here, the one he kept at the airport. Silvia laughed as he practically ran with her to the car.

"You think this is funny?" he asked, caging her against the side of the car.

The streetlights cast a warm glow over her features, and he realized he wanted to be the man who kept that smile on her face. He wanted to be the one to put that sparkle in her eyes.

Before he could delve too deeply into his emotions, Nick leaned in to brush his lips across hers. When she sighed and opened for him, Nick devoured her. He settled his hands on her hips, pulling her closer to where he ached most.

Silvia threaded her fingers through his hair, knocking his glasses askew.

Nick eased back, righted his frames and raked his thumb across her damp mouth.

"The plane is waiting," he murmured, more than ready to get her back to Green Valley and show her exactly how much he wanted her.

"Nick. Did you hear me?"

Nick rubbed a hand over the back of his neck and gripped his cell. Silvia had left around ten the night before, after they'd gotten back from their impromptu donut run. He'd been up most of the night trying to put his feelings into perspective, but all he came up with was that where Silvia was concerned, he was damn confused. He wanted the hell out of her.

There was nothing more he could want, nothing more he deserved. But was she seeking that family life she'd never had? Even if he wanted to offer one big, cozy, happy family, Nick feared he wouldn't even know how.

But before he could continue driving himself crazy with his chaotic thoughts, Sam called with some startling, unexpected news.

"Say that again," Nick stated.

"I said there's a rumor that Rusty has been skimming from Milestones," Sam stated. "All the money that his employees donate each year and he claims to match, well, the talk is that he has not only *not* been matching it, he has also been taking the monthly donations."

Nick pushed away from his desk and came to his feet. He turned to stare out the back window and across the mountaintops as far as the eye could see.

"I want to say I'm surprised, but nothing that man does shocks me anymore, even if it's illegal. Rumors have circulated around him for years." Nick sighed as a ball of unwanted emotions formed in his stomach. This crooked bastard was his father. "But the fact that he's stealing from a children's charity is a new low."

Milestones was a charity in Tennessee with the mission of helping children under seventeen who suffered from any handicap, mental or physical. The money funded summer camps and educational programs to target the kids' strengths and give them hope for a better future, regardless of their disability.

"That bastard publicly promotes that he urges his employees to donate and that he'll match any amount they raise each month," Sam added. "He preys on the weak to boost his own ego and reputation. I don't have proof, but I have a reliable source that claims Rusty is being investigated regarding these accusations."

Nick gritted his teeth. Was that why Rusty hadn't returned his call from the other day? Was that why he hadn't given in to what Nick demanded? Maybe Rusty was too preoccupied with attorneys and untangling his web of lies.

What would he need to take that money for? Lockwood Lightning brought in millions each year.

Maybe Rusty had a gambling problem or maybe he was paying off more mistresses who claimed to be pregnant with his baby. Who knew what the real problem was.

No matter what mess Rusty was in, Nick would ultimately get what he wanted. Rusty's issues weren't Nick's, and Nick didn't give a damn what Rusty had gotten messed up in.

"If he's stealing from any charity, I don't care who does his books, that's pretty damn difficult to hide," Nick claimed. "He'll get caught eventually. But we need to keep up the pressure. You up for another card game this weekend?"

"Can't," Sam replied. "I'll be out of town for the next few weeks. I'm acquiring two more restaurants on the East Coast and finalizing renovation plans."

Nick turned from the window and stared down at the monitor showing the security footage from cameras covering various portions of his property. A deer ambled by near his back patio, but other than that, absolutely nothing stirred on this early morning.

"I'll keep on Rusty while you're gone," Nick promised. "Maybe all the pressure will be too much for him and he'll finally relent."

"It would have to be something major for him to loosen his grip on those city council members. That good ol' boys' club goes back decades."

That might be, but Rusty didn't know he had a son. And thanks to his mother's insightful note, Nick knew he wasn't the only Lockwood bastard running around. In a perfect world, all three boys would come together and take down the bullying mogul. But Nick didn't live in a perfect world. He had realism running through his veins.

"Rusty is getting sloppy," Nick argued. "That good ol' boys' club won't last forever, especially when the members see there's more money to be had by opening up the liquor laws to a broader spectrum of entrepreneurs. The more liberal they are with the licenses, the more tourism comes into this area, the more the city council and taxpayers benefit. It's simple math and common sense."

Sam laughed. "Remind me to keep you on my good side."

Another call came through Nick's phone, and he

glanced to the screen only to see an unknown name. He couldn't assume the caller was a telemarketer, not in his line of work.

"I need to take another call," Nick said. "I'll be sure to keep you posted while you're gone."

"I'll do the same if I hear any more."

Nick disconnected the call with Sam and took the other.

"Hello?"

"Mr. Campbell?"

"Speaking."

"My name is Gertie. I'm Rusty Lockwood's personal assistant. He wants to meet with you at eleven this morning."

Nick glanced to the antique clock on his desk and noted it was just after nine. Had Rusty come around? Was he ready to talk business? No matter what he wanted, Nick was eager to get there.

"I'll be there at ten thirty," Nick stated, simply out of spite. "I have a meeting later that I can't miss. Thanks for calling."

He disconnected before Gertie could give him another time or argue that only eleven would work. Nick didn't know what Rusty wanted, but he had to believe it had something to do with the liquor license. Not that Nick thought the old man would back down so easily, but Nick was relieved that his bluff had captured Rusty's attention. With this recent rumor about the investigation into the charity, maybe Rusty was ready to relieve some pressure any way he could.

Whatever the reason for this sudden meeting, Nick was more than ready to tackle Rusty—and hopefully he wouldn't have to pull out the daddy card.

Thirteen

Silvia smoothed a hand over her flat belly and pulled in a deep breath. She hadn't gotten sick at work before this morning, but now she couldn't seem to stay out of the restroom.

A tap on the door had her groaning. She wasn't sure it was safe enough to exit, but she could always go to the restroom up on the next floor...she only hoped she could make it that far without getting sick again.

She splashed some water on her face and dabbed her cheeks with the backs of her hands. One glance in the mirror and she realized nothing she did would make her look perky or like she was ready to go back to her desk.

Whatever. She couldn't hide in here forever, no matter how nauseated or weak she felt.

Silvia shoved her hair behind her shoulders and straightened her jacket. As soon as she opened the door, she came face-to-face with Edwin, the office manager, just as he was about to knock again.

"Oh, Silvia." He took a step back to allow her to pass. "Um...are you okay?"

Was she okay? Between getting pregnant from a one-night stand and then developing feelings for a man who would likely never reciprocate them, no, she actually wasn't okay.

"Do you need to go home?" Edwin asked, still studying her face. "The last time I saw a woman this pale and shaky was my wife, when she was pregnant with our son. He's a month old now."

Silvia attempted a smile, though her nerves were even more on edge now. The last thing she needed was some busybody coworker outing her secrets.

"I'll be fine in a bit," she assured him. "My breakfast just isn't agreeing with me."

Understatement, but Edwin seemed to believe her, so she excused herself and made her way toward the elevator. She'd rather hang in the bathroom until she was positive it was safe to sit at her desk and go on about her day.

She turned down the hall, spotting the elevator at the end...but her boss stepped right in front of her, blocking her path.

"Silvia."

Clark's voice seemed to boom, which irritated her. She just wanted some privacy and a commode. Was that too much to ask?

"I stopped by your office and couldn't find you," he went on. "I know there was an accident at the Campbell project. I wanted to know what was going on with that claim or if the client had everything settled."

Silvia pressed a hand to her stomach. "My client opted not to file a claim, and the worker who was injured is fine. He was honest about his negligence and has been released from the project."

Clark nodded, seemingly fine with her response. "That's good to hear. I was concerned this would reflect badly on the company, but you handled it like a pro. You're really fitting in quite well here. I see a permanent spot for you, possibly a promotion. We like employees who are determined and focused. The way you put the job first and foremost in your life tells me you're serious about being here and taking on more responsibility."

Silvia's smile widened, though guilt about her secret weighed heavily. She knew that being a mother in this male-dominated office would immediately make her look less committed to her role here. "I really appreciate that. Working at this firm has been a dream come true for me."

"Keep up the good work," Clark praised.

He stepped around her, and Silvia continued on toward the elevator. She wasn't ready to fill them in on her condition. They were pleased with her work, and they saw how devoted she was. If they thought she was going to put her baby first, which she was, and that she would be taking time off for maternity leave, which she also was, she worried they'd pull her from Nick's project. Though she knew Nick wouldn't let that happen, she didn't want Nick or anyone else to have to come to her defense.

As the elevator doors closed, Silvia shut her eyes and rested her head against the cool metal. She could have a successful career and be the doting mother her baby deserved. There was no reason she couldn't do both. It would just take some juggling and plotting…that's all.

For now, and for the next several months, she had to push through. She had to continue to prove herself within the company. She had to give them no reason to doubt her abilities so that when the time came for her to take maternity leave, they would be begging her to come back. This job meant more now than ever, because she had to be the sole provider for not just herself, but for her baby.

The memory of all of those foster homes she'd rotated in and out of filled her mind. She wanted stability for her baby, which meant she couldn't be distracted or confused by where Nick stood in her life. She had to define their relationship and stick to it.

So where did Nick fall in with her long-term goals?

That was her biggest fear…that maybe he couldn't.

Nick stepped into Rusty's office and closed the door behind him. Rusty stood at his desk with his hands in his pockets, clearly expecting Nick.

"Are we ready to put an end to this game you're playing?" Nick asked in lieu of a traditional greeting.

"I don't play games when it comes to business," Rusty countered. "I do, however, want to discuss what you have on me, or what you think you have."

Nick sighed as he stepped farther into the spacious office. "We've already been through this. I'm not telling you, and I promise, I have proof. So if that's why you called me here, you've wasted your time and mine."

Rusty stared across the space, and Nick didn't waver or back down. He hadn't come all the way down here to leave without getting what he wanted or at least move a step toward that ultimate goal.

Nick wondered if he should allude to the charity. Maybe that's the angle that would work for now.

"If you're in some kind of trouble, maybe you should just do the right thing for once," Nick added.

Rusty's bushy brows drew in. "What trouble do you think I'm in?"

Nick laughed and took another step closer. Clearly Rusty was into playing games by pretending he didn't know what Nick was talking about. "A man of your position and immoral compass is always going to be in some type of scandal."

"Scandal? I'm not part of any scandal."

Rusty scoffed like Nick was absurd for even mentioning such a thing…which told Nick all he needed to know. Rusty was worried, and that would go a long way in getting Nick what he wanted. Rusty would be desperate to be seen as an upstanding businessman in light of all that was happening. He would need to do something to redeem himself because no matter how many cronies he had in his back pocket, even they wouldn't be able to stand by him if Rusty was indeed stealing from a children's charity.

"Trouble, then," Nick stated. "So, what do you want from me?"

Rusty's face studied Nick. "You're an arrogant bastard, aren't ya?"

Like father, like son.

Maybe, if he was lucky, that was the one and only thing Nick had received from his biological father.

Nick didn't reply; he simply crossed his arms and waited. Patience was key in gaining everything he wanted. He wondered how much patience he'd have with Silvia—and then he immediately wondered why that thought had popped into his mind. He'd never wanted a family; he'd been just fine married to his career. Now here he was with a baby on the way and rolling into a relationship.

No matter what they said to the contrary, there was no denying the fact that something neither of them had expected was happening.

And yet he still wanted more.

"I'm not giving up anything," Rusty finally stated. "You want to play with the big boys, then you'll have to show your hand, because I'm calling your bluff."

That's exactly what Nick had been afraid of, but he wasn't about to cave. If he could continue the veiled threats, hopefully Rusty would see that Nick wouldn't be scared off or give up. Not going to happen.

"Then you'll be sorry," Nick fired back. "It's your life and reputation you're gambling with. Either way, I'm going to get what I want. You just have to figure out if you want to give it up quietly, like the upstanding man you think you are, or with a very public scandal. Totally your call."

Rusty didn't say a word. He barely blinked, and Nick knew the man was sweating beneath his cheap suit. The old man might have made millions illegally and then tapped into a billion-dollar industry once laws were changed in his favor, but that didn't alter the truth. Rusty Lockwood was just a criminal with no ethics and still working every illegal angle in an attempt to hoard his money.

"I'm not giving up anything," Rusty growled. "If you

don't want to tell me the information you have, then I have to believe you have nothing."

"Then that's your mistake."

Nick was not waiting around to argue any more. Without another word, he turned and left the office, letting the door bang against the wall on his way out. Maybe he would have to give up his secret even though he wasn't quite ready yet.

He would press every other angle first. Revealing his paternity would be a last resort.

Nick made a stop at the florist after he left the office and bought flowers for the two women in his life. He decided to go by the cemetery, since he hadn't been since the funeral. He needed a quiet place to think and wanted to feel closer to his mother.

What would she want him to do? She'd given him this information for a reason, even though she'd known Rusty and Nick had never gotten along. Did she just want Nick to finally know the truth, or did she want him to go to Rusty with what he knew? The cryptic letter produced as many questions as answers. And the longer Nick sat on the bench in front of his mother's grave, the more confused he became. He wasn't finding answers in the silence.

Nick had never felt this alone before. Even though he had hundreds of employees and multiple businesses across the globe, that didn't replace having an inner circle he trusted and could lean on.

It couldn't replace the bond he'd had with his mother.

But he could take comfort from the woman she'd been. His mother had never given up. Until she drew her last breath, she'd loved with all she had and worked toward her dream of owning a beautiful mountain resort.

Nick searched through his heart, his mind, and couldn't come up with one single dream of his own. Oh, he had goals and career aspirations, but an actual dream that he was working toward? Not really.

Beating Rusty, finishing the resort and taking care of his baby were the three main focal points in his life right now. Maybe he'd honor his mother by pursuing a dream, something she would be proud of. Because, even though she was gone, he would work every day to continue her legacy.

Nick came to his feet and traced his fingertip around his mother's name on the stone. "Love you, Mom."

When he turned, Nick swiped the dampness from his eyes and set out to make sure he accomplished everything his mother had started.

Fourteen

After last night, Silvia was surprised she hadn't heard from Nick. Not a call, not a text, nothing. There hadn't even been a professional check-in regarding the resort.

Silvia swung by Mama Jane's and ordered double fried chicken, potatoes, rolls and banana cream pie. It was early enough in the evening that she could surprise Nick and return his sweet gesture from last night. Though, after that heated encounter on the plane, she'd say they were pretty equal.

Still, amazing sex aside, she found she wanted to take care of him, to offer comfort where she could. He was going through so much right now and even if they went nowhere romantically, she wanted to be someone he could count on.

Silvia turned up the steep incline toward Nick's drive and stopped at the gate. She punched the button to announce her arrival and waited. She hoped he was home.

That was the drawback to surprises. But if he wasn't, she'd take all this food home and eat really well for the next few days. She still had some leftovers in her fridge from his delivery, but she wanted to have a casual dinner with him tonight.

Finally, the gate slid open, and Silvia eased her car up the mountainside. She curved around each turn until the stone-and-log home came into view. The magnificent structure matched the owner: strong, bold, demanding.

Silvia couldn't ignore the flutter that curled through her belly...one that had nothing to do with nausea and everything to do with the man inside that house. She'd dated over the years, but she never recalled getting schoolgirl giddy over anyone before.

Ridiculous, really, to have these innocent, adolescent feelings when she was expecting the man's baby. A little late for crushes and giggles.

Silvia pulled to a stop in the circular drive right in front of the extended porch. Nick didn't step outside like he had before to greet her, which she found odd. He knew she was here, but perhaps he was busy on a call or something. He did have a life beyond her, and she had to not only remember but also respect that.

Just like she wanted to stay guarded, Nick did as well. He was still hurting from his loss, and Silvia would do well to remember that he could just be seeking comfort from her and nothing more.

Ignoring those weighted thoughts, Silvia gathered the takeout bags and headed up the stamped concrete steps to the front door.

She was trying to figure out how to juggle the sacks when the large double doors opened. Immediately she knew something was wrong. His hair was a mess, his glasses were on top of his head, he had on a fitted black tee—which did amazing things for those sculpted arms and shoulders—and he was barefoot. He seemed at home and relaxed, save for the disheveled hair and the sadness in his eyes.

Similar to what she'd seen the other day when he'd pushed her away.

"Did I interrupt something?" she asked, stopping on the third step.

Nick shook his head and pulled his glasses off. He shoved them in his pocket and came down the steps toward her to take the bags.

"This is fine," he told her. "And if this is dinner from Mama Jane's, then it's even more fine."

Mama Jane's was a little hole in the wall that had been at the foot of the Tennessee mountains for decades. It was a local hangout with the best fried chicken and homemade potatoes she'd ever had in her life.

"Please tell me you got dessert, too," he said as he gestured for her to go ahead of him into the house.

"If you don't like their banana cream pie, then you're wrong."

Nick followed her into the kitchen and started unloading the bags. He didn't say anything as he pulled out plates and drinks and silverware. She watched him carrying everything out to the patio, still in silence. Once she realized he intended to eat out there, she gathered what she could and followed.

When the silence stretched, Silvia couldn't take it another second. If he didn't get whatever this was off his chest, he was only going to grow more miserable, and then where would that leave them?

"Something bothering you?"

He set his plate on the table and moved around to take hers and do the same. Then he pulled out her chair.

"Nothing worth discussing," he told her without looking her in the eye.

An unease came over Silvia, and worry settled in deep. Did he want to tell her he'd met someone? Had he decided this secret relationship wasn't working out? Maybe he was worried about the emotional state he was in right now, or that getting involved was a bad idea.

She couldn't argue with that last one, but her heart didn't know common sense. Her heart only knew what she wanted—and she wanted Nick.

Heartache was inevitable. She knew it. She'd told herself over and over that long-term relationships couldn't stem from a passionate fling, and he'd never given any indication he wanted more. Yet she hadn't been able to stop her feelings from turning serious any more than she could stop the sun from setting.

"You don't seem fine," she pushed, taking a step toward him and ignoring her chair. "You can talk to me, you know. I'm a pretty good sounding board, and you clearly need to get something off your chest."

Nick glanced out toward the mountains and the glowing sun, but she didn't take her eyes off him. The muscles in his jaw clenched, and he gripped the back of the chair.

"This might not be a good night for you to be here," he murmured. "I'm just… I'm not in a good space and I won't be good company."

Ignoring his statement, Silvia took another step, then another until she came to stand right next to him. She covered his hand with hers, and every muscle in his body tensed.

"If you're this upset, this is the perfect night for me to be here."

He turned his attention to her, and the torment in his eyes tore at her heart. He opened his mouth, and she waited for him to let her in on what had hurt him, but he ultimately shook his head and took a seat.

"I'd rather eat."

OK. Shutting her out, yet again. She didn't want to ignore his pain, but she couldn't make him open up. She couldn't make him understand that she was here for him. No, he had to come to that realization himself.

And somehow Silvia recognized that his issue wasn't really so much about not wanting to share with her. It was more that he didn't want to face this himself, which he'd have to do if he shared it with her. That was all the more reason he needed to open up. Or maybe it was all the more reason for her to snap back to the reality that they weren't in a normal relationship. She wasn't even sure what a normal relationship entailed, but this certainly wasn't it.

He had his own life and she had hers—she'd do well to remember that once they moved on and only had a baby in common, she had to have a solid career. That was the only stability she had, and she would not only maintain it, she would grow that part of her life so she could be the best mother and provider for her baby.

Silvia took a seat, served herself a hearty helping of potatoes and dug in. Might as well push beyond the emotional turmoil and deal with what she could—eating.

"You don't want any chicken?"

Silvia shook her head. "I had a rough day, so I'm afraid to put anything too heavy on my stomach."

His fork clattered to the plate as he stared. "Are you okay? You didn't have to bring me dinner. Damn it. I've been so preoccupied with my own issues, I didn't think to ask how you were doing."

"I'm fine," she assured him.

He was obviously trying to deflect and keep the focus on her when he was the one clearly hiding something. She'd thought they were at least friends. Did he not trust her? If he just didn't want to talk, she could understand it, but if he was keeping her shut out for another reason, that stung a little.

She finished eating and didn't attempt any more conversation. When she was done, she simply picked up her stuff and took it back inside. She was rinsing her plate when strong arms came around her. Nick's head dropped into the crook of her neck, and Silvia shut off the water.

"Be patient with me," he muttered against her skin. "I just don't want to think or talk or worry. Just for tonight."

That raw honesty tugged at her heart. He didn't owe her any explanations...that's not why she had pushed. She genuinely wanted to help him through a difficult time. Because right now, even though she hated to admit it, they only had each other.

Silvia turned in his arms and looped her wet hands around his neck. "Tonight," she agreed and covered his mouth with her own.

Nick lifted her up, and she wrapped her legs around his waist. He carried her and she held on, pouring herself into him, letting him take what he wanted. She didn't care where they went, so long as he didn't let her go.

That mentality is what would wind up breaking her heart, but she didn't want to think about that right now. She didn't want to think at all.

She felt the warm evening air on her skin and knew he'd stepped back outside. He gently laid her on the swinging bed suspended beneath an old oak. Nick shed his clothes as he kept his eyes locked on hers. Silvia's body responded, her ache becoming more than she could bear.

Before he finished undressing, she was working on her own clothes, tossing them wherever, eager to feel his skin against her own.

Nick eased onto the bed beside her, sending it swaying gently in the wind. With a quick grip of her hips, he had her up and straddling his lap. She'd never felt so exposed, not even when they'd had sex in the lounger. Here, they were out in the open, in the dusk with the sun still not quite set, and she was completely vulnerable to Nick's stare.

When he reached up to cup her breasts, Silvia arched into his touch. She leaned forward and braced her hands on either side of his head, then lined up their bodies before easing down on him.

Nick's lips thinned as his jaw tightened, but that dark gaze never wavered from her. The way he looked at her made her feel so empowered, so sexy. How could she not fall for this man when he made her feel things she'd never known were possible? How could she not fall for the man who made her want more of everything he was willing to give?

His vulnerability and raw state only made Silvia want to shield him from any more pain. He needed her, and she'd never had anyone actually *need* anything from her. The realization had her falling even more deeply.

Perhaps they needed to heal each other so they could move on together.

Nick's hands roamed down to the dip in her waist and over the flare of her hips. He held her in place as he jerked his hips rhythmically. Silvia groaned as she absorbed all of his emotions, his strength.

The swing swayed, and Nick's fingertips bit into her. Silvia moved with Nick as she leaned down and slid her lips across his. Her hair curtained them both, and she coaxed his mouth open. Nick's hands cupped her backside as his hips pumped faster. The climax built, and Silvia tore her lips from his as the sensations spiraled through her. She eased back, holding her body upright as she pumped her own hips.

Nick gripped her waist and tensed beneath her as his body bowed and he followed her pleasure. Silvia squeezed her eyes shut, not wanting any of her true feelings to show—not now when she was too vulnerable and on the edge of completely falling in love with Nick Campbell.

When their bodies settled, she relaxed down onto his chest. The swing kept swaying with a soft momentum, lulling her into a peaceful state. She hadn't been this calm for quite some time.

Nick's arms wrapped around her, and Silvia kept her eyes shut. She just wanted this moment, with this man.

Whatever problems he shouldered could wait. At this minute, all was right with their world.

Fifteen

"My mother left me a letter."

Nick didn't realize the words were going to slip out until it was too late. But he wasn't sorry. He needed to purge these feelings before they consumed him and turned him into someone he didn't recognize. He hadn't wanted to talk, because saying the truth out loud only made the ugly facts more of a reality.

But Silvia had changed him.

She shifted in his arms. He had no clue how long they'd been lying here completely bare and utterly vulnerable to each other. The sun had set, but he had no desire to move.

"Her attorney gave an envelope to me after her death," he went on, thankful for the darkness, save for the landscape lights around the pool. "I carried it around for a few days, scared of opening it. I guess I thought if I didn't open it, there was still one more conversation to be had with her. I just didn't want to let that go."

Emotion clogged his throat as Silvia turned. She fisted her hand on his chest and rested her chin on top. He didn't look her in the eye—he couldn't. If he saw pity or sadness from her, he wasn't sure he'd make it through.

"I finally opened it at the cemetery." He cleared his throat, recalling the punch to the gut when he'd first read the words. "She revealed the truth about my biological father."

"You don't seem happy about this news."

Happy? He was utterly disgusted and part of him wished he'd never found out. The other part of him... No, there was no other part. He wished he'd never had to associate himself with Rusty Lockwood, especially not by blood.

"I found out who my biological father is, and he's a total bastard." Nick blew out a sigh, likely from the relief of getting some of this out in the open. "He doesn't know I even exist. Well, I'm sure he knows he has children, but he doesn't know one of them is me."

Silvia flattened her hand against his chest and pushed up. Now he did look her in the eye, and he wasn't surprised at her wide eyes and open mouth.

"Is it someone here, in Green Valley?" she asked.

Nick nodded. "Rusty Lockwood."

She gasped, which seemed to mirror his gut reaction when he'd discovered the truth, too.

"Now you know why I've been so moody, so out of sorts," he told her. "I guess I'm still in shock myself."

"Are you positive?" she asked. "Did you talk to him?"

Nick glanced back to the starry sky. "I've spoken to

him, but not about this. He doesn't know about the letter. I highly doubt he even remembers who my mother was."

There was an anger in him he hadn't realized before. An anger that Rusty could just dismiss Nick's mother like she was nothing and let her fend for herself and the baby they'd made. Men like that literally thought money could solve all of their problems, and Nick believed it had for Rusty for a time. But now, the old man might find himself in too much turmoil and no amount of money could save him.

Nick's arm tightened around Silvia. "I don't know how the hell to be a father. I mean, is it better to have no dad or a terrible dad? I don't even know the answer to that. But I do know I'm going to try to be the best father I can be, because walking away is an immediate failure our child doesn't deserve."

"Oh, Nick."

The sadness in her voice broke him. Tears pricked his eyes, but he blinked them away. Weakness had no place here. Of all the times in his life, this was when he needed to be the strongest—for himself and for his baby. Hell, for Silvia, too. She needed someone stable in her life.

"I don't want pity," he told her, meaning every word. "I'll be there for this baby, but where Rusty is concerned, I battle back and forth on revealing the truth or just keeping it as the ace up my sleeve."

"Are you sure he's really your father?" she asked.

"My mother wouldn't lie about something like that. If she wasn't sure, she never would've told me. And I know that's why she waited until she was gone to let me know. She knew the news would be devastating."

"I don't doubt your ability or your determination

to be a great dad. I have no idea what I'm doing in the motherhood department, either. I didn't have the best examples." Silvia sighed. "But with your own father… I don't even know what to say."

"There's nothing to say. I just had to tell someone, and considering I've been a jerk at times, I wanted you to know my mood has nothing to do with you and everything to do with the fact that my life blew up in my face."

Her fingertips skimmed over his bare chest. Her soft, soothing touch affected him in a way he never could have imagined. Maybe hurt recognized hurt. Silvia was the strongest person he knew. She'd been through so much as a child that she was able to listen without judgment. Right now, he didn't necessarily need advice; he needed a sounding board.

"There's more," he told her, sliding his hand over hers on his chest. "My mom mentioned siblings. Brothers."

"What?" She gasped again.

Nick sat up, sending the swing swaying, as he kept her hand clasped against his chest. "I have no idea who they are. She said she sent letters to them as well. At this point, I can wait on brothers to come to my door, or I can confront Rusty and see if he knows anything."

Silvia scooted closer and rested her forehead against his. "I saw you with the letter that day at the cemetery. I wondered what was happening, but I was so consumed with my own problems that I assumed you were just grieving when I saw the pain on your face."

Nick swallowed back his emotions and refused to lose control. "There was so much to take in all at once," he admitted.

"And then I told you I was pregnant."

Yeah, that had been the trifecta of life-altering news. Losing one parent, finding another and learning he was going to be one. Honestly, he was pretty damn proud of himself for holding it all together.

"So what now?" she asked. "Do you want to tell Rusty the truth? Do you want to hire someone to find your brothers?"

Nick eased back and reached up to tuck her hair behind her ear. Trailing his fingertips along her jawline, he watched as she studied him. What he thought earlier had been pity was so much more, so much deeper.

Silvia stared back at him with compassion, determination, as if she was ready to slay those dragons for him. There was nothing sexier or more appealing than a strong woman who wanted to protect her man.

Wait. Her man?

No, that's not what was going on here. He didn't know if he could be a proper father, let alone be in a real relationship with Silvia. He had no experience with either role, and the fear of failing was a serious struggle. She'd had enough people fail her in her life—he didn't want to be added to the long list.

"There's so much I want, I'm not sure where to start with Rusty," he admitted. "But with you, hell, I'm not sure what to do there, either. Do we date? Do we co-parent? I'm lost here, Silvia. I know I want you, that much is obvious, but what can I offer you beyond that?"

Silvia's eyes softened. "Nick—"

He framed her face with his hands, stroking his thumb across her bottom lip. Exposing any vulnerability was far removed from his comfort zone, but he also couldn't keep certain feelings to himself.

"I can't be in a public relationship with you," she stated before he could go on. "My career is too important right now. I was just told today there may be a promotion on the line, and that's what I've been working for. If my boss knows that I slept with a client, that I'm carrying a client's baby, I can kiss that promotion goodbye. I bounced around so much from one foster home to the next when I was growing up, not only do I need this career and stability for myself, I need to provide for our baby. I can't be dependent on anyone else."

Anger filled him. On one hand, he understood her drive to want to be at the top of her game and find the success she'd worked so hard for. But the other part of him—the alpha side—wanted to tell her that he would provide everything she or the baby could ever want or need.

"You are human, Silvia," he told her. "I could see if there was a professional issue with our project, but there isn't. I wouldn't cancel contracts with your firm, if that's what they'd be worried about."

Silvia shook her head and scooted off the other side of the swing. Her sudden movements had Nick swaying and confused.

"You don't get it because you're a guy," she insisted. "If a man messed around with a female client, it would seem fun and flirty, but because I'm a woman, and new to the firm, new to town, and I got involved with my very first—and right now only—client, do you know what that will look like to them?"

Once again, anger bubbled up within him, and he swung his legs around to stand.

"Don't say it," he ordered. "Don't think of yourself

like that, because I sure as hell don't and anyone who does can go to hell. That firm is damn lucky to have you, and if they don't see it, then they don't deserve you."

Silvia jerked like she was completely shocked at his outburst, at his support of her talents.

"I'm not ready to tell them about the baby," she finally admitted. "Just be patient."

He understood her fears, but he also wanted her to understand that he wouldn't just leave her to fend for herself. Did she worry about abandonment? Because of her upbringing, was she concerned that he'd leave her and the baby?

They were both a mix of strengths and vulnerabilities, and Nick worried the clash might leave them both in a bigger mess than when they'd started.

"Go talk to Rusty," she told him, her tone pleading. "You're going to wrestle these demons until you do. You're not going to get some loving father/son reunion, but at least you'll have the truth out in the open and he can decide what to do from there."

Nick knew at some point he'd have to tell Rusty the truth, as leverage or as closure.

"I don't want to talk about Rusty any more," Nick stated as he circled the swing. "I want to take what I can for now and not worry about anything else...just for a little while."

Silvia's shoulders dropped, the tension visibly leaving her body. She took one step, then another, until she was in his arms.

Nick smoothed her hair down her back, then framed her face and grazed his lips across hers.

"Stay," he murmured. "For as long as you can. Stay."

He found he was always telling her that, and he wondered if this temporary arrangement would slide into permanent.

Nick leaned back in his office chair and stared at the double doors. He'd ordered Rusty to a meeting here, on Nick's turf. Nick knew the old man wouldn't turn down the request. Rusty was too on edge, too worried that Nick might actually have something to make public.

Their volley back and forth was about to come to an end.

"Mr. Lockwood is here to see you."

His assistant's low tone came over the desk speaker, and Nick remained in his seat. He wanted to appear as relaxed as possible, though he felt anything but.

A week had passed since he and Silvia had opened up to each other. She'd been spending her nights with him and going to work the next day. They'd fallen into a regular pattern that seemed natural, perfect.

The double doors opened, and Nick's assistant glanced at him before silently gesturing for Rusty to enter.

"Thank you, Natalie," Nick said. "Why don't you go ahead and take the rest of the day off?"

She smiled and nodded. "Thanks, Nick."

Once she closed the doors, Nick and Rusty were alone. Nick watched as his father glanced around the room, his gaze ultimately landing on Nick.

"You always dismiss employees early on a weekday?"

Nick shrugged and leaned back in his chair. "Happy employees stay loyal, and loyalty keeps the business running smoothly. You run your business the way you want and let me worry about mine," Nick added.

Slowly, he eased from his desk chair and came to his feet. "Care for a drink? I can offer Blanton's, Eagle Rare or Pappy."

"I'm not here for bourbon," Rusty scoffed. "Tell me what you want and let's get this over with."

Nick crossed to his minibar and pulled out a tumbler embossed with his company's logo. He popped the top off a bottle of Hawkins gin and added some tonic and lime. He took his time, purposely irritating his guest.

"Have a seat," Nick said as he crossed back to his desk.

Rusty remained standing near the doorway, but Nick stood by his chair. He held on to the back while gripping his drink in the other hand.

"You ever marry, Rusty?"

Obviously surprised by the opening question, the old man blinked. "Married? No, I didn't. What the hell does that have to do with anything?"

Nick shrugged and took a sip. "Just curious. I believe you knew my mother."

Nick's heart quickened; his palms grew damp. He hated that his mother had had any involvement with this arrogant bastard, but what was done was done.

"Lori Campbell," Nick added after a beat.

Rusty's brows drew in, then he shook his head. "Name doesn't ring a bell. Was she an employee?"

Nick swallowed. "She worked at a hotel you used to own years ago."

He waited for some realization to dawn or any spark of recognition.

Nick gritted his teeth and pulled in a deep breath. "Are you aware of any children you fathered?"

"Children?" Rusty scoffed. "What the hell are you hinting at?"

"I'm your son."

Nick hadn't meant to blurt it out, but he couldn't contain the truth anymore. He set his glass on his desk and stared back at the wide-eyed man.

"Lori Campbell was my mother," Nick stated. "She worked for you, and you got her pregnant."

Rusty's face turned red, his nostrils flaring. "If you think you can blackmail me because of my wealth—"

"Your wealth?" Nick mocked. "I don't give a damn about that. I could buy you out ten times. I care about the fact that you ignored a woman who was having your child. You paid her money to go away, but it wasn't nearly enough and now your past is coming back to haunt you."

Rusty hadn't paid Nick's mother nearly enough. She'd still worked two jobs to make ends meet and looking back on how hard she struggled only pissed Nick off even more.

Rusty took a step forward until he flattened his palms on the desk. "I don't have a son," he ground out. "Any woman I dealt with was compensated. So whatever you're wanting from me now, forget it."

Compensated? Nick nearly felt sick at the thought of this heartless prick paying women to exclude him from the lives of his own children. Nick couldn't imagine how he'd feel about not seeing or knowing his child. How crass would someone have to be to just toss some money and move on?

And that was the obvious difference between Rusty

and him. Maybe they did share the same blood, but Nick wasn't a cold-hearted bastard.

"My mother left me a letter before she passed," Nick stated. "I'm aware that I have half siblings. Do you have any idea who or where they are?"

Rusty pushed off the desk and crossed his arms. "Like I said, I paid enough not to be included in what those women did. I had a business to run and no time for kids running around."

Nick circled his desk until he came to stand directly in front of his nemesis. "I was better off without you in my life. My mother more than filled the void of not having a father, especially a deadbeat dad like you. I wonder what your cronies would think of you paying off women you impregnated. Doesn't sound so noble and loving, like the man you want people to believe you are."

Rusty opened his mouth, but Nick went on, taking another step until he loomed over the pudgy man.

"Couple that with your newly uncovered issue regarding Milestones, and I'd say you have a hell of a scandal on your hands."

If he thought Rusty's face was red before, it was nothing compared to now. He also had a flash of fear in his dark eyes.

"So, do you want to talk about those liquor licenses or are you going to continue to play this game?"

Rusty took a step back. "That's your proof? A letter from a dead woman?"

Nick fisted his hands at his sides and forced himself not to punch the man in the face. "My mother had no reason to lie. In fact, I'm sure she wished anyone else was my father. Why do you think she kept the secret until she was gone? She never wanted to admit she had anything to do with you."

"So you want to blackmail me? Is that it?" Rusty sneered. "Go right ahead. Smaller people have tried to take me down. It comes with being so successful."

Nick snorted. "Bullshit. You're successful because you started out doing something illegal. You've always been crooked—you just hide behind a corporation now. But I'll expose every one of your skeletons if it's the last thing I do. And you can bank on the fact that I'll track down your other children. Your days of running everything in this region are over."

Rusty's lips thinned. "You'll hear from my lawyer."

Nick smiled. "Oh, I'm looking forward to it."

Rusty stormed out, and Nick stared at the open door for a moment before going back to his forgotten drink. He tossed it back and welcomed the refreshing taste of gin with lime.

If Rusty wanted to fight, Nick was more than ready. Nick refused to be a man like Russ—a worthless father, a jerk to the women in his life.

But the fact remained: Rusty was his father, and Nick had a legitimate fear of that man's blood running through him. Maybe that's why he wasn't ready to commit to Silvia. He didn't even have commitment in his DNA.

Sixteen

Nick slid his hand into Silvia's as they stepped from the doctor's office. She'd had an ultrasound two weeks ago and then her regular visit today. So far, the baby seemed healthy and strong. Nick was still dying to know the gender, but he could wait if that's what Silvia really wanted.

He escorted her toward her car. They'd driven separately, but planned on meeting at the resort site. Still, they couldn't show up together, because she hadn't told her employer they were seeing each other. She'd all but moved her stuff into his place, but she wouldn't just say they were seeing each other.

Not only that, her boss still didn't know she was expecting a baby. Nick didn't know how much longer he could remain quiet.

Silvia pulled out her keys and released his hand.

"Are you heading straight to the site?" she asked, turning to face him.

Nick rested an arm on top of her car. "I'm going to stop and grab something to eat, and then I'll be there. Want me to pick up something for you?"

"I'm good," she told him. "I'm swinging by the office first, and I have some things in my fridge. So, I'll see you there in about an hour?"

Nick pulled in a deep breath and tucked a crimson strand of hair behind her ear. "Maybe you should tell your boss about the baby."

Silvia's eyes widened. "Nick, I will, I just—"

"Need time. You've said that for weeks." He stepped into her and traced a finger down her jawline. "But they're going to find out about the pregnancy and the secret is just added stress that's not good for you or the child. Not to mention you're practically living with me."

"I have my own house," she argued.

"Where you rarely stay," he reminded her. "I don't want them to find out from someone else. That would be much worse than if you just be honest."

"I'll tell them," she promised. "Soon."

"Today?"

She leaned up and slid her lips across his. "Soon," she repeated.

With a pat on his chest, she eased him back so she could open her car door. He watched as she got in and drove from the lot. She was still keeping barriers between them, still worrying about letting him fully in.

He would never be part of her life if he kept his own barriers in place, either. Damn it, he wanted more. Even though something inside him doubted that happiness and long-term commitment were even a possibility.

No, he didn't deserve her, but that didn't mean he didn't want her. Once he'd dealt with all of this mess with his father, his next step would be thinking about moving forward with Silvia.

Rusty had the nerve to block every call and visit, so that wasn't going according to plan. No problem. Nick had a meeting scheduled with the entire city council on Monday morning. The meeting was supposed to be private and secretive, meaning no Rusty, but that didn't mean the shady mogul wouldn't find out.

It was time for action…action in all aspects of his life.

Nick adjusted his glasses and crossed the parking garage toward his SUV. He was ready to take control and claim everything he wanted.

"Are congratulations in order?"

Silvia froze in the midst of grabbing a yogurt from her office refrigerator. Glancing toward the door, she spotted Kevin with a wide smile on his face, holding up his phone, wiggling it like it held some great secret.

Dread curled in her belly as she faced him. Her eyes locked onto the image on the screen, and every fear came crashing down on her.

No. This couldn't be happening.

She'd just left the doctor twenty minutes ago. How could a tabloid already have this photo online?

Silvia stepped closer. Above the image of her and Nick in an intimate embrace beside her car, the headline read, From Mogul to Daddy?

Her eyes scanned the rest of the wording and caught phrases like "mystery lady" and "is Nick Campbell ready to be a dad?" as well as her name and her employer's name. That had been fast detective work from the journalist.

What could she do now? There was no backpedaling and she had no valid excuse as to why she'd kept the secret.

"I had no idea," Kevin continued, oblivious to the turmoil spiraling through her. "And Nick Campbell? Girl, you wasted no time. Does Clark know you guys are…well, you know?"

Silvia's mind whirled. She hadn't even seen anyone lurking, but she also hadn't been looking for anyone, either.

Nobody even knew there was a secret to be kept other than her and Nick. He'd lingered by her car for longer than usual. Had he been giving the photographer time to get the perfect shot?

She didn't think he'd do this, but who else would have anything to gain from exposing their relationship?

Maybe Nick wasn't the man she'd hoped he could be. She'd been disappointed before by those she'd cared about.

"Excuse me," Silvia said, pushing past Kevin.

She had to get to Clark's office now. If he saw that image or if another employee got to him first, Silvia would have a difficult time explaining why she'd not come forward sooner. She'd been working with Nick for nearly six months, but she didn't know if Clark would believe that the affair started less than two months ago.

Her heart beat quickened with each step she took toward her boss's office. She should've been up front with Clark from the beginning. But she'd been so afraid of either losing her job or losing her heart. Because she'd known that the moment she admitted she was pregnant, the discussion would've snowballed and revealed the identity of the baby's father.

Silvia had so many reasons why she hadn't wanted to tell people, but right at this minute, they all seemed irrelevant. How could she provide financial security and stability for her child if she was out of a job?

She pulled in a deep breath as she reached Clark's double doors. When she tapped on them, they eased open, and there was Clark's assistant beside his desk with his phone. The way both men glanced up at her, she knew.

"Well, Silvia, come on in," Clark greeted. "I was just reading some fascinating news about you. And I assume congratulations are in order."

"Thank you, sir."

His assistant pocketed his cell and excused himself, leaving Silvia and Clark alone. She'd never been this nervous or anxious in her life.

"I had planned to tell you about my condition," she started the moment they had privacy. "Since I'm new here and my pregnancy was unplanned, I was trying to find the right time."

"Understandable," Clark agreed as he eased back in his seat. "And I really did mean congratulations on your pregnancy. I have five children of my own and three grandchildren. They're a blessing. I have no qualms about the pregnancy whatsoever. I do, however, have issues with you getting involved with a client while you're working on his project. One of the firm's most prestigious projects, actually."

Silvia clasped her hands in front of her and remained still. Her heart beat so hard, her stomach curled with tension and knots. But she wasn't going to show fear or worry, because she needed to remain strong, not just for her future, but for her boss to see she was an asset to this company.

"We don't condone this type of behavior," Clark went on. "It's not my business what you do in your spare time, but it is my business when it involves our biggest client. I can't exactly let this pass."

Silvia nodded. "I understand your concern, sir, but I assure you that my involvement with Mr. Campbell will not reflect on this company and will not hinder the project."

"This is already going to affect the company because of the media coverage," he countered. "You know how fast and far these stories travel."

"I also know that the next story will come along and mine will be forgotten," she informed him. "You just commended me on my performance and on how well I'm doing. Let me continue to do well for this company and prove what an asset I am to you."

He stared at her, his gaze unwavering, and she wanted nothing more than to run from the room and find out who was responsible for making that photo public. But she had to fight this battle with Clark first, before she could move on.

"Why don't you take a week off—paid, of course," he quickly added. "Let's see what happens and if there's backlash. This firm has a remarkable reputation, and I cannot allow my newest employee to tarnish what I've worked so hard to attain."

A week off? She didn't like the sound of that. He was making her feel like she'd done something wrong when all she'd done was fall into the arms of a man she'd been unable to resist. There was no policy here against fraternizing with clients. She'd only wanted to be extra cautious by keeping it secret. Was being human with basic needs wrong? Had she not gotten pregnant, her boss never would've known about her sex life, but now it was suddenly all over social media and fodder for office gossip.

"You should know I have an impeccable reputation as well," she added, more than ready to defend herself. "I'll be back in one week, and I will continue to do my job with as much excellence as always. The client I'm working with and all of my future clients will not care about my private life and you, sir, shouldn't, either."

She'd never normally talk disrespectfully to the one who signed her paycheck, but she also needed to stand her ground. She wasn't sorry for her actions. She hadn't left a black mark on the company, and she'd bet that if she started digging, she'd find at least one employee who'd had a fling with a client.

"I'll see you next week," she told him as she turned on her heel and walked calmly out the door, shoulders back and head high.

Her walk down the hall was quick. Whispers filtered from offices, but she didn't glance around. She didn't care who was talking about her, because she had bigger problems to worry about than what gossipmongers were saying. They had no effect on her life. Finding out who had shattered her small bubble of trust took precedence right now.

She had a week, right? Well, Silvia figured she'd find the culprit in the next few minutes...as soon as she met him at the site.

If he wasn't the man she'd thought he was, what

would she do? She wasn't sure how she could raise a child with someone she couldn't trust. She knew he was all alpha, wanting to provide for her and take care of her.

Had he let this secret out as a way to make sure she needed to lean on him even more?

Silvia was about to find out.

Seventeen

Nick walked through the third floor, examining all the new framework for the suites. He glanced at his phone again and wondered what was keeping Silvia. It wasn't like her to be late, but maybe something had held her up at work.

He bypassed the second floor, where the crew was working for the day, and went down to the main lobby. Still no sign of her, so he headed toward the back of the building and stepped out onto the expansive wrap-around deck with breathtaking views. This was where they would host parties and private receptions and even weddings. His mother had created a very detailed packaging plan for guests. He couldn't wait to see the end result come to fruition.

Out of all the businesses he'd worked on, this was by far his favorite. Unlike those others, which he'd flipped and sold, this one he would keep forever. Perhaps his child would want to take over this resort one day. Maybe this could be the start of a legacy. Nothing would've made his mother happier than to know her grandchild would one day take the reins.

A thrill of hope about a future with Silvia burst through him. What would she say if he asked her to create that family, that dynasty? With her architectural skills and his business sense, they could create a hell of a company. Of course, they could stay based out of Green Valley, but traveling with their child and exploring the world and flipping old buildings into something grand would be amazing.

And maybe that's the dream he'd been waiting for. Maybe that was the life that had been calling to him. He'd just had to find the right woman to share it with.

Nick knew his mother would've loved having a grandchild, and she likely would have been gooey and all smiles over how Nick and Silvia had found each other in the most difficult of circumstances. Now he just had to convince Silvia that they were right for each other, that her past didn't have to dictate her future.

Nick stared out over the mountains and instantly envisioned a wedding here. His wedding to his beautiful bride, glowing with pregnancy.

He smiled, unable to prevent happiness from bursting out. He loved Silvia. Maybe he'd been falling in love from the moment he'd met her, but now he knew he didn't want to be without her.

Raising their child in the kind of home they'd both missed out on would be their ultimate testimony to love and commitment.

And knowing he was building an even bigger legacy than he'd ever dreamed filled him with a burst of hope. He truly wished his mother could be here to see everything.

"Tell me you didn't leak the story."

Nick jerked around. Silvia stood in the open doorway, her wide eyes locked on his.

"What?" he asked.

"The story splashed all over social media." She pulled her phone from her pocket and held the screen out to him. "Did you do this?"

Confused, Nick closed the distance between them and took her phone. He stared at the photo of them, obviously taken just a while ago outside the doctor's office when Nick had been easing her hair behind her ears. There was another shot of when he'd kissed her.

The headlines, the comments, the hashtags—all were claiming the business mogul was becoming a father, and Silvia's name was mentioned, as well as the name of her firm.

His eyes darted back to hers and there was no mistaking she was serious about her accusations.

"I told you I would tell them," she insisted. "I told you to give me time. Why would you do this?"

"Wait. You truly think I did this?"

He waited for her to deny it, but the way she stared at him with so much hurt and anger, he could see she truly had convinced herself that he'd had a hand in outing them.

Did she immediately think the worst of him because of his confession about his biological father? Rusty was a total bastard, but Nick worked damn hard not to be like that. He'd always tried to be straightforward and honest, even more so now that he knew the genes he fought against.

"Who else even knew we had a secret?" she asked, her arms out wide. "I certainly didn't have someone ready to take our picture outside my OB's office. I assume you wanted a valid reason for me to rely on you, a reason for me to let you do everything for me like you wanted to do from the start. You thought a few pics and a clever headline would get the truth out there and speed that process along."

Nick didn't know what feeling lay so heavy on his heart, but it certainly wasn't the happiness and hope that had been there only moments ago.

"And you really believe I did this?" he asked again, giving her another chance to say something else.

"Did you?" she asked.

Nick pulled in a slow breath and glanced around at the mountains. That image he'd had of the two of them pledging their lives to each other had vanished.

He focused his attention back onto her. A fresh new slice of pain hit him hard. Maybe he was fighting a battle inside himself over what it meant to find out he was Rusty Lockwood's son, but that struggle didn't mean he would purposely, maliciously hurt someone he loved.

"The fact that you're even asking me really crumbles every ounce of trust I've built with you."

Her eyes widened, then closed. She blew out a sigh and shook her head.

"My first thought was that you planted someone there so it would pop up on social media and hopefully get back to my boss—which it did, by the way."

Nick eased his hurt aside for a moment, concerned with her well-being. "What did he say?"

"I was given a week's paid leave until they see if

there's going to be a scandal or a smear on the firm's reputation."

Nick's fury volleyed between Silvia's mistrust of him and her dumb-ass boss not believing in her. How dare that man say something to her about the relationship she had outside of work hours? Yes, Clark had a reputation to uphold, but he also had to be considerate to his employees and treat them all equally.

"If you tell me you didn't do this," she said, "then I'll believe you."

Nick shoved his hands in his pockets and stared back at her. "I don't have to say anything," he told her, the hurt growing deeper and deeper. "You either know my character or you don't. And the fact that my betrayal was your first suspicion says nothing about me, but a lot about you and your fears about us."

She jerked as if he'd smacked her.

"I didn't leak anything," he went on, forcing himself to close down the anguish he was feeling and just be honest. "I'm as blindsided as you are."

Silvia's bright blue eyes filled. "You can't blame me for wondering if you had something to do with those photos. The timing was too perfect."

"Maybe it was perfect," he agreed, a gnawing ache settling deep. That fear that maybe he wouldn't ever be good enough for long-term, that he and Silvia weren't meant for each other, consumed him. "But if you'd taken just a few seconds to think before jumping to a damning conclusion, we wouldn't be in this spot now."

"And what's that spot?" she whispered, one tear spilling down her cheek.

Unable to stop himself, Nick reached out and swiped away the moisture. He hadn't known it possible to physically hurt so badly from being heartbroken. The loss of his mother, the discovery of his father, now this. It was all too much.

"Back at the beginning, where we don't fully trust each other," he answered, dropping his hand. "Go take that week of vacation, but I can't be part of it. I can't make you happy. I'll be around if you need to tell me anything about the baby, but other than that, I can't be with you, Sil. It's too painful to love you and know you don't believe I'm the man you deserve."

He moved around her and walked through the lobby and out the front door. He bounded down the steps and straight to his truck. His vision blurred as tears pricked his eyes, and he blinked them away.

Over the past few weeks, there had been so many emotions that had completely taken over. He had no idea when he'd ever feel completely whole again or how he'd get his life back on the track he needed it to be.

All he knew was he'd never hurt like this. Between his mother and now Silvia, there was only so much pain he could handle.

Nick pulled away from the site and gripped the wheel as he tried to keep his emotions in check. How could she believe he'd ever do such a thing, especially after she'd told him how important it was for her to keep things secret?

All he could assume was that she truly didn't know him, and having such a vengeful, wicked man as his father didn't help his case. Hadn't Nick believed all along that he wasn't good enough for her? He'd wanted to prove himself—he'd even gotten his damn heart involved when he'd known good and well that was a mistake.

Nick found himself driving toward Silvia's firm before he realized what he was doing, but since she'd had her say with them, Nick figured he wanted his, too. He was their client, after all, and his working relationship with Silvia was the reason for her paid time off.

As Nick pulled into a parking spot, his cell chimed. He killed the engine and picked up his phone. Rusty's name lit up the screen, and Nick swiped open the message.

Immediately the photo that had surfaced on social media filled the screen, and Rusty's message read, Like father like son.

Rage bubbled within Nick, and he shot off a reply.

I take responsibility...like mother like son.

He put his cell on silent and stepped from his truck. He didn't need that reminder that there could be any of Rusty's negative traits inside Nick. He'd been raised by the strongest, most amazing woman ever. She had done all the parenting, so there should be no trace of Rusty inside of Nick.

Ignoring his niggle of worry about somehow ending up like his father, Nick went straight in the main doors of the office and requested to see Clark immediately. The receptionist—Kevin, if Nick recalled—fumbled with the phone and made a quick call. Apparently, Nick's face gave him away. It must have revealed that he wasn't going to wait and he wasn't here for small talk.

"You can go on up," Kevin stated as he hung up the phone.

Nick nodded his thanks and moved to the elevators.

Moments later, he marched through the fourth floor of the firm and straight to Clark's office, where the doors were open.

"Nick," Clark greeted as he came to his feet. "Great to see you. Come on in."

Nick stepped in and shook the man's hand. "I'm sure you know why I'm here."

"I can guess," Clark replied, then gestured toward the bar along the wall. "Can I offer you a drink?"

"I won't be long," Nick stated. "I just want to make it clear that if Silvia is taken off this project or if she is removed from her position here, I promise, I will take my business on this project and all future projects elsewhere."

Clark's smile vanished. "I gave Silvia a week off with paid leave."

"I'm aware of that," Nick stated, refusing to back down on this topic. "I'm also aware that's your way of figuring out what to do with her. It's your business, of course, and you can do what you want, but I'm just making my position clear. So you know where *my* business stands on the matter. I'm positive you could find another employee who had an outside relationship with a client. Your firm is too large—you've done too many projects. Silvia's not your first."

Clark's jaw clenched. "I'll take your words under advisement. Thanks for stopping in."

Nick knew that was his cue to go, which was fine. He'd come for what he wanted, and he'd made his case clear. He also knew Silvia wouldn't like that he had come to her defense here, but he didn't give a damn. His name was associated with this story as well as hers, and even though he was angry with her, she still deserved to have someone standing in her corner. She'd never had that, and damn it, he loved her.

No matter what went down between them or where they landed, he couldn't just turn off his emotions.

Besides that, she'd worked too hard for her career, and she deserved to do the job she excelled at.

As Nick marched back to his car, the message from Rusty slid to the front of his mind, and Nick knew in that instant who had leaked the story. That's something Rusty would do—underhanded, scheming, having Nick followed to look for dirt.

Nick didn't care, though. The truth would have come out eventually, and if Rusty thought this would make Nick back down, Rusty was an even bigger fool than Nick had thought.

He headed back to his house. With his heart so heavy, he'd rather work from home than deal with any employees or questions…especially today. No doubt if any of his staff had popped onto social media, they would've seen the pictures.

Right now, all he could do was focus on the resort, like his mother wanted. Silvia and that stab of betrayal would have to take a back seat in his mind—and in his heart.

Eighteen

Silvia walked into the spare bedroom and flicked on the light. She'd tried to go to bed around midnight, but thoughts kept swirling around in her mind. Between her boss, the baby and Nick, her entire world had been flipped every which way. She honestly didn't know what to do next.

After two hours of staring into the darkness, she decided to come into the room she'd envisioned as the nursery. Right now, she utilized this space as a library. She'd put up an entire wall of shelves. The bay window made a perfect lounge area to curl up and read...not that she'd had much time to do that lately.

She padded barefoot across the plush pale pink rug and took a seat on the window cushion. Silvia grabbed a fluffy white throw pillow and hugged it to her chest as she stared out at the starry sky and the full moon over the mountains.

Sleep wasn't going to come any time soon for her. Whether her eyes were open or shut, all she saw was that pain in Nick's eyes. She hadn't flat out accused him, but her question had made it seem that way. He'd told her she should've known his character enough to trust that he wouldn't betray her. And she did. Damn it, she did. Nick was the nicest, most considerate, most protective person she'd ever met in her life. How could she think—even for a moment, even when all evidence seemed to point his way—that he would purposely hurt her?

Everything he'd said had been accurate. She was afraid of happiness. She'd never fully had that in her life before now, and she wasn't sure how to react.

All of which were lame excuses for being so hurtful to the one man she loved.

And she did love him.

Silvia hadn't heard from or seen Nick in three days. She was absolutely miserable. Her bed was lonely; her days were lonely. She desperately missed him.

She also hadn't heard a word from Clark, which really irked her. The longer she thought about her position at his firm and his response to her pregnancy, the more she re-evaluated what she wanted. She really wanted to work for a prestigious firm, but more so, she wanted to be proud of herself at the end of the day. Her work was damn good, and she wasn't vain in thinking that. Nick and his mother wouldn't have hired her if they hadn't liked her portfolio.

Silvia had decisions to make. She could continue to be miserable without Nick and go back to work in four days for a man who might or might not still be thinking she was the black sheep of the office. Or she could take control of that happiness she'd found, apologize to Nick and see what this next chapter of life would bring her way.

Silvia stared around the room and wondered what Nick would want to do…if he forgave her. Would he want to live here or in the home he'd built? Would he want to work with her on more projects after this resort?

There was no guarantee he'd trust her again. He'd said they were back at square one. But Silvia was going to push aside her fear of heartache and let herself love him.

Nick had been hurt, too, and he had freely opened himself to her. Then what had she done? She'd taken his vulnerable heart and crushed it. Knowing she'd hurt him only made her insomnia that much worse. She couldn't stand knowing he was likely still in pain when he'd never done anything but lift her up and encourage her, all while dealing with the death of his mother.

Silvia rested her cheek on the throw pillow and figured she'd have to get some sleep so she could tackle her new attitude and new life goals come morning.

She couldn't help but feel a slight burst of hope. Clark and Nick wouldn't have a clue who this new Silvia was… She just prayed she was making the right decision where all parties and her future were concerned.

Nick adjusted his tie and stared at his reflection. Yesterday morning he'd received a text from Silvia requesting that he meet her at the airport wearing black-tie attire. She'd told him she had some news. She'd added that she knew she didn't deserve for him to show up, but she was just asking for a few minutes.

He had no clue what she planned to tell him or why he had to be dressed up to hear it, but there was no way he would miss this meeting. He'd been damn lonely without her. When he'd had dinner last night, Nick had eaten three pieces of bread and realized he should have one more, to make it even.

It was memories of those silly little quirks that filled his days. That wide smile of hers that would make her eyes glisten. He missed her in his bed, in his home, hanging by the fire outside late into the night. He missed everything about her.

Receiving her text had been the biggest relief.

He wanted the chance to apologize for the way he'd reacted. Instead of talking things through, he'd ended it and walked away. That's not the man he wanted to be, and that's sure as hell not the man she deserved. He was ready to prove he could be the man for her.

Nick had given her space, given her time to think. He'd hoped she would come around, but he didn't want to push. Silvia needed to come to every conclusion on her own, and Nick knew she was strong enough to do just that.

Her only flaw? Fear.

Well, he'd been scared, too. Scared she wouldn't come back, scared she'd push him away for good, scared she would throw away all they could've been.

So he hoped this text and meet up was about their future.

Nick stopped fidgeting with his tie and grabbed his keys and phone. Twenty minutes later he pulled into the lot that housed his plane.

He gasped as he took in the scene before him. His Cessna had been pulled out onto the runway. A mini runway of candles ran from the parking lot to the plane, where Silvia stood. His breath caught again at the sight of her in a strapless white dress with her red hair down and curled around her shoulders.

Nick parked and stepped from his SUV then made his way down the path of flickering candles toward Silvia.

"Did you pull my plane out?" he asked when he reached her.

"Don't be mad," she told him, wrinkling her nose out of nerves. "I called the manager of the airport and incorporated his help."

Mad? He wasn't mad. Intrigued? Definitely.

"And what do you have planned that you need my plane?" he asked, sliding his hands into his pockets to keep from reaching for her.

"You said I should know your character. So I'm counting on the fact that you said you love me. I'm counting on you giving me another chance even though I don't deserve it. I'm counting on you taking me on this plane and going to a destination I chose and filed in your flight plan."

Shocked and more than impressed, Nick took another step toward her. Now he did reach out, smoothing her hair from her shoulders. She was so damn breathtaking, he could hardly stand it. Being away from her for any amount of time had been pure hell.

"I know your character," she went on. "I know you're the best thing that's ever happened to me. I know you're going to be the best father to our baby, because you push when you should and you give me space when I'm being a jerk."

"It wasn't me that leaked the pregnancy," he told her.

"It was Rusty. I'm dealing with him in my own way, on my own time, but he had a photographer following me trying to dig up dirt on me for blackmail."

"I'm sorry he's your father," Silvia murmured. "Sorry he's causing you more hurt."

Yeah, he was sorry, too, but that wasn't important now. Rusty had no place here, in this moment, and Nick would definitely deal with him later.

He framed her face and smoothed the pad of his thumb over her bottom lip.

"I also know you went and talked to Clark," she added with a quirk of her brow. "You know I can take care of myself, but that was sweet in a protective sort of way."

"Clark and his firm don't deserve you," he told her.

Silvia smiled. "No, they don't. Which is why I plan on turning in my resignation. Now, don't worry, I'm working on a few plans. I don't intend to be unemployed and living off your wealth."

Nick couldn't stop his grin. "Is that right?"

"I paid for this little trip, though, so that's not on you," she stated. "But I do need you to fly this plane, because I'm not quite that good."

"And where are we going?" He closed the minuscule distance between them, making their bodies line up perfectly. "Because I'm fine with going back to my house and showing you a little more about my character."

Silvia curled her hands around his neck. "We're taking a trip first, because we need to talk, and we need to get away."

Hope overcame him for the first time since they'd fought. "I agree. I'm sorry for how I treated you the other day. That's not who I want to be for you."

Her fingertips threaded through his hair. "I know that's not the real you, just like me assuming the worst in you isn't the real me."

Nick feathered his lips across hers, unable to stop himself from seeking more of her touch, her affection.

"I can't stay angry with you when you were only running because you were afraid," he murmured against her mouth. "You had a terrible childhood, but I'm here to make sure the rest of your life is nothing but happiness and memories you want to keep."

She eased back with a wide smile. "That's going to go really well with my plan."

"And what plan is that?"

"What do you say about a quick flight to the coast, a wedding at sunrise and then...who knows?"

Nick stilled, his heart kicking up at the prospect of being with Silvia forever. "A wedding?"

Silvia stepped back and took his hands in hers. "Will you marry me? Can we be that family neither of us had? Can we grow more and more in love each day with our baby?"

Nick laughed. "I can't believe you're proposing to me."

Her smile faltered. "Does that mean you don't want—"

He scooped her up off her feet and spun her around. "Don't finish that sentence," he commanded with a quick smack on her lips. "I'll marry you anywhere at any time. But a beach wedding sounds perfect. How did you pull all of this off? Were you sure I'd say yes?"

"I pulled some strings," she informed him, her smile so wide it stole his breath. "And I told you, I know your character. I was certain you'd say yes."

Nick kissed her, claiming the woman he'd always wanted but hadn't known he'd been missing.

"I love you, Silvia."

She rested her head on his chest. "I love you, Nick. I just have one stop on our way to the coast."

"What's that?"

She focused her eyes back on his. "Double Down Donuts has a special order for us in lieu of a wedding cake."

Nick's heart swelled. "You thought of everything."

"I thought it was a way to include your mother in the day. The owner is making her favorite donut into a double stack cake."

"Double," he repeated. "Of course."

"There's only one thing I want one of," she told him.

"What's that?"

She kissed him. "One lifetime with you."

* * * * *

ONE WILD KISS

JESSICA LEMMON

For John.

I'll never forget the moment you called me out by asking, "Are you flirting with me?"

Why, yes. Yes, I was. ;)

One

Breathe in. Breathe out. He's just a guy.

Just a devastatingly handsome guy wearing an impeccably tailored navy designer suit.

Just a guy whose eyes were the color of bourbon enjoyed fireside.

Just a distractingly gorgeous guy whose hair was the perfect rumpled pattern of his own fingertips—or maybe some lucky woman's.

Just a guy who'd taken up residence in her heart and mind and soul for the past year who also happened to be her boss so he was Off Limits.

He's just a guy.

Addison Abrams started each of her workdays reciting that mantra before stepping into the ThomKnox building, entering the glass-walled elevator and zooming to the top floor of the multibillion-dollar tech company where her office was located.

When she accepted the position of executive assistant for the president of the company one year ago today, she'd expected said president to be older. Much older. Not six months older than her and closely resembling a model on the cover of *GQ* magazine. Granted, she hadn't done a ton of research on who she'd be working for. She saw the opportunity to work for a higher-up at ThomKnox and sent in her résumé so fast her own head had spun.

"I couldn't resist," that guy said now, setting a lone cupcake—vanilla with buttercream frosting, her favorite—in front of her. He lit a single gold candle with a match and then shook out the flame. She followed that trickle of smoke up to the face she saw every weekday. Once again, his sheer male beauty floored her. Seemed unfair to every other man on the planet that this one was hogging the good genes.

"Should I sing 'For She's a Jolly Good Executive Assistant' or 'Happy Workiversary to You'?" Brannon Knox gave her a wide smile, which disarmed her completely.

She'd been trying—fruitlessly—to stop admiring him, to stop longing for him, to stop looking at him like she wanted to take a bite out of him, for goodness' sake. Thank God for her poker face, because she hadn't yet been successful at getting over the crush she'd been harboring since the moment he extended his hand in greeting during her final interview.

Hi, I'm Brannon Knox. You can call me Bran.

"Singing is below your pay grade." She bent forward and gently blew out the flame. "This was unnecessary, but I appreciate it. Thank you."

Brannon Knox wasn't only the most beautiful man she'd ever laid eyes on, he was also kind and ruthlessly intelligent. Funny, tall, charming…and damned sexy. As if she hadn't thought about that enough already.

"I'm lucky to have you." He shoved his hands into the pants pockets of his suit and glanced over his shoulder as if making sure they were alone. "I should have thrown a big party, but I'm hopeless at doing anything without you." He winked, and even sitting, she felt her knees grow weak.

Oh, how she wished that was true. That he needed her in other rooms besides the boardroom.

Like the bedroom. *Yum*.

"I'm happy to hear I'm indispensable." Practice made it possible for her to keep her smile cool and her fidgeting to a minimum. The throbbing heat working its way from her chest to her lap was the hardest to ignore, but she was doing her best. She'd convinced herself she couldn't help her physical reaction to him, since looking at Bran and wanting him came hand in hand.

But recently, she'd had a wake-up call. Her mind was made up. Even if her body was slower on the uptake.

"I'd give you the day off if we didn't have ten million things to do." His brow crinkled. "What am I doing today, anyway?"

She rattled off his schedule from memory: a conference call and two meetings.

"Plenty of time to grab a cup of coffee before the day starts." Once again, he peeked over his shoulder. "I don't see any sign of the big bad CEO. Let's get out of here."

The *big bad CEO* was Bran's older brother, Royce Knox. A few months ago, Royce and Bran had both been contenders for the position when their father retired. Bran insisted that Royce won out because he was older, and she supposed that was true. Bran was amazing at what he did and every bit as capable as his older brother. In her eyes, he was the obvious number one choice for everything.

Once CEO, Royce had received more exciting news. He was going to be a father. The mother of his child, Taylor Thompson, was ThomKnox's COO—better known as a childhood friend to the Knoxes and the woman Bran used to *date*.

True story.

Addi had behaved like a jealous girlfriend during the short time Bran and Taylor dated. Though "dated" could be in quotation marks for as tepid as the romance had been. She would lay money on the fact that those two had never shared more than a kiss—though she'd never seen them kissing, either.

That unbecoming version of Addi was the old her. She was moving on with her life—disassembling the crush she had on Bran one swoony sigh at a time. She had to. Her job was important. Her pride was important. She wouldn't spend another moment longing for a guy who was uninterested in her.

"Coffee sounds amazing, but I really should return these emails." Best to keep work at work. They spent a lot of one-on-one time together discussing schedules and pertinent business information—a given for an executive assistant—but whenever she'd seen Bran outside these walls she began thinking of him as accessible. And, as she'd recently learned, he *wasn't* accessible. At least not to her.

"Come on, Addi." He leaned both hands on her desk, his jauntily patterned tie dangling between them. When he added an entrancing "let me take you out of here," she caved.

Old habits died hard.

"Fine, but I want an extra shot of espresso and two extra pumps of vanilla syrup." She pulled her purse from the bottom drawer of her desk and slung it over her shoulder. "And whipped cream on top."

He leaned in, his cunning smile further scrambling her brains, and added, "For your ThomKnox birthday, Addi, you can have anything on top you like."

Like you?

His innocent comment flooded her sex-starved body in a tidal wave and washed her all the way back to square one. This was going to be harder to do than she'd originally believed.

Her recent wake-up call had come courtesy of Bran's ex-girlfriend, Taylor. She'd innocently suggested that Brannon and Addison would "look good together," which meant Taylor noticed Addi's crush on him. The worst moment of Addi's life wasn't when she realized that Bran had overheard Taylor's matchmaking comment. It was the moment he'd reacted. In the long corridor bisecting the copy room, his face went slack, his expression pained.

Addison had wanted to die.

He might as well have held up a sign in all caps that read I DON'T FEEL THAT WAY ABOUT YOU, ADDISON. A sign she'd overlooked for way, *way* too long.

And since she loved her job and wanted to preserve what was left of her pride, burying her feelings was the wisest course of action. She'd had years of practice being independent. All she had to do was apply that same principle to her heart.

Tricky.

But necessary. If she had learned one thing from her parents, and it very well might be the only thing, it was that she couldn't rely on anyone else for anything. Not money, not friendship and certainly not love. A fact she'd forgotten as soon as she'd laid eyes on the younger Knox brother. A fact she was going to pound into her head with a sledgehammer if she had to—whatever it took to survive the travesty of a grown-up crush.

Maybe having coffee with Brannon would be a good thing. Platonic coworkers had coffee together all the time. And reaching the lower echelon of platonic coworkers was the goal. Not a very exciting goal, but she'd had enough excitement for a while.

"Get over him," she murmured, digging through her purse for her cell phone.

"What was that?" Bran asked as they stepped outside.

"Oh, nothing." She smiled up at him and her heart squeezed. An organ she'd recently determined had not one ounce of common sense.

The awkwardness continues.

Ever since Bran had dated Taylor, broken it off with Taylor and learned Royce had been named CEO, his work life had been challenging. Addison Abrams seemed to be another domino that had been reduced to rubble.

His executive assistant was irreplaceable. A trusted confidante who always had his back. She'd fit in since day one and brought with her an ease and efficiency that had helped him excel in his role as president. If she left, he'd...

Well, he couldn't think about it without seeing a mushroom cloud in his mind's eye. The saying went that behind every successful man was a strong woman. He'd made the epic mistake of believing Taylor was that woman. Now, he saw it was Addi.

Lately his relationship with Addi had been strained, and that blame could be placed directly on one rogue comment from Taylor Thompson. He didn't know if it was Taylor being in love with Royce or if it was pregnancy hormones that had made her say it, but she'd suggested that Addi should be more than his assistant. That they'd be good together. He and Addi had locked eyes wearing matched expressions of panic. His stemming from complete shock and hers from what appeared to be fear. Seriously. It was like a scene right out of Hitchcock's *The Birds*.

Fresh off the grave error of dating Taylor in the race to win the CEO role, Bran was determined not to follow that mistake with another. But he could admit that since it'd happened, he'd started noticing Addison.

Like, *noticing.*

His plan with Taylor had been shortsighted. Misguided. But at least he could explain it away. He thought having her at his side would make him appear more CEO-worthy. See? Misguided. After a few awkward dates, he thought he'd better their chances by...proposing.

It made sense at the time. Now, he swiped his brow in relief that they hadn't slept together. That would have made family holidays really awkward.

So. How did that tie in with Addi?

On the tail of the CEO race ending with Royce holding the baton, on Taylor becoming pregnant with Bran's niece or nephew, Bran found himself at the office more. Paying attention to his assistant more. Addi, whether she was trying to smooth over the uncomfortable suggestion that they should date or simply trying to soothe his ego, had been in his space more than usual.

He'd noticed her poise and passion when she discussed even the blandest work topics. He'd noticed her legs, long and lithe, and wondered if she was a runner or if hers was a yoga body. He'd noticed that she brought takeout from a local restaurant frequently, and she stayed to work late when he did.

In short, he'd noticed she was *single*.

Taylor's suggestion had taken a foothold in his subconscious. He'd begun thinking of Addi regularly—and not professionally. Which had led to the disastrously uneasy exchange this morning. Unbelievably, the aftereffect with her was proving harder to hurdle than the almost-proposal to Taylor a few months ago.

Today being Addi's one-year anniversary at ThomKnox was significant. If he intended on keeping her around for another year, he had to fix what was broken. He wasn't sure if coffee and an anniversary cupcake would be enough to usher the pink elephant out of the room, but it was a good start.

Outside in the gorgeous California sunshine, the office building towering over the green lawns dotted with reaching palm trees and colorful flowers, they crossed to the coffee shop that was a permanent fixture on the ThomKnox property. The Gnarly Bean served the best coffee in the state—he was hooked.

"I love this place." Addison's lips curled into a smile that made her blue eyes sparkle. She was dressed in yellow, her fair hair swept back into a cute ponytail. It was impossible not to notice how gorgeous she was. He'd sort of noticed since the day he hired her. But he could compartmentalize. He'd been great at compartmentalizing before the CEO obsession.

He pulled on the sleek silver handle of the glass door and gestured for her to enter ahead of him, pausing to inhale in appreciation. Was there any better indulgence in life than coffee?

Automatically his eyes tracked to Addi's legs. *Just one.*

"I'm buying," he reminded her when she reached for her wallet. He could've sworn her bright blue eyes flicked to his mouth a second before her own beautiful lips formed the words "thank you." Probably he was projecting.

The worst part about what went down a few months ago was that he'd behaved so out of character he'd hardly recognized himself. He hadn't asked Taylor to date him because he was attracted to her, but because he'd hoped their partnership would make him a better contender. It was like an alien had taken over his body. Bran was the easygoing, playful Knox brother; robotic pragmatist described Royce.

"We should do this more often," Bran said.

She watched him carefully, her expression unreadable.

Oh-kay. Going well so far.

"Morning, Addi." The barista met her at the counter, smiling around a beard and subtly flexing the tattoos on his forearms.

Pathetic.

"Hey, Ken. How are you?" Addi greeted him warmly

and Bran felt a twinge of jealousy. Beard and tattoos? Was that what she was into?

Suddenly he felt like a stodgy guy in a suit whose only importance was signing her paychecks. He never used to notice who Addi smiled at—until she stopped smiling at him. God, he missed the simplicity of the good ol' days. Back when he saw himself in the role of "boss" and her in the role of "assistant" and never the twain shall meet.

Before Taylor pointed out that they'd look good together.

Before Royce suggested the girl for Bran was right under his nose.

Before Bran starred in his own personal remake of *Invasion of the Body Snatchers*.

He used to live life day by day without worrying about the future. Those were the days.

Ken said something stupid and Addi laughed—surely to be polite. Bran stepped between them and Ken's smile turned challenging.

"She wants whipped cream on top, and I promised to give her whatever she wants. It's our one-year anniversary today. Isn't it, Ad?"

Her cheeks turned pink, but her smile was genuine and focused on Bran for a change.

"It is," she agreed.

"Congratulations," Ken said as he tapped the screen to add the upcharge. Bran didn't think he meant it.

And even though he was setting a course to win back the trust of his trusty executive assistant, he saw no harm in making sure that Ken, here, didn't tread where he wasn't welcome. Addi could do better than a hairy barista, anyway, so Bran had no problem reminding this guy of his station.

After all, what were bosses for if not to protect their most treasured coworkers?

Two

Addison was contemplating Bran's behavior at the Gnarly Bean yesterday when Taylor Thompson stepped into her office.

"Knock, knock. You should demand a door. Anyone could barge in." Taylor was referring to the dividing wall separating Addi from the rest of the office, and Bran's office, which was to the left of her desk.

"You are the COO. Barge away."

"Ugh. Let's stop talking about barges. I already feel like one." Taylor smoothed a hand over the small baby bump protruding from her black Dolce & Gabbana midi dress.

"Stop it. You look amazing. How's everything going?" Addi asked.

"Do you mean with work, the pregnancy, the engagement or moving in with Royce?" Taylor's eyes widened slightly. Her life had changed drastically over the last few months, so it must be hard to wrap her head around. It wasn't long ago that Addi had flipped the light switch on for the copy room and stumbled across Royce and Taylor making out in the supply closet.

Thank goodness those days were behind them. At the time she'd been so jealous of Taylor and Bran's relationship. Now Addi could hardly believe how immature she'd been. It was obvious Taylor had found her other half in Royce.

Addi had since apologized for being rude—while avoiding mentioning that it was because she was half in love with Bran—and because Taylor was at once charming and classy, she'd apologized right back and asked if they could be friends.

Taylor lowered into the guest chair in front of Addi's desk. "I've never been so busy and yet I feel like I'm exactly where I should be. Does that make sense?"

"Complete sense." Addi smiled. She used to believe she was exactly where she should be. Before Bran started acting weird around her. What was with that display with the barista yesterday morning, anyway? Ken and Bran seemed to be having some sort of modern-day Wild West standoff.

Men made no sense. Maybe it was time to stop trying to figure them out.

"It's incredible that I get anything done considering I can't have caffeine right now." Taylor grimaced.

"I'd die." Addi tucked her coffee mug behind her computer screen to hide it from view.

"That's the price of having a healthy son or daughter. It's strange not knowing what to call my baby. I can't very well say 'it,' can I?"

"You don't want to know the sex?" Addi didn't know if she could stand the suspense if she were pregnant.

"I do. And I don't. Everything about my and Royce's relationship has been a surprise. Why not surprise ourselves with a little girl or boy?" She rubbed her round tummy.

"I'm happy for you." Addi meant it. Taylor was glowing and not just from the pregnancy. Whenever she was with Royce, the other woman lit up like the northern lights. "Have you set a wedding date yet?"

"Ho boy." Taylor admired the gigantic diamond solitaire on her left hand. "I know the engagement will lead to a wedding, but we're not sure when. We're taking things a day at a time."

Unplanned pregnancy and closet kisses aside, Taylor had handled life's many curveballs with a grace Addi hoped one day to possess.

"Happy belated anniversary, by the way. I saw Bran with a pair of cupcakes yesterday."

"Funny. He only gave me one." Addi narrowed her eyes playfully, trying not to let any of her feelings for him show. Walking around half in love with him was not healthy—and behaving like a lovesick woman in front of Taylor was asking for it. "I'm lucky to work for people who care. I've had bosses who didn't."

A lot of them. She'd shunned her parents' money when she didn't follow their rules for her life. Seceding from the union five years ago to pave her own way had come at a price. There were a lot of ramen noodles in her past, and plenty of bills that had been paid late. But that was in her past. When she landed the position at ThomKnox, she knew she was in the right place. They paid her well, and the higher-ups actually cared. Jack Knox, Bran's dad, had always treated her with respect and addressed her warmly.

And recently she'd almost blown it. Over what? A schoolgirl crush? No more.

She would never go back to scraping by or working for companies that gladly stepped on the "little people" to pave their mansions' driveways with gold bars. The Knoxes—and Taylor would soon be one—were good people. Addi was a good person. And she was no longer going to let a silly attraction distract her from what was important.

"Now for the real reason I came here. When's Brannon back?" Taylor glanced at his dark office.

"He had an early meeting before work. He should be here soon." Addi glanced at the clock. "You're welcome to wait."

"No, that's okay. I'll track him down later." Taylor stood and seemed to quietly debate before asking, "Are you and Brannon...okay?"

"Of course!" Addi said a little too loudly. "Why wouldn't we be?"

"Come on, Ad. Just us girls here. I see the way you look at him."

Was she so transparent? "He's...very nice. But I'm not interested in him like that." *Starting right now.*

"That's too bad." Taylor's mouth quirked.

It really was.

"We're fantastic coworkers." It was such a dry, stale definition for how she felt about him, Addi internally cringed.

"Right." Taylor nodded but didn't look convinced. "Tell him I stopped by. And enjoy some of that coffee for me."

Addi watched Taylor go, her stomach pinching. That happened whenever she didn't tell the truth. She appeased her conscious with the reminder that soon, it would be true.

One day she'd be as immune to Bran as he was to her.

Three

When Taylor strolled by, Bran stepped out of the copy room and intercepted her path. He'd been en route to his own office when he'd heard her and Addi's conversation. He'd rerouted before his presence was known and made everything between him and his assistant worse. If that was possible.

"Bran, hey. I was just at your office."

"I know." He folded his arms over his chest. "I *heard*."

To her credit, Taylor winced. But she followed it up with a justification. "You can't blame me for trying!"

Gently, he gripped her biceps and towed her into the copy room where he closed the door. "You have to stop doing this."

"Doing what?"

"You can't make two people fall in love because they're both good-looking." He lifted an eyebrow and complimented them both. "As well you know."

"Ha ha. And that's not the only reason."

Something was suspicious in the way she examined the floor.

"What's the *other* reason?"

"What do you mean?"

He knew her well enough to know that her innocence was one hundred percent feigned. *"Taylor."*

"I just…want you to be okay. I worry."

Ah, Taylor. She really was so sweet.

"About me?" he asked.

"Yes. You almost proposed to me, Brannon."

"A mistake."

"Obviously. But I would like to see you with a nice girl. And Addi likes you. I don't care what she says."

"A nice girl—Taylor, you're not my mother. You don't have to fix me up. And you should care what Addi says. You're freaking her out and I need her to keep this job or else I'll be demoted to the tech department with Cooper."

Jayson Cooper was Bran's ex-brother-in-law. Taylor chuckled, understanding that Bran was joking. Cooper and Bran's sister, Gia, worked side by side in the tech department. It was the heart of ThomKnox.

"You deserve to be happy. That's all I'm saying."

See? Sweet.

He touched her shoulder, grateful to have a friend who cared that much about him—even if it was slightly emasculating. "I'm in the process of putting everything back where it goes. I'm not jealous of Royce about CEO, or anything else." He gave her a meaningful look. "And dating Addi isn't going to help me be happier. If anything, it'll end badly and I'll be more alone than ever. You don't want me to hire an assistant like Royce's, do you?"

Melinda was an ace, but she was also sort of terrifying. As if reading his mind, Taylor shuddered. *"No.* Let's keep Addi."

"Yes, let's." He opened the copy room door. "Now what was it that you wanted to talk to me about? Should we grab a conference room?"

"Actually I'm starving." She patted her belly. "How about we grab a snack?"

"We can do that," he told her and they walked to the elevator. "And just so we're clear…"

Taylor turned, wide-eyed innocence worn like a mask.

"Addi and I are trying to make our way back to professional coworkers after you kicked open the 'Bran + Addi' door. Can you do me a favor and let us close it?"

She sighed, her shoulders slouching in her designer dress. "*Fine.* But I won't like it."

He pressed the button for the elevator and smiled. "I'm sure you won't."

After his impromptu breakfast with Taylor, Bran strolled toward his office. He came to an abrupt halt when he saw Addi scrambling in the lap drawer of her desk for a tissue, fresh tears wetting her cheeks. She pasted on a smile that wasn't the least bit sincere.

"Hey," he said, unsure what else to say.

He had a mother. He had a sister. Seeing either of them in tears made him feel two things: helpless…and helpless. He felt the same way now.

"Morning," she said. "How was the meeting with Frank?"

He could pretend not to notice. Save her the embarrassment. But what kind of jerk would he be if he did that? His goal was to keep her from leaving and if her tears had to do with something he could help with professionally he needed to know about it.

"The meeting went well. I ran into Taylor on the way back."

"Oh good. She was looking for you." Addi blinked damp eyes at him, but she didn't appear to be reeling from Taylor's visit.

No, Addi's eyes were filled with sadness. Something

had broken her heart. Or someone. Did he guess wrong about her being single? Did she have a boyfriend she never talked about?

He lowered himself onto the corner of her desk, catching sight of cream-colored card stock and a black envelope. Fancy. The kind of paper used for—

"A wedding?" he guessed.

Those sad blue eyes turned up to his, her expression both startled and vulnerable.

"The invitation," he clarified. "Weddings aren't always good news." Especially if, for example, the groom was her ex.

"Oh, um, no. It's a family...reunion." She stuffed the invitation into her planner. Formal for a family reunion, but okay.

"Everything all right?" he asked gently.

"Yes! Completely fine." Her smile was shaky. "Family can be tricky."

"Try working with them every day."

Her smile was genuine this time and made this awkward interchange worth it in every way. "I couldn't walk by and pretend not to notice. I'm not that obtuse."

"Ha!" She slapped her hand over her smile, then waved the air in front of her. "I'm sorry. Ignore me. I'm fine. Honestly."

Against his better judgment, he captured her smaller hand in his. "You're human. It's okay to cry."

Warmth between their palms radiated up his arm, attraction snapping the air between them like a leashed alligator. Meanwhile, Addi regarded him like he *was* a leashed alligator.

He gave her hand a squeeze before dropping it and standing from her desk. "If you need to take off—"

"No. Thank you." Her tears had dried already, her smile glued into place.

"Don't say I didn't offer." He pointed at his office door. "You know where to find me."

He shut himself inside and sat in his chair, eyeing the Post-it stuck to his laptop that read, *Taylor stopped by. Not urgent.* Addi's handwriting was pretty and delicate, like she'd been a moment ago. Whatever family thing was going on—if that was the truth—he didn't like how it'd affected her.

His cell phone buzzed with a reply to his earlier text to Tammie. When he'd sent it, he wasn't sure if he was hoping she'd reply or hoping she wouldn't. Similarly, he wasn't sure whether or not to read it.

He grabbed his cell phone anyway, too curious to ignore her reply.

Been a while.

A long-ass while.

In an effort to put everything back to normal, there was one issue to contend with that he hadn't talked about with anyone.

His roving libido.

He hadn't had a woman in his bed in a long time and had become suddenly distracted by Addison Abrams. Which was detrimental to the balance he was trying to restore at the office.

This morning, the *situation* had escalated. He'd woken hard and ready, unable to think of anything but sex. Sex with Addison.

He blamed the dry spell that had yet to end. From now on, his work and personal life had clear lines of demarcation. He needed to get laid, and obviously the best choice was to find someone outside of work to satisfy that urge.

The simplest fix was a sure thing by the name of Tammie. He'd sent her a text after a, um, *rejuvenating* shower, inviting her out for drinks.

Too long, he typed.

Her reply lit the screen half a second later. Thursday at 7? Vive?

Vive was a dark, classy bar with rich red velvet on the booth seats and cozy, sexy nooks filled with shadows.

Perfect. Meet you there.

He tossed his phone on his desk. Sex with Tammie would fix more than his blue balls. Sex with Tammie was a time machine back to before the whole "who will be named CEO" fiasco. Back when he knew how to lighten up. Back when "work hard, play hard" was his motto. Hell, this year all he'd done was work hard and then work *harder*.

Was it any wonder Addi had followed him around, staying late to make sure he was okay?

He glanced out his window at her. She was typing on her keyboard, her attention fixed on her computer screen. The pull he felt toward her, the concern he had for her, was alive and well, but he wouldn't allow it to harm their friendship or their working relationship.

She deserved to feel comfortable at work and he didn't need her—or Taylor—worrying about him. What he needed was to focus his physical attention on a woman who wouldn't worry about him for longer than one night.

His phone buzzed with another text from Tammie. A red lips emoji.

By Friday morning, this situation with Addi would be resolved.

I'm not that obtuse.

Addison hadn't meant to literally laugh out loud, but come on. He'd been pretty darn obtuse! Not only had he bought her lie about a family reunion but he'd also completely missed the way she'd drooled over him for the last year.

Obtuse or not, him consoling her when she'd been crying had tugged at her heartstrings.

"Just when I decided to get over him," she mumbled to herself.

She reached for her cell phone to text her friend. Carey was out of the country traveling for work, but Addi needed to talk to someone, even if the conversation was one-way.

She texted, Just cried in front of my boss. Go me! and sat back in her chair, her eye catching the invitation in the inside pocket of her planner. The very card stock she'd been holding when Bran caught her crying.

Behind the paper was a black envelope on which her name and address had been meticulously scripted in gold ink. Grief weighed heavy on her chest.

Joe was too young to die.

The invitation had arrived yesterday but she'd neglected to check her mailbox until this morning. As a result, she'd shoved it into her planner and promptly forgotten about it. When she finally remembered and tore open the envelope, she was shocked to see that it contained an invitation to Joe's "celebration of life."

He'd passed away over a month ago and had been cremated per his wishes. According to his family, funeral plans were "forthcoming." Joe, as it turned out, had arranged those plans before he passed away. He'd selected a group of friends and family to attend an intimate but luxe party at a resort in Lake Tahoe. He'd covered the expenses for guest rooms and had prearranged an itinerary and catering. The lush surprise was so…him.

The last time she'd seen Joe had been around Christmas. It had broken her heart to see him so frail, and it'd broken his heart for her to see him that way, too. *Don't you dare come back here, Addi,* he'd told her. *I don't want you to re-member me like this.*

She'd swallowed tears she'd promised not to shed while sitting next to him. They'd drifted apart—and hadn't hung out in years—but he'd meant a lot to her. Losing someone was hard. Losing someone she'd known and cared for as long as she'd known and cared for Joe had seemed insur-mountable.

It wouldn't surprise her if that visit had been what turned up the volume on her crush on Bran. She'd mentioned her boss to Joe at the time, if only to change the subject. Joe had encouraged her to "go for it." But he had lived a big, brave life thanks to a family that was drowning in money and eagerly showered it on him. She'd reasoned it was eas-ier to be brave when there was a few billion in the bank.

Receiving the invitation to his life celebration had brought the grief of that December day back in an instant. Addi was a private person. She reserved messy emotions for when she was alone. If Bran's attention hadn't been so welcome, she might've been embarrassed about carrying on like that at work.

She shut her eyes against the memory of how great Bran had smelled sitting so close. Like mountain pine and cit-rus—

That's enough.

Operation Get Over Him was a new endeavor, but an important one. Focusing on her independence would for-tify her job, which would keep her housed and well-fed, as well as heal her heart.

The upcoming trip to Lake Tahoe would bring closure to another wound in her past—she hadn't seen Joe's par-ents since she stopped working for Hart Media, and as a result royally pissed off her own parents. While a resolu-tion with her parents was too much to count on, maybe the Harts would surprise her.

After a quick call to the inn where Joe's life celebration was being held, she learned that her room had been reserved, the cost covered. Travel was easy since the lake was a four-hour drive away. A trip even her questionably reliable car could handle.

Onward.

Satisfied that at least her personal life was moving forward, she jotted the trip into her planner. The only thing left to do was schedule her time out of the office and a temp to fill her chair for a few days.

A long weekend celebration was a perfect sendoff for Joe, and the perfect time to bury her crush on Brannon Knox.

Out of sight, out of mind and all that.

Four

In a traffic-clogged lane on the freeway, Addison worried her lip with her teeth as she watched a trail of smoke snake out from under the hood of her hatchback. She was no mechanic, but she guessed that smoke coming from any part of her car was *bad*.

She was twenty minutes into her trip with several hours to go. She just needed a little bit of luck. She shut off the air-conditioning, hoping that taking the AC out of the equation would encourage her antique car to complete its journey as far as the next exit, but her beloved rust bucket jerked forward one final time before wheezing and, ultimately, stalling.

Lady Luck had given her the finger.

Honks sounded in the air, along with a few choice swear words from her fellow commuters. Like she *decided* to break down? She was tempted to shout back at them. Something to the effect of, "Oh, you know, just taking a breather here in the far right lane!" Instead she bit her tongue, grateful that she'd managed to steer onto the shoulder at least partially.

Her entire morning had been frustrating.

She'd forgotten to halt her mail and discovered this morning that the post office's website was down. So she'd physically driven to the post office and waited in line and then filled out one of those stupid forms. As a result, her planned departure from River Grove at 10:00 a.m. had been delayed two hours.

And now this.

Well. She was going to have to call for help.

Her parents weren't an option and hadn't been for some time. Discussion of a broken-down car would lead them to remind her how if she'd stayed "at Joe's family's company," she'd not only have reliable transportation but also would have funded her retirement by now. She guessed they still held her responsible for the fracture in their relationship with the Harts, but Addi refused to take the blame. She'd worked hard to get where she was in life. Her parents might not give her credit for thriving without their money or connections, but she was proud of herself.

She typed tow trucks Silicon Valley into her phone. Approximately six million options popped up on the screen. How was she supposed to know who was reliable? Who wouldn't overcharge her? Who would be the fastest?

She debated for the count of three drivers who sped past and flipped her off before calling the most logical person. If there was a silver lining for this crappy day, it was that her car had chosen to croak ten miles from ThomKnox headquarters.

"Mr. Brannon Knox's office, may I help you?" answered the temp currently stationed at Addi's desk.

"Hi, this is Addison Abrams, Brannon's executive assistant. Is he available?"

"One moment."

A brief pause later, Bran's silky voice was caressing her ear canal. "Couldn't stay away, I see."

"My car broke down. I was hoping you could recommend a towing company." She rattled off the nearest exit and then had to repeat herself when some jerk swerved around her, horn blaring.

"What the hell was that? Are you okay?"

"Apparently it's frowned upon to have car trouble on the 80."

"You realize you could wait an hour or two for a tow truck to arrive, and that's optimistic."

She grunted. "That sounds about right for today."

"I'll pick you up myself."

He'd...what?

"Oh, no. I didn't mean for—"

"Addison." Those three sternly spoken syllables locked her throat. "Sit tight. I'm coming for you."

Congratulations! You've just unlocked another Brannon Knox fantasy badge.

Her car's hood was up, Bran's upper half hidden under it. His suit jacket was tossed over the front seat of his shiny red sports car, which he'd parked in front of her car and off to the side. A tow truck was on its way, but he'd insisted on having a look himself. Before this moment, she would've bet her life savings that Bran didn't have a clue about cars. Why would he? He was a billionaire. Everything was probably done *for* him.

But no, of course he knew enough to climb on in and make another of her sexual fantasies about him bloom to life. He pulled this wire and that, checked a dipstick here and twisted a cap there. All while she admired the ropey muscles of his forearms and the way his white shirt stuck to the muscles of his back thanks to a damp pool of sweat.

He cranked something or another, grunting with exertion while she silently lectured her lady parts. Him attempting to resuscitate a vehicle was hands down the sexiest thing she'd ever seen him do. There was no desk hiding his long legs, encased in charcoal trousers and leading up to a spectacular ass. She'd always admired Bran's backside, and now she could do it without worry of being caught.

She wrenched her eyes from his amazing physique to watch those hands twisting and tightening. The longer hair on top of his head fell over his forehead, sweat trickled down his face as he grimaced with effort. Her gaze wandered south of its own accord as she pictured him exerting himself elsewhere, same sweat, same hair on his forehead, only he'd be over top of her. Or beneath her.

Oh, yes.

"Well." He emerged from under the hood and she jerked her attention from his butt. "Your radiator's shot. Probably more than the radiator, but that part I know for sure." There was an oil streak on his face and his hair was more rumpled than usual.

Sexxxxy.

The meager progress she'd made getting over him had suffered a major setback thanks to this circumstance. Heaven help her.

He dropped the hood with a bang and wiped his hands on what looked like an expensive pocket square. It was paisley—silk, she'd bet. Not to mention the shirt that stretched over his ample chest, covering three-quarters of those capable arms, was ruined as well.

"Your *wardrobe* is shot. You'll have to take it out of my paycheck."

He grinned and she nearly swooned on the side of the freeway. "Sounds like me. Help out a damsel in distress and then dock her pay. What kind of a guy would I be if I let you fend for yourself?"

"A practical one?"

Her reward was his husky laugh that made her ankles

tremble. Interestingly enough, no one had yelled at her since Brannon arrived. It was as if they understood they were in the presence of power.

"Come on, I'll give you a ride to the office."

She retrieved her purse from her front seat while he transferred her luggage to the trunk of his incredibly shiny car.

"Is this new?" she asked as she sank into the butter-soft leather passenger seat. She could swear she'd never seen this car before.

"Very new. She's one day old. Had her delivered last night." He settled in the driver's seat, picked his moment and smoothly pulled into traffic. "I haven't been able to drive her anywhere but work, but I'm itching to take her out."

"I'll bet."

He put his foot on the gas and the engine growled, sending tingles through her feet and up her legs.

"You were headed to Tahoe, right?" he asked.

"Yeah."

"For a reunion."

He wasn't technically wrong, so she nodded. "How long do you think it'll take for my car to be repaired?"

"Hard to say. Depends on whether the mechanic has the parts he needs, and if he has five cars in front of yours or fifty."

Her shoulders sagged. That piece of crap car was her only means of transportation. And if repairing it cost more than the vehicle's worth—a probability—she'd have to go through the hassle of buying a new one.

"Why are you driving a car in that bad a shape, anyway? Tell me it's not because I don't pay you enough."

"No! Oh my gosh. Not at all." He took very good care of her in the money department. "It's... I keep it for sentimental reasons."

"Really?" His dubious expression said what he didn't. How could she be sentimental over such an ugly hunk of metal?

"That car was the first big purchase I made with my own money." She'd hunted countless dealerships and sifted through online classifieds. She'd taken care of the transaction herself. It'd been scary at first, but then enthralling. That was the day she knew that she didn't have to be scooped under her parents' wings to make it in life. That she was capable of surviving on her own.

Though she'd sort of been scooped up under Bran's wing today. It was past time to reclaim that plucky woman who had ventured off on her own. To be as independent as she'd once been.

"I remember my first car," he said wistfully.

"Was it a Maserati?"

"Maybe." He flashed her a quick smile and she had to laugh. "When do you need to arrive in Tahoe?"

"My reservations are for tonight."

"You should take a jet. You'd be there before you know it."

Sure. She'd just *charter a jet*.

"I don't fly. But thank you."

"You *don't* fly?" One judgmental eyebrow climbed his forehead.

"No. I *don't* fly. I like the wheels touching the road at all times during my commute." Feeling more and more like a problem he had to solve, she asked, "Can you drop me at a car rental place? There has to be one nearby."

She'd arrive later than she wanted—way later—but at least she'd be there.

"Why don't I take you?"

"What? No. I mean, no, thank you," she added, not wanting to sound ungrateful. "I wouldn't dream of putting you out."

"Did I not say I needed to take this car on a road trip? This is the perfect excuse for me to spend some time with her." He stroked the dashboard and gave the car a gentle pat. Then he slid Addi a wink and she melted into the interior.

"B-but you'll have to drive back. Won't you be tired?"

"I'll grab a room. Wouldn't hurt to have a night away. Maybe you can take a break from your family and grab a drink or dinner with me. It'll be fun."

Fun? She might die if she spent four-plus hours in the car with a winking, eyebrow-raising Brannon who had a smudge of oil on his cheek.

He slid over three lanes of traffic with barely any effort, ignoring a blaring car horn when he did. Pedal to the floor, he whipped around a truck and opened up the engine.

"Gotta love turbo," he said over the feral growl. "Give me ten minutes to change and pack and we'll be on our way." He slanted her a look, seeking permission. "Okay?"

"What about the office..."

"I'm a big boy. I can take off work to deliver my valuable assistant safely to Lake Tahoe. Unless you don't want to hang out with me." His tone was more of a dare than a question. "Am I skeevy? Is that it?"

"That's not it. Stop making fun of me!" She nudged his arm and felt the hard muscle there as he shifted gears. Touching him casually wasn't her norm. He felt like a solid wall. A very warm, solid wall. *Whew.* Was it hot in here? She fiddled with the vent and aimed the AC at her face.

"You're very hard to treat. I practically had to beg to take you out for coffee on Monday morning. Now you're going to make me beg to let me drive you to Tahoe when the very thing you need and want most is travel to Tahoe?"

Oh trust me, that's not what I want most.

But she couldn't refuse him. This sexy billionaire with a healthy dash of confidence was her undoing.

"Say thank you, Addi."

"Thank you, Addi," she said with an eye roll.

"That's more like it." He adjusted the vent in front of her. "Better?"

The best. Watching his fingers press the temperature control nearly gave her an orgasm. She really needed to get out more.

"A-as long as you're sure I'm not interrupting any of your plans."

"Nah," he said as he weaved around a line of cars and angled for an exit. "I don't have any plans tonight."

Five

Nothing that can't be canceled, Bran amended.

His date with Tammie was tonight—something he'd remembered, oh, about thirty seconds ago. She'd forgive him. Probably.

Addi crossed her legs primly, one calf sliding over the other, one sexy wedge heel stacked on the other. In the tight confines of his new car, those legs looked a mile long. Long enough to make his breaths shorten and his mind wander. Was it any wonder she'd wiggled into his fantasies?

He'd gone back and forth deciding if she had a boyfriend, but this situation had given him the definitive no he'd suspected. If Ad was dating someone, she'd have called him, not Bran. And no decent guy would let her drive that rattletrap of a car, either. Unless she'd started dating the barista. Who knew what Ken would allow her to do? Bran wrinkled his nose.

Leaving Addison standing alone in the middle of the highway was not an option. She could be hit by an oncoming truck, or *hit on* by the tow truck driver. Anything could happen to a beautiful woman in the center of the freeway.

He understood that she liked to rely on herself, a quality he respected. He had no problem with a strong woman. But she had to know when to let someone take care of her. Today he'd had the time, the means and the inclination to pick her up. He'd have done it for anyone.

But driving her to Tahoe? That wasn't something he'd have done for just anyone.

That was something he'd offered to do for Addi. *And why is that?*

Why didn't he arrange a rental car for her instead? Why didn't he talk her into taking the corporate jet? Why did he insist on delivering her personally to safety?

Because we're friends.

Because she's a valuable employee.

Because I want her to know she can count on me.

Damn.

He'd never thought of himself as having a white knight complex, but that last reason was a touch more honest than the other two. When he'd offered to drive her to Lake Tahoe, her shoulders had dropped from their position under her ears. Setting her at ease was enough, even if they never closed the chasm between them.

The offer of dinner tonight was as casual as the coffee the other day, he further defended. But it wouldn't stay that way if he kept eyeing her legs.

He was fairly certain he'd felt an answering sexual awareness the moment they settled into the bucket seats of his car. Despite her saying she wasn't interested in him, he'd felt that bolt of lightning when she'd touched him. He had a hard time believing that zap only went one way.

Regardless. He wasn't pursuing her. The two things he'd focus on during this road trip were not Addi's legs. That would be safe travels and the new girl in his life: his Misano Red Audi RS 7 Sportback.

There.

Now that he'd justified that half to death...

Twenty minutes later, he pulled into his driveway and parked. When she didn't get out behind him, he opened her door, narrowly avoiding eyeing those long legs again.

"I'll wait here," she said.

"You sure you don't want to come inside?"

"No. No, no, no." She'd turned him down—four times, no less—with a smile.

"I'll be quick."

"Okay." She pulled out her cell phone and began scrolling, busying herself with something other than a tour of his place. Maybe it was inappropriate to invite her into his house since she'd never been here before.

When he'd hired one Miss Addison Abrams, he'd been pleased when she lived up to her résumé. Her work record was impressive. She'd been employed for several large companies and understood corporate regimens. She interviewed well, too. She was confident, poised and beautiful. Which he wasn't supposed to take into account, but her attributes were impossible to dismiss.

Bran never considered himself to have a "type" but he did love a California girl, and Addi was golden, blue-eyed and blonde. His weakness.

"Well, you're going to have to be strong," he reminded himself as he stuffed clothes into a bag. He'd done a fine job of compartmentalizing her until recently. Damn Taylor.

He changed from his suit pants and oil-streaked button-down into jeans and a T-shirt and tied his sneakers. At the last second, he grabbed a fresh suit, too, in case dinner was formal.

He jogged downstairs with his bag, excited at the prospect of taking a break. Hell, if tonight went well, maybe he'd stay the weekend. He'd felt no such excitement about meeting Tammie at Vive. Which reminded him...

He texted Tammie a quick message: Have to cancel tonight. Something came up. By the time he'd locked his front door and was sliding into the car next to Addi, he'd almost forgotten he'd sent it. Leaned back in the passenger seat of his car, her blond ponytail blowing in the breeze, her elbow resting on the window's edge… She looked damn good in his car. Any guy who caught sight of her looking this tempting would forget his own name.

His phone buzzed from its resting spot on the gear box and Addi's eyes went to it at the same time his did. A photo of Tammie's low-cut top and plentiful cleavage flashed onto the screen.

"Shit." He picked up his phone. "Sorry about that."

"No judgment here." She held up a hand.

Beneath the lewd photo, the text read, Can I change your mind?

He replied, Going out of town. Rain check.

We'll see came Tammie's reply.

He shook his head. Not because he'd messed up his "sure thing" but because he didn't remotely care about seeing her once he was back home. What had he been thinking? That the attraction he felt for Addi could be painted over with a girl like Tammie? Impossible.

Not the point. He wasn't pursuing Addi.

"I didn't peg you for a clean lines kind of guy," his adorable assistant said, her eyes on his house and, he noticed, not on his phone.

"I don't like clutter."

She hummed but didn't look at him. He had an idea how to get her attention, even if it was a tad immature.

"Sorry you can't go topless."

He earned a wide-eyed look of surprise.

"I almost bought a convertible, but I couldn't resist the sleekness of this model. Was that joke too soon?"

She held her finger and thumb an inch apart and peered at him through the gap. So damn cute.

"Windows down okay?" He pressed a button and both driver's and passenger's windows lowered. "Some women don't want to mess up their hair."

"Like the woman on your phone?"

"Oh-ho! I sense a little bit of judgment." He mirrored her earlier gesture and held his own finger and thumb an inch apart. "I canceled my date with her tonight. I guess that was her way of trying to change my mind."

"That lacks creativity." Addi tilted her head and a flirty smile crossed her lips. He could feel them sliding back into the comfortable groove they'd worn in at the office.

The only new part was that the joking was starting to feel a lot like flirting.

An excited glint lit her eyes before she slipped on her sunglasses. "I'm okay with the wind in my hair."

She shouldn't care what Bran was doing or who he was doing it with. After all, she was leaving Crush Island and setting sail for Independence Cove.

She shouldn't care. But she did.

Sigh.

The woman who'd texted him wore a skintight dress that left little to the imagination. Her chest was unmistakably the subject of the photo, but Addi had caught sight of a cute, pert nose and full red lips. She still couldn't believe he'd canceled his date with that woman to ferry Addi to Lake Tahoe.

A rock song played on satellite radio and he sang along, slightly out of tune. She smirked, liking his voice no matter how imperfect the pitch.

"Are you laughing at my singing?" he asked, the wind from the open windows whipping his hair around his head.

"Not at all," she lied.

"Yes, you were." He turned the volume down. "It's okay. My sister's been laughing at me since she was born." They watched the road for a beat before he added, "I haven't been to Tahoe in about five years. Last time I was there, I nearly died on a bunny slope."

"You mean there's something you can't do?" She gasped.

"I can't do a lot of things. Ski, propose, land CEO." He said it with a self-deprecating smile and followed it with one of his signature knee-weakening winks. Maybe one day when he did that, her knees *wouldn't* weaken. #Goals.

"I've only been there once. Joe's family brought us. I don't like skiing—it's cold and hurts when you fall down. But he was an amazing skier." That trip with the Harts was eons ago and mentioning it made her miss Joe anew. This weekend promised to be full of old memories that were hard to think about.

"Who's Joe?" Bran glanced over. "Old boyfriend?"

"We were friends."

"Ah, so he had a thing for you and you shot him down."

"Nothing like that. Our families were friends." Emphasis on the *were*. Her parents blamed her for quitting her position at Hart Media and "driving a wedge" between them and their wealthiest friends. Emphasis on the *wealthy* part. She'd always wondered if her parents were enamored more with the Harts' financial status than them as people. They were billionaires, after all. Like the man sitting next to her.

"Nope. I don't buy it. A romantic ski trip together—"

"We were seventeen!" she argued with a laugh.

"Even worse! He was probably dying for you to notice him."

Bran didn't know that her friend had, in fact, died. But that reference wasn't what caused her eyes to mist over. It was remembering the good times she and Joe had together. That ski trip was one of the best weekends of her life. They'd grown apart after she'd stopped working for his parents. Years later they'd reconnected for a double date, but she felt the distance between them. She recalled vividly the sad smile he'd given her while his girlfriend at the time and Addi's frat-boy date were talking about a football game.

She blinked away fresh tears and turned to focus on the passing landscape out her window.

"Oh, hell. What happened?" Bran asked. "You okay?"

"I'm fine." She gave him a watery smile. "Joe and I drifted apart. It was...hard."

"Oh." Bran drew out the word with a sage nod. "You liked him and he didn't like you, right? I'm sorry, Ad. That sucks."

She had the sudden urge to laugh. Or punch him. Or maybe laugh and *then* punch him. Did he hear himself? She liked *him* and he didn't like her back and it did suck! "We were friends. And now..."

She shook her head, the lump in her throat cutting off the rest of her sentence. She cleared her throat and tried again. "This weekend is Joe's life celebration. He prearranged three nights in Tahoe for close family and friends before he died."

The only sounds in the car were the low volume of the radio and the wind sliding off the sleek sports car as they glided down the highway.

"I'm so sorry, Addison. I didn't know."

"How could you have?"

"How'd he die?"

"Bone cancer. From diagnosis to the end, he only lived nine months. The same amount of time it took for him to come into the world was the same amount of time it took for him to leave."

He squeezed her hand. "That's why you were crying in the office."

Bran would be so easy to lean on, to confide in. To trust with her deepest, darkest fears and secrets. She slipped her hand from his to dig through her purse for a tissue and found herself doing just that.

"We grew apart after I went to college," she said as she dried her eyes. "It wasn't as hard as I thought it would be. Maybe we outgrew each other."

"Yeah. I know what you mean." His comment was thoughtful, and she wondered if he was referring to Taylor, who'd been a family friend for decades before Bran and she had dated.

Joe didn't have a girlfriend when he died. He'd never married. When Addi heard he was sick, her own life seemed shorter.

Which was why it was a good idea for her to get over Brannon. She could be dating someone who was madly in love with her, not torturing herself by hoping her boss might someday notice her.

She punched the volume button on the radio to drown out those thoughts.

"I love this song!" she called out.

"Yeah, me, too!" he called back, cranking the volume louder.

She didn't know if he was letting her off the hook or if he really did love this song, but she was going to embrace the opportunity to stop being so damn needy. So far, their road trip had consisted of awkward pauses, tears for Joe and jealousy over the woman that would have occupied Bran's bed tonight if Addi's car hadn't broken down.

She'd learned a long time ago that relying on others for her basic needs came with strings, rules and, if Addi didn't follow those rules to a T, rejection. She was grateful to Bran for a lot of reasons—her job, primarily, but also that he cared enough to console her and drive her to Lake Tahoe.

But.

Her heart was a terrible translator. Her heart would read that professional concern as "true love" and fill her pragmatic mind with head-in-the-clouds fluff.

She was done pretending they might someday march down a long, white aisle. It was time to buckle down and be practical. Find that independent version of herself and put *her* in charge of her life for a change.

Six

The last hour had passed easily. Addison was a good dee-jay, even though she was cranking a country station. Not typically what he preferred but he could tolerate Florida Georgia Line. Besides, she looked cute singing along to every word.

He hadn't gotten over the news that a funeral was her "family reunion."

She kept her personal life a hell of a lot closer to the chest than he'd previously thought. He knew she was a private person, but good God. How had she not trusted him enough to confide that a close friend of hers had passed away?

What he knew about Addi wouldn't fill a shot glass. For good reason. Work stayed at work and she was at work. Now with the rare opportunity of having her outside of work, he was finding out all sorts of things about her. Like that she didn't like skiing. That her family wasn't close. That her late friend Joe was the son of the Hart Media Harts—a behemoth that made ThomKnox look like a garage start-up company.

Meanwhile, she'd clammed up. She was a lot like the

tide. Advance, withdraw. Advance. Withdraw. He still felt as if she was hiding something from him.

But what?

He thought back to his conversation with Taylor—when she confessed she was worried about him. He suspected Addi was doing the same. And as much as he appreciated it, he needed to let her know that he was just fine, thank you very much. There was no reason for her to take on his personal life—only his professional one.

As he caught sight of her mouth moving to the words of the song, again he felt attraction vibrate the air. It was so much stronger outside the office.

He rolled up the windows and, risking potentially embarrassing both of them, tapped the Off button for the radio on his steering wheel.

"You don't like that song?" she asked.

"We've been politely skirting a very big issue since Taylor insinuated that you and I should date."

Addi froze.

"In this space, I'm not your boss. You can say whatever you like to me and I'll respond honestly. The impact of what we say will never leave the confines of this car. Agreed?"

She said nothing, watching him cautiously.

"I never should have dated Taylor." It was the most he'd said to Addi on the topic, but the air needed clearing. "She and I are friends, great friends. Hell, we never even slept together."

"Thank God," she breathed and he shot her a startled look. "For your brother's sake, I mean. And your niece's. Or nephew's. I'm sorry, go on."

"Uh, right. Point is, you don't have to worry about me. I wanted CEO but I also love what I do. And while I admit I find you very attractive and funny and smart, I also know you are irreplaceable, and I'd never compromise our most important union. The relationship we have at work."

More silence from her side of the car, but she did nod. Eyes on the road, he continued, content to fully bury this hatchet once and for all, "I have no plans to ask you on a date, Addison." He glanced over at her. "None. Dinner tonight will be a couple of coworkers hanging out, and that's it. If you're uncomfortable or if you feel I've overstepped, say the word. It's not worth ruining our friendship."

She didn't respond to that either, watching out the windshield, eyes unblinking.

Granted, this wasn't the easiest conversation to have. The promise never to ask her out was as much to reassure her as to remind himself that she wasn't going to grace his bedsheets. Before their joking was misconstrued as flirting, or his lingering gazes made things worse for both of them, he had to set them back on course.

"You've been at my side as my executive assistant for a year and just so you know, I see that as a lateral position. You're every bit as important as me to ThomKnox. If I lost you, Ad, I'd be lost. And unlike your friend Joe, I know in my gut—to the soles of my feet—that you don't like me that way. You don't have to worry about me assuming otherwise."

She'd started out shocked, slipped into nervous and advanced to royally pissed off during Brannon Knox's monologue. He'd made a ton of assumptions despite promising he wasn't. He wanted to be honest? Oh, *she* could be honest.

How many arguments had she had with her parents over the years where they claimed to know exactly what she wanted? Exactly what she *needed*? Piano lessons. Modeling sessions. Cheerleading practice. She'd kept her mouth shut then, too, not wanting to disappoint them. Afraid that if she disagreed, they'd cut her off.

Then one day they did.

She'd barely graduated college before her parents were shoving her into an admin position at Hart Media. In a short while, she'd been "promoted" to accounts manager and hated every second of it. She tried for a year and a half to make it work—always at the encouragement of her parents not to lose out on the huge opportunity of working at Hart Media. When she was finally brave enough to walk away she'd never felt freer.

Her parents had been furious.

They were so certain they knew what was best for her, but never bothered asking her what she thought. Just like Brannon was doing now. By the time he got to the part of his speech where he said *I know you don't like me* she couldn't hold her tongue any longer.

"I do like you, you idiot!"

The words bubbled from her throat like lava from an active volcano, spewing out way too much truth for the confines of a car. Static electricity charged the air between them as her heart rate ratcheted up. She'd *never* yelled at him before. She had no idea what to expect. Was he going to yell back at her? Pull over and tell her to find her own way to Lake Tahoe? *Fire her?*

She hoped not. She needed her job. Liked her job. Liked him.

With nowhere to hide and the object of her infatuation a mere six inches away from her, she folded her hands in her lap and waited for his retaliation.

He didn't respond the way she expected.

"Oh."

That was what he said. *Oh.*

"I'm sorry," she blurted. Lame.

"It's fine."

But he didn't look fine. His mouth was a firm line, his elbows straight, his hands on the wheel in the ten-and-two position. She'd either blown up their friendship or lost her job. Neither of which she could face right now.

She stabbed the radio button and loud music crowded in with the heavy air in the car.

Seven

They arrived at the inn exactly when his car's navigation system said they would. Addison remained stoically silent for the remainder of the trip, and Bran, who was still trying to decide what the hell to think about their conversation, had remained silent as well.

She liked him.

And she'd called him an idiot.

He swallowed another laugh. Truthfully, that'd been cracking him up on the inside since she'd said it. He'd never heard her speak to him with anything less than professionalism and respect.

Which meant something he'd said *really* bothered her.

It was damn interesting, if you asked him.

Here he'd been barely banking his attraction for her this entire trip only to learn that the street went two ways.

He'd made a decision not to pursue her, to go have sex with someone else and dismiss the idea of him and Addi in any relationship other than the one at the office, but now...

Hell.

Now.

Screw the justifications he'd been making. Work was important, but hadn't he also argued that play was just as important? Plus, he and Addi weren't at work right now, were they? He'd thought she'd been offended about Taylor's suggestion that they should date each other—that Addi didn't want anything to do with him. Now he knew that wasn't true and it opened up a whole host of ideas, none of them rated PG.

The real bitch of it was that Taylor had been right. Hell, *Royce* had been right. He'd been the one to tell Bran that a woman who liked him was right under his nose. Bran had blown off the comment, convinced that the hearts-in-their-eyes couple had sipped from Cupid's Kool-Aid cup.

He parked and shut off the engine, leaning forward to take in the building in front of him. The inn was swanky and posh, smaller than he'd expected and fairly secluded. Surprising, considering the tourist-rich town. On the lake below Jet Skis and boats zipped along its surface.

He retrieved his bag from the trunk and, after a back and forth of "you don't have to" and "I got it," also won the right to carry in Addison's bag as well.

They were adults. They could navigate attraction. Especially away from work. Here, Royce and Taylor and Gia, or even his father Jack who popped in on occasion, weren't lurking around every corner. Here, they were just Addi and Bran. Which was new…and exciting.

At the front desk, Addison gave her name. The woman behind the counter consulted her computer.

"Lucky you!" the woman exclaimed. "We have a king-size room available. You two won't have to share a double."

The laugh that'd been trapped in his chest nearly escaped. This poor lady and her horrid timing…

"No, no," Addi told her. "We're not sharing. He's my boss."

"Yowch," he said in response. Addi ignored him.

"My apologies for the assumption." The woman—Ava, her nametag read—tapped her computer. "In that case, I'll put one of you in the king room and one of you in the double. They're the last two rooms we have available for occupancy, and side by side. So you're still lucky."

She took this mix-up a lot better than his coworker, who appeared, at best, mortified.

Ava smiled at him. "Are you with the Joseph Hart group as well, sir?"

"Sort of."

Ava flicked her gaze from him to Addi and back again.

"Uh, thanks for the ride." Addi grabbed the handle of her suitcase and her key card. "I'll settle in."

She fled the scene and he watched her, half bemused, half confused.

"Will you be staying the entire weekend, Mr. Knox?"

He'd planned on staying the night and driving back tomorrow morning, but that was before Addi admitted she "liked him." Not to be an eighth grader about it, but that seemed significant. Especially since she hadn't looked him in the eye since.

What the hell? He'd committed to playing harder, hadn't he?

"Yes, the entire weekend."

That overthinking part of his brain could stay dormant for all he cared. There was another side to him that hadn't been around nearly enough lately. The fun guy. The laid-back guy. That guy would have leaped at a spur-of-the-moment weekend in Tahoe. And with a woman who was as attracted to him as he was to her.

Ava slid a sheet of paper across the counter. "Here is the itinerary for Joseph Hart's life celebration. In case you and your employee cross paths this weekend." There was pure mischief in her smile.

"Thank you." He looked over the schedule. Cocktail hours, dinners, water activities and a masquerade ball. Weirdest funeral he'd ever heard of. "Looks like I'll need to pick up an outfit or two while I'm here. Can you point me toward the best shops in town?"

"Certainly, Mr. Knox."

He finished checking in and strolled to his car, his bag in hand. He had no idea how Addi would react to hearing he wasn't going anywhere. Guess he'd find out tonight.

She'd agreed to dinner regardless of what had happened during their car ride from River Grove, and he was holding her to it.

"You're the one who said you *liked me*," he said aloud as he turned over the engine. "No denying it now."

Whistling, he pulled away from the inn and toward the shopping area the clerk had told him about. Tonight was proving a lot more fun than his original plans, after all.

After Addison hung her dresses in the wardrobe and tucked the rest of her clothing into the dresser, she hopped into the shower. Just a quick rinse before she changed for dinner with Bran.

He was holding her to it—he'd texted her to confirm the time. She thought about canceling but canceling would be less mature than sprinting away from him like her hair was on fire. She couldn't hide forever.

But she could concoct a believable story.

Tonight, she would be courteous and professional…and apologize. She intended on remedying that rogue moment of stark honesty the only way she knew how.

By lying about it.

Blaming her outburst on grief would work, even if it wasn't fair to Joe. But grief was the only excuse she had. She couldn't erase what she'd said from Bran's memory, so she was forced to explain it.

This uncomfortable mess would be over in a few hours. One dinner with Bran and then he'd leave come morning. There would be a nice lengthy gap between today and Monday at the office. Which reminded her, she needed to book a rental car so she could drive herself home.

She swept her hair into a chignon and smoothed her hands over her jade-green cocktail dress. She'd had no idea how to pack for a funeral disguised as a party. Her closet at home was choked with bright or pastel colors, but she'd packed her lone black dress just in case. She couldn't very well show up in fuchsia for the official goodbye. She'd die of humiliation.

Don't be dramatic, Ad, said Joe's voice in her head.

He was right. If she hadn't died admitting to her hot boss she liked him, humiliation wasn't going to be what took her out.

She'd just finished applying her lipstick when there was a knock. Heart hammering in her chest, she gripped the handle, took a deep breath and plastered a smile on her face. When she opened the door, there was no one standing outside of it. She leaned her head into the corridor and looked left then right. Empty.

The knock came again, this time from behind her. From the shared door between their rooms. Of course he'd do that. She resteeled her spine and replastered her smile before opening it.

Bran was, unsurprisingly, suited and sexy, his hair a tempting mess. His smile, unlike hers, wasn't manufactured. His stance mimicked hers, his hand resting on the handle of his own dividing door as if they were looking at each other from either side of a fun house mirror.

"You didn't have to give me the king bed," he said.

"You're bigger than me." Her eyes trickled over his shoulder to his room. The clothes he drove here wearing were folded neatly on top of the stark white bedding, his shoes side by side on the floor. His suitcase was open, still packed, which made sense. He was only staying one night. She took in each of the details as an observer, trying her damnedest not to imagine him sleeping, mostly naked, on that bed just a breath away from her room. She wondered if she'd hear him showering through the walls…

She silenced the thought since fantasizing about him while standing in front of him was poor form.

He shut his own door and strolled into her room, breaking that invisible fun house mirror glass to stand in her space.

"You're as organized as I imagined you would be," he said. "Clothes put away, suitcase tucked into the closet." Her heart fluttered when his eyes scanned her from head to toe. "Outside of work, I'm allowed to tell you you're beautiful in that dress, right?"

"Thank you," she managed. Barely. Outside of work and inside of her hotel room, there were a lot of things he could say and do that she could allow. Like a soft kiss to the corner of her mouth or a roll on the bed that would leave the comforter twisted into a knot.

Wait, no.

She had a plan and it didn't involve acting on her feelings for him. This weekend was about reclaiming her heart as much as her independence. He'd stated clearly that tonight was nothing more than two coworkers hanging out and she was going to honor his wishes. Just because she'd foolishly admitted she liked him didn't give her carte blanche to coerce him into her bed.

Suddenly hot, she stepped away from him—and the bed—to grab her purse. "We should get going."

"I booked a reservation on the balcony, if that's all right."

Sounded romantic, but then again when it came to him, even "good morning" sounded romantic to her. He offered his elbow and she placed her hand on his corded forearm and let him lead her from her room. Soon they'd be on the same page again and she could lull her feelings for him into a deep, forever sleep.

Eight

When Bran knocked on their attached room doors and picked Addi up for dinner, he didn't count on his body tightening at the sight of her standing in front of a bed. Seeing her, rosy cheeked and smiling up at him, had been the stuff of his recent fantasies—if she were wearing a lot less clothing.

Tonight, she wore a bright green dress the color of jungle leaves. The color made her eyes appear piercing turquoise rather than blue. Her pale blond hair was swept up, revealing her neck, and the dress had a demure square neckline that didn't show what she was hiding beneath. Unlike Tammie, Addison was a mystery. Not knowing only made him want to unwrap her more.

White wine poured, their appetizer arrived. Crab and cream cheese wrapped in cigar-shaped, deep-fried wonton wrappers served with sweet chili sauce. Bran wolfed down three of them before coming up for air.

"Damn, those are good."

"They really are." She blotted her mouth with her cloth napkin, having only made it through one.

"So, tell me—" he leaned back in his chair "—what's it like to eat somewhere other than Pestle & Pepper?"

Teasing her about her favorite restaurant in River Grove was low-hanging fruit. A takeout bag from P&P was sitting beside her desk at least three times a week. He'd needled her about it before.

"Have you *been* to Pestle & Pepper?" Her smile was confident, her voice strong. He liked this much better than her wide-eyed and dashing away from him.

"Never. Though considering how many times you come back with leftovers or carried-in lunch makes me wonder if I'm missing out."

Their dinners arrived—fish and vegetables for him and a chicken pasta dish for her. They each ate a bite before she spoke.

"You only know half of it. I eat there as many times for dinner as I do for lunch." Her nose wrinkled. "I'm not much of a cook."

"Me, neither. I love to grill."

They shared a not-uncomfortable beat of silence. Progress.

"What's so great about that place, anyway? Do they have some signature dish I should know about?"

"Their food is incredible. But the atmosphere, the people, are even better than the food. After college, I ate dinner with my parents a lot, but that changed." She was silent while she wound pasta on her fork. "I missed that feeling of home—a home-cooked meal. Pestle & Pepper is a close second."

It was the most he'd ever learned about Addi's personal life. In his efforts to treat his assistant with professionalism, he'd unintentionally kept their relationship on the surface. Shame.

"Family dinners weren't a regular occurrence in the Knox household. Dad worked a lot." Jack Knox was far from an absentee father, but it wasn't as if they were going to the zoo or the beach every weekend. Building Thom-Knox had taken a lot of his dad's dedication and time. Bran thought of his own brief obsession with CEO. Temporary insanity was the only explanation. No way did he desire a schedule that demanding or pressure that intense. "Dad was right about naming Royce CEO. I was the wrong choice."

"Not wrong. Just…different."

"You must've thought I lost my mind this year." His eyebrows jumped as he considered her point of view for the first time.

She pressed her lips together like she had something to say but wasn't willing to share it yet. They'd get there.

"Consider yourself lucky you won't have the privilege of meeting my parents. They're arriving tomorrow afternoon." She lifted her wine glass and took a sip. "I assume you'll leave for River Grove early?"

Again, he sensed there was something she wasn't asking. Was she wondering if he'd be around for breakfast? Or attempting to ferret out his schedule in order to avoid him?

"Not sure yet," he answered. Now seemed the wrong time to drop the "I'll be here all weekend" announcement. "So, the staff at Pestle & Pepper treat you like family?"

"The owner, Mars, does." Her eyes warmed. "Last week he asked me to taste a new dessert they were adding to the menu. He took my advice on the cinnamon. Always more cinnamon." Her tempting lips curved into a smile of pride.

"I don't have that sort of treatment anywhere. Don't they know who I am?"

"It's not about status." She took the joke the way it was intended and consoled him by patting his hand. "I have a delicate palate."

He imagined kissing her and having a taste of her delicate palate. As he held her gaze, the air snapped with a now familiar electric current. Then she broke eye contact and steered them onto bumpier terrain.

"I need to apologize for what I said in the car. Again." She put her fork down and put her hands in her lap. "First off, you're not an idiot."

"Why, thank you."

"A-and I meant it when I said I like you—" her cheeks stained pink "—but I hope you didn't take it the wrong way."

He wasn't letting her off the hook that easily. "Which way would that be?"

"I like you. You're a good boss. A good work friend."

He felt his mouth screw to one side. *Work friend* made him sound like a balding, potbellied old dude.

"I think of you the same way you think of me," she added.

Naked, sweaty and in his bed? Because that's how he thought of her.

"Look at us." She gestured at their shared table. "Just a couple of coworkers hanging out at dinner."

That was verbatim what he'd said to her in the car. Satisfied with her speech, she smiled. She'd been so matter-of-fact while giving them the out they needed. She was hitting the undo button on accidentally admitting her feelings for him.

He could let her off the hook. He *should*.

But he wanted to live in the now, not the future. He wanted to work hard but play harder. Since learning the attraction to Addi was mutual, he couldn't care less about steering himself to a safe and sandy shore. Bring on the rocks.

"My emotions were unstable. Probably due to my grief over Joe," she continued, acting as her own defense counsel. "I was tired. Frustrated about my car. Worried about you leaving the office to drive me here. I didn't really know what I was saying."

The lady doth protest too much, methinks...

"I'm sorry. That's what I'm trying to say." She let out a soft laugh. "My reaction was completely out of context— I'm not sure why I said it."

He returned her smile and she eased back into her chair. She'd said her part. She'd made her peace. All he had to do was accept her apology and return to his dinner. Instead, he looked into her gorgeous cerulean eyes and said what he was really thinking.

"Bullshit."

Addi stared at Bran, fairly certain she was about to have an out-of-body experience. If she could consciously detach from her body and float away from this table, she'd do it.

She felt as trapped as she had in the car this afternoon, but now he didn't have to take his eyes off her to drive. Shouldn't he be relieved to hear she hadn't meant it? He was supposed to grab onto her explanation like a lifesaver and then float away, comfortable in the knowledge that his executive assistant expected nothing from him.

He wasn't doing that.

He ate a bite of his dinner like nothing had happened. She watched him chew, swallow and go in for more. Completely unfazed.

"I'm staying the weekend," he announced. *Fork, chew, swallow.* "Looks like I'll meet your parents after all."

Her vision doubled and she blinked at her wine. She'd drunk half a glass, so she couldn't blame that.

"I had to find a costume for the ball on Saturday, but this town is equipped for strange requests. I also bought swim trunks." He continued eating, listing various items on the itinerary as casually as if he'd been invited. "I'll stand in as your date tomorrow at Joe's wake. I'd feel strange being there alone since I never knew him."

"What?" she finally said. "Why would you come to Joe's wake?"

"For you." He lifted his wineglass and took a drink and she stared at him some more. "I was going to take in the sights but hearing how upset you are about being here and how nervous you are to see your parents…" He shrugged, a casual lift of one broad shoulder beneath his dark suit jacket. "A *work friend* wouldn't let you go alone."

"That's hardly your responsibility." She didn't exactly snap, but her tone was definitely clipped.

"Well, who knows why I do anything. You did say I was an idiot." He flashed her a smile.

Groaning, she dropped her forehead into her palm. "I apologized for that."

"And for saying you liked me, I heard. Thing is—" he pulled her hand away from her face "—I don't believe you were overcome with grief. I believe you were pissed off that I said I wanted nothing to do with you personally, physically. *Sexually.*"

He paired the word "sexually" with the arch of one eyebrow and she had the irrational urge to dive under the tablecloth.

"At the time, I was trying to reassure you since I overheard you and Taylor talking at work. You said I was 'nice' which is the equivalent of you finding me as attractive as the calamari over at that table."

"Nice isn't an insult." But she had lied when she said she wasn't interested in him romantically. "I don't think you're calamari."

He ignored her awkward compliment. "We're in neutral territory here, Ad. This isn't work. I'm not your boss. Not here."

She swallowed thickly, her nerves jangling… It'd be so easy to say yes.

"We have the weekend. Why not?"

She blinked at him, pretty sure she was having that out-of-body experience she'd wished for a moment ago.

We have the weekend.

His wasn't an offer to explore their friendship and beyond, it was an offer for sex. At least she was pretty sure it was. And wasn't that what she wanted? Sort of. She wanted him, yes—she'd just wanted…more than his man parts.

Still, how could she turn down the offer for *those*?

She was so confused. And overheated. She shouldn't consider what he was offering—what he was *sort of* offering—but her brain was too busy throwing a party to hear her over the noise. "We, uh, work together."

There. That was logical.

"We work together well."

"Wouldn't this…" God. She couldn't say it. "This weekend change that?"

"It wouldn't have to." He watched her with a steady gaze, fork in hand.

She shakily reached for her wineglass. Sleeping with Brannon Knox would change everything for her. But not for him. He was suggesting they sleep together out of convenience, but she wanted something deeper than convenience.

"I'm not the kind of woman who texts pictures of my cleavage," she said, setting her glass aside.

He frowned.

"You can't swap me for her like we're interchangeable."

"I know." His head jerked on his neck like she'd genuinely surprised him.

"You shouldn't go to Joe's wake. You weren't invited, and you being there will make things awkward." She stood abruptly, drawing attention from the surrounding tables on the balcony. "Thank you for dinner."

She dropped her napkin onto her plate, grabbed her clutch and weaved her way through the crowded restaurant. She didn't look back.

"Way to go, Addison," she mumbled to herself as she punched the button on the elevator. She'd wanted Bran more than anything, and then when he offered himself to her, she turned him down?

Sanctimonious, Joe's voice announced in the back of her head.

"Shut up," she whispered as the doors to the elevator opened. The older couple inside gasped. "Not you," she reassured them as she stepped inside.

She could swear she heard Joe laugh.

Nine

She didn't spot Bran the next morning when she ventured out of her hotel room for breakfast. Nor did she run into him at the pool in the afternoon. There was no sign of his shiny red sports car from her window, but then again she only had a partial view of the parking area.

Evidently he'd changed his mind about staying the weekend, which ushered in feelings of relief and regret simultaneously. She knew turning him down was the right thing to do, but her hormones didn't.

She'd lain awake last night and thought of how she could have handled their conversation better. She could have talked to him about it—logically. She could have discussed parameters. She could have politely said she wasn't interested and then finished her dinner. Instead she'd overreacted, stood and stormed out.

God, she might have lost her job...

Not that Bran would fire her for turning down a weekend tryst. He'd never technically mentioned sex. He'd told her he wasn't her boss here. Which meant whatever happened between them happened outside of her contract at work.

Yes, definitely she could have handled last night better.

She chose the understated knee-length black cocktail dress for the somber gathering tonight. Joe wouldn't like it, but then again, he wasn't here. *So there.*

She blinked back tears, wishing he was here. He'd know what to say to her about this mess with Bran. Hell, he'd said it last Christmas when she'd shared in passing that she had a crush on her hot boss.

Go get 'im, Addi. Life is short.

Remembering those words made her suspect that she really had screwed up last night.

The wake was held in the Violet Ballroom. After passing the Clover Room and the Poppy Room, she'd figured out the ballrooms were named for flowers and not for colors. The decor in the Violet Ballroom wasn't purple but an understated and masculine navy and gold. A wide chandelier cast warm lighting over patterned carpet and the well-dressed crowd, mostly in black attire, milled around with drinks in hand admiring the photographs dotted throughout.

Joe's handsome, smiling face, surrounded by a gilded frame, welcomed visitors at the front. A table with candles and memorabilia and more photos stood at the back.

She'd arrived a few minutes before they were scheduled to start and the room was already packed. Some people she recognized as Joe's friends or family, others she'd never met.

His parents emerged from a small group and spotted her. The last time she'd seen Elsa and Randy Hart Addi had been packing up her desk at Hart Media. Since then, her parents had shared that the Harts didn't think much of her leaving them in a lurch.

"Beautiful Addison." Elsa Hart extended her arms and pulled Addi into a brief hug. Addi embraced Joe's mother, taken aback by the affection. "It's been too long."

"Yes. Yes, it has."

"Addi, Addi. Oh, we've missed you." Randy kissed her lightly on the cheek.

"I'm so sorry about Joe. I was honored to be included on the guest list."

"As if there was any doubt. You meant the world to him." Elsa's smile was warm. "He had it all planned, paid for and arranged." She blinked away fresh tears.

Randy wrapped his arm around his wife's waist in support.

"Are your parents coming?" Elsa's voice went flat, clearly hinting there was some love lost between them.

"No. Not yet."

"Well, do send them our way. It's been too long since we've spoken. And help yourself to a cocktail," Elsa added, cheerier than before.

"I'm told the emcee will be making some sort of announcement soon." Randy grunted. "After all that boy put us through, he's springing a surprise emcee on us, too?" He winked to show he was joking, his own eyes misting over. They all missed Joe so much.

Addi moved to the back of the room and meandered along the table stacked with trophies, ribbons and report cards Joe's parents had displayed. She smiled back at another large photo of Joe. His cheeks were healthy and full instead of skeletal like they'd been when she'd seen him last. Next to the framed photo was a memory board filled with photos from his life.

She traced her fingertip over the photos of her and Joe—one of him kissing her cheek, eyes closed while she grinned at the camera. That was Joe's twenty-first birthday. And another from a few years later, of them dancing at his parents' wedding anniversary party. The photo showed a scene more intimate than she remembered. Addi's eyes were focused across the room, but Joe's gaze was unmistakably pinned to her.

She'd never seen this photo before, and now that she was older and wiser, she saw something there she'd never seen before. *Longing.*

Joe was looking at her the way she looked at Bran. She watched Bran with a similar want. Meanwhile Bran lived his life in ignorant bliss.

Heart thudding, she turned away from the photo to catch her breath. It couldn't be true…could it?

She replayed her conversations, emails and text messages with Joe over the years. She recalled the final time she'd seen him. She'd sat with him on the couch at his parents' home. He was weak, but refused to let her see him lying down in his hospital bed.

"Promise me something," he'd told her, taking her hand in his colder one.

"Anything."

He glanced at their intertwined fingers before locking gazes with her. "Live a beautiful life, Addison. Not an acceptable life. Not an okay life. A *beautiful* life. One where you have the desires of your heart and leave none of them behind—including that boss of yours you're in love with."

A sad smile crossed her lips.

"Go get 'im, Addi. Life is short."

She'd been more concerned about keeping her tears inside than she'd been about reading between the lines of his speech. Had he left his desires behind? Had he wanted her but never told her?

"Oh, Joe," she whispered to herself.

She lifted a glass of bubbly from a passing tray and took a fizzy gulp, remembering how she and Joe had laughed any time his parents or hers had insinuated they should be together. Joe hadn't taken them seriously. Or so she'd thought.

Tears balanced on the edges of her lashes, she started at

a voice behind her. Joe's brother, Armie, stood next to Joe's framed photo, speaking into a microphone.

"Good evening, everyone." Tall, with thick, dark hair, Armie looked like his younger brother. He waved an envelope in the air. "The outside of this envelope literally reads, 'Do not open until my party or else I'll cut you out of the will.'"

The crowd laughed softly. Addi couldn't find her laugh yet, even though she did send an eye roll to the heavens.

I saw that, Joe seemed to say. Funny, he'd been stone silent on the revelation she'd had a moment ago.

"I'm the mystery emcee, by the way. Another of Joe's surprises." Armie's eyebrows jumped. "Let's start, shall we?" He read from the paper in his hand, "To my beloved parents..."

Yes, Joe had plenty of surprises in store for this evening, she thought as she finished her glass of champagne.

Bran had already been to the Violet Ballroom. He'd introduced himself to Joe Hart's parents. When they'd asked how he knew Joe, he told them the truth. He didn't. He told them he was here in support of Addison, but hadn't seen her yet today.

He then visited the table of memorabilia and perused the photographs on a board. Addi was younger in the photos and still drop-dead gorgeous. There was litheness to her frame, as if her womanly curves had come later. She was polished and regal, like she was now, but her smile was brighter and wider in those photos than it had been lately.

In the one of her and Joe dancing at what appeared to be a formal event, Bran didn't miss the way Joe was looking at Addi. Like he wanted her to be *way more* than a friend.

Poor guy.

Bran had never longed for a woman he couldn't have—that he wouldn't allow himself to have—until recently. Addi had captured his attention. If not the same way as Joe's, damned close. She'd left last night asking him not to come tonight, but when he finished up his dinner and paid the check, he decided he wasn't going anywhere.

She was used to doing things by herself, but maybe she shouldn't be. And at a venue like this one, definitely she shouldn't be alone. Sometimes being strong meant leaning on someone you could trust.

He was a man she could trust.

Back at the entrance of the ballroom, he paused to let a couple walk in ahead of him.

The crowd was facing front, where a man on the stage read from a sheet of paper. "To my brother, Armie," he started, his voice wobbling. Joe's message to his brother was funny and heartfelt, and by the time the emcee sniffed and made a joke, it was obvious that *he* was Armie.

Bran sidled along the edge of the group before spotting Addi. She stood, hands gripping a forgotten champagne flute, her face twisted with sadness.

"The last message I have from Joe reads as follows," Armie said into the microphone, "Addi, you're the one woman I loved for as long as I can remember." Armie's eyebrows raised in surprise as he scanned the crowd. "We, um, we never made it down the aisle, but you have my undying devotion. Even though I'm dead. Go, beautiful girl, and grab ahold of that incredible life we talked about. Go get him, honey."

Addison's expression could only be described as shell-shocked. Every eye in the room swiveled to her. She blinked a few times in quick succession, her fair skin turning an impressive shade of rose. Bran could practically see the question marks over Joe's parents' heads.

Bran wasn't surprised even a little.

She turned to slip from the crowd and he moved to intercept her, but an older couple blocked her escape before he could reach her.

"That's quite the announcement," came the man's stern tone.

"Hi, Daddy." Addi's shoulders curled in and Bran frowned. He'd never seen her withdrawn before.

The band in the corner started up the music again as the crowd dispersed and mingled. Bran hung back, close enough to overhear Addi and her parents, though she hadn't spotted him yet.

"Joe was in love with you? How could you walk away from him knowing that?" asked an older blonde woman.

"I didn't know, Mother." Addi's tone was less subservient, more impatient. "Joe and I were friends. I had no idea he felt that way about me."

"And who is this 'man' you're supposed to fetch?" Her father's bushy eyebrows were so low they obscured his eyes. "He'd better make a good living. God knows you don't."

"Is this mystery man the reason you quit working for Hart Media?" her mother squawked, hand to her chest. "Think of the life you could have had if you'd stayed! An amazing career. A marriage to Joe."

"And after all we did for you, placing you in that company. You could have been a millionaire by now! Never listens," her father grumbled to her mother.

Addi's chin began to tremble. Bran had seen enough. He walked up and slipped a hand around her waist. "Sorry I'm late."

Three sets of eyes were on him and he wasn't sure who looked more surprised—Addi or her parents.

"Hi, I'm—"

"Brannon Knox," Addi's mother breathed, stars in her eyes.

"Yes, actually."

"My boss," Addi interjected.

"And her date." Neither of her parents offered their hands, which was fine with him. He suddenly wanted nothing to do with them.

Addi's face flooded with alarm and gratitude simultaneously. She looked like she wanted to slap him and then hug him.

Or kiss me.

Sounded good to him.

"Missed you," he said and then he bent and pressed his lips to hers.

Ten

The entire building had burst into flames.

At least that was what it felt like the moment Addi finally, finally sampled Brannon's delicious mouth.

The kiss couldn't have lasted longer than a count of three. He hadn't ravished her while onlookers gasped. It was a simple kiss hello, but for her, there was nothing simple about it. For her, it was a slo-mo climax in a sweeping romance. Her senses were filled with the warmth of his mouth, the enticing scent of his soap and the low hum in his throat as he ended the kiss with a soft "mmm."

Hand on her back, he steadied her where she stood and she schooled her expression.

He pulled her flush against his body and having nowhere else to put her hand, she rested it over his taut abs. Just for a second, then she decided it was more appropriate to dangle her hand at her side. God. He smelled *amazing*.

"Glad to hear we have Joe's blessing," Bran said. "He was very special to her."

"The love of his life," her mother said. She smiled at

Addi's suitor, appearing less disappointed that she'd failed to splice the Hart and Abrams family trees than before.

Addi's family didn't come from money, but they had it. They partnered with the right people, kept their wealthy alliances strong. Addi had heard so many behind-the-scenes conversations about how to "align" with wealthy people that she'd sworn never to use someone for her own financial gain.

Perhaps she'd course corrected too much.

Her job at Hart Media was fine, it was. But it was also not her calling. She wanted to work her way up, not be handed a position because of her status.

Her parents encouraged her to exploit their connections, to "get rich quick" rather than slow. Addi, frankly, didn't gave a damn if she was rich or not. She only wanted to be loved. Love in her family came at a steep price.

"ThomKnox is a very prestigious company," her father said to Bran, cheeks turned up into a plastic grin.

"Addi is exceptional, is she not?" her mother chirped.

"She is." Bran gave her a squeeze. She liked his arm around her way too much. "I don't know what I'd do without her."

"And now you're together," her mom cooed, "which I'm sure will mean advancement in the near future."

"Well…"

Before Bran wasted his time being polite, Addi spoke. This was one relationship she wouldn't allow her parents to exploit. "I'm executive assistant for the president of ThomKnox. That's pretty advanced."

"She's more than that." Bran squeezed her waist again, his eyes warm on her. Not only had he not gone home, he didn't seem the least bit upset over her leaving him to eat dinner alone.

Joe's parents approached, and she saw the perfect excuse to duck out.

"If you'll excuse us. Bran hasn't had a bite to eat all day. Shall we?" She widened her eyes at her "date," and he picked up where she left off, bailing her out beautifully.

"Another glass of champagne for you, as well. Nice to meet you, Mr. and Mrs. Abrams," Bran added politely.

Her mother called after them as they left, "Lena and Kerry, please!"

Addi steered Bran to an unoccupied corner of the room as the Harts descended. "At least my parents have to be civil when they're here."

"That was them being civil?" Bran asked, his eyes going to the foursome. Joe's mother embraced Addi's mother and Addi felt suddenly bamboozled. Maybe things hadn't been as tense as her mother suggested.

"My mom does enjoy making me feel guilty," she murmured to herself.

"They want what's best for you. Everyone's parents do." He snagged a glass from a waiter's tray. "Champagne?"

"Thank you. For that. For everything. I've been…awful."

"You've been incredible." His smile was sincere.

Once they had a small plate of food each, she took her first full breath since she'd heard Joe's letter. She and Bran stood at a highboy cocktail table with a candle in the middle. Reminded of their dinner last night, she once again found herself in the position of apologizing. This time, though, she meant it.

"I could have communicated better last night," she told him. "Sorry for leaving on my high horse."

"It's okay. I finished your pasta. It was really good."

She smiled, giving him a headshake. He was too much. And too charming for his own good. "It was kind of you to show up here. I didn't know I needed saving, but here we are."

"No one should attend a friend's funeral alone. Though I'm questioning the 'friends' part after hearing his message to you." He watched her as he popped a sausage puff into his mouth.

"Aren't we both."

"What was with the part about you two never making it down the aisle?"

"I have no idea." She pinched the bridge of her nose. As if that would set the world right again. "Half of me wonders if this is an elaborate practical joke. If Joe is going to stroll through that door and yell 'gotcha!' He always was the life of the party." She realized what she said and offered a wan smile. "Ironically."

Bran's eyebrows rose. "A practical joke wherein he fakes his own death so that he can admit that he's in love with you at his own funeral?"

"Yeah. Probably not." She sipped her champagne, troubled by that observation as much as everything else that'd gone down so far during this trip. Her eyes tracked to her parents, still talking with the Harts. "I had to sneak away before I broke his mother's heart. I have no idea what to say to her."

"Don't say anything."

"Well, she can't go on believing that Joe and I were in love."

"Why not?"

"Because..." But Addi didn't know why not. If it was true on Joe's side, and made his family happy to believe he'd found love during his short stay on this planet, why not, indeed? "That's actually practical."

"That's no good. I'm fighting practicality these days."

"I noticed." That small kiss was the least practical act imaginable.

"I was practical to a fault earlier this year. I'm a man who can learn from my mistakes." He sucked in a deep breath. "I should apologize for the kiss."

Her lungs deflated. This was the real reason she didn't

"go get 'im" as Joe had suggested. Bran had never shown any interest in her before, so why would one little kiss ignite a five-alarm fire in him now?

"You don't have to apologize," she said, hoping she hid her disappointment.

"That's not what I mean." His voice was low and sultry. She faced him, the candlelight reflecting in his bourbon-colored eyes. They were nearly as warm as the flame itself. "I mean I *should* apologize, but I can't. I liked that kiss way too much."

She could only stare. "Y-you did?"

"Did you?"

Color him pleased when she didn't stammer or hesitate in her response.

"Yes," she stated clearly. "Yes, I did."

Now that was what he liked to hear.

Reaching across the table, he lightly touched her arm before taking her hand in his. "Have you thought further about my offer last night?"

Addi's bright blue eyes darkened enticingly. "I thought you'd gone home upset with me, so no, I hadn't."

"And now?" He lifted her hand and brushed her knuckles with his lips, kissing her once before lightly touching his tongue to her skin. Her lips parted but no sound came out at first.

"I—I'll have to think about it."

"Successful leaders make decisions quickly," he told her. He wanted another kiss like the way-too-brief one he'd stolen from her earlier. He wanted to give her time to respond. Let her explore and find her way. She seemed curious and he would be more than willing to let her explore that curiosity until both of them were panting for air.

"Brannon. We work together." Her eyebrows bent almost desperately, but the heat was alive in her eyes.

"Yeah, I heard. You're my executive assistant."

"Don't joke."

"I'm not joking." He was content to throw caution into the windstorm given their borderline combustible attraction. "Remember what I said. I'm not your boss this weekend. Just a guy who'd like to have a few more close encounters with you." He remembered her words to him at the restaurant last night. "And for the record, I don't think of you and Tammie as interchangeable."

"Of course. I knew that." She closed her eyes as if embarrassed by her behavior last night. He didn't like that look of shame when he saw it earlier with her parents and he sure as hell wouldn't stand for it now.

"I only asked Tammie out to take my mind off you," he admitted.

"Off me?"

"Yes. You've been taking up a lot of space up here lately. Too much." He tapped the side of his head. He could see she didn't know what to make of that. "Everything I've said and done lately is to make you feel more comfortable around me. In the process I began to see you differently than before. The easiest way to distract myself was…"

"With Tammie?" Addison finished for him.

"Guy math. One and one equals I'm an idiot."

At least she smiled.

"I'm so sorry to interrupt." Elsa Hart approached the table hand in hand with her husband. "I just spoke with your parents. Evidently this gentleman is Brannon Knox of ThomKnox. Which he did not disclose when we met earlier…"

The band of tension between Bran and Addi snapped. Unfortunately, she threw him to the wolves, probably relieved not to have to address his offer head-on.

"One and the same," Addi answered. "I'm Brannon's executive assistant. I've worked at ThomKnox for a year."

With no polite way to extract himself from the conversation, Bran indulged Addi and Joe's parents. He came here for Addi, anyway, so had no other choice but give her what she needed.

And, if she decided to explore what could be between them physically, he'd give her that and more.

Eleven

Addison went to bed that night exhausted from…well, everything. Joe's gathering had taken a toll on her, alongside some extra unwanted attention after she'd been outed as the love of his life.

Bran was right in suggesting she didn't have to explain Joe's one-sided love for her to the Harts, though. They didn't ask about it in front of Bran, anyway, so there was no reason to bring it up.

It was healing to reacquaint herself with Elsa and Randy. She'd worried over the years that they'd hated her for leaving Hart Media and growing apart from Joe, but it turned out they didn't feel that way at all.

Once the Harts had interrupted her and Bran, Addi grabbed onto the distraction like a lifeline. Eventually they'd left the ballroom to retire to their individual rooms, and Bran hadn't brought up what Addi and he had talked about before.

Not that it mattered. His claim of "I'm not your boss this weekend. Just a guy who'd like to have a few more close encounters with you" kept her up, tossing and turning for quite a few hours.

Brunch the next morning was held in the second-floor lobby and since the inn was mostly filled with Joe's friends and family, it was impossible not to bump into someone she knew. So, she put on a happy face, poured herself a ginormous cup of coffee and went out to mingle.

Bran hadn't rapped on their connected doors this morning to wake her, but he'd beat her down here. He was in line for breakfast, chatting with a pretty redhead.

Addison watched them together—the way the woman tucked her hair behind her ear and batted her lashes. She was petite, wearing a pale green dress and sandals. Charm oozed naturally from Bran so Addi wasn't surprised to hear the other woman laugh, warm and inviting. All-too-familiar jealousy propped its hands on its hips with indignation.

She'd had enough of that emotion to last two lifetimes.

"There she is," he said when he noticed her standing off to the side. "Addi, darling. Come over here."

Addi, darling. Swoon.

He opened an arm and tucked her against him. She inhaled his clean, soapy scent. In the office, she'd hadn't had the privilege of being this close to notice.

He rubbed his palm on her bare arm. "I wanted to let you sleep." The suggestive lilt paired with a kiss to her forehead sold the assumption they'd spent the night in the same bed.

The redhead introduced herself. "I'm Rebecca."

"Nice to meet you."

"He's told me so much about you. You two make a cute couple. Bran is very charming." To her testament, Rebecca didn't say that with an ounce of animosity. "Later we should hang out. Bran and my husband have a lot in common."

Ahh, she was married. That explained why she didn't mind hearing Bran was attached. *Fake* attached, but still.

"Allen's a tech guy, too. And I, like you," she said to Addi, "run the show at the office. We should have a drink tonight. Al has so many great stories about Joe."

"I'd like that."

Rebecca bid them adieu and took her full plate to a table occupied by her husband.

"Did you think I was flirting with her?" Bran asked.

"What? No!"

He raised an eyebrow but didn't call her on the lie. "Want some eggs?"

"Yes. Please."

Holding his plate and hers, he dished out a portion of eggs for each of them.

"You don't have to take care of me, you know."

"So you keep saying. Potatoes?"

"Please."

"I like a girl who likes her carbs." He dished out a spoonful each onto their plates. "You take care of me a lot, Ad. Remember, I'm not your boss this weekend. I'm your date."

"So you keep saying," she repeated.

All he did was grin.

"I appreciate your efforts with my mom last night," she said once he chose a table for them and placed her plate in front of her. He'd served her nearly as much as he'd served himself. She couldn't eat half of the food on the giant plate.

"What do you mean?" He ate a bite of potatoes.

"Talking to my parents isn't as easy as talking to yours. If we'd have stood there any longer, I'm sure my father would have asked a lot of questions about ThomKnox shareholders, company worth and other impolite matters."

Bran chuckled. "I'm used to it."

She scooped up a bite of her own breakfast. "At least Joe's parents didn't grill you."

"They couldn't care less about our shareholders. They

have more money than God. Seriously, ThomKnox doesn't have a tenth of what Hart Media has. Damn monopolies." He winked to let her know he was kidding.

"Don't you? Have more money than God?"

"We're up there."

And she wasn't. They were from two different worlds. Her crush on him had always been safe. Distant. It wasn't the stuff of real life. It was a fantasy, pure and simple. Only now the lines had blurred. It wasn't clear what was happening between them.

"Money aside, your family is amazing," she told him. "I remember when I first started working there and I met you one at a time. Gia, Royce, you…and then your dad and eventually your mom. I decided that day I wanted to be a Knox when I grew up." She winced, realizing what she'd implied. "I didn't mean that in a creepy way."

"Sure you didn't." He kept eating, unfazed.

"My family's never been as generous with their love. It always had to be earned."

Who wanted to earn love? She drank from her coffee mug and raised her eyes when she felt Bran watching her.

"Hence the family dinners at Pestle & Pepper."

He didn't miss a thing.

"You don't have to earn love when you can pay for it," she followed that with a "ha ha," but he didn't laugh. In fact, he was watching her a little too intently. Like he was seeing clear down to her soul.

"Maybe we can stop by there on the way home," she said, happily changing the subject. "I'm having withdrawal. I mean…assuming you're driving me home."

"Of course I'm driving you home," he said, amused.

"I'll give you some gas money."

"Addison." He dropped his fork and swiped his mouth with his napkin. "Do you hear yourself? What kind of assholes have you been dating, anyway?"

"I don't date. *Because* they're assholes. Except for pretend funeral dates. Oddly enough, those turn out really well."

Earning another laugh was like being handed a million dollars. Who needed riches when she had Brannon Knox?

Four-plus more hours in the car with him to look forward to after an entire weekend spent in his company. She wouldn't know what to do with herself come Monday morning when he was in his office and she was stationed outside of it.

This weekend was originally meant to be the beginning of the end of her Bran obsession. Now Operation Get Over Him held another meaning entirely. Like getting *over* him. Or under him. She wasn't picky.

She smothered a laugh by coughing.

"The masquerade ball is tonight," he said.

"Oh, I don't expect you to attend that. It's a whole thing, with masks and formalwear." She waved a hand. It wasn't a big deal, so why was her heart pounding a nervous staccato, like she was about to be asked to prom? "If anyone asks where you are I'll say you were tired."

"And let you go by yourself? Forget it." He ate a bite of eggs and then added, "Who knows who will dance with you if I'm not there."

"I don't think people are looking for a date at a funeral."

"No, I guess not." He settled back in his chair and lifted his own mug of coffee. "Which brings us back to the discussion we didn't finish last night."

Dammit.

Silence settled between them. She didn't know what to say, especially since he hadn't yet asked her a question. But then he did.

"Have you thought about us?"

Only every day for the past year.

She sure as hell couldn't say *that*. While she watched

him carefully, debating how to answer, a smile spread his mouth.

"Listen, Addi." He leaned forward, his voice lower and, if possible, more seductive. "You don't have to say yes. We can finish out the weekend as friends and, much as it pains me to offer, I won't kiss you again. If that's what you want, say the word."

His low voice swirled around her like a vortex, threatening to suck her in. She *really* wanted him to kiss her again.

"But—" he took her hand and held onto her fingers, his gaze unwavering on hers "—I really, really want to kiss you again. And again *and again*."

Oh, Lordy. Easy for him to say. He hadn't had his heartstrings tangled in knots over her for the last twelve months. He hadn't agonized over his own emotions because she was suddenly dating someone in the office.

She could either tell him no—but how, when he wanted her as much as she wanted him?—or she could consider this weekend a once-in-a-lifetime opportunity. An all-access pass to Brannon Knox.

Her earlier justification that sleeping with him was a bad idea had grown stale since the kiss. Since he'd approached her so openly and honestly. As long as she maintained some control in this situation, she could have what she wanted and escape unscathed.

"Okay, but I need to set a few ground rules."

He put an elbow on the table. "I'm not much of a rules guy anymore."

"We can call them guidelines." She nodded succinctly. She didn't want any bizarre vibes once they were back in the office. Setting parameters would help both of them know how to behave. "Tonight and that's it. Once the ball is over and we...do whatever we do, then that's the end."

"Okay." He nodded slowly. "I agree to your terms."

She smiled and he smiled back and there they sat at

brunch, having made the craziest agreement of all time. She was buoyant, excited…and slightly nauseous.

One night with Brannon Knox. She was going to make it *count*.

"Should we shake on it?" She disentangled their hands and held out her palm, which he shook officially. Before he could pull away, she added the caveat, "I have a strict curfew of midnight."

"No worries, Cinderella." A barely banked heat darkened his eyes. "I promise to have you in bed before then."

Twelve

When she was preparing to come on this trip, Addi looked up "what to wear to a masquerade ball" on the internet. She'd never attended one, though she remembered Joe's parents having one at their house about seven or eight years ago. She hadn't been able to attend, but she'd seen photos online of Joe in his tux and mask, a pretty girl on his arm.

A costumed ball seemed so...impractical. At the time she'd been working her tail feathers off at corporate headquarters for a company that made athletic wear. Rhinestones and ball gowns weren't exactly part of her wardrobe.

Joe either had fond memories of the party, or he wanted his parents to experience another. Or maybe, like her, he found the idea of a ball preposterous and was having a laugh over forcing his friends to attend.

She'd done research before she chose her outfit, and learned that masquerade balls were formal and classy. Loathe as she was to admit it, shopping for a ball gown was fun—and bonus, she'd found one to rent. Logical, since this occasion was quite literally a once-in-a-lifetime event.

The elegant rhinestone-studded gown was sky blue and sparkled like a sea of diamonds wherever the light hit. It was formfitting and cut into a low V at the back, which was almost chilly in the cooler air of the lobby. The mask she'd purchased online. With its matching blue and silver gemstones, she hadn't been able to resist.

At the rental shop, she'd been floored not only by the elegance of the gown, but how she felt in it. Beautiful. Captivating. Shivers streaked down her arms as she spotted the Sunflower Room, where the event was being held. When she'd rented the dress, she had no one to captivate. Now she did.

Unfortunately, like the dress, she'd have to return Brannon after only one night. But oh, what a night it was going to be.

He insisted they find each other at the event. "A masquerade is cloaked in mystery, Ad," he'd told her. "Where's your sense of adventure?"

The ballroom's interior was strung with fairy lights, but otherwise filled with shadows. A band played quietly in the corner, soft jazz that added to the almost romantic, and definitely mysterious, ambiance. Many women wore dresses similar to Addi's, but in a rainbow of colors, bedecked in rhinestones and jewels. The men were in black, most donning formal tuxedos, though she spotted a few velour jackets.

She didn't know what Bran was wearing, so she scanned the crowd. Seeking him out in a group was nothing new—she always looked for him first—but knowing he was looking for her caused her stomach to knot.

She'd agreed to be his date for one night, and here they were, the masquerade ball a preview of what was to come. Her goal for the evening was simple, but not the least bit pure.

She wanted him.

Tonight, she was going to be adventurous when it came to Bran—it might be her only chance.

A woman in a slim black dress, her long, dark curls falling over her shoulders appeared in front of Addi.

"Choose your fate." Deep brown eyes blinked from behind a black mask as the woman offered up a basket of gold envelopes. "One of these cards is destined for you. Which will it be?"

Addi swallowed a laugh. Fate? In this basket? She highly doubted it. She chose her own fate. But, what the hell? Once-in-a-lifetime experiences should be savored. She held her hand over the basket and closed her eyes, wiggling her fingers over the envelopes before choosing her "fate."

"It's a good one. I can tell," the woman told her before leaving to offer an envelope to another guest.

Addi stepped off to the side of the room and tore open the envelope. Inside was a note in handwritten calligraphy that read:

Find someone wearing a gold mask and ask them to dance. Your future awaits.

Addi giggled as she dropped the envelope into her purse. It was like reading a fortune from one of those machines at the fair. "What is up with this, Joe?"

"You read my mind," came a female voice from over her shoulder. Addi turned to find a red-haired woman in a stunning red dress, a red mask obscuring her face. "Rebecca. From breakfast. What a beautiful gown."

"Right, hello. Sorry, I didn't recognize you."

"The point of this event. What did your card say?"

"To ask someone wearing a gold mask to dance. What about yours?"

"Mine says I have to buy a stranger a drink. And you're about to let me off the hook." Rebecca looped her arm in

Addison's and walked with her to the bar. "We barely know each other. You count."

After they each had a glass of sparkling white wine in hand, Rebecca asked, "Did you come with Brannon?"

"I'm his date, but we decided to meet here."

"Ohh, young love. It's too sweet." Rebecca flashed a bright white smile behind painted red lips. "Allen probably won't last long. A wild night for us ends at eight thirty. Is Bran wearing a gold mask?"

"I don't know." Addi scanned the crowd for him again. "I haven't spotted him yet."

"To a night of intrigue." Rebecca clinked their glasses and excused herself, wishing Addi luck.

There were a lot of people here, but no sign of her parents. It was unlike them to skip an event this bougie.

She sidled by couples in clusters chatting. Some of the men hadn't bothered with masks, and she wondered if Bran had even worn one—let alone a gold one. The card commanded she ask someone to dance, and while she knew she could ignore it, she wanted to believe that fate had something special in store for her. Mystery and adventure seemed more in tune with Bran's world than hers, but in the spirit of Joe's final wishes, she would have faith.

Her eyes wandered over the crowd anew before she turned in the other direction and nearly plowed over a man in a black tux. Her eyes flitted from his bow tie to a face she'd seen in her dreams on multiple occasions.

Brannon Knox's staggeringly handsome face was obscured by a mask. A black one. She drank in the sight of him, from those whiskey-brown eyes behind the mask to his foppish hairstyle to his furrowed brow.

"Excuse me," he said, his smile measured and polite. Recognition lit his eyes a half second later. *"Addison."* His smooth voice sailed along her body like a caress. "You're—

that's a dress. Sorry, I'm completely floored by how beautiful you are."

"A first," she joked.

"No, not even close. But tonight will be full of firsts."

Yes, she supposed it would. She pulled out her card and handed it to him. "You chose poorly." She gestured to her own mask. "Gold was the winning color."

He read the card before tearing it into pieces and tossing it over his shoulder. "Wrong again, Cinderella." From his pocket, he pulled his own card. It read:

A lady in blue is the one for you. Enjoy your evening together.

"I don't believe it," she said through a laugh.

"Well, I slipped the lady in black twenty bucks."

"No!"

He laughed, his throat bobbing above his bow tie. "I'm kidding. I drew it fair and square. Honest. Dance with me?"

"It's tempting fate, but how can I resist?"

He took her champagne glass and set it on a nearby table. "You can't. Which is my secret weapon."

The wink was a little cheesy, but not on Brannon. It only made her want him more.

On the dance floor, he pulled her close, his hand brushing her bare back. "This is some dress. I look forward to seeing you wear it into the office sometime."

"Sorry to disappoint you, but it's a rental."

"Bummer. You could've livened up the next staff meeting." He looked down at her, sincere. "I mean it, though. You are incredibly beautiful. In that dress or out of it."

She felt her mouth drop open.

"I didn't mean it that way." He hoisted an eyebrow so high it winged over his mask. "Or did I?"

"With you, who knows? Where has this funny, open guy

been all year?" She'd meant it as a teasing statement but his chest lifted and dropped in a heavy sigh.

"I was different when you started working at Thom-Knox. More laid-back. More fun. Lighter, in general. Dad handing off CEO..." He shook his head. "I didn't want anything I was running after at the time. Isn't that something? I didn't realize it until later."

A great metaphor for tonight. He was running after Addi now, but in the future would he realize she was wrong for him? Would he look back and see how he'd behaved out of character this weekend, too? The possibility of losing her heart was a bigger risk than losing her job, and that was saying something. No matter how much fun she was having in fantasyland tonight, she had to keep her head on straight—for her heart's sake.

They swayed to the music—a mix of jazzy undertones and pop beats that was steady and smooth—like Bran's steps.

"You can't sing, but you can move," she said.

"Oh, honey, I can move."

She squeezed his biceps. "Not what I meant."

"And yet, our minds keep going there. Are you excited for tonight?"

"Very," she breathed.

"Good." He leaned close and spoke into her ear. "I have plans for you."

"I have plans for you, too." Emboldened by the mask, she'd said that aloud.

"Really."

She hummed, enjoying talking about what was to come.

"Care to share?" he asked.

She shook her head. "I'm more of a show than tell kind of girl."

Where did this brazen vixen come from? She smiled, liking the power she wielded. Especially when Bran tucked her so close the hard ridge along his zipper pressed into the front of her dress.

"How much longer do we have to stay?" he growled in her ear.

"A good, *long* while." She purred up at him. "I know it'll be *hard*, but I promise I'll make it worth your while." She erased the space between their bodies and he grunted when she brushed his erection. If what she felt against her was any indication of what it'd feel like without their clothes in the way, she was in for a great time tonight.

As if it could be bad.

Good point.

"Haven't we waited long enough?" Again, his voice was a husky growl. She'd never heard him talk like that, like he was balanced on the very edge of desire. She'd never seen—or felt—him turned on before. It was *wonderful*.

"I want you to want me a little longer before we go upstairs." She wanted him to long for her, to imagine her naked, to watch her, wondering how he could survive another second without her lips on his. After all, she'd felt that way about him for over a year.

"I didn't peg you for a masochist, Addison Abrams." He swept her in a smooth circle and she followed his lead. "I like it."

"Maybe, Brannon Knox," she said, swaying with him to the music, "you should have been paying closer attention."

Thirteen

Who is this masked woman?

Addi had danced with him for a few more songs. He liked holding her, being near her. The delicious anticipation of what would come later. *Her*. He'd guarantee it.

This weekend would forever be marked in her memory, and his. He was going to make it that good.

They found a seat in a dark corner. She sipped a glass of wine slowly while dropping double entendres. He flirted back, glad for the table blocking his lap—she turned him on more than anyone he could remember, and with just the hint of a smile. She was driving him crazy and he was more than ready to get the hell out of here.

By the time Rebecca and her husband, Allen, joined them at their table, Bran had been ready to *howl*.

If Addi wanted him to want her, goal achieved.

When she and Bran finally left the party, it had taken every ounce of restraint he possessed not to press her against the elevator wall and kiss her until they were both out of their minds.

He waved the keycard over the sensor on his door, looking forward to the feel of her hands on his body beneath this tux. To discovering what she was hiding beneath her dress. He wanted those full breasts in his face, in his mouth. He wanted to grip her ass and graze her neck with the edge of his teeth.

He wanted her with an animal need that was unfamiliar to him—had he ever wanted a woman this badly?

To keep from busting out of his tux like the Hulk, he reined in his libido as he popped open the door. She'd probably want a drink or conversation first. He wasn't going to maul her the second they stepped over the threshold. He was more man than beast…at least he thought so.

"After you."

She stepped in ahead of him. The room had been cleaned, the bed neatly made. He'd put his clothes away and tucked his suitcase aside earlier. Mentally, he mapped a path to where he stashed the condoms he'd picked up in town that first day. Wishful thinking at the time.

She set her purse on the entertainment stand and turned to him. The mask still covered her face, her bright blue eyes even brighter behind it. He'd taken his off at the table while they were still at the party and hadn't bothered finding it again when she suggested they leave.

He liked that she'd left hers on, liked the mystery of her, the idea of unwrapping her—every part of her.

Now he reached for the ribbon tied at the back of her head. "May I?"

"You may." Those pink lips. He hadn't had a taste of her tonight and was looking forward to a kiss more than anything. Their first kiss had been in public. Neither of them had reacted the way they wanted at the time, but now they were alone. She could go *wild* if the spirit moved her.

He kept his eyes on hers as he slowly untied the satin and lifted the mask from her face. Revealing her rosy cheeks made him look forward to revealing other parts of her. He kissed the apples of each of those cheeks and murmured into her ear, "I'm kissing every pink part of you tonight, Addison."

She didn't laugh. She didn't speak. But she did touch him. Her hands on his chest, she slid her palms north and tugged his bow tie free. Behind his crisp shirt and jacket, his heart thundered. The anticipation of wanting her had been sheer torture.

She unbuttoned his shirt, her hands shaking over the first three buttons.

He palmed her cheek and thumbed her bottom lip. "Nervous?"

"Excited," she admitted with a grin.

"You can't do anything I won't like. I promise." He wanted her to enjoy herself. Hell, he wanted her to have the time of her fucking life tonight. No pun intended.

"I, um… I don't know where to start. It's like seeing everything I've ever liked all in one place."

Damn. That was flattering. He watched her, wondering how he'd overlooked her for so long. How had he seen her day in and day out and not acted on the attraction so obviously vibrating between them?

"Start where you left off," he told her, placing her hands on his buttons. Seemingly over her case of nerves, she made swift work opening the rest of his shirt and stripping it from his shoulders. Leaving his arms trapped in the sleeves, she smoothed her hands over his bare chest.

"Mmm. That's better." She leaned forward and closed her mouth over his pectoral before dragging her tongue to the other and giving his nipple a light bite.

He sucked air through his teeth but she only smiled up at him. God, what did she have planned for him? Half of him wanted it right now and the other half of him wanted her to take her time and torture him some more.

Greedily, she explored his chest with her mouth and

hands and he lost himself in the sensation of being wanted. He was used to doing the pursuing. He normally initiated the touching, the kissing.

He liked this dynamic.

She yanked his shirt from his arms and pushed him toward the bed. He sat, watching as she tugged her skirt up to her thighs and pressed one knee into the bed, the other straddling him. Once she was astride him, he had no option but to look up. To her fancy updo, a few locks of hair that'd come undone curling around her face, to her blue eyes, bright and seeking. Her mouth was a bow, her tongue the arrow as it darted out to wet her lips.

"How are you doing down there?" she asked.

He was as hard as rebar and just as unyielding.

"Keep doing what you're doing." He tucked a stray curl behind her ear. "I'm here for it."

He was entranced. Completely under her power. And he didn't mind one damn bit.

Fingers on his belt, she slowly undid the leather, feeding it through his belt loops and throwing it on the floor. She stroked his erection over his zipper and unbelievably, he grew harder.

When she unzipped his pants, she gasped. If she'd wondered whether he was a boxers or briefs guy, that conundrum had been definitively answered.

"You don't...wear anything under your pants?"

"Not a thing." He grinned, loving the hunger in her eyes.

"Ever?"

"Never."

"Wow. The office will never be the same." When her smile hitched, it snagged him in the gut, pulling him forward like a fish on a line.

"Kiss me." If he didn't taste her soon, who knew what would happen.

She tenderly laid her lips on his, stroking into his mouth

with her tongue. He closed his eyes and drank her in, lying back and pulling her with him. His hands found her bare back, where her dress dove into a deep V, and he caressed her agonizingly soft skin. Slowly, ever so slowly, he dragged the zipper down over her backside, pulling away from her mouth to say, "I've been waiting for this moment all night."

She sat up, a feisty twinkle in her eye when she said, "I've been waiting longer."

He sat up with her as she shrugged out of the dress. Beneath, she was naked, her breasts pert. Beautiful, with pale peach-colored nipples and tan lines that made his mouth water. He reached up and cradled those breasts, pleased when they barely filled his large hands. They were so delicate. So Addi. He swept his thumbs over her nipples. His eyes fastened to them as they pebbled in the cooler air of the room.

"Oh, that feels nice," she praised.

"That ain't nothin'." He set his tongue to one, the taste better than the feel. She raked her hands into his hair and encouraged him to make his way to the other. He was a man who was willing to serve.

He swirled his tongue around and around, sucking her deep. As her breaths quickened, her hips moved of their own volition. She rode his lap but fell short of where he wanted her—where he needed her. Palms splayed over her back, he moved to lay her down but she stopped him with both hands on his chest and shoved him down on the bed.

"Stay," she instructed.

He obeyed, watching, amused, as she climbed from the bed to shed the remainder of her sparkly ball gown and kick off her high-heeled shoes. Then she undressed him, which was something he didn't recall experiencing with a woman *ever*—he could say that with certainty. She tossed his shoes aside, peeled off his socks, dragged his pants down his legs and tossed them on the floor. Then she gave him another show, turning her back to him and tucking her thumbs into her panties. Bending, she peeked over her shoulder at him as she rolled the last bit of clothing over her temptingly round ass, past her thighs and finally off her feet.

His chest heaved, his fists mangling the neatly made bedspread. She came to him and leaned over, her small breasts brushing his chest as she crawled up his form.

Her lips barely touching his, she murmured, "Good boy."

Cupping her soft breasts, he accepted the kiss she offered, nearly exploding then and there when she kissed him long and deep. She took her time to explore his mouth while he gently pinched her nipples. When she gripped him and gave him a stroke he wondered if he'd die before he came.

"Bran." Her whisper was almost frantic. "I want you."

Best damn news he'd heard all day.

"I noticed." Sliding his hand between her legs, he found her warm and wet. He stroked her center, while he kissed her, timing his tongue with his fingers. But she wasn't able to hold her mouth over his whenever he touched that tiny, sensitive nerve bundle. She pulled away on a gasp.

"Condom," came her broken sentence. "Where?"

"Bag in the bathroom."

She moved to climb off him, but he stopped her with a "not yet."

"But—"

He reversed their positions, him over her, and with one knee spread her legs wide. Then he found the heart of her with his fingers and renewed his efforts, kissing her nipples instead of her mouth this time. She squirmed beneath him, her hands fisting his hair, her breaths high and tight. By the time an orgasm rocked her, he moved from her breasts to kiss her neck, then her cheek and then her mouth.

"That's what I wanted," he told her, his lips against hers before finishing her off with a succinct kiss.

He watched her descend back to earth, shaking off the

haze of the orgasm slowly. A smile crested her full mouth, her eyes barely open. "Thanks."

"My pleasure."

Somewhere she must've found a hidden source of energy. Next she pushed on his chest and rolled over him, kissing his neck and chest. Halfway to where he wanted her sweet mouth, she hopped off him and sent him a smile over her shoulder. Her hair was a wreck, and combined with the wiggle of her heart-shaped ass as she left the room, quite possibly the most tempting she'd ever looked.

Every moment he'd spent with Addi on this trip had taken him by surprise. It was a refreshing change from him trying to wrangle and orchestrate every detail of his life. With her he could just *be*.

When she returned, his head cleared of all thoughts save her. She straddled him, settling over his waist and waving the condom packet between them. "Ready, cowboy?"

He moved before she expected him to, pressing her back to the bed and snagging the condom at the same time. A laugh exploded from her chest, one of pure delight. He couldn't help grinning, too. "Are you ready?"

Her teeth on her bottom lip, her smile transformed into one that was at once demure and wanton. He knew why a second later, when he felt her hand grip him firmly before tickling his balls with her fingernails.

He'd fantasized about having her tonight, so sure he'd have to ease her into it. Take his time. He thought she'd be shy. That he'd need to coax her out of her shell by first kissing her from head to toe.

How wrong he'd been. Delightfully wrong...

He rolled on the condom, notched the head of his cock into her and her head bucked. Eyes closed, she hissed the word "yes" three times in a row. Her fingernails scraped his shoulders as he slid in the rest of the way, burying himself to the hilt in her tight heat.

Once there, he paused long enough to meet her open eyes, to admire the blush of her cheeks. "Ready, Addi?"

She gave him a squeeze with her inner muscles, grinning like a goddess while he nearly blacked out. In his ear, the silken caress of her voice announced, "I've *been* ready, handsome. Now start moving."

If he wasn't convinced before, now he knew for sure. Sex with Addison would be the best sex of his *life*.

Fourteen

Addi's goal for her one night with Brannon Knox was to take everything she wanted and leave nothing undone. She'd vowed to make it *good*. Evidently she overshot the mark, because sex with Bran wasn't good. It was freaking fantastic.

Epic.

Mind-blowing.

And when he'd stopped letting her run the show to take over, she was just as thrilled with the outcome.

But.

She still wanted to run the show.

"I want to be on top again," she told him as he stroked into her. "*Please*."

She could tell that he didn't want to say yes, to give up control of her pleasure. But there was more to her pleasure than he knew—most of it would come from being in charge of his.

Her *please* must have swayed him. He allowed her to climb on top of him, settling beneath her. Straddling him, she admired his hair ruffled in the pattern of her fingertips—*bucket list item!*—on the backdrop of a snow-white pillowcase.

She eased down onto him, and he filled her, the length and girth of him even more substantial in this position. Still, he didn't let her do all the work, his hands clutching her hips as he rose to meet her.

After a few gentle glides, he clutched her hips and slammed her down onto him.

"Oh!" What a lovely surprise that had been.

He repeated the motion, his gaze never leaving hers. Another orgasm crept along her spine, threatening bone-melting pleasure.

"Like that?" He pulled her down and hit that precious, perfect spot again.

"Oh!" He'd coaxed that reaction from her without trying.

"Yeah, you like that."

So proud of himself.

"You like this." She rotated her hips and watched as his smile was replaced by a look of pained pleasure. "Don't you?"

"Keep working, honey," was his gruff answer.

She kept working, he kept rising to meet her and his thumb brushed against her clitoris in time with each long, smooth stroke. It was that move that sent her over. Hands on his chest, she rode out her orgasm with her eyes shut. Wave after wave hit her mercilessly, her insides clutching him greedily. He took over for her, pistoning his hips while she had the most delicious orgasm she'd ever experienced. A loud growl followed—his release—paired with his tight grip on her hips. So tight she wouldn't be surprised if his fingertips left imprints.

When she was finally able to open her eyes, she'd collapsed on top of him. Her breasts were smashed flat on his chest, her nose tucked into his throat. She took a long inhalation before biting his neck and soothing it with a kiss.

He spoke first.

"Damn, Addi. That was… That was…" His chest moved with a deep laugh and she used the reserves of her strength to lift her head. He quickly lost his smile and kissed her tenderly, moving his lips on hers.

"Incredible." He kissed her nose. "Unexpected. You're a cowgirl in the bedroom. Who knew?"

Delirious from her earth-shattering orgasm, she muttered, "Only with you."

"I'll take it." He dropped his head back and blew out a breath. "I owe you a few hours of foreplay, but if you give me a few minutes to recover…"

A few minutes.

Well, they'd have to hold her funeral right after Joe's because she must have died from ecstasy. No way was Brannon Knox asking her for a round two.

She looked into his dark eyes. "You're—are you serious?"

"Usually it wouldn't take me so long to recover." Ever so gently, he slid from her body and placed a kiss on the center of her lips. "Honey, you ruined me tonight." With a wink, he climbed off the bed and went to the bathroom.

That seemed fair. He'd ruined her a long time ago.

He strolled back into the room a minute later and she feasted on the sight of him. Wide shoulders trickled down to a broad, defined chest to chiseled abs. His penis hung heavy to one side. At half-mast, it was still impressive.

"Hey, I'm up here."

She rerouted her gaze to his face to find him grinning.

"Nah, I'm kidding. I like the way you look at me." He peeled back the blankets and invited her under them with him.

She went, cuddling into the crook of his arm. "This has been… You've been… I don't know what to say except for thank you."

He responded sincerely, his lips pressing against the top of her head. "I know this is a tough weekend for you. I'm glad I could make it better."

She rested her hand on his chest. "I'm glad you're here."

"It went fast. The weekend's almost over."

Right. Almost over.

Almost time to load up the car and drive back to River Grove where she would sit at her desk come Monday morning. Almost time to forget that Bran wore nothing under his suit pants—impossible. Almost time to pack her feelings for him into a deep, dark crevice and forget about them.

"But not yet." He was suddenly gone, her head falling to the pillow with a soft *whump*. His head ducked beneath the covers, his hands on her breasts while his mouth kissed her torso then lower, lower and...

"Oh God." She arched her neck and closed her eyes. Definitely she'd died and gone to heaven.

Heaven was the only way to describe Bran's mouth.

Brannon woke the next morning to an empty bed.

After a *very* late night with Addison, he'd pulled the room-darkening curtain so they could sleep in—which he'd had zero problems doing. He could have slept through a 10.0 earthquake. She'd thoroughly worn him out.

He climbed from bed, scrubbed his face with his hands and opened the drapes. "Ad?"

Sunlight filled the bedroom, highlighting the tangled white sheets. He squinted against the brightness, smiling at the pillows they'd knocked to the floor during their exploration of each other. Shuffling to the bathroom, he checked the dark room but she wasn't in there, either.

Well. That was a first.

He'd never *lost* his date from the previous night. Not that he'd had many one-night stands. And after how good last night was, they'd be crazy to only indulge in one night. He hadn't had enough of Addi.

Before they'd fallen asleep, he'd gone down on her and she'd climaxed several times. They'd had sex again, and he went slow so he could watch each satisfied microexpression cross her face. She'd fallen asleep snuggled against him, and dead arm be damned, he was content to let her lie there as long as she liked.

Now, she was a ghost? It made no sense.

The clock on the nightstand read a little after eight in the morning. He knocked lightly on their joined doors, assuming she'd fled to her own bed in the neighboring room.

No answer.

He knocked again. "Addi?"

When there was no answer, he tried the knob. Locked.

He knew damn well she'd enjoyed herself—several times. She hadn't faked her reaction to him any more than he'd been able to fake his reaction to her. She'd turned him inside out, surprised him and made him want more. So how was it that she wasn't around this morning for the more he was ready to give her?

He showered and dressed before venturing downstairs. Brunch was in full swing, and he saw some familiar faces from the weekend festivities. At the coffee bar, he spotted the face he'd been expecting on the pillow next to his this morning.

Approaching from behind, he leaned over Addi's shoulder and dropped his voice low. "Excuse me, have you seen the woman who was in my bed last night? She vanished without saying goodbye."

She spun around, her mouth pulled into a soft "O" of surprise. "Brannon. Hi. I was… I couldn't sleep."

"That's funny. I could barely wake up."

"I noticed. You snore." She poured cream into her coffee.

He started to argue, but she spoke before he could.

"Would you like coffee?"

"Sure."

She poured him a mug, then added cream and the perfect amount of sugar. She knew how he took his coffee and he had no idea how she took hers. She'd been paying attention to him for the last year she'd been working for him and he'd been... Well, not ignoring her, but definitely not paying close *enough* attention.

She handed him the mug. "Here you go."

Before she vanished a second time, he gripped her arm. "Where are you going?"

"The pool?" A closer look at her white linen dress showed the shadow of a yellow bikini underneath.

"How about some breakfast?"

"I thought you might be in a hurry to leave for River Grove so I was going to grab a quick swim before we check out."

One of them was in a hurry today, but it sure as hell wasn't him.

"Now that you mention it, I could use a swim. *After* breakfast. Join me."

She turned and walked to a table, her spine straight and her shoulders pulled back. Proper. Elegant. She was icing him. No easy smiles or flirtatious side-eyes any more. Even her offer of coffee had been as generic as if they were back at the office already.

They'd barely lowered into their chairs when a waitress approached and took their breakfast order. There were limited choices on the menu, which made choosing easy.

"Pancakes sound good. I almost ordered that," Addi said conversationally after the waitress left. "Just let me know when you're ready to leave. I can be packed in a matter of minutes."

Again, so formal.

"What gives?" He knew when he was being dismissed. He didn't care for it.

"What do you mean?"

"You left my bed." And now that he'd said it aloud, he realized how much it pissed him off. Not because she owed him anything, but because he'd invited her there. She could have done him the courtesy of telling him she was leaving. Or hell, leaving a note. "I had to scour the grounds to find you and when I do, you treat me like we're in the middle of a business transaction. So again I ask, what gives?"

He sipped his coffee. It was perfect, which irked him for some reason.

"You knew what this was." Her voice was barely above a whisper. "One night and a clean break."

He felt his eyebrows jump. "I didn't realize there was such a defined line between Saturday night and Sunday morning."

"I said midnight—"

"We went well past midnight." Last time he'd checked the clock over Addi's naked, sated body, it was nearly 3:00 a.m.

"I was trying to be practical." Her cheeks stained pink as she studied her coffee.

"I'm not big on practical any longer. Remember?" *Practical* hadn't helped him land CEO. *Practical* had him asking out a woman he had no sexual chemistry with whatsoever. *Practical* had him purchasing an engagement ring for the same woman, one he didn't love. As far as he was concerned, practical was damn *impractical*.

He'd insisted enjoying the weekend with Addi for one reason: he wanted to. Granted, he hadn't expected to enjoy himself as much as he had or he never would have agreed to her one-night rule.

"I don't want it to end like this," he grumbled, frustrated. "Not over pancakes before a four-hour car ride home."

She watched him, silent.

"Have you had enough of me already?" Having asked that he realized she could answer the affirmative, which left him weirdly exposed.

"No." She sighed, and in her hesitation he sensed she was feeling equally vulnerable.

"Okay, good." Great, actually. "How do you feel about extending the weekend? Is there any reason for me to be in the office tomorrow? Any big meetings? Unmovable conference calls?"

"I—I'd have to double-check but I don't think so."

"Even if there is, we can cancel. There's nothing more important going on than this."

She offered a gentle smile, and his shoulders relaxed some. He didn't often crave approval, but hers meant a lot to him.

"Addison—what's your middle name?"

"Jane."

"Addison *Jane* Abrams—" he reached for her hand on the table "—would you be willing to stay another night with me? The *entire* night. Through morning. No vanishing."

She nodded.

"I'm going to need to hear the word."

"Yes," she answered and pride flooded his chest. "As long as my boss doesn't care if I skip work on Monday, I'm willing to stay another night."

"I see no bosses here."

The waitress delivered their breakfasts and he was forced to have an annoying interaction to specify that *yes*, he was fine and *no*, he didn't need butter. When she finally left, his eyes tracked back to Addi, who hadn't so much as picked up her fork.

"I'll try to leave you with enough energy for work on Tuesday."

Elbow on the table, she propped her chin on her fist. "I make no such promises."

Damn.

He liked her like this. Bold and fun. Open and lively. So much better than the controlled, *practical* woman he'd bumped into this morning.

"The entire night," he reminded her as he cut into his pancakes. "I might save some of this syrup for later."

As he took a big bite, she laughed. He loved hearing it. He also made it a point to ask the waitress for some syrup to go when she returned to the table.

Fifteen

The surface of the pool sparkled in the sunshine. They were on the rooftop, overlooking the lake, trees and mountains. Plenty of boats were out today, their passengers sunbathing on decks or following behind on water skis.

"Rather be boating?" Bran asked from beside her. His tanned body was stretched out on a lounge chair, arm thrown over his head, sunglasses hiding his closed eyes, a pair of yellow swim trunks covering her favorite part of him. Although, to be fair she had a lot of favorite parts of him. Starting with his hair, followed closely by the sharp straight nose, contoured perfect mouth, the column of his throat leading down to his wide chest. Her eyes traveled down to the bumps of his abs, a perfect "innie" belly button and long strong legs. He even had nice feet.

"I can feel you staring at me." One of those eyes peeked open and he turned to face her. His white, sharklike grin was cunning and reminded her of every yummy thing they'd done last night. If there was anything that made her want to leave the pool or the precious sunshine, it was the promise of more Brannon Knox.

"I'm not staring," she lied. "I'm thinking and happened to zone out on you."

He pulled off his sunglasses and sat up. And no, she did not miss when his abs contracted with movement. "Thinking about what? The hours of foreplay thing? I meant that. Say the word. Our rooms are a short elevator's ride away."

She couldn't hide her smile, and his answering one told her he'd read her mind.

Early this morning, she'd woken and rolled to her side to admire him asleep next to her. She'd realized with a gut-wrenching certainty that keeping her heart out of the bedroom was more challenging than she'd previously imagined.

By leaving his bed and climbing into her own, she'd hoped to pull herself up from the emotional tailspin she saw coming. She worried if she'd stayed there awake next to him, she would've watched him sleep, counting his thick, numerous lashes, or tracing the outline of his amazing body under the sheet so that the night would forever torment her memory.

And she thought she needed to forget about him. Because last night wasn't supposed to happen—and sure as hell wasn't supposed to happen *again*.

Now she'd agreed to stay another night with him for one reason and one reason only: she still wanted him. She'd had a hard time compartmentalizing. The memories of the time they spent together followed her from bed to breakfast. By the time he admitted he wanted her again she'd been powerless to resist.

"I was serious before," she started.

"About?"

"About stopping by Pestle & Pepper on the way back. Since you've never been there." It was likely her only chance to take him. P&P was technically in River Grove, but she reasoned that driving by the exit counted as part of this trip. "Would you like to stop?"

"Heck, yes." With that, he slid his sunglasses back onto his perfect nose and closed his eyes to soak up some more sun.

It must be nice to not worry about the future. Then again, he'd worried plenty earlier this year. She remembered him taut with frustration when Royce had been named CEO. Bran had come a long way. She understood why he didn't want to think any more. Why he wanted to indulge in the present.

The difference was, his indulgence was a fun sex-filled weekend. Hers risked her very heart and soul.

Drama queen, Joe's voice whispered in her ear.

Am not, she argued back, but he was sort of right. Indulging in Bran didn't mean she had to be emotionally crippled once she arrived home. She should give herself some credit.

That's better, Joe encouraged.

"Look who it is," a familiar voice said—a real one this time. She shielded her eyes as her mother approached, Addi's father behind her. "I thought we'd missed you."

"Nope, just grabbing some sun before we, uh, check out." No way was she telling her mom and dad about staying another night.

"We were on our way out, but we can stay for a drink. Brannon, darling, would you like a drink?" her mother sang.

"He's sleeping," Addi said at the same time Bran said, "Sure."

So agreeable.

"Let's move to the café, dear." Her mother lowered her voice but not low enough when she said, "Much as I like admiring his chest, he should dress before discussing business."

"I'll hand it to her," Bran told Addi as they strolled inside. "Your mom has some balls."

She groaned. Her mother had been an embarrassing disaster. She'd grilled him about everything but his banking information, and even then, Addi had half expected her to ask.

"I'm sorry. They're completely embarrassing."

"It's fine. I was the one who agreed to a drink. Nothing I couldn't handle." His hand in hers, he towed her in for a quick kiss. She was going to miss that when they arrived back home.

At the front desk, Bran stopped.

Ava, the same woman who'd checked them in, smiled in greeting. "Good morning, Mr. Knox. Ms. Abrams."

"Morning, Ava," he said. "I need to extend our reservations one more night if you have the space. We're not ready to check out yet."

"I'm happy to extend your reservations." Ava's smile was smug, as if she'd known something they hadn't. As if Bran and Addi had been wasting their time by not sharing a room in the first place. "Are you extending reservations for one room or for both?"

"One," they said at the same time and Bran sent Addi an approving smile.

Ava tapped a key on her keyboard. "Which one?"

His eyes on Addi, enough heat in them to start to start a forest fire, Bran answered, "Mine."

"Good choice." A few more key taps later, Ava looked up. "I have you down for one more night in the room with the king bed. Shall I send up a bottle of champagne or strawberries this evening?"

Addi laughed.

Bran didn't. "Both. Thank you."

As they walked to the elevator, his hand went to her back. "You're learning."

"What does that mean?" she asked as the doors opened and they stepped inside.

"You let me treat you without any pushback. Pretty soon, you'll have no problem letting me take care of you." The doors shut and in one smooth move he had her back pressed to the elevator wall. "How about I take care of you now?"

"N-now?"

He reached for the big red emergency button and she grabbed his outstretched hand in both of hers. "Brannon. *No*."

He tsked at her. "So practical."

He shook off her hold, swiped her hair behind her ears and cradled her jaw. Then he lowered his lips to hers for a warm kiss. He smelled of coconut-scented sunscreen and really, really good sex. Or maybe she was projecting that part.

"You're mine tonight, Addison Abrams. What do you think of that?"

"I think you'd better start as soon as possible." She grabbed his ass. "What I have in mind for you is going to take a while."

Turned out they had to first move her luggage into Bran's room before they—*ahem*—indulged. After a few hours of indulgence followed by a much-needed nap, they emerged from their shared room in search of a late dinner. The strawberries and champagne were lovely, but not filling.

In the downstairs bar, they ran into two other couples. Rebecca and Allen and two men Addison had never met before who were newlyweds: Dave and Cameron. Rebecca had waved Addi and Bran over and asked them to join them at the bar.

Bottoming out her second glass of wine, Addison decided she didn't want this day to end. But Dave and Cameron had an early flight, and Rebecca had hidden more than one yawn behind her perfectly manicured fingernails.

"I can't keep up with you West Coasters." The cute redhead didn't bother hiding her yawn this time. "In my head, the time hasn't changed."

"Don't listen to her. She's always in bed by seven," Allen joked.

"Same here," Dave said. "Cam and I have gone to bed at eight o'clock every night while we've been here."

"Well, we're not twenty any longer," Cam said. "Hell, we're not thirty any longer."

This led to a discussion from both of them that Bran and Addi should "enjoy their youth."

"What about you, Ad? Are you tired from your exhausting day?" Bran asked, pure mischief in his smile.

"Actually I'd love another glass of wine." They had time for another round of epic sex or three, even if she stayed at the bar a little longer. Bran had nothing if not stamina.

"Allow us." Dave dropped a twenty-dollar bill on the bar top and kissed Addi on the forehead. "Enjoy."

"To Joe." Cameron polished off his whiskey sour, and Rebecca and her husband toasted their late friend and then finished their drinks as well.

Once everyone had cleared out, Addi let out a wistful sigh. After spending a few hours reminiscing about Joe and hearing how each of the couples met, she decided that practicality was overrated.

If she'd stuck with her plan to "Get Over Him" she never would have experienced the wonderful moments they'd had together this weekend. Some of the best of her life. Because she'd followed Bran over to the *light side*, her afternoon had been filled with surprises. Including an evening of swapping stories about Joe, which had been cathartic and so very needed.

In a way, Joe's death had brought her and Brannon together.

Bran ordered another round and when two full wineglasses were delivered, they settled into a comfortable silence. Remembering the life Joe left unlived added weight to the room.

"You know, if Joe really did think of me as the love of his life, that's sad."

"Why? Did you want to fulfill his dream?" Bran asked.

"No." She gave him a playful poke to the ribs. "The opposite. I would have had to let him down easy. I might've broken his heart. He was my friend. I never wanted more than that." Her own heart felt broken admitting that aloud.

"You did love him. As a friend. What if that was enough for him?"

"Hmm. Love's tricky."

"The trickiest," he agreed.

"My parents love me, but their love has always felt like an exchange. Like if I behaved and did what they asked, I could trade my good behavior for some of that love. I longed for the unconditional kind. The kind of love *your* family has so much of it's bursting at the seams."

"I've met your parents a few times now. They love you. I can tell they want what's best for you even if they have a harsh way of showing it. Their scheming is born of worry."

"I never thought of it that way." She'd only felt criticized or punished. "I guess I was too busy trying to hustle. Trying to make something of myself—trying to prove them wrong. Have you ever felt like you don't measure up?" She wanted to eat those words as soon as she'd said them. Of course he had. "You must've. With your dad. With Royce."

He held her hand, their elbows resting on the bar top between their drinks. "I know it's hard to believe because of my daunting physique, but I am only human."

She rolled her eyes, though she had to agree with the daunting part.

"Like you, I put a lot of pressure on myself," he said, serious now. "I felt like I needed to win. Royce didn't do anything wrong accepting CEO. Taylor didn't do anything wrong by falling in love with him. Listen, I can't argue with you about my family. They're incredible. Gia, Royce and I, we stick together. We have each other's backs. I've always felt loved and know that no matter how many times I screw up they'll *still* love me."

"You are now witnessing the jealousy of an only child." She pointed to herself but was only half kidding.

"My family adores you, too, you know. I've told them again and again how lucky I am to have you. You're a crucial part of ThomKnox. You want a family to appreciate you? You don't want to be alone anymore? *Addi*." He kissed her knuckles. "You're not alone."

Hearing that healed some hidden part of her. A wound she didn't know was there. She'd admitted she wanted family, but had never truly accepted that she'd had one all along. "Thanks for saying that."

"I mean it." He kissed her knuckles again before releasing her hand and then lifted his wine glass. "To family."

She raised her glass and clinked his, feeling very not alone for the first time in a long time. "To family."

Sixteen

Three and a half hours into a four-hour-long car ride and Addi was *still* buzzing from last night. Not only had Bran assured her she had a place in his family's heart, but he'd implied she had a place in his. And after he'd promised her she wasn't alone, he'd taken her to bed and made the most tender love to her. He'd been present and focused solely on her needs. She knew it was dangerous to project, but she could swear what he couldn't put into words he'd said with his body. She hadn't imagined their conversation afterward, as they lay snuggling and cozy in bed, talking.

"If I have kids, I'm having more than one," she'd told him. "I'd love to have a sibling or two."

"I always thought three was a good number," he'd said, tickling her forearm with his fingertips and sending chills down her body. "Royce and Gia and I have always been close. If one of us is acting like an idiot, at least there are two other honest opinions and no possibility of a tie."

She'd laughed at that, as she did at most of their conversation. Even though he hadn't outright admitted he wanted to have three children himself, that's what she heard. Her mind had offered up a vision of a small child on her hip, another's hand in hers, and a third one chasing Bran along the ocean's shoreline.

A fantasy, surely.

But what came next seemed to confirm it.

"I have a proposition for you," he said now, from the driver's seat.

"Sounds important. Let me prepare myself." She smoothed her hair—down since they'd left the windows up—and straightened her spine. "Okay, I'm ready."

"Honestly, when did you become such a smart-ass? I ruined you this weekend."

He so did, but not in the way he meant. He'd successfully thwarted her plan not to fall for him. She'd tried to keep her heart out of the bedroom but how could she when he'd been all heart?

"Which brings me to my question." One hand on the wheel, he spared her a quick glance before looking out the windshield again. "How would you feel about spending more nights together once we return home?"

Delighted. Thrilled. Sign me up!

"I'm having fun. You seem to be having fun." He lifted one shoulder in a shrug. "Why not?"

Not the profession of love she was hoping for, but that wasn't going to happen—not so soon. She might've been in love with him for a year, but he'd recently been through the wringer. He was stoic about how Royce and Taylor and the role of CEO had affected him, she knew Bran—she knew he was still feeling his way forward.

She wanted to be more than his soft space to land. What they needed was more time to uncover what they could mean to each other. Exactly what he was offering. But. There was a real world to consider outside of this car.

"What about your family? What about work?"

"We can keep it to ourselves. Not because I'm worried

about backlash, but who needs the pressure, you know? Who needs outside opinion on what we're doing when we know what works for us?"

Coming from anyone else, she might consider it a blow off, but this was Bran. She knew Bran. And she wanted Bran. So much she'd be willing to do almost anything he asked.

Almost.

"And this won't affect my working with you?" she asked.

"Not on my end. It might lead to a couple of very interesting private meetings—" his mouth quirked "—but I don't want you to worry that anything that happens between us will affect your job. I meant it when I said I needed you at ThomKnox, Ad. I do."

She needed him, too, but wouldn't dare mention it.

"I appreciate the transparency. I'm not ready to shut this down, either." She clucked her tongue and offered up a sarcastic, "Poor Tammie, though, what will you tell her?"

He chuckled. "You're never going to let me live that down, are you?"

"Probably not."

He reached for her hand and lifted it to his mouth. "A small price to pay."

A few minutes later, he swiftly pulled over several lanes of traffic and angled for an exit she knew well.

"Pestle & Pepper," he said in explanation.

"My home away from home."

"Let's have a celebratory lunch. I'm starving. Plus, they're going to wonder if you fell off the planet. Probably think their best customer was abducted."

She was still on the planet. But she was fairly certain her heart was orbiting Earth at the moment.

She was *so* screwed. Or was she?

Independence didn't have to mean being alone forever,

did it? Couldn't she find a way to be at work with Bran and then be at home with Bran afterward?

Of course you can.

She wasn't about to miss out on being with the man she was already half in love with. She was going to carpe diem. He'd teased her about being too practical and arguably, he was right. Every fun thing she'd experienced this long weekend had been a result of her following her heart, not heeding the warnings offered up by her brain.

"Wait'll you have their lava cake," she told Bran as he pulled into the P&P parking lot. "You may have had lava cake before, but trust me, you haven't had Pestle & Pepper's lava cake."

"I trust you." He shut off the engine and climbed from the car. "With a lot of things bigger than lava cake."

She took his hand and they walked toward the entrance. Though she tried to stop it, her next thought was *like with your heart?*

She wasn't kidding about the lava cake.

It was damn good. The satisfying moment where the chocolate ganache oozed onto the plate was almost as good as watching Addi lick her spoon.

He'd had a hard time not thinking about her tongue elsewhere during the car ride back to his house.

"So this is my place," he told her from his front door. Before she could leave the foyer, he shut the door behind him and pressed her against it. "And this is you in my place."

She laughed, but he covered her mouth with his, tasting the chocolate on her tongue.

"But your luggage," she said as he kissed a trail down her neck.

"I don't need any clothes right now." He reached for the hem of her short dress and lifted it over her beautiful hips. "And neither do you."

He wasn't over how well this weekend had gone—and hell, it was Monday and they were *still* going.

He'd spent most of the car ride home thinking about Addi and work. He loathed the idea of boxing them in with more rules, or *guidelines* as she liked to call them, but Tuesday would come regardless. And he could admit they needed at least a loose plan.

He was as confident in her professionalism as he was in his own. No matter what the future held for him—or how far into the future they ventured—he was certain they could survive.

She unbuttoned his jeans and stuffed her hand inside, humming her approval. "Can I say again how much I like that you are not a fan of underwear?"

"I'm a big fan of underwear," he argued, his thumbs hooking the sides of her cute, lacy pink pair. "On you." Then he thought of what he'd said and quickly amended, "No, you're right. I don't like you wearing them, either."

He worked those panties down her legs and she lifted one foot, then the other to step out of them. While he had her here, he decided to have a taste of her, too.

Ten minutes later, one knee over his shoulder, Addi cried out, her shout echoing off the walls of his house. He liked her voice echoing off the walls of his house.

"I'm really glad we agreed not to stop," he told her as he kissed his way up her body. He tucked his tongue into the cups of her bra to tease each nipple while she gripped his hair.

"Where is your bedroom? Knees are weak," she mumbled.

He lifted her into his arms and started for the stairs. "I'll give you the full tour later."

"*Much* later."

"Much later," he agreed.

She held onto his neck, her blue eyes at half-mast, her

smile his reward. A warning bell sounded in the depths of his mind but he ignored it. He was no longer the guy who was going to talk himself into a proposal or go running after a goal that had nothing to do with what he really wanted. He was smarter now, and he refused to plague himself with future plans and arrangements.

Addi was here with him now, and now was what mattered. Now was all that existed.

And *right now*, he was going to blow her mind in the bedroom and follow that with a long, lazy Monday off.

Seventeen

"Are you…whistling?" His sister, Gia, hovered in his office doorway, one eyebrow so high on her head she resembled a cartoon character.

"Can't I have a good day?"

Or a good week? A good *couple of weeks*?

He and Addison had fallen into a great rhythm since they'd returned to the office. They worked together, flirted with each other, and yesterday she'd come into his office and shared her Pestle & Pepper takeout.

She'd spent a few nights at his house when the evening went too late. No arguments from him. He liked her in his bed. Even if she was grouchy in the morning before coffee.

"You can have a good day—" Gia dropped a file folder on his desk "—but when you smile like the Joker, it makes me suspicious."

Addi sailed by the doorway but evidently didn't notice Gia until she blurted, "Hey, handsome… Oh, uh, I meant to say Bran. Wow. So unprofessional. Hi, Gia. I didn't know you were here."

Nice recovery, Ad. No way was Gia going to let that go.

"Hi, Addi. How are *you*?" Gia folded her arms, her smirk evident.

"Fantastic." Addison straightened her shoulders and pasted on a smile that was a little Joker-y as well. "I was coming in to update Bran on his schedule."

"Do you mean 'handsome' here?" Gia jutted a thumb at her brother.

"Leave her alone." He stood and crossed the room, both females' eyes on him. He kissed Addi's forehead and faced his sister. "You caught us. We've been…dating. Try not to run and tell everyone within earshot so that we can have some peace, will you?"

"Well, well. Will office romances never die?" His sister's eyelids narrowed.

"You're one to talk."

"Jayson and I don't count."

"Uh-huh." He leaned forward to murmur into Addi's ear. "We'll talk later."

"Yes, um, sir. Bran. Thanks." Addi left the office, shutting the door behind her.

"You should be nicer," he told his sister.

"How in love with you is that girl?" Gia shook her head.

"She's not in love with me." He scoffed. "Who needs love?"

"Everyone on the planet?"

Ignoring that, he opted for a cavalier response. "Don't worry about me, sis. I get plenty of lovin'."

Gia groaned.

"Addi and I have compatibility. Companionship. We like spending time together."

Gia chuckled. "So you feel the same about her as you did Rusty."

"Best dog over." He gripped his chest. "I can't talk about him. It's too soon."

"You were *eleven*."

"Don't put a bunch of labels on Addi and me. It's not healthy. As far as you're concerned, we're just—"

"Dating?"

"Yeah."

What was wrong with that? No way was Addi *in love* with him. She wasn't clingy. Even the nights she stayed, she mentioned how she should be going home. He'd told her she was welcome to do whatever she liked, but if she chose to stay, that was fine with him. He'd grown accustomed to her rental car sitting in his driveway.

"It's working fine the way it is," he said. "We both know the deal. She's cool, by the way. You'd like her if you came out of your dwelling every so often to see what we do up here."

"I know what you do up here. My *dwelling* is only one floor down from this one, and tech is the command center of this entire operation." She spread her arms. "I see all."

"Now who sounds like a cartoon villain?" He didn't want to break Gia's heart and remind her that she couldn't have seen much if she'd only just now noticed he and Addi were seeing each other. They'd been discreet, but Gia was supposed to be the genius of the family. Though she was the first person to notice, so that counted for something.

"Mom's having a big cookout for the Fourth of July at the summer home."

"Already? I thought she was redoing the kitchen."

"She is, but she wants to 'encourage progress.'" Gia used air quotes around the words he'd heard his mother say multiple times. "She figures with a tighter deadline, the contractors will hustle harder."

Their parents' summer home was a huge estate in wine country perched on top of a hill overlooking a vineyard. It had been in the family since ThomKnox became a household name. It was also where Gia and Jayson spent their honeymoon. Which was, Bran guessed, the reason for her deep frown.

"Been a while since we've been up there," he said.

"Yeah." She sighed. "Jayson's invited."

"You're the one who made him family." Once a Knox, always a Knox. She'd been adamant about Jayson not being treated differently after the divorce.

"I know that." Her eyebrows crashed over her cute nose. "I just... How will I bring a date if he's everywhere I am?"

"Do you *have* a date?" His sister had been as single as a slice of Kraft cheese for as long as he could remember.

"I don't, but what if I did?"

"You would show up with your date. And then Jayson and Royce and I would talk behind your back about what a dope he was."

"Shut up!" That brought forth her smile. "I am perfectly capable of meeting a nice guy."

"I know you are." He wrapped his arm around her and gave her a squeeze. She was syrupy sweet underneath her Naugahyde exterior.

"Are you going to bring your adorable blond date?"

He slipped his arm from his sister's shoulders, dread settling on his back. Being at work and taking a little ribbing from Gia was one thing. At an *event* where they'd be clearly coupled off invited a lot of opinions and expectations. He didn't want to be under a microscope—not again. "I don't know…"

"You can't hide her forever." She pretended to zip her lips. "I won't say anything to Royce or Taylor—or Mom and Dad—but if you're really dating Addi, you can't exclude her from basic family gatherings."

She blew him a kiss and left his office, leaving him with a live grenade.

Addison at his family's cookout crossed a lot of boundaries he hadn't known were there. It opened them both up to everyone's assumptions. He wasn't eager to subject either of them to that. What they were doing was working. He saw no reason to complicate it.

This was, however, a great opportunity to tease her.

He popped open the door and affected his sternest expression. "Ms. Abrams. Come in here for a moment."

Addi smoothed her pink dress as she stood and walked to his office. With her blond hair swept up at the back of her neck, she looked like a dessert. One he wanted to taste. He folded his arms over his chest and leaned on the edge of his desk.

Worry crimped her forehead and he almost felt bad. He'd make it up to her soon enough. "Close the door."

She did as he asked, her hand resting on the doorknob like she was ready to make a swift escape. "I know what you're going to say. I'm so sorry. I had no idea your sister was in here. Obviously. I should have looked. That's no excuse. We're at work and I know better than—"

He crooked a finger, beckoning her forward. When she was within reach, he put both hands on her hips and pulled her to stand between his legs. "Kiss me like you mean it."

"Wha—"

Closer now, his lips brushed hers. He repeated, "Kiss me. Like you mean it."

She placed her soft lips on his and the brief worry he'd had about boundaries and who knew and who didn't dissipated. Addi went pliant beneath him, draping her arms around his neck while her tongue danced with his.

She lowered to her heels, her eyes opening slowly. "So, you're not upset?"

"Have you met me? When am I upset?"

Why should he care what anyone said about who he was with? He was an adult. No one could tell him not to date Addison Abrams except for Addison Abrams.

He kissed her again and she pressed against him, breasts

to thighs. This time when the kiss ended, he didn't loosen his hold on her.

"You *really* shouldn't encourage me." He was fighting a full-on erection at work. He was going to have to hide behind his desk until it went away, which at this rate might be tomorrow.

"And you shouldn't go to your next meeting wearing Think Pink lip gloss." She swiped his lips with her thumb.

"You are such a tigress. Had I known..."

"You'd have called me in here sooner?" She gave him a grin.

She wasn't wrong. If he'd known how much fun they could have together, he'd have called her in here a hell of a lot sooner.

An entire *year* sooner.

"It's been too long," Addi told her friend Carey as she sat down across from her at Pestle & Pepper. Typically, she met her best friend once a month for a girls' night, but this month had flown by. Must have been because Addi was so damned happy.

"It has! The last text I had from you was that your car blew up on the highway on your way to Lake Tahoe." Carey flipped her sleek, black hair over her shoulder, showing off envious cheekbones. They'd worked together a few jobs ago and had kept in touch. She was now an ad executive in Palo Alto.

They chatted about Carey's latest overseas trip, but Addi hadn't filled her in on any of the bigger changes in her life.

Carey glanced over her menu. "Is the car in the car graveyard yet?"

"Ugh. Yes. I have a rental while I shop." Despite Bran insisting she use a company car, she couldn't allow herself to do it. See? She was plenty independent! "It takes time to find a good used car. And I've been...busy."

"Aw, hon." Carey looked up from her menu. "Has work been hard?"

Addi swallowed her laughter. Their server dropped off their appetizer—fried avocado slices with jalapeño ranch dip.

"These are *evil*."

"Calories don't count on girls' night," Addi reminded her friend. They both dipped a wedge into the ranch before sipping their chardonnays. "Work's been great. I've been busy...elsewhere." She let the comment hang.

Her friend accurately gleaned there was more to that statement. *"Oh?"*

"I haven't had a chance to tell you... Well, I have but I didn't want to jinx it." Addi couldn't hide her smile. When she'd busted in to find Bran's sister in his office, she was sure he wasn't happy with her. Instead, he'd pulled her against his amazing body and commanded she kiss him. Uh, no problem there. Since then she'd on Cloud 999.

She'd been treading lightly since they'd been sleeping together, making sure not to crowd him. Making sure she didn't presume too much too soon. Bran showed no signs of slowing down. And before she left work today, he'd asked her if she had plans for the Fourth of July. Granted, not the most momentous of holidays, but it *was* a holiday. She'd told him she was free and he hadn't said more, only sent her a sly smile.

"There's this guy..." she started.

Carey's sharp, high-pitched cheer turned the heads of the patrons at three neighboring tables. "Oh my God, tell me everything! Is he hot, rich, great in bed?"

"Yes to all of the above. He's also my boss..."

But he was so much more than that. They'd spent many nights in bed talking after having amazing sex. They'd spent as many days ironing out work issues—working together as seamlessly as they always had.

She shared the highlights of her recent trip to Tahoe. From Bran driving her to staying next door to her hotel room to extending their trip one more night and then extending their affair.

"Is affair the right word?" Addi wrinkled her nose. "Sounds so scandalous."

"Agree. Let's call it a hot billionaire hookup," Carey said it so matter-of-factly that Addi burst out laughing.

It felt good to laugh. It felt good to be with Bran. Part of her worried she was in way over her head—with her heart dragging her further and further out—but for some reason that felt good, too.

As loathe as she was to admit it, she was enjoying living in the now.

Eighteen

Bran's calendar alert chimed on his phone and he tapped the screen without looking. Today had been hectic as hell, and the very last thing he wanted to do was walk to the other side of their floor and into a conference room to meet with Bernie Belfry, an old golfing buddy of his dad's who also happened to be a premium investor in ThomKnox.

Thank God Addi had arranged the necessary paperwork. He grabbed the bundle, neatly stapled in one corner, from the inbox on her desk.

His mood lightened some as his thoughts turned to Addi. It was hard to be upset about anything when they had a date tonight at her place. Sex made for a great release valve after work, which he'd always known. But sex with her was also completely hassle-free. That was a nice perk.

He passed Royce's office, intending to flip him off for sticking Bran with Bernie, but his brother didn't look up from his computer screen.

In the corridor, Bran came to the last conference room on the right and stopped, considering. They rarely used this one unless the others were full.

He was surprised to find the door shut, and even more surprised to find it locked. Before he could wonder what Bernie was doing in there, the lock disengaged and the handle turned easily under his grip.

"Catching a nap before the meeting?" Bran asked as he stepped in. He opened his mouth to continue the how's-the-weather and how's-the-wife small talk, but when he laid eyes on the person in the room, every thought shot out of his head.

Addi eased onto the conference table, her legs crossed. He took her in by snatches, his eyes moving too fast to focus. There were simply too many good parts to look at all at once.

Skirt: black and rucked to her thighs, revealing lacy garter straps attached to black thigh-high stockings.

Blouse: bright pink and unbuttoned halfway, revealing a wealth of cleavage.

Hair: down, tumbling over her shoulders in loose, light waves.

Hands: braced on the edge of the table.

High-heeled shoes: swinging in a rhythm that matched his own escalating heartbeats.

He shut the door behind him, grateful for the lock. Really grateful.

"Hello, Mr. Knox," she purred, her mouth spreading into a smile.

"Hello, Ms. Abrams." He held up the papers as he stalked toward her. "Guess I don't need this?"

She shook her head, pursing those tempting pink lips to say, "Nope."

He chucked the report into the wastebasket. A conference room romp hadn't occurred to him. Okay, okay, it had, but only in his fantasies. Being caught flirting was one thing, pants around his ankles in his place of work was another altogether.

But then that sounded too roped off and rules driven for his taste. He wanted to put as much distance as possible between him and the work-hard guy he'd been earlier this year. Taking Addi up on her offer of a boardroom tryst ought to help in that endeavor.

His eyes snapped from her chest to her legs. Damn. He had no idea where to start.

She solved that conundrum for him, grasping his hands and putting them on her breasts. Next, she snagged his neck and tugged his mouth down to hers for a scintillating kiss.

"How far?" she asked between kisses, running her fingers along the buttons of his shirt.

"What?" He blinked stupidly. "How far, what?"

"How far do you want this to go? My plan was to tempt you, but I respect that this is our place of work and if you—"

He smothered the rest of her words with his mouth and unbuckled his pants, dropping them to his ankles as she laughed into his kiss.

"How much time do we have?" He didn't want to rush.

"Your three o'clock is with Royce and Taylor."

That gave him about thirty minutes before he met with his brother and soon-to-be sister-in-law. They'd forgive him if he was a few minutes late.

"You didn't give me long." He unbuttoned the rest of her shirt and opened her bra, freeing her beautiful breasts.

"I wasn't sure—" she gasped as he suckled her nipple "—how much you'd want to do in here."

"More than we have time for," he said on a growl. He tossed her shoes to the floor and lifted her skirt. The garters and stockings could stay right where they were. By the time he'd rolled her black panties down her legs, he was as hard as iron.

He slipped his fingers along her folds and found her wet

and warm. Head dropped back, blond waves brushing the top of the conference table, she was a fantasy come to life. Behind her, a view of the mountains in the distance interrupted a perfect blue sky through the tinted windows, but the view before him was ten times as appealing.

"We need a condom, Addison. Did you prepare for that, too?"

She sat up on her elbows, her cheeks flushed. "Under the plant."

"Seriously?"

She nodded.

Sure enough, under the large potted plant in the corner was a square of foil. They were home free.

"You've done this before?" he asked, the condom scissored between two fingers.

"Yeah, right." She laughed, a glorious sight with her breasts bared in the air-conditioned room and framed by her bright pink shirt. "Who do you think I am?"

He rolled on the protection, shaking his head. "At the moment, I'm not sure."

Tugging her legs so that she met him at the edge of the table, he cupped her ass and held on tight. She wrapped her ankles around his back and gripped his shoulders as he slid in the first few inches. Her moan wasn't quiet.

Good thing those other two conference rooms were vacant.

He continued working them into a sweat, gently shushing her whenever her high-pitched cries threatened to be overheard. She covered her mouth with her hand, her smile evident beneath her palm. God, she was beautiful. And fun and incredible. He'd had no idea a vixen lurked beneath the polished veneer of his professional executive assistant. She was like having a naughty librarian on call.

Probably it was too much to hope for to gift her with an orgasm in the limited time they had, but it wouldn't keep him from trying. He navigated his thumb between their bodies as he entered her over and over again. By the time he lowered his tongue to her breast, he felt her tightening around him, her breathy sighs curling into his ear.

Her orgasm came not a second too soon. His release followed hers, though he was better than she was at monitoring the volume of his voice.

"Sorry. Loud," she panted before she kissed his ear. A shudder climbed his spine and zoomed down again.

"I hope I don't have to think in this meeting," he said. "Can't."

"Mmm. Worth it if you ask me." She kissed his cheek.

"Totally worth it." His hand on her jaw, he angled her mouth toward his when a sharp knock came at the door, followed by the jiggling of the handle.

"Helloooo? Is someone in there? We have a three o'clock for this room!"

Taylor.

Bran pegged Addi with a look. "You booked the same conference room?"

"The other rooms were booked for three o'clock!" she whispered. "I didn't, ah, think this would take that long?"

"You underestimate me." He gave her a hard kiss. "Don't let it happen again."

Taylor knocked and this time he responded. "Keep your skirt on, I'll be right there." Then to Addi, he said, "You should probably put yours on. Panties optional."

"What are you doing to me?" she asked with a smile as she scurried to redress.

He could ask her the same thing.

Addison's hands shook along with her legs. It was like she'd been submerged into a Jell-O mold.

Not only had Bran turned her on in minutes flat, but he'd done it at work. She'd been excited all day, planning her sexy surprise in the conference room. The hidden condom was wishful thinking. She hadn't counted on actual sex, which explained why she hadn't considered the piggybacked meetings.

What was with her lately? She'd gone from consummate professional to hair-blowing-in-the-wind free spirit.

But she knew what she was doing. She was testing him. How far would he let her go? How far did he *want* to go? He hadn't said no to anything she'd offered yet.

That kind of power was heady. A rush that made her feel, well, feel a lot like she felt right now, only with a teensy bit of nausea at the idea that Taylor might've overheard. Addi had *not* been quiet while having sex with Brannon.

"Ready?" He wore a cocksure smile, his hand at the ready on the door handle. So proud of himself, and who could blame him? He'd taken her to the edge in record time.

"Ready," Addi said, not sure she was. He unlocked the door as she pulled his discarded papers from the wastebasket.

"I heard some...thing..." Taylor's gaze jerked from Addi to Bran. The other woman's darker blond locks were pulled into a neat ponytail at the back of her head, her navy blue dress outlining her baby bump. She looked gorgeous and professional...and suspicious. Her eyes narrowed. "Hi, Bran. Hey, Addi."

"Hi, Taylor," Bran said, sounding much more at ease than Addi felt.

Taylor's expression was blatant approval. "Well, don't you both look amazing."

Addi bit her tongue so she wouldn't laugh. She *felt* amazing.

"Thanks. I've been working out." He smoothed his tie, which was tied *not at all* right. The bottom was a good inch or two too high. Addi ducked her head to hide a giggle, then noticed she'd buttoned her shirt wrong. "Crap!"

"I knew it. You've been too happy," Taylor said to Bran.

"First Gia, now you? What's wrong with me being happy?"

"Nothing. At all," Taylor said sincerely. "I'm happy for you. And also—" she gave him a pointed look "—I was right."

"You better not have interrupted to gloat," Bran warned as he retied his tie.

"I came in here to have a meeting. Remember?" She waggled her ThomKnox tablet. "Addi, can you join us? Bran could use a second brain. His seems to be disconnected from his vertebrae at the moment."

Bran's eyes hit Addi and warmed an incremental amount. "Stay."

Her cheeks infused with heat and she couldn't prevent her smile. The request wasn't dissimilar to what he'd said to her on a handful of nights at his place. He'd wanted her to stay then, too. And him admitting it in front of Taylor was even more significant.

Royce appeared in the doorway next, tall, regal and frowning. His usual. Bran's tie was back to normal and the buttons on Addi's blouse were even, thank God. "Everything all right in here?"

"Why wouldn't everything be all right?" Taylor asked as she settled into a chair at the head of the table.

"I don't know. Seems...strange in here." Royce took a long look at Bran before his eyes landed on Addi.

"He's learning," Taylor said to Addi. "Men become more perceptive if you teach them. It's the repetition. Like training a puppy."

Addi snorted, while Royce and Bran argued against Taylor's assessment. Then they settled down for the meeting, Addi at the very spot where she and Bran had their own "meeting" a few minutes earlier.

While Taylor spoke, Addi thought about how she'd long

dreamed of being a part of a big, loving family. And now here she was, one step closer to being folded in by the Knoxes. It was almost too much for her heart to handle.

Nineteen

By Friday morning, Bran couldn't figure out what the hell was wrong with him.

He should be in a phenomenal mood. The week had started with conference room sex, last night he'd fallen asleep next to Addi on her couch, and now they had the weekend to look forward to.

And next week was… *Fourth of July weekend.*

It suddenly dawned on him what was bothering him.

That warning bell that'd rang in Tahoe was back. He couldn't ignore it. The last time he'd ignored his gut had been when he and Taylor were dating. When he'd ordered a Tiffany & Co. diamond online.

Who ordered an engagement ring online?

A desperate guy, that's who.

There was no reason for him to freak out, which might be *why* he was freaking out. Royce and Taylor and Gia knew that Addi and Bran were dating. They didn't care. Mom and Dad were retired. They sure as hell didn't care.

The only person who seemed to have an issue was *him*.

He hadn't officially invited Addi to his parents' house at

the vineyard—and now he wondered if he shouldn't. She might not care if she went or not. Maybe a family gathering was too much too soon for both of them.

He blew out a breath of relief that brought his shoulders out from under his ears. He felt better now that he'd let himself off the hook. God, when was this day over?

He glanced at his wrist only to find, again, his watch missing. He'd left it at Addi's, he was sure of it, but every time he thought to ask her, he'd been in the middle of something else work-related. He was glad it was Friday—he needed a weekend like his next breath.

"Boxing tomorrow?" he asked Royce, poking his head into his older brother's office.

"No can do." Royce stood from his desk, his leather laptop bag in hand.

"Where the hell are you going? It's only—" Bran glanced at his wrist again before consulting the clock on the wall "—two o'clock."

"Home. I'm the CEO and I say none of us needs to stay another minute." He cocked his head, staring down Bran as if he could see through him. "Why are we boxing? Have some pent-up rage you'd like to take out on me?"

"Exercise this time, promise." Bran held up a hand and swore the truth. The last time he'd invited Royce out to his backyard boxing ring, they'd worked out some unfinished business. They'd both been feeling the pressure about who would be chosen CEO and their father had joked that they should box it out. There might also have been a come-to-Jesus talk from Bran that led to Royce breaking up with Taylor, but it all worked out in the end. Boxing had helped sort out the brotherly stuff between Royce and Bran, though.

"Everything okay?" Royce asked.

Not really, but that made no sense. "Of course. See you tomorrow."

"Yep. Have a good one."

Addi was at her desk when Bran entered their semiprivate corner. He stopped in front of her, nearly forgetting what he was going to say. Blame the low-cut top. She'd never worn low-cut tops before, unless he hadn't noticed. He was certain he would have noticed.

"I left my watch at your apartment."

"Yes. I noticed." Her tender smile reminded him of that night. She'd found a new toothbrush in her hall closet and invited him to stay over. He hadn't planned on staying, but she was so damn sweet, he hadn't been able to say no.

Come to think of it, he hadn't slept much that night. He'd laid there for a long while, mind racing, eyes watching the ceiling. Addi staying at his place had never caused that reaction, so what made him itchy about staying at hers? His head was a jumble lately—maybe he was just stressed about work.

"I'm having the battery replaced and the face cleaned," she said. "You ruined your surprise. I'll pick it up after lunch."

The warning this time was a blare. Having his watch serviced and delivered as a surprise sounded like something she'd do for a boyfriend. Boyfriends led to marriage, which led to babies. See: Taylor and Royce. Then again, they weren't even dating when Taylor discovered she was pregnant and they weren't married yet.

Bran was suddenly overly warm.

"Thanks, uh, I appreciate it." He pasted on a smile. "I'll just… be in there."

He followed his pointing finger into his office where he drew the blinds and shut the door. Then he stared at his desk for a long while.

At the beginning of this year, he was sure he was going to be the CEO of ThomKnox, that Taylor Thompson would be his fiancée. That his life was on a fast track in a known direction.

Then it went off track.

His solution? Enter the unknown. Don't worry about consequences. Stop planning his life and live it instead.

"And now you're doing nothing but thinking of the future. No wonder you're losing it." He laughed to himself as he sat and opened his laptop. "Ad's right. You are an idiot."

And even though he mentally shook it off, he couldn't get past the idea that something had changed between him and Addi. Something she knew that he didn't.

Something that was going to threaten everything he'd just decided.

Forty-seven minutes later, Bran dropped the handset of his phone on the cradle and leaned back in his chair. Scrubbing his face, he buried a yawn in his palms. A soft knock on his office door preceded Addison peeking through. He waved her in.

"That man could talk a caffeinated squirrel to sleep." He expected a laugh but all he received for his lame joke was the barest flinch of her lips. "You didn't have to wait for me."

"I—um." She handed him a black velvet bag. "I wanted to give you this. It's your watch."

He dumped the Rolex into his palm and examined the shining face. "Thank you. You didn't have to go to the trouble, but I appreciate it."

He unclasped the band and laid the watch on his wrist.

Addi sank to her knees in front of him, her eyes cautious, her smile shaky. "I wanted to ask you something."

"Whatever it is, the answer is yes." Especially if she was going to take off his pants and dive under his desk.

She let out a nervous laugh. "Oh, boy. You're not going to make this easy on me are you?"

He cupped her jaw. "I will *absolutely* make it easy for

you." Get her a pillow, move to the conference room. Anything.

Her throat moved delicately as she swallowed but her ocean-blue eyes never left his. "Brannon."

That earlier premonition pricked its ears.

"Addison," he said carefully.

"You've meant a lot to me for a long time. A long, long time. I had no idea how much more to me you could mean. This…this has been a whirlwind and I wasn't expecting it. I know you weren't expecting it. I know that right now, the last thing you're expecting is this."

Warning! Warning! Abort mission! Clear the area!

But there was nowhere for him to go.

Addison was on her knees giving him a speech. And with her earnest words bouncing around the room, there was only one way the speech would end. She wasn't offering a kinky in-office sex act, but something very, *very* different. Something he recognized, because he'd nearly attempted the same thing with Taylor, to his detriment, at the Valentine's Gala this year. A mistake he was saved from making by Taylor and Royce kissing at the gala.

Addi was about to make a similar mistake. He had to stop her before she said or did something she regretted—something she couldn't take back.

She flipped the watch over in his palm.

There, on the back of the face, was an engraving that hadn't been there before. An engraving she'd had carved into his seven-and-a-half-thousand-dollar watch. Two words, one question mark.

Marry me?

His heart hammered against his ribs like it was trying to escape. And because his mouth was dry and his tongue was welded to the roof of his mouth, he hadn't formed any words yet.

"I love you," she continued. "I'm totally and completely in love with you. I know you've had a rough year, but if I learned anything from attending Joe's celebration of life, it was that if I feel something I should say it. Before it's too late. You want to live in the moment, Brannon. So do I." She rested her hand over his and the watch and smiled. "This moment is real. It's happening. What we have is bigger than sleepovers and shared Pestle & Pepper. And by the way, can we go there for dinner because I'm *starving*?"

Her smile shook, but she glowed with happiness. With surety. She was waiting for his answer.

God. He was being proposed *to*.

He'd never seen this coming. That explained the tightening of his gut. The feeling that something was lurking just outside of his peripheral vision. He'd been wrong about her thinking of him as a boyfriend. She'd been thinking of him as a *husband*.

"You seem surprised," she said because he still hadn't thought of how to say no.

And he had to say no.

She'd gotten the wrong impression and that was his fault. He'd assumed they were operating with the same game plan, not that she'd gone rogue and created one of her own. The night he'd spent at her house flashed in his mind. Before she'd fallen asleep, she'd kissed him on the side of the mouth, her arm wrapped around his waist, and murmured "goodnight" followed by...

You're everything.

Which could mean literally *anything*...except not now. Not with a proposal engraved into the back of his watch. Now it could only mean one thing. He was everything to Addison, and while she was a lot of things to him, he simply couldn't be *everything* to anyone.

Trying to be *everything* had nearly cost him his relationship with his brother. Had left him with one hell of an identity crisis. Had taught him to take life a day at a time without scheduling every one of them in advance.

He'd taken a chance on Addi. He'd been so sure she was on his side. Not on the side of...

God.

Marriage?

He set the watch aside and grasped her hands to help her stand. He couldn't shoot her down while she was on her knees. He could barely do it now that she was standing, both her hands in his and raw hope in her expression. There wasn't any way avoiding it, so he'd have to say it. Say the truest, fairest words he could think of and then offer her an escape hatch.

"You weren't supposed to fall in love with me."

Confusion crinkled her forehead before a new emotion sent her expression careening in another direction. Fear. Sadness. Maybe a combo of the two.

"I'm so sorry, Addi. I thought we were cool with the way things were. Right now I'm not looking for—"

"Oh, no." She pulled her hands from his and rested them over her stomach.

"Listen, listen, it's okay." He rubbed his palms on her upper arms. "Here, sit in my chair."

"I can't sit. I have to leave."

"You don't have to leave, Ad." He wasn't sure how to fix this. But he had to. He needed her—here at work. And he liked her a whole hell of a lot after work, too. There was no reason to blow up everything they had just because she'd jumped the gun. "We can still go to P&P for dinner. Nothing has to change. This was a misstep, that's all." He pointed to the watch. "I'm sure they can remove the engraving."

"A misstep," she repeated, not sounding convinced.

"One I'm familiar with. I know how you feel—"

"You have no idea how I feel. Did you hear anything I said to you?"

"I heard every word." She loved him. It was a gift. But the other thing… The proposal… "But, Addi, I can't marry anyone right now."

"Say what you mean, Bran. You can't marry *me*."

He didn't know if he'd *never* marry Addison, but well, hell, he didn't want to plan that far out.

"I've been off course for most of the year," he said, attempting to explain. "Normally, I don't get wrapped up in the thrill of the chase. I don't want to win to say I won. And yet, CEO came up for grabs and that's exactly what I did. Before our trip to Tahoe, I swore to myself I wasn't going to do that again. Not ever. I've been free-falling with you, Addi. It wasn't about landing you and letting you go. I was the one who asked to extend the trip, remember?"

As her eyes flooded with tears, he realized that this wasn't mostly his fault. This was one hundred percent his fault. "And then I asked you to continue once we were home." And then he'd invited her to stay the night again and again. "I didn't mean for you to take this as me wanting more. I'm sorry."

His apology lit her temper on fire. Anger reddened her face. "You never wanted more than sex."

"No!" Hell, that wasn't what he meant. Not really. "Well, sort of. It sounds bad when you say it."

"I've been in love with you since I started working here," she snapped, a fat tear perched on the edges of her eyelashes. "I was in the process of trying to fall out of love with you. But you wouldn't let me compartmentalize after one night in Tahoe. *You* were the one who wanted more, Bran," she added quietly. "You might not have made promises with your words, but your body painted a future with me in it. And now you're telling me I wasn't supposed to fall in love with you? What is it you thought we were doing?"

"I thought I'd finally found someone who understood me." His voice raised an octave. "I wasn't promising you anything. I was living my life one day at a time, which, by the way, is the lesson you should have learned from Joe."

Her head jerked on her neck. A quiet voice warned him not to keep talking. He ignored it.

"If your friend had lived his life to the fullest, he'd have kissed you long and hard, before you knew what was happening. And then you would have told him no and broken his heart. And then—" Bran sighed, hating hurting her. Hating watching that tear tumble out of her eye and knowing there was no way to undo this horrible situation. "You would've had to give him a similar speech to the one I'm giving you now.

"You mean a lot to me, Ad. We work together well here and we are incredible at home—at either of our homes. You're not convenient. You're not a pastime. I still want you. Just not like this."

She shook off his hold, grabbed the watch off his desk and dropped it into his mug of coffee with a *bloop*.

"Fuck you," she added before rushing out of his office.

Shocked and incensed, he grabbed the coffee mug and followed her. "What did you expect? *What?*"

Her eyes darted around behind him but he didn't care who was overhearing him.

"For us to get married and live happily-ever-after?"

"What was *your* plan? For us to have sex and keep our hearts out of it?" she countered.

"I don't want a plan."

She lifted her chin with determination. "No problem. I won't be here to make any plans for you or with you. I quit."

She lifted her laptop and dropped it unceremoniously

into the trash can next to her desk, then pulled her purse over her shoulder.

"Have fun running ThomKnox *without a plan*!" she shouted as she stormed by him.

He let her go, growling under his breath and not sure who he was more pissed off with—himself or Addison. Or maybe he could blame Joe. That'd been a good move.

"Dammit, Addi."

He fished his watch from the coffee and dried it off with his tie. It was waterproof. She should have known that. She should've known a lot of things, but she didn't. He'd talked her out of practical, and apparently had fully won her over to his way of thinking.

Because she was in love with him.

But he wasn't denying who he was or what he wanted—not again. He'd followed someone else's dreams before and where had that gotten him?

This was Addi's dream. She wanted *him* more than anything, or had before he'd turned her down. He was honored. He was floored. But he couldn't say yes, even though saying no meant incinerating the best relationship of his life.

He took one last long look at the engraving on his watch before dropping it into the wastebasket on top of Addison's laptop computer.

If she didn't understand why he'd said no, or appreciate his honesty, then they were better off apart.

Twenty

Addison inhaled deeply, intent on appreciating the scent of her recent purchase. Nothing smelled as heavenly as "new car." Unfortunately that scent also reminded her of Bran's sports car and the trip to Tahoe.

But of course.

She'd spent the weekend car shopping, and while agreeing to a five-year loan wasn't the most intelligent move now that she was jobless, purchasing the car had made her feel better. Or at least more independent.

Anyway, she wasn't broke right away. She had a savings account and she'd been in this exact position before. Each time she'd been out of work, she'd found more work. Although she'd given notice at each of those places and in this case, there was no way she could work through a notice. There was no way she could face Brannon Knox again.

She loved him.

He'd used her.

Things hadn't only ended, they'd ended very badly. There was no recovering from a botched proposal. Apparently, Bran was reserving the love he had to give for a special occasion. And him turning her down had made her feel very *un*special.

Not that it mattered. She was heading to the copy center to print her résumé since she didn't own a printer. All her personal printing was previously done at work.

Soon she'd have a new job—a different job—and before she accepted the job, she was going to make sure her boss was a curmudgeonly, unattractive old guy with no sense of humor. She wasn't going to make the same mistake twice.

Yeah, right. Because you fall in love with all your bosses...

No. Just one.

One she'd wanted to build a life with. She'd talked herself into proposing, so sure that Bran would realize his dream from earlier in the year was meant to be with Addison instead of Taylor. He'd wanted a family—he'd said so himself. Addi wanted a family. They were compatible. They were right for each other.

But she hadn't given him a single moment's warning before she popped the question. What a disaster.

Her cell phone rang from her purse as she pulled onto the highway. Before she could dig through her bag to find it the screen on her dashboard announced the caller's name: Brannon Knox.

She reached for the Decline button as a car nearly swerved into her. She gripped the wheel, moved safely out of the way...and accidentally hit the green Answer button instead.

Shit, shit, shit!

She tried to find the End Call button in between watching the road but didn't succeed.

A second later Bran's voice filled her car. "Addi?"

"Hi. You're on speakerphone. I don't know how to operate this thing."

He offered a dry laugh. "I wondered why you picked up."

She angled for the next exit with the office supply store logo on the sign.

"It's Monday. You should be here. I pulled your laptop out of the trash."

Coming into ThomKnox would only solve one problem. A monetary one.

"I'm not coming back, Brannon."

"Why not?"

"Are you serious?" How could he ask her that? "Because... I mean. Honestly? I'm humiliated."

"Yeah, I can relate. I'm also a member of the recently-rejected club."

"You didn't propose. And you didn't love Taylor. She didn't love you. Your heart wasn't involved, Bran. You said so yourself." Their situation was nothing like Bran and Addi's. Hot tears pooled in her eyes as she pulled into the practically empty parking lot of the office supply store. She parked in the back, her eyes on the big red logo. Maybe they were hiring.

"Marriage is a big step," was all he said.

"I know that. One you were willing to take in order to land a raise but not when the woman you're sleeping with professes her feelings for you. I thought you loved me, too. Obviously, or I never would have asked."

"I know." He sounded miserable. "I'm sorry for bringing up Joe. I was out of line."

"I'm sorry I proposed to you," she said, frustrated by his clinical tone. "It wasn't appropriate work behavior."

"Don't do this, Addison. You have a place here. You belong here. I can't do this without you."

She'd thought something similar when she stormed out on Friday. That she couldn't *live* without him.

Know what she figured out? She could.

It hurt. It hurt like hell and she was going to love him for a long, long time, but pulling herself up by her proverbial bootstraps was nothing new for her. Her parents' love came with strings, and she'd done without their manipulation for years.

"You know, I was fine with a one-night stand." She swiped at the tears running down her cheeks, angry that she was so emotional.

"You were not."

"Don't be a pompous ass."

"You tried to be someone you weren't," he argued. "I recognize that quality well. You were trying to *pretend* you were fine with a one-night stand."

"And what were you doing?"

"Enjoying myself! What the hell is wrong with everyone? Why can't we hang out and work together and have amazing sex?" He lowered his voice like someone might overhear. "Listen. This isn't why I called. I called because I made a mistake."

Her heart—her stupid heart—leaped with hope.

"Remember when I asked you what you were doing for the Fourth of July? I had a plan in mind, but I talked myself out of it. I didn't want anyone to pressure us into becoming something we're not. Come with me to my family's cookout on Saturday. They'd love to see you and you could use the reminder of why you liked it here. Let's fix this. You're an integral part of ThomKnox. I don't want you to work anywhere else."

What a profession! He would love for her to come work with him and his family sure liked her, too. Her heart broke into a thousand pieces hearing the impassioned, incredible man she'd fallen for compartmentalize their relationship so thoroughly.

"And then what?" she asked with a sniff. "Am I allowed to kiss you? To come home with you? To sleep with you?"

"There are no rules. We're taking this a day at a time,

not crafting a future everyone else wants. I know why you proposed."

Because she loved him. Duh.

"You feel alone and unloved," he answered for her. "You are not alone. You have me, my family. You have your job. You don't have to orchestrate a wedding to fulfill a need your family failed to supply."

Her tears dried in the heat of her rage.

"You think this was about me not wanting to be alone?" As she said the words, she only grew angrier. "You think I was filling the hole in my heart with a *marriage*?"

There was a slight pause before Bran said, "Yeah. I do."

"I proposed because I'm in love with you. Because I had a glimpse of a future with you in it." Bran and her and their three children. "You have your head so far up your ass with this 'live in the now' credo that you don't see what's right in front of you! You said there were no rules, but you lied. I broke a very big one when I asked you for more. I won't live another moment feeling way too much for someone who gives me so little. Goodbye, Brannon."

She tapped the End Call button on the screen and stared straight ahead. Outside the window, the giant storefront blurred as she blinked away more tears. They'd probably never end at this rate.

"I won't be told how I feel or what I want. Not by anyone," she said to herself. She refused to feel bad about being transparent. About being herself. She was a treasure. A prize. A goddamn rare find. If he couldn't see that, then the only mistake she'd made was letting him talk her into bed in the first place.

He wanted to live in the now? Well, he was going to have to live with the consequences of not planning for his future.

As for her, she had her own future to plan for. One without him in it.

She blotted her face with a tissue and pressed on some

powder. Before she stepped out of her new car, she smiled at her reflection in the rearview mirror. Not great, but it would do.

She was capable of being everything she needed in life. She'd practiced at it enough. This misstep wouldn't slow her down.

Heavy, she trudged into the store, her "you go, girl" speech feeling more and more false with every step.

The truth of the matter was, she wasn't angry at Brannon for not loving her any more than Joe wasn't angry with her for not loving him. She was angry at herself for not reading the signs, for not proceeding with caution, for *not* making a plan.

She should have known better.

From now on, she would.

Twenty-One

Brannon's temporary assistant was sweet, showed up on time and had neat handwriting. She'd also forgotten to remind him about his conference call on Wednesday and he'd missed it. She'd delayed in handing him his messages, and today he'd put off having lunch with an important client until next week to help wade through them.

He missed Addison.

For reasons that far outnumbered professional ones.

"See you, Peg," he said to his new assistant. She was pulling on a light jacket and waved, her desk cluttered and disorganized.

"See you Monday, Mr. Knox."

Not a chance.

He'd have to find another temp in the interim. He'd made attempts all week to woo Addi back to work. She must have figured out her Bluetooth because he was unsuccessful reaching her on the phone again. He'd had P&P delivered to her front door, had sent flowers and candy and fruit, every one of them arriving with a version of the same note: *Come back to work. We need you.*

If he could talk her into sitting behind her desk again, everything else would work out. He knew it. He couldn't think without her here, let alone examine how he'd been feeling in the week since he'd touched her. Kissed her.

He missed her like crazy.

He wanted her in his bed and in his world. She belonged here. She loved it here. Why was she being so stubborn?

On his way to the elevator, he was intercepted by Royce.

"Are you going straight to the vineyard from here?" Royce asked. "Taylor and I are staying the night."

"That's the plan." Bran didn't feel like celebrating but he didn't want his parents and siblings talking about him. And if he wasn't there—they would. He didn't want anyone worrying about his state of mind or well-being. He was a grown man, dammit.

They stepped inside the elevator and Royce pressed the lobby button. "Is Addi coming?"

"No, she's, uh. Busy." Ignoring him, but still.

"You know no one bought your bullshit excuse about her finding another job, right? You two split up, didn't you?"

"Yes, but it's fixable." Bran had no idea how to fix it, but he was working on it. She was going to come back. She had to. "We need her here."

Royce remained stoically silent during the short walk from the building to their executive parking spots. "See you there," were the last words his brother spoke before he backed out of the lot and left. Before Bran could follow suit, his sister shouted from behind him.

He turned to find Gia in tall high-heeled shoes jogging after him, a weekender bag in hand. "Can I ride with you? Are you going straight there?"

"Yes, actually. You mean you don't want to carpool with Jayson?"

"Assumptions," she reminded him.

"Get in." He didn't have the energy to argue and she was already climbing into the car anyway.

During the hour-and-a-half drive north, she finally pulled her wireless headphones from her ears and faced him.

"I know the last thing you want to do is talk about it, but for the record I told you Addison was in love with you. You didn't listen."

"Congratulations," he grumbled, turning up the radio.

She turned it off. "Did you really not see a proposal coming?"

"How—how did you…?" How the hell did she know about that?

"The watch," she answered. "I saw it in your lap drawer. I was looking for a sticky note to leave you a message."

"I knew I should have left it in the wastebasket."

"You didn't!"

"Who else knows?" He slid her a glare.

"Come on. You know me. I'm assuming that's the real reason she left? Because she proposed and you said no?"

"You've always been the smart one."

"What a gesture." She smiled softly. "That was really sweet."

"Addison has a huge heart."

"Why'd you say no?"

He chuffed and this time watched her for a beat before watching the road again. "Are you serious? You think I should have agreed to marry her?"

"Why not?" Gia shrugged.

"Uh, hello, my divorced sister. Don't you have a list of reasons why *not* to marry?"

"Jayson and I are different." She waved a hand. "Stop changing the subject. Just because my marriage didn't work out doesn't mean I don't want you and Royce to be happy. Don't you love her?"

"Love is a big word with a lot of bigger consequences, Gia. I don't understand this need to label and define everything. Why can't Addi and I just be together? Be present in the moment?"

"Because, you jackass, being 'in the moment' leads to a future," his sister said as he pulled into their parents' driveway. "People are who they are. You can't cordon off only the parts of them you want. And you shouldn't."

Bran sighed, tired. "All I know is that being around her made me happy."

"Yeah. I know that, too." She touched his hand. "Sorry, bro. It's hard for a lot of people to compartmentalize. Except for me. I handle that like a boss."

"You are the coolest," he said, meaning it.

His mom and dad had hired caterers and the entire open-air patio smelled like grilled meat and veggies. Once the family table was set, Bran lifted his beer to another of his father's toasts.

"My family," Jack said. "I love you all."

Royce sent Bran a bland look that Bran mimicked. Their father so enjoyed grandstanding. While he went on and on about how much he adored the legacy he was building and the great role his family played in it, Bran took a look around the table.

His father and his mother, Macy. Royce and Taylor. Gia and Jayson, even though they weren't together, were sitting next to each other.

If Addison hadn't been so damn stubborn, she could have been a part of this. Isn't that what she claimed she wanted? To be part of a big, loving family? It hadn't been easy for him to call her and offer her a seat at this table tonight, but he'd done it. For her.

Evidently she wanted all or nothing. He didn't understand. Wasn't some better than none? He hadn't landed

CEO, and as a result, found that the role of president suited him better. If Addi would open up to the possibility of having some of what she asked for, she could have almost everything she wanted. Sometimes almost was as close as you got.

Frustrated, Bran excused himself from the table, taking his wineglass and half a bottle of cabernet sauvignon with him. He tracked to the stone firepit at the edge of the hill overlooking acres and acres of vineyards.

The sun was waning, the air chilling. He refilled his glass and plopped down in the grass to watch it disappear completely.

"What's up, man?" came Jayson's low voice a minute later.

"I'm not sharing," Bran told him, eyes on the sunset.

"Brought my own." Jayson settled next to him and rested a bottle of wine on the edge of the firepit. It would be a good night to light it. The air was brisk up here.

"What happened, Coop? Did you draw the short straw?" Bran took a swig of wine.

"Are you kidding? No one wants to talk to you when you're moping."

"I'm not moping. I wanted to be alone. There's a difference."

"Yeah, I recognize the difference." Jayson chuckled. "If you haven't noticed, Gia and I have a turbulent but amicable relationship since the divorce. But it took a while to get there."

Bran turned to ask him what his point was, but Jayson was studying the sky.

"Before we could get to the zen state which we find ourselves in now, she and I had to admit how we felt about each other before the divorce. We were in love when we were married. And we had every intention of making it work. After the divorce, we were angry. Would have been easier to say we never loved each other. In other words, it would have been easier to *lie*."

"Is there a point to this diatribe?"

Jayson turned his head. "If you want Addison back in any capacity, you have to be honest with her."

"Gia told you. I should have known."

"Spouses don't count."

"You're not a spouse."

"I was. I'm grandfathered in. No getting rid of me." He grinned. "Addison proposed and you turned her down."

Thanks, Gia. A whole hell of a lot.

"I was honest with her." Bran could not believe he was explaining this again. "She was on her knees in front of me, pouring her heart out." She told him she loved him. She painted a picture of family and future. She'd been honest and transparent. "I hated telling her no, but I had to tell her the truth. And she hates me for it."

Jayson kept his gaze on the vineyards below, the dark rows and their shadows stretching in the waning light. "Is that why she hates you? Or is it because you lied to her about how you were feeling? Did you take a single second to absorb what she was saying to you?"

It was like his ex-brother-in-law was begging for a fist-fight. "Did I take a moment to absorb she was asking me to marry her?"

"Yeah. Did you soak in the professions she dropped at your feet while she was on her knees? Sounds like she was vulnerable, and you were an asshole."

Jaw welded shut, Bran spoke through his teeth. "I'm sure that's the way she saw it. Hence her quitting."

"How *do* you feel about her? Did you feel anything for her at all? Or were you passing the time?"

"I'm not sure why everyone makes that sound like such a bad thing. What is there but time? And we're here on Earth for a relatively short period of it," he said, liking this line of argument. It felt sensible. And making sense felt good. "Maybe I won't wake up tomorrow morning. Maybe this wine's gone bad and I'll die in my sleep." They raised their glasses and took long swigs, tempting fate. "Doesn't it say something that I chose to spend each day with her?"

"Oh, so she should be grateful."

"I was." The honesty of those words shook him. "I was really damn grateful to have her in my life. I learned all these things about her I didn't know. We had a lot more in common than I thought. She sees the Knoxes as some kind of dream family. I don't know, I think she was trying to surround herself with us."

"Are you that unlovable? I doubt she would have proposed unless she was over the moon for you." Jayson narrowed his eyes. "I don't see it. But I know what she means about your family. Why do you think I never left?"

"Maybe she was caught up." Bran shook his head, his mind back on the conversations they'd had. When the night was quiet and their voices were the only sounds in the room. They'd been naked in more ways than one. "I gave her the wrong idea."

"Or the right one. I don't think you've thought it through yet."

"I don't want to marry anyone, Coop."

"But she isn't anyone. She's Addison Abrams. The woman who turned you from an egotistical, hustling boar into a guy I used to hang out with a lot more often."

Bran frowned.

"You were a dick this year." Jayson leveled him with a look.

"Thanks a lot."

"And then you weren't. The right woman can bring out your best. How did she take the no?"

"She was devastated," Bran said before he thought about it. He remembered the acute pain in her eyes when he attempted to let her down easy. Devastated was a great description. "And pissed off."

"Broke her heart. I did that once." Jayson looked over his shoulder at Gia. "What were you thinking when she asked?"

"What do you think I was thinking?" Bran raked a hand through his hair. "I was agonizing over bringing her here. Worried that bringing her to a family event would be putting too much pressure on us. I had no idea she was thinking of—Cooper, what would I do with a wife?"

Using Bran's shoulder as leverage, Jayson stood, his smile evident in the grainy, fading light.

"Love her." Jayson slapped Bran's shoulder. "And hope for the best."

Twenty-Two

After a week of ignoring Bran's repeated attempts to woo her back to work, Addi decided to give her friend Carey a call. One, for emotional support, and two, was Carey's company hiring? Over a lunch at a Mexican restaurant in Palo Alto, Addi learned that no, they weren't hiring. At least she could count on her friend to be there for her emotionally. Carey might well be the only person left.

"I know you're proud, but if you need money..." Carey was saying.

"No, no! That's not why I invited you out. I'm not flat broke." Not yet. Even though the car purchase had put a healthy dent in her savings account.

"I can't believe you quit. You love ThomKnox." Carey's eyes widened. "Oh, no. It's your boss. Who you were sleeping with. He screwed it up, didn't he?"

Addi nodded, swallowing past a lump in her throat. "He did. That's the other reason I wanted to talk to you. You're my person."

Carey's hand landed on hers. "Of course I am! Lay it on me."

All Addi had to do was make it through the story with as few tears as possible. Easy peasy. "The reason I'm not working at ThomKnox any longer is because I quit. And the reason I quit is because I proposed to Brannon Knox." She felt the tears well in her eyes despite her trying to dam them. "He said no."

"Oh, honey."

Addi shared about the watch and the proposal given from her knees. Then she shared that Bran had helped her stand and told her what amounted to *let's forget this ever happened.*

"I don't know if I'm more humiliated that I proposed, or more humiliated that I love him and he feels nothing for me."

"You don't know that."

"I do, actually. He's been texting and sending flowers and P&P takeout."

"That's sweet." Carey cooed, but promptly covered her lips with one hand when Addi shook her head.

"He wants his assistant back. Although I'm sure he would appreciate more sex in the conference room." Addi ate a chip. She was so miserable her taste buds were on strike. It tasted like salted cardboard. "I was caught up," she admitted.

"Babe. *Of course* you were caught up! You were in a relationship."

"Not according to him." According to Bran, they were in a live-in-the-moment sex-a-thon. "Sex changed nothing for him and everything for me. I thought we were building a life."

"You acted from the heart. That's never wrong. It's not your fault he's emotionally crippled." Carey paused to order another margarita for each of them. "Never hold back. Follow your heart. Joe didn't follow his heart, and don't you wish he would've? If you would've told him you didn't want to date him, he would've known how you felt about him."

"Funny, Bran brought up Joe, too. He said if Joe would have confessed how much he loved me, I would have had to turn him down the same way Bran turned me down."

"And Joe would have accepted it *because* he loved you." Carey's mouth twisted to the side. "What a catch twenty-two."

Carey was right. She didn't know Joe, but Addi had told her a lot about him. Addi could easily picture the scene Carey painted. Him telling Addi how much he loved her, and her letting him down gently. He would've joked and said he never expected a yes anyway. He would've let her off the hook.

The same way Bran was trying to let her off the hook now.

The reality hit her with such a suddenness, she felt dizzy.

"Bran doesn't love me," she said as a fresh margarita was set in front of her. "And I'm punishing him because he didn't say yes. That's as unfair as if Joe would've hated me for not loving him back. And he wouldn't have. He *didn't*. He probably kept his feelings to himself to spare mine." Oh, Joe.

It's okay, sweetheart, Joe said in her head.

"Is it better to know or not know?" Addi asked Carey.

"To know."

Carey was right. Addi was better off knowing that Bran didn't want to marry her. She could've gone another year aching for him and waiting for him to ask *her*.

"You know what? I'm going back to work. I can't leave the work I love because he didn't want to marry me. That'd be as bad as him firing me if I didn't sleep with him. Being independent doesn't have to mean burning down every bridge from your past."

Even if it did seem to mean being alone.

She thought of her relationship with her parents and how rough things had been. After she left here, she was going to pay them a visit. What if they'd been reading each other wrong this whole time? What if there was healing around the corner? What if one conversation where no one held back would finally clear the air? And if her parents felt the same way as they always had, that, too, would be an answer.

Knowing *was* better.

"I have the perfect job with an amazing company. And I spent a really great month with a really great guy," Addi said. The silver lining was there, even if it hurt to think about it.

"That's very mature of you." Carey's eyebrows bent with sympathy. "You don't have to be okay right away, you know."

"I'm not." Addi gave her friend a brittle smile. "But I will be. I'm strong. I'm professional. I'm practical." It was her heart that was *im*practical and *un*professional.

If Bran was willing to let the whole proposal thing go and invite her back to work, and after she'd dropped a big F-you at his feet, she'd be crazy not to accept his offer.

She'd been out in the real world, and knew she could find another job. But ThomKnox was more than a job. It was a passion.

So she and Bran weren't going to be married and live happily ever after. That didn't mean she had to forgo her professional future at ThomKnox.

Monday morning, Bran stepped into the office, half expecting Peggy the temp to be there in spite of him canceling her contract last week.

Maybe that's why he wasn't surprised to see someone standing at Addison's desk. But he hadn't expected a trim, beautiful blonde wearing a teal green dress. Her hair was down. Sleek and straight and brushing her shoulders. She turned her head and saw him and he froze in his tracks.

It was the first full breath he'd taken since she left. The first time he felt a sliver of hope that she might not hate him.

"Addi." It wasn't much of a greeting, but he couldn't think of a single other thing to say. He'd been trying to bribe and beg her to come back, and here she was. "What are you doing here?"

She'd told him to fuck off. She'd quit. And the day he called her to explain himself, he'd been a bigger ass than he had the day she proposed.

She came out from behind the desk and smoothed her hands over her dress. She looked so soft and touchable, and he wanted to touch her. Touch her and reassure her that he didn't mean any of what he said last week, except the part about wanting her to come back.

"Unless you've changed your mind since last week, I would like to resume my position as your executive assistant," she said, her mouth firm. "Maybe in the future I can find another position within ThomKnox, but for now, if you'll agree, I can work with you until you find my replacement."

He didn't want a replacement. At this desk or by his side.

"The point is," she continued, as beautiful and brave as he'd ever seen her, "I can't leave the best job I've ever had. Or the best family I've ever worked for. Are you willing to forget everything that happened and move on?"

Absolutely not. He didn't want to forget it. He wanted to revel in it.

After he'd spoken to Jayson after dinner, Bran had lain in the guest bedroom of his parents' house, wide awake. Anger, frustration and guilt took turns throwing punches until he gave up on sleep and climbed out of bed. He went back outside to sit in the same spot he was in before, but this time, stars dotted the dark sky and the twisting grapevines were gnarled fingers reaching from the ground.

What was he afraid of?

Addison had handed over her heart, so bold, and he'd been a total pussy. And he'd continued trying to stuff her into the limited space he'd reserved for their relationship when they expanded far past it. The sex was fun but it was also so much more. They'd laid out their hearts and dreams to each other. Addi was right when she accused him of making promises with his body. He had.

He'd sat on that patch of grass until the sun rose over the vineyards the next morning. Only then did he stumble inside and make coffee, greeting his siblings and parents with a hazy "good morning." The conclusion he'd come to in those hours alone made him sick and hopeful at the same time.

He'd fallen in love with Addison Abrams, and he hadn't even known it.

He'd decided a long time ago what love looked like but nothing in his immediate world matched the picture in his head. He'd never imagined being proposed to, assuming he'd be the one down on one knee. He'd be the one delivering the big speech and the profession of love.

Addison had ripped the rug from under his feet and he'd fallen on his ass. When she asked him to marry her, he wasn't ready. And what really threw him off was that if she hadn't asked, he might *never* have been ready. If she'd let them continue to be the underdeveloped version of themselves, they could have gone on the way they were for months. *Years.* What a loss that would have been.

As hard as he'd fought against planning anything in life, he'd done it anyway. Not making a decision *was* a decision. Not having a goal was, in its own way, a goal. Declaring that him and Addison were one thing meant they couldn't be more.

"I had a great time with you, Brannon." Her voice was small, tender. Her eyes weren't tear-filled, but they reflected the anguish he knew she'd suffered. "I don't regret it. Not any of it."

It was killing him to see her like this. He wanted to kiss her. Scoop her into his arms and apologize for every dumb thing he'd done since their shared road trip. Tell her that he didn't hold her at fault, but he held her in his heart and wanted nothing more than to hold her in his arms.

"I haven't changed my mind about wanting you," he said, but the moment she frowned, he hurriedly added, "here at work."

Damn. This was hard. It'd taken a lot for her to be so vulnerable with him—so honest. Now that he knew how he felt about her, admitting it was downright terrifying. He could blurt out everything and be shot down, which, arguably, he deserved. She'd bared her heart before and he'd stomped on it.

He swiped his brow, nervous for the first time in a very long time. Facing a live tiger while nude in the jungle would be less frightening.

"Great. I'll just…get started unless anything has changed in the week I've been gone?" She hesitated, giving him an opening, but the timing was off, so he addressed her question.

"Peg probably left you a pile of emails to sort through. And I answered some of them personally."

"You didn't." Addi's lips pulled down at the sides. "I'll have to do damage control."

She was joking. She was here. She was back. It was everything he thought he wanted. Only now that he'd quieted down to give his heart room to talk, he realized he didn't want her like this. He wanted everything she'd give him. He wanted the original vision of him in his head. *He* wanted to be the one to propose. To give a speech. To profess his love for *her*.

The phone on her desk rang and she answered it, lowering into her chair as she did. She hung up a moment later, having already slid back into her efficient pre-sleeping-with-him self.

"Did you want to review your schedule for the week?"

"Actually, there's something I have to do. Can we postpone?" What was a few more minutes when soon, if she agreed, they'd have the rest of their lives?

"No problem."

She began reorganizing her desk and he headed back to his office and shut the door. On his desk sat his watch. He'd had every intention of having the words she'd engraved onto it filed off, and then selling it to the jeweler. Thank God he hadn't.

Now a different impulse came. One that was risky and bold—every bit as brave as what Addison had done.

Or stupid.

He'd nearly proposed once before and narrowly avoided the mistake of his life. But now... He watched out of his window as Addi picked up the phone and held it to her ear. She sent him a professional smile and quickly averted her eyes.

Now he was going to propose to the right woman.

He could only pray that what he had in mind would be enough to win her back. If not...

Well, if not, he'd keep trying. The future mattered as much as the moment. The mistakes made had been his and had brought them here, to a future he *didn't* want.

When she hung up, he pressed the intercom button on his phone.

"Yes?" she answered.

"Let's catch up on what you missed over dinner. I was thinking Pestle & Pepper if that's okay with you?"

"Uh—okay."

"I'll have to meet you there. I have a lot to do today—none of which is on your calendar." What he had to do didn't exist until he'd seen her at the office. Before then, his goal this week had been to try her again on the phone. To text her. To deliver flowers personally and then serenade her from her front stoop if he had to.

Now that he was looking at his watch, he had a better idea. A *bigger* idea. And it'd better work. For both their sakes.

For the future.

For their forever.

She deserved no less.

Twenty-Three

Beautiful girl, you can do hard things.

Like having a professional work dinner with Brannon Knox on her first full workday after she returned to Thom-Knox since proposing marriage to him.

Sure thing. No problem.

She was trying desperately to compartmentalize him, and work, and now that she'd entered Pestle & Pepper, she was determined to enjoy her damn self. There was a lot to be grateful for. Whenever she needed to feel loved, all she had to do was step foot into this warmly lit restaurant, be greeted by Mars's infectious smile and order her favorite meal.

As if on cue, the owner, Mars, appeared around the corner like he'd sensed her. Round with heft showing he enjoyed his own cooking a great deal, he embraced her in a bear hug. She hugged him back, reminding herself that red eyes and a snotty nose was no way to greet her friend. Plus, Bran would be here any moment. She refused to let him see her in pieces.

"Your favorite corner booth," Mars said as he walked

her to the back of the restaurant. She liked being close to the kitchen, where she could hear the clatter of pans and Mars's big voice. "We've missed you. Brannon Knox has been ordering takeout in your absence. Are you two sharing all those meals he's having delivered?"

A safe assumption, but sadly...

"No." She hated seeing her friend's face droop with worry, so she added, "But he had quite a few of them delivered to me. They were delicious and amazing, of course. I'm meeting him here tonight, by the way. For work."

"For work." Mars sighed and took the seat across from her in the booth. "I'm sorry, love. That's a shame."

"Yes, it is."

Mars nodded solemnly. "I will send out a special dessert for you. You can enjoy it while you wait."

"Oh, that's not necessary."

"You're my best taste-tester," He peered at her over a small pair of wire-framed glasses, his eyes filled with wisdom and love. "It's necessary."

It was nice to have someone care about her this much. Tired of her own melancholy, she said, "I actually do have good news."

"Oh?" Pausing at the end of the table, Mars waited.

"I visited my parents and we had a long, long talk." She'd once told Mars he was like a surrogate father. When he asked if her father had passed, she said no, and told him a truncated version of her family drama. Since then, he'd proudly referred to himself as Papa Mars. "They want me to be more goal-oriented, but they love me. They're worried about me. They want the best for me."

"They sound like good parents to me." He gripped her shoulder and gave it a squeeze. "Dessert first. I insist."

She nodded and he hustled away.

She'd settled in at ThomKnox with little fanfare today. Other than a visit from Royce and Taylor and later, Gia, the Knoxes welcomed her back like she'd never left. It was a huge blessing. That was the part of her work her parents didn't see. She wanted to be part of a team. She wanted to matter. At ThomKnox, she did. They needed her—even if Bran didn't.

But she couldn't ask for more than he was willing to give. She understood that now. The next time her heart ran away with her brain like the dish with the spoon, she'd first have a conversation with the man she was dating to make sure he loved her *back* before she proposed.

A server delivered a glass of water while she kept an eye on the front door for her boss, a man she used to have dinner with followed by sweaty, delicious, naked time.

She couldn't regret the time she'd spent with him, though. Life was a series of highs and lows, and even if what she and Bran shared was destined to end badly, she'd do it all over again. Loving Bran might well be part of her DNA. There was no removing it, so the only option left was learning to live with it.

"Dessert." Mars settled a small, white ramekin in front of her with the addition of a glass of white wine. "Chocolate mousse with a surprise inside. I can't come up with a name for it, though, so think about it for me, yeah?"

The chocolate dessert was topped with two strawberry slices in the shape of a heart and dusted with a delicate coating of powdered sugar. "It's too pretty to eat."

"Don't tell my guest chef that. This is his first creation. But be honest," he added, his tone low and serious. "Honesty is best."

Mars was staring at her so she nodded her promise. "I will."

Before she could lift her spoon, a figure appeared from the front door. Silhouetted in sunlight, Brannon Knox approached. God, he was beautiful and…wearing a tux?

At the table, he stood over her in, yes, a full tuxedo, his

face partially obscured by a black mask. The same outfit he'd worn to the masquerade ball.

"What…are you doing?"

"May I sit?" he asked.

"O-of course." She stared at him, fairly certain he'd lost his mind. A few other patrons at P&P watched him with curious smiles.

"This was better in my head," he said, removing the mask and setting it aside. His tentative smile made her heart leap. She ignored that leap. Her heart had caused enough trouble already.

"This past spring, I learned the hard way you can't make a future happen that isn't meant to be," he said. "I was angling and strategizing for CEO. Plotting. Planning. *Scheming.* I made a lot of mistakes. A lot of very wrong assumptions. I never want to do that again."

She wished he'd stop talking. She wanted to reach over the table and stuff her napkin into his mouth. She'd already come to this conclusion. She'd made a lot of wrong assumptions about him, and about her future, too. If he was trying to explain why he turned down her proposal, she could do without the fanfare.

"You didn't agree to come to the vineyard over Fourth of July weekend, and to be honest, I'm glad you weren't there."

Well. This was just getting better and better.

"Bran—"

"Let me finish." He held out a hand.

She quieted, but didn't know how much more she could take.

"I have been moving forward without ceasing since everything blew up in my face a few months ago. I didn't want my past to catch up with me. I didn't want the future to come, and then you proposed."

She winced.

"I wanted to stop you before you said or did something

you'd regret, but I wasn't fast enough. You forced me to turn you down, Ad."

"I know, okay? I know!" She lowered her voice when a couple at the next table turned to stare. "I screwed up. Just like you. We're the same. Go us. Can we *please* stop talking about this?" she whispered.

His crooked smile flooded her chest with the love she still felt for him. Even being shot down again, she couldn't stop loving him.

"I owe you an apology."

"You don't," she was quick to say. She couldn't let him do this. Every next thing he said was bringing her closer to tears. She didn't want to revisit any of this. "You were right about moving on. When you suggested forgetting what happened."

"I *can't* forget. More important, I don't want to. It took not having you in my arms for me to realize that I fell in love with you, too, Addi. That nauseous sick feeling I had when I was telling you no? That was my gut screaming at me that I was making a mistake. I was losing you in real time and there was no way of stopping it. There is no moving forward without you—not if I ever want to be happy again."

Dumbfounded, she blinked. He—what?

"I'm sorry for ignoring the love right in front of me," he continued. "And I'm sorry for my reaction when you proposed. When you offered me everything and I acted as if it was nothing." He kept those bourbon-colored eyes on hers, regret swimming in their depths. "If you forgive me, I'll spend the rest of my life loving you so hard you'll never feel alone again."

He folded his hands on the table, his tux jacket sleeve sliding up and revealing the Rolex she'd engraved. She stared some more. He waited in silence.

Her brain scrambled to put the puzzle pieces together

between what she believed he'd been thinking and what he'd *actually* been thinking.

Amazing how wrong she could be twice.

"And if I don't forgive you?" she finally managed, because that was really the question, wasn't it? If this was an ultimatum, there had to be a flip side.

"Then you can look forward to ideas a lot stupider than me wearing a tux and masquerade ball mask to dinner, because I'll never stop fighting for you, Ad. Never."

Warmth filled her chest and flooded her face. It was everything she wanted and the man she loved more than anything was offering it to her.

"Part of living in the now is doing what's right in the moment." Bran reached for her spoon and dunked it into the mousse, coming out with a string attached to what looked like...*oh, God.*

He tugged the string until a chocolate-covered ring appeared from the dessert. A ring with a diamond in the center, and it wasn't a small diamond.

He dipped the chocolate-covered jewelry into her water glass and swirled, fishing out the shining, and now clean, platinum diamond ring. With that string, he dangled it in front of her like a pocket watch on a chain. And like she'd been hypnotized, she replayed everything he'd said.

I didn't want the future to come, and then you proposed.

There is no moving forward without you—not if I ever want to be happy again.

I'll spend the rest of my life loving you so hard you'll never feel alone again.

"At least read the inside of the band," he said.

With shaking fingers, she took the ring from his hand. Cold water dripped on her fingers as she tilted the band with the very big diamond centerpiece in the candlelight so that she could read it.

The engraving was one word.

Yes.

"It's what I would have said if I wasn't ignoring my feelings. If I didn't have my head so far up my ass I couldn't see sunlight. I wasn't wrong, Addi. Not about all of it. Life is about being present. But we don't have to let it cost us a future we deserve. The family we both want." He shook his head, a tender smile pulling his mouth. "It's not an accident that you're in my life and I'm in yours."

Tears stung her nose as she continued staring at the ring. Everything she thought she'd lost was being handed to her, and it was almost too much to process.

"I love you, Addison Abrams." Bran stood and then lowered to one knee at her side of the booth. "If your proposal hasn't expired yet, I accept."

Bran only *thought* he knew how Addison felt when she proposed. Now, he *knew*. Knew what it was like to leap without a safety net and risk everything. All the flowers, delivered food and begging in the world wouldn't win her back. Only baring his soul and telling her the truth would. At least he hoped it would.

He was at her mercy. Addison could truly ruin him. Could turn him into a fool if she told him no.

She couldn't tell him no.

She won't.

He was praying and hoping and wishing that she believed him. He loved her. More than anything. He'd been too stubborn to see it sooner. The blinders he wore to protect himself had handicapped him in the end. Now all he could do was kneel before her and hope he wasn't too late. That she didn't instantly write him off. That there was some scrap of love for him still left inside her. That he hadn't destroyed everything they'd built.

She was holding the ring—a good sign—but her face

was unreadable. He could hear his own heartbeats, so close together he lost count at four. After what seemed like an eternity, she finally looked at him.

Bright blue eyes lifted her rosy cheeks into the barest hint of a smile. It was like the morning he'd watched the sun rise over the vineyards behind his parents' house. The very moment he'd come to the conclusion that he loved her, and had been loving her the entire time they were together. The moment he'd felt at once free and devastated because he had no idea how to win her back.

His beautiful, brave girl clasped his face with both hands and kissed him solidly on the mouth. He kissed her back, feeling the competing warmth of her lips and the coolness of the metal band of the ring in her grip against his cheek— but mostly relief. So much relief.

He ended the kiss and, before she could rethink her answer, slipped the ring on her left finger. Clasping both her hands in his, he became aware of the low echo of applause around them and the blur in his eyes from an unshed tear or two of his own. Her next words released them.

"I love you, too." Her grin was wide, her eyes misted over. Then she was kissing him again and damming the words he was going to say in his throat.

That was fine by him. Those four words were the only words he needed to hear until the day they said *I do*.

Epilogue

Addison stood in her wedding gown looking out at the vineyards and mountains beyond. The sun had set, but only just. The sky was a deep navy blue.

"Mrs. Knox," her husband said from behind her, sliding his hands around her waist. Brannon kissed her ear and lower on her neck as she breathed in the clean scent of him.

The night he proposed in the restaurant, they went to his house after and made love in his bedroom. This time each kiss, each touch, each long slide of him inside her was paired with an "I love you." They hadn't spent a night apart since.

It'd been a whirlwind, from their trip to Tahoe until their wedding, with plenty of missteps—with each of them pulling in opposite directions. But somehow they'd ended here, in a beautiful place, after a beautiful ceremony, with another beautiful surprise she'd yet to share…

His parents' vineyard mansion had been packed with family and friends, their "small backyard wedding" a crowd of one hundred and fifty people. Her parents, Joe's parents, and friends new and old were the only guests from her list.

Brannon Knox had come with an entourage, but she'd expected no less, she thought with a smile.

Now most of the guests were filtering out to the parking area behind Jack and Macy Knox's vacation home, their cars forming a motorcade down the hill.

Reaching behind her, she stroked her husband's stylishly disheveled hair. "Thank you."

"For?" He placed another kiss on her shoulder and she shivered. She'd come outside, overheated from dancing, but in the night air she realized her off-the-shoulder dress wasn't warm enough to thwart the November chill.

"For being you. For making my dreams come true. For giving me a whole new family in addition to the one I have." She turned and encountered his handsome face, a sight she'd never grow tired of. "I love you."

"I love you." He leaned in to kiss her and she leaned in to accept when a sharp, panicked shriek cut into the air.

They jerked apart and turned toward the patio. Taylor was gripping her very pregnant stomach with one hand and her husband-to-be with the other.

"Here we go," Bran said, gripping Addi's hand and walking with her.

"Someone get those goddamn cars out of the way! *Now!*" Royce shouted, pointing at the parade moving slowly down the hill.

Jack Knox appeared from nowhere like a superhero. "I've got it! I'll take the bike down."

"Dad," Royce warned, but Jack didn't listen, only ran for the garage to extract his new Harley.

Royce sent Bran a look of worry-slash-irritation. "Now we'll have to take him *and* Taylor to the hospital."

"Ohhh, God!" Taylor cried, her face twisted in anguish, her fingers choking the material of Royce's shirt.

Addi ran to support her other side while Royce held onto his fiancée with both arms.

"You two are ready for this," Addi reminded them—but mostly Royce, since he looked like he needed to hear it more. "Bran, honey, why don't you start the car?"

"Got it."

"Oh, Ad. I didn't mean for this to happen on your wedding day. I didn't expect this baby to be a week early!" Taylor hissed another tight breath, sweat coating her brow. "Those doctors swore I'd be on time!"

"Taylor, I'm honored to share your baby's birthday," Addi assured her. "Soon we can finally find out whether I have a niece or a nephew!"

"Right now it feels like an elephant," Taylor growled as Royce shoved a chair underneath her.

"How about an ice-cold washcloth for the ride to the hospital?" Addi offered, and Taylor nodded an enthusiastic yes.

"Make me a gin and tonic while you're in there," Royce said, his tone dry.

Addi laughed to herself—and only once she was in the house. She bypassed Bran's mother, Macy, who was gathering her purse and running for the back door.

"A baby! Oh, Addi, I'm so excited!" Macy squeezed Addi's arm before she darted outside. Addi might be as excited as her mother-in-law about meeting a new member of the family.

Family.

She paused in the hallway en route to the linen closet to appreciate that she had a family. Not only her parents, who had come and gone today already, but a family who *chose* her. The Knoxes had always been supportive and amazing, and now she could claim relation to them. Her dream had come true.

Addi grabbed a washcloth from the linen closet as a door opened at the back of the hall. A sharp whisper that sounded a lot like Gia's said, "You go first! Go!"

Jayson stepped from the bedroom, Gia shoving him with

both hands. They froze when they saw Addi and did their best impression of deer in headlights.

Gia's lipstick, if she'd been wearing any, was gone, her lips plump like she'd been recently and thoroughly kissed.

"Addison! Hi! Is Taylor in labor?" Gia smoothed her hair away from her face and grinned, as if a grin would hide that she'd been making out with her ex-husband.

"We heard something." Jayson straightened his shirt but then noticed his zipper was down. He swore and turned his back to close up shop.

Addi couldn't repress her smile at the couple who *used to be* a couple caught *nearly* coupling. Especially since Gia had busted Addi and Bran not so long ago.

"That was Taylor," Addi confirmed. "And yes, she's in labor. She has amazing timing."

"Yeah. Amazing," Jayson mumbled, pushing a hand through his hair.

"I'm taking her a cold cloth."

"I'll do it. You two check on her." Gia took the cloth from Addi, quickly ran it under the sink in the bathroom and then raced outside.

Jayson offered his arm and Addi hooked her hand around it, lifting the edge of her slim, satin wedding gown while she walked. When Gia was out of earshot, he said, "Macy's ceiling fan wasn't working."

"Okay, sure." Addi shot him a grin and he returned it with a smile. She suspected there was more to his smile, and more to finding him and Gia together. Maybe because it was her wedding day and love was all around. Or maybe because she was perceptive. Or maybe, because she liked Gia and Jayson so much, she was hoping with everything she had that they'd end up together again.

"You make a beautiful bride, Addi. I'm happy for you and Bran."

"Thank you, Coop." She rested her hand over his arm. "And thank you for intervening when Bran needed it most."

"He told you about that, huh? Sometimes the best men need a kick to the 'nads. We're not all that bright."

They exited the patio, both laughing as Bran came back to announce the car was ready. "Dad managed to make it down the hill safely and actually moved traffic quite a bit. Need help, Tay?"

Taylor was surrounded on all sides by her mother, Royce and his mother, and now Jayson. "I feel like a parade float with this many handlers. I think I'm good."

"I'll just collect my wife, then." Bran came for Addi, which sent an arrow straight into her heart with Cupid's signature on it. "Hello, gorgeous. Where'd you disappear to?"

"Wait! I'm coming!" Gia shouted as she chased after the group.

"I went in to wet a washcloth for Taylor and found your sister and Jayson, um…preoccupied. He claimed he was fixing a ceiling fan in a back bedroom."

"A ceiling fan," Bran repeated.

"Who knew ceiling fan repair required one to remove his pants?"

"Maybe I should have a look at it." Her husband scooped her against him.

"We have to go to the hospital." She pointed in the direction of Taylor being loaded into an SUV.

"We have time." He kissed her and all reason flew out of her head.

"Lovebirds!" Mars interrupted next. Pestle & Pepper had catered the wedding—their availability the reason they'd chosen this date. "Go be with your brother. Looked like he needed you. I'll lock up and clean up."

"Actually we were going to—" Bran gestured to the house.

"Do just that," she finished for him. She leaned forward and kissed Mars on the cheek. "Thank you for being here."

"Are you kidding? I'm the reason you're married!" He patted Bran's back. "My wife had our first baby twenty minutes after arriving at the hospital. You may not have as much time as you think you do. You kids have fun!" he called as he went back inside.

Somewhat reluctantly, her husband walked her to the car. He opened her door for her as she scooped up the bottom of her white dress.

"It is exciting, a baby, isn't it?" Bran asked.

"It's very exciting." She waited until he rounded the car and was buckled in to share her own news. "Especially since we'll be doing this approximately nine months from now."

The color washed from his face, his finger hovering over the ignition button in his shiny red sports car.

"I'm sorry to say you're going to have to drive something that can hold a car seat. I know how you feel about Red, here." She patted the dashboard. She was sentimental about the car, too, as it was the beginning of her and Bran.

"You're... Are you serious?"

"Telling you about the positive pregnancy test was going to be my wedding present to you tonight. But since we don't know where tonight will take us, I thought I should tell you now."

Gripping the back of her neck, he towed her close and kissed her, taking his time which was so, so precious considering the circumstances.

"What was that for?" she whispered as Royce started down the hill, honking the horn.

"You've given me everything I've ever wanted," Bran said, never taking his eyes off her.

She kissed him once more, knowing the clock was ticking but unable to resist. "You started it."

* * * * *

COMING SOON!

We really hope you enjoyed reading this book. If you're looking for more romance, be sure to head to the shops when new books are available on

Thursday 2nd April

To see which titles are coming soon, please visit

millsandboon.co.uk/nextmonth

MILLS & BOON

THE HEART OF ROMANCE

A ROMANCE FOR EVERY KIND OF READER

MODERN

Prepare to be swept off your feet by sophisticated, sexy and seductive heroes, in some of the world's most glamourous and romantic locations, where power and passion collide.
8 stories per month.

HISTORICAL

Escape with historical heroes from time gone by. Whether your passion is for wicked Regency Rakes, muscled Vikings or rugged Highlanders, awaken the romance of the past.
6 stories per month.

MEDICAL

Set your pulse racing with dedicated, delectable doctors in the high-pressure world of medicine, where emotions run high and passion, comfort and love are the best medicine.
6 stories per month.

True Love

Celebrate true love with tender stories of heartfelt romance, from the rush of falling in love to the joy a new baby can bring, and a focus on the emotional heart of a relationship.
8 stories per month.

Desire

Indulge in secrets and scandal, intense drama and plenty of sizzling hot action with powerful and passionate heroes who have it all: wealth, status, good looks…everything but the right woman.
6 stories per month.

HEROES

Experience all the excitement of a gripping thriller, with an intense romance at its heart. Resourceful, true-to-life women and strong, fearless men face danger and desire - a killer combination!
8 stories per month.

DARE

Sensual love stories featuring smart, sassy heroines you'd want as a best friend, and compelling intense heroes who are worthy of them.
4 stories per month.

To see which titles are coming soon, please visit

millsandboon.co.uk/nextmonth

JOIN US ON SOCIAL MEDIA!

Stay up to date with our latest releases, author news and gossip, special offers and discounts, and all the behind-the-scenes action from Mills & Boon...

 millsandboon

 millsandboonuk

 millsandboon

It might just be true love...

MILLS & BOON

MODERN

Power and Passion

Prepare to be swept off your feet by sophisticated, sexy and seductive heroes, in some of the world's most glamourous and romantic locations, where power and passion collide.